Desert

*In the heat of the desert,
a lifetime of desire...*

**Praise for three best-selling authors—
Emma Darcy, Helen Brooks
and Mary Lyons**

About Emma Darcy

'Emma Darcy dishes up a spicy reading
experience.'
—*Romantic Times*

About Helen Brooks

'Helen Brooks pens a superb story.'
—*Romantic Times*

About Mary Lyons

'Mary Lyons presents a sexy tale.'
—*Romantic Times*

Desert Destinies

THE SHEIKH'S SEDUCTION
by
Emma Darcy

THE SULTAN'S FAVOURITE
by
Helen Brooks

ESCAPE FROM THE HAREM
by
Mary Lyons

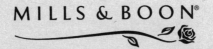

MILLS & BOON®

*MILLS & BOON and MILLS & BOON with the Rose Device
are registered trademarks of the publisher.
Harlequin Mills & Boon Limited,
Eton House, 18-24 Paradise Road, Richmond, Surrey, TW9 1SR*

DESERT DESTINIES
© by Harlequin Enterprises II B.V., 2001

The Sheikh's Seduction, The Sultan's Favourite and
Escape from the Harem were first published in Great Britain by
Harlequin Mills & Boon Limited in separate, single volumes.

The Sheikh's Seduction © Emma Darcy 1998
The Sultan's Favourite © Helen Brooks 1994
Escape from the Harem © Mary Lyons 1986

ISBN 0 263 82773 9

05-0501

*Printed and bound in Spain
by Litografía Rosés S.A., Barcelona*

Initially a French/English teacher, **Emma Darcy** changed careers to computer programming before marriage and motherhood settled her into a community life. Creative urges were channelled into oil-painting, pottery, designing and overseeing the construction and decorating of two homes, all in the midst of keeping up with three lively sons and the very social life of her businessman husband, Frank. Very much a people person, and always interested in relationships, she finds the world of romance fiction a happy one and the challenge of creating her own cast of characters very addictive.

Emma Darcy is the author of more than 75 novels, including the international bestseller, THE SECRETS WITHIN, published by MIRA® Books. She enjoys travelling and often her experiences find their way into her books. Emma Darcy lives on a country property in New South Wales, Australia.

Look out for

THE SWEETEST REVENGE by Emma Darcy

in Modern Romance™, June 2001

THE SHEIKH'S SEDUCTION

by

EMMA DARCY

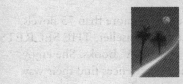

CHAPTER ONE

"MY NAME is Sarah Hillyard. My father trains race-horses in Australia…''

The artless words of a twelve-year-old child.

A child he'd liked and remembered seven years later when he'd come to choosing a trainer in Australia.

Sheikh Tareq al-Khaima shook his head in self-derision. Stupid to have let a sentimental memory influence his judgment. He'd hired Drew Hillyard, entrusted him with the progeny of some of the best bloodlines in the world, and the man had proved to be a cheat and a crook, wasting what he'd been given in favour of sure money, bribe money.

It was an effort to remain civil, sitting beside him in the Members' Stand at Flemington Racecourse, waiting for the Melbourne Cup to be run. Recognised as one of the great races on the international calendar, The Cup was a prize coveted by trainers and owners. It made reputations. It sealed a horse's fame. It was the return on an investment.

If Firefly won today, Drew Hillyard might earn himself another chance. If Firefly lost, the trainer could kiss Tareq's string of thoroughbreds goodbye. The moment of truth was fast approaching. The horses were being boxed, ready for the start of the race.

"He should run well," Drew Hillyard said reassuringly.

Tareq turned to Sarah's father. The older man's brown

5

curly hair was streaked with lustreless grey and cut so short, the ringlets sat tightly against his scalp. His dark eyes were opaque, as though he'd fitted blinds over the windows of his soul. The memory of Drew Hillyard's daughter flashed into Tareq's mind—a glorious mop of burnished brown curls framing a fascinating face with eyes so dark and brilliant he'd loved watching them. He didn't want to even look at her father.

"Yes, he should," he answered, and returned his gaze to the track. Firefly had been bred from champion stayers. If he'd been trained properly he should eat this race. He *should*, but Tareq wasn't banking on it. None of the horses he'd placed in Drew Hillyard's stables had lived up to their breeding. The initial promise of the first two years had been whittled away by sly corruption.

Susan Hillyard claimed his attention. "Did you place a bet on Firefly, Tareq?"

He looked at her, wondering if she knew the truth. Drew Hillyard's wife—second wife—was a thin, nervous blonde. With every reason to be nervous, Tareq thought darkly. "I never bet, Mrs. Hillyard. It's performance that interests me. On every level. I like to see my horses fulfil the promise of their bloodlines."

"Oh!" she said and retreated, her hands twisting worriedly in her lap.

Sarah's stepmother.

My father's marrying again. Since my mother's made her home here in Ireland now, she's arranged for me to go to boarding school in England. So she can more easily visit me, she says. I get to go home to my father in the summer break.

A lonely, disillusioned child, her world torn apart by divorce. Tareq wondered what had become of her, where she was. Not here at Flemington. He'd looked for her, curious to see the woman she'd grown into. He was tempted to ask about her but revealing a personal interest went against his grain in this situation. Sarah, the child, was a piece of the past, eleven years gone. Comprehensively gone after today, if Firefly failed.

A roar went up from the crowd, signalling the start of the race. Tareq stood with the rest of the people around him, binoculars lifted to his eyes. The commentator's voice boomed over the loudspeakers, whipping up excitement. Tareq focused all his attention on the horse that had brought him here, a magnificent stallion who'd be worth his weight in gold if he won.

He was poetry in motion, well positioned for the early part of the race and running with a fluid grace and ease that was exciting to watch. He took the lead at the halfway mark and streaked ahead of the field. Too soon, Tareq thought. Yet he held a gap of three lengths into the last hundred metres. Then he visibly flagged, other horses catching him and sweeping past to the finishing post. Eighth. Respectable enough in a class field of twenty-two horses, people would say. Except Tareq knew better.

"Ran out of puff," Drew Hillyard said, his weather-beaten face appropriately mournful with disappointment.

"Yes, he did," Tareq coldly agreed, knowing full well that a properly trained champion stayer did not run out of puff.

"Want to accompany me down to talk to the jockey?"

"No. I'll have a word with you after the last race."

"Fine."

He and his wife left. Tareq was glad to see the back of them though he'd have to confront them later.

"Do you want me to do it?"

The quiet question came from his oldest friend, Peter Larsen. They'd been through Eton and Oxford together and understood each other as well as any two men could. It was Peter who had investigated Drew Hillyard's notable failure to make champions of champions. The paper evidence left no doubt as to the reason behind the obvious incompetence. To top it all, Drew Hillyard had even sacrificed a chance at the Melbourne Cup.

Tareq shook his head. Peter had saved him trouble on innumerable occasions but this wasn't usual business. "I was fool enough to choose him. He's mine, Peter."

A nod of understanding.

Drew Hillyard had broken a trust.

That was always personal.

CHAPTER TWO

SARAH helped her little half-sister to bed. Jessie had grown strong enough to move her legs herself but she was tired, her energy spent on all the anticipation, excitement and disappointments of the day. The latter had dragged her spirits right down and there was nothing Sarah could say to cheer her up.

Despite sitting glued to the television for hours before and after the running of the Melbourne Cup, Jessie hadn't seen the sheikh, whom she'd imagined in flowing white robes. Sarah had suggested he would probably be in a suit. Not a well-received comment. To Jessie's mind, a sheikh wasn't a sheikh unless he wore flowing white robes. Either way, the television had failed to put him on display.

And Firefly had lost. After looking as though he might take out The Cup for most of the race, the stallion had faltered with the finishing post in sight. A flood of tears from Jessie. She'd loved Firefly from the moment she'd first clapped eyes on the beautiful colt and she'd desperately wanted him to win.

''Mummy didn't call,'' she now grumbled, adding another disappointment to her list of woes.

Sarah tried to excuse the oversight. ''It would be a busy day for her, Jessie, what with having to entertain the sheikh and everything. They've probably gone out somewhere.''

Big blue eyes mournfully pleaded the injustice of it

9

all. "It's not fair. Daddy's had the sheikh's horses for four years and this is the first time he's come to Australia and I didn't even get to see him."

Neither did I, Sarah thought ruefully. Though it wasn't so important to her. Just curiosity to see what he looked like after all these years. Funny how some childhood memories remained vivid and others faded away. She'd never forgotten Tareq al-Khaima, nor his kindness to her over that first lonely Christmas in Ireland with her mother.

He'd been a young man then, immensely wealthy and strikingly handsome. Everyone at her mother's house parties had wanted to know him. Yet he'd noticed a forlorn child, eaten up with the misery of feeling like the leftover, unwanted baggage from her mother's first marriage, best out of sight and out of mind. He'd spent time with her, giving her a sense of being a person worth knowing. It was her only good memory from being twelve.

"Maybe there'll be a photograph of him in the newspaper tomorrow," she offered as consolation.

"I bet there isn't." Jessie stuck to gloom. "There hasn't been one all week."

Which had been surprising with the Spring Carnival in full swing and the social pages packed with photographs of visiting celebrities. Either the sheikh was not partying or he was camera-shy for some reason.

"And he's not coming to Werribee to see his other horses, either. Daddy told me he'd only be at Flemington."

"Well, the sheikh owns horses all around the world, Jessie." He'd been buying them in Ireland when she'd met him. "I don't suppose any particular string of them is special to him."

She wondered if he remembered her. Unlikely. Too brief a connection, too long ago. It was just one of those coincidences in life that Tareq's agent had assigned the sheikh's horses in Australia to her father to train. There'd been nothing personal in the deal.

"He came to see Firefly race," Jessie argued.

"That's because the Melbourne Cup is special." Having settled her half-sister comfortably, Sarah stroked the wispy fair hair away from the woeful little face and dropped a kiss on her forehead. "Never mind, love. I'm sure your mother will tell you all about the sheikh tomorrow."

Disgruntled mumbles.

Sarah ignored them as she made sure everything was right for Jessie; the electric wheelchair in the correct position for easy use when she needed to go to the bathroom, the night-light on, a glass of water on the moveable tray. It was amazing the amount of independence the little girl managed now. In fact, Sarah knew she really wasn't needed here at Werribee anymore. It was time to move on with her own life. Once the Spring Carnival was over, she would broach the matter with Susan.

Having completed her check list, Sarah moved to the door and switched off the overhead light. "Goodnight, Jessie," she said softly.

"Mummy didn't call and she promised she would."

The final petulant comment on a day that had not delivered its promises.

Sarah quietly closed the door on it, privately conceding Jessie had cause to feel let down. Her mother should have called. That had been a real promise, not a wish or a hope. Real promises should be kept.

Sarah grimaced at the thought as she moved along the hall to the twins' room. It was so hopelessly idealist in this day and age where keeping promises was a matter of convenience. Wasn't her whole life an illustration of not being able to count on them? It was about time she accepted the real world.

She looked in at the boys. Her seven-year-old half-brothers were fast asleep. They looked as innocent as babes, mischief and mayhem cloaked with peaceful repose. The problem with children was they were innocent. They believed in promises. When disillusionment came it hurt. It hurt very badly.

Mummy didn't call…

The words jogged memories of another Melbourne Cup day. She'd been ten, the same age as Jessie, and left behind at Werribee in the care of the foreman's wife. *Her* mother hadn't called, either. She'd been too busy with Michael Kearney, planning to leave her husband and daughter and go off to Ireland with the promise of becoming the fourth wife of one of the wealthiest men in the horse world.

Her mother had made good on *that* promise, and when Michael Kearney had chosen wife number five, the divorce settlement had been astronomical. It had certainly helped make the ex-Mrs. Kearney an attractive proposition to an English Lord. Sarah could safely say her mother had never looked back after leaving Werribee. She'd been appalled when her daughter had rejected "the chances" lined up for her, returning to Australia to help with Jessie.

Sarah didn't regret her decision. It was strange how

far away that life in England seemed now. The question was…where to go from here? She wandered into the living room, curled up on the sofa and gave the matter serious consideration.

She'd always loved books. They'd been her escape from loneliness, her friends and companions, doors that opened other worlds for her. She'd had her mind set on getting into some career in publishing. Maybe her degree in English Literature would still hold her in good stead there, though she had no work experience and probably openings at publishing houses were few and far between. Still there was no harm in looking for a position.

Melbourne? Sydney? London?

She instinctively shied from going back to England.

A new life, she thought, one she would make on her own. Though how best to do it kept her mind going around. When the telephone rang it startled her out of a deep reverie. She leapt to pick up the receiver, glancing at her watch simultaneously. Close to nine-thirty.

''The Hillyard Homestead,'' she rattled out.

''Sarah… I promised to call Jessie. Is she still waiting?''

Susan's voice was strained. She didn't sound herself at all. But at least she hadn't forgotten her daughter. ''No, she was tired,'' Sarah answered. ''I put her to bed at eight. Do you want me to see if she's awake?''

''No, I… I just thought of it and…oh, Sarah…'' She burst into tears.

''Susan, what's wrong?''

Deep, shuddering breaths. ''I'm sorry…''

''It's okay. Take it easy,'' Sarah soothed, trying to contain her own fast-rising anxiety. ''Try to tell me what's happened.'' Please, God! Not another dreadful accident!

"The sheikh…he's taking all his horses away from your father.''

"Why?'' It made no sense. Unless… "Surely not because Firefly didn't win the cup?''

"No. There's…there's more. The past two years…but you know what they've been like, Sarah. It was hard for Drew to keep his mind on the job.''

What was she justifying? Had her father mismanaged the training?

"It'll ruin us,'' Susan went on, her voice a wail of despair. "It'll make other owners uneasy. You know reputation is everything in this business.''

"I don't understand.'' She'd been too busy with Jessie to take an active interest in what was happening with the thoroughbreds in her father's stables. "What is the sheikh's complaint?''

"It's all about…about performance.'' She broke into tears again.

"Susan, put Dad on. Let me talk to him,'' Sarah urged.

"He's…he's drinking. There's nothing we can do. Nothing…''

Not if you're drunk. Sarah bit back the retort, knowing it was useless. All the same, her father's growing habit of hitting the bottle could be at the root of this problem. It was all very well to seek relief from stress but not if it led to shirking responsibilities.

"Tell Jessie I'll call her tomorrow.''

The phone went dead.

No point in holding the receiver. She put it down. The living room suddenly felt cold. If her father was ruined, if that sent him further along the path of drinking himself into oblivion…what would happen to his and Susan's marriage? What would happen to the children? It was always the innocent ones who were overlooked.

Sarah shivered.

Did Tareq al-Khaima realise what effect today's decision would have? Did he care? How bad was the situation?

Sarah shook her head helplessly. She had no idea to what extent her father had failed in giving the sheikh satisfaction.

But she did know the circumstances behind his failure.

Tareq had been sympathetic to her once. If he remembered her…if she could get him to listen…

It was worth a try.

He was staying at the Como Hotel. She remembered her father mentioning it. If she went there as early as possible tomorrow morning…

Anything was worth a try to stave off disaster.

CHAPTER THREE

SARAH glanced anxiously at her watch. The drive into the city had taken over two hours. The morning was slipping away from her. It was almost eight o'clock and she was still locked in Melbourne traffic. A sleepless night and a heavy weight of worry wasn't doing much for her judgment on which were the faster transit lanes, either.

She'd left Werribee as early as she could but not as early as she would have liked. It had taken time to instruct one of the stable hands in the house routine so he could look after the children until the foreman's wife could come. It wasn't the best arrangement but this was an emergency situation.

Her main fear was the possibility she was already too late to make any difference to Tareq's decision. He may have acted yesterday, lining up another trainer to take his horses. Or he could be at Flemington right now, discussing business. The Spring Carnival wasn't over yet. It was Oaks Day tomorrow. Many owners gathered with trainers at the racetrack at dawn each morning, watching the form of favoured horses.

On top of which, even if Tareq was at his hotel, there was no guarantee he would see her. Or talk to her. Let alone listen to what she had to say. All Sarah could do was hope and pray for a chance to change his mind before his decision became irreversible.

When she finally reached the Como Hotel, she did a

double take. Despite its being in South Yarra, outside the main city area, she had expected a big, plush, ostentatiously luxurious establishment, the kind of place one automatically associated with oil-wealthy sheikhs. The Como was relatively small, almost boutique size. Sarah hoped it meant Tareq was more approachable.

She found a parking station just off Chapel Street, left the jeep there, and walked back to the hotel.

The moment she entered it, the decor screamed class—quiet, exclusive class—marble floors, black leather sofas, floral arrangements worthy of being called exquisite modern art. It might not be ostentatious luxury but it was just as intimidating to anyone who didn't belong to the privileged people.

Sarah could feel herself bridling against its effect and mentally adopted a shield of untouchability to carry her through gaining entry to Tareq's presence. She knew from experience with her mother's high-strata world that her appearance would not be a critical factor. The dark brown corduroy jeans and fawn skivvy would pass muster anywhere these days. The wind had undoubtedly tossed her unruly curls but that didn't matter. Neither did the fact she wore no make-up. ''Being natural'' could be just as fashionable as designer clothes.

The concierge directed her to the reception area, around to the left and down a flight of steps, privacy from the street effectively established. One elegant free-standing desk was apparently enough to serve the guests. The woman behind it smiled invitingly. Sarah willed her to be obliging, too.

''I've come to call on Sheikh Tareq al-Khaima. Is he in?''

''Yes, Ma'am. Whom should I say is calling?''

"If you'll just give me his suite number…"

"I'm sorry, ma'am. That's against our security rules. I can call up to his suite for you. What name should I give?"

Security. Of course. This place was probably as tight as Fort Knox—no unwanted visitors allowed past the steel doors of the elevator. "Sarah Hillyard," she stated flatly, resigning herself to the inevitable. If Tareq didn't want to see her, she couldn't force him to.

Her nerves knotted as the call was made and the message passed on. There seemed to be a long hesitation before an answer was given. Sarah's tension eased slightly when the receptionist smiled at her, indicating no problem.

"He's sending Mr. Larsen down to fetch you. It should only be a minute or two, Miss Hillyard."

"Fetch me?"

"There's a special key for the executive floor. The elevator won't take you up without it."

"Oh! Thank you."

Relief poured through her. Past the first hurdle. Though Mr. Larsen, whoever he was, might prove to be another barrier. She wondered how big Tareq's entourage was. He wouldn't have come alone to Australia and might well have taken over the whole hotel. Such information hadn't been of interest to her until now and it was too late to ask her father or Susan for more facts.

When the steel doors opened, a tall, fair-haired man, impeccably dressed in a silver-grey suit, emerged from the elevator. His face was thin and austere; high cheekbones, long nose, small mouth, and very light eyes. He looked to be in his early thirties and carried an air of lofty authority. He inspected Sarah as though measuring an adversary; a swift, acute appraisal that left her highly rattled.

One eyebrow was slightly raised. "Miss Hillyard?"

"Yes. Mr. Larsen?"

He gave a slight nod and waved her into the elevator. No smile. His eyes were a silver grey like his suit. Very cold. He didn't speak as he used a key to set the compartment in motion, nor did he acknowledge her in any way as they rode upwards. Sarah felt comprehensively shut out from this man's consciousness.

Fighting another rise of tension, she inquired, "Have you been with Sheikh Tareq al-Khaima for a long time, Mr. Larsen?"

He looked directly at her, his mouth curling slightly. "You could say that."

Oxford accent. Upper-class English. "Are you a friend or do you work for the sheikh?" she asked, needing to place him.

"I'm his trouble-shooter. Are you trouble, Miss Hillyard?"

A hatchet man, she thought. "Am I seeing him or you?"

"The sheikh will see you personally."

The man's superior manner provoked her. "Then I hope I'm trouble, Mr. Larsen."

"Brave words, Miss Hillyard."

And probably foolish. Getting anyone close to Tareq offside was hardly good politics.

Mr. Larsen turned away, though not before Sarah saw a flicker of amusement in the light grey eyes. A chill ran down her spine. This man's amusement would undoubtedly be aroused by the anticipation of seeing someone cut to pieces. It did not augur well for her meeting with

Tareq. But at least she was seeing him, which gave her a chance at persuasion.

Sarah clung to that reassurance. The elevator stopped. Mr. Larsen led her along a corridor, stopping at a door on which he knocked before using a key to open it. Poker-faced once more, he ushered Sarah into a suite full of light.

The blinds had been lifted from two huge picture windows, allowing a spectacular view over the city. Tareq stood at the window. Although his back was turned to her and he was anonymously clothed in a navy blue suit, Sarah had no doubt who it was. The thick black hair, dark olive skin, his height and build, brought an instant wave of familiarity, despite the passage of years between their meetings. Yet Sarah was just as instantly aware of something different.

She remembered him as carrying an air of easy self-assurance, confident of who he was and what he wanted from life. To a child who felt no security about anything, it had seemed quite wonderful to be like that. Now she sensed something more, a dominant authority that didn't bend.

Perhaps it was in the square set of his shoulders, the straightness of his back, the quality of stillness telegraphing not only total command of himself, but command of the situation. Even the plain dark suit implied he needed no trappings to impress himself on anyone. He didn't have to do anything. He certainly didn't have to turn to her need to appeal to him.

Her formidable escort had followed her into the suite and shut the door behind them. He waited, as she did, for Tareq to acknowledge their presence. Waiting for the entertainment to begin, Sarah thought, and wondered if she should take the initiative and greet Tareq. The silence seemed to hum with negative vibrations, choking off any facile words.

"Did your father send you, Sarah?"

The quiet question had a hard edge to it. Without moving, without so much as a glance at her, Tareq had spoken, and Sarah suddenly realised he was standing in judgment. She sensed his back would remain turned to her if her answer complied with whatever dark train of thought was in his mind. She didn't know what he expected to hear. The truth was all she could offer.

"No. It was my own idea to come to you. If you remember, we met in Ireland when…"

"I remember. Did your father agree to your coming here?"

Sarah took a deep breath. Tareq al-Khaima was not about to be swayed by reminiscences. He was directing this encounter and she had no choice but to toe his line.

"I haven't even spoken to my father. Nor seen him," she answered. "I was at Werribee yesterday, looking after the children. Susan, his wife, phoned last night. She was terribly distressed…"

"So you've come to intercede for him," he cut in, unsoftened.

"For all of them, Tareq. It doesn't just affect my father."

"What do you intend to offer me to balance what he's done?"

"Offer?" The concept hadn't occurred to her. No way could she compensate for whatever had been lost. 'I…I'm sorry. I have no means to pay you back for…for my father's mismanagement."

"Mismanagement!"

Her heart leapt as he swung around. The vivid blue
blaze of his eyes shot electric tingles through her brain,
paralysing her thought processes. Her whole body felt
caught in a magnetic field. Her stomach contracted.
Goose bumps broke out on her skin. She couldn't even
breathe. Never in her life had she felt such power coming from anyone. She was helpless to do anything but
stare back at him. His gaze literally transfixed her.

The initial bolts of anger transmuted into laser beams.
It felt as though he was peeling back the years, remembering how she'd been at twelve, then piling them on
again, rebuilding the woman she was now, studying her,
seeing if she measured up to whatever he thought she
should be.

Sarah struggled to reclaim her mind. He had changed.
The shock of such blue eyes—an inherited gene from
his English mother—against his dark complexion still
held fascination but she saw no kindness in them, nothing to encourage hope. His strikingly handsome face had
matured into harder, sharper lines, his softer youthful-
ness discarded. She knew him to be thirty-four, yet he
had the look of a man who wielded power at any level
and commanded respect for it. He was armoured, in
every sense.

His mouth suddenly curved in a half-smile. "How can
dark chocolate shine so brightly?"

They were the teasing words he'd used about her eyes
the morning he'd invited her to ride with him on her
stepfather's estate in Ireland, she on a pony, he on a
thoroughbred stallion. Sarah floundered in a wash of
memories. She had no reply to the remark, any more
than she'd had then.

"You haven't learnt any artifice, Sarah?" he asked.

The abrupt change to a more personal line of conversation confused her. "I don't know what you mean."

The half-smile took on a cynical twist. "You're a grown woman, yet I still see the child. The same rioting brown curls. The same appealing face, bare of make-up. Clothes that are nothing more than clothes. Perhaps that was intentional. Artifice in lack of artifice."

She blushed at his dissection of her appearance and hated herself for letting him make her feel gauche. "Look! This isn't about me," she implored.

"The messenger always carries many messages," he stated, his eyes mocking her assertion. "You're a beautiful young woman. Beautiful women usually know and use their power."

His gaze dropped to her breasts, making Sarah acutely conscious of the stretch fabric of her skivvy hugging their fullness. Then he seemed to mentally measure her waist, the wide leather belt she wore undoubtedly aiding his calculation. The curve of her hips and the length of her legs were inspected, as well, much to Sarah's growing embarrassment.

His appraisal of her feminine *power* increased her awareness of the strong sexual charisma which, at twelve, she'd been too young to recognise in him. It was certainly affecting her now, so much so it prompted the realisation he was probably used to women throwing themselves at him. Wealth alone was considered an aphrodisiac. With his looks...

An awful thought occurred to her. When Tareq had asked what she intended to offer him, had he imagined a proposition involving sexual favours? Was he summing up her desirability in case she took that line of persuasion?

Sarah almost died of mortification. She wouldn't even know how to go about it. Men hadn't featured largely in her life, none in any intimate sense. As for Tareq…she was losing all her bearings with him.

"The question is…how grown up are you?" he mused, the glitter of speculation in his eyes discomforting Sarah even further.

"I'm twenty-three," she replied, fervently wishing everything could be more normal between them. She remembered feeling safe with Tareq all those years ago. She didn't feel safe now.

"I know how old you are, Sarah. Your age doesn't answer my questions."

"I told you…this isn't about me."

"Yes, it is. It's very much about you. How long have you been at Werribee?"

Was this a chance to start explaining? "Two years," she answered, and it was as though she'd slapped him in the face.

She physically felt his withdrawal from her. There was the merest flicker in his eyes, a barely visible tightening of his jawline, no other outward sign. He remained absolutely still, yet she felt every thread of connection with her being ruthlessly cut.

"So…you've been assisting your father," he said coldly.

Sarah realised he'd just cloaked her with her father's sins, whatever they were. "Not with the horses. I've had nothing to do with them," she rushed out. "I've been helping with Jessie. She's ten years old, Tareq. My little half-sister. And she's a paraplegic."

A muscle in his cheek contracted.

Sarah plunged on, wanting him to understand the

background. "Two years ago, Susan was terribly ill, being treated for breast cancer. Then Jessie was injured and Susan couldn't cope. There were the boys, too…"

"Boys?"

"My half-brothers. Twins. They're seven now but they were only five when I came back to Werribee to help."

"You were asked to do so?"

"No. Susan wrote about Jessie."

"Where were you then?"

"London. I'd just finished my finals at university."

"And you dropped everything to help them?"

He made it sound incredibly self-sacrificing but it wasn't. "I've always loved Jessie. How could I not come when she had to face never walking again?"

He frowned. "You stayed with her…all this time."

"I was needed." It was the simple truth.

His eyes bored into hers and she felt the reconnection. It was a weird sensation, as sharp and quick as a switch being thrown, making her nerves leap and jangle, an invasion she had no control over.

"The child belongs to its mother, Sarah," he said quietly. "She is not the answer to your loneliness."

Her heart pumped a tide of heat up her neck and into her cheeks; burning, humiliating heat. He knew too much about her. He was plucking at her most vulnerable chords. It *had* felt good to be needed. And wanted.

Her reluctance to cut herself off from those feelings had influenced her choice to stay in her father's home longer than was strictly necessary, but she did realise it was time to move on. Though this latest disaster confused the issue.

"I can't desert them now. Don't you see?" she

pleaded. "My father will be ruined if you take your horses away. What will happen to the children?"

"It is not your responsibility," he retorted harshly. "Your father brought this outcome upon himself."

"Did he? Did he?" she cried, and plunged into a passionate defence. "Was it his fault his wife got cancer? Was it his fault Jessie was crippled? There were astronomical medical bills and the house had to be renovated to accommodate a handicapped child, a special suite built on with all the aids for Jessie to learn to be independent, a special van bought to transport her. There were so many adjustments to be made, and the continual cost of physiotherapy, masseurs... Do you wonder that my father was distracted from doing his job properly?"

Sarah was out of breath from the frantic outpouring of words. Her eyes clung to Tareq's, begging understanding. If he could see through her so easily, couldn't he see this, too?

Or did he see an ongoing problem?

"But things are better now," she hastily declared. "Susan's been cleared of the cancer. She's fine. No trace of secondaries. And Jessie has made fantastic progress. It's amazing how much she's learnt to do for herself. The boys have become good at helping her, too. So you see...my father no longer has so many worries on his mind. He could concentrate on the training if you'll just give him another chance."

Her plea seemed to be falling on deaf ears. There was no visible reaction to it on Tareq's face, no trace of sympathy. She needed some response, some hint of whether he was reconsidering his stance or not.

His brick wall silence tore at her nerves. It went on for an agonising length of time. Sarah fought against a mounting sense of defeat. Was there anything more she could say that might touch him?

"Leave us, Peter."

The quiet command startled her into jerking her head around. She'd forgotten the presence of Mr. Larsen behind her. He was still there, a witness to everything that had been said. His gaze was locked on Tareq, the chilling light eyes slightly narrowed, as though trying to discern the reason behind the command, or perhaps sending a silent warning that a witness was a wise precaution against trouble.

Whatever he thought, he left without a word, not even glancing at Sarah. The door clicked shut after him, emphasising the continued silence and making Sarah intensely aware she was alone with Tareq. She spun her attention back to him, fighting a rush of inner agitation. Her heart beat chaotically as he started walking towards her.

"You fight very eloquently on your father's behalf," he said, though he didn't look impressed. "I find that quite remarkable since he didn't fight for you. He gave you up, freeing himself to marry again without any encumbrances and have this family you care so much about."

"Whatever my father's shortcomings, the children are innocent," she argued, inwardly quailing as Tareq came closer and closer. "It's more for their sake that I'm asking you to reconsider your decision."

He stopped so close she had to tilt her head back to look up at him. His eyes burned into hers with mesmerising intensity. "And if I don't reconsider, you are willing to give them more devoted service. More of your time," he said, stroking her cheek with feather-light fingertips as though seeking to get under her skin and feel all she was.

Sarah's legs turned to jelly. His nearness was over-powering, his touch insidiously weakening both her mind and body. She'd never experienced anything like it in her life. Movement was beyond her. She could hardly think.

He raked back some curls and tucked them behind her ear, his eyes simmering into hers, holding them captive to his will. "I like your giving heart, Sarah. It's a rare thing in today's world."

She swallowed hard, trying to rid herself of the con-striction in her throat. "Can't you give, too, Tareq?"

"Perhaps."

"You were once kind to me," she pleaded.

"And I'll be kind to you again, though you may not appreciate the form it comes in."

"What do you mean?"

"A bargain, Sarah. You want me to give your father another chance. I want something in return."

She literally quaked. He was still fiddling with her hair, winding curls around his fingers, tying her to him. It took all her willpower to force out the words, "What is it you want?"

"For the length of time it takes for your father to prove he can be trusted to do his best by my horses, you will stay with me. Let us say...you will be a hostage to his conscientious efforts to redeem himself."

Dear God! He did mean to tie her to him! Sarah tried to rally her wits out of their state of shock. "You mean...like a prisoner."

"No need to be so grim. You can be my travelling companion...my social secretary..."

Euphemisms for current mistress? Or was her imagination running riot, along with her hormones?

"Staying with me should not be a hardship," he assured her. "I'll pay you a generous salary for your devoted service."

"Like what?" Sarah's mind was spinning, unable to decide what was real or unreal. How *devoted* was the service to be?

"What did your father pay you for all the hours you gave to his family?"

She flushed. "It's my family, too."

"Two years of unpaid labour, Sarah? Two years of putting your life on hold with nothing to show at the end of it?"

"Is there a price on love, Tareq?"

"Oh, yes." A taunting twist of his mouth mocked her naivety. "There's always a price. You've been paying it. And you'd pay more. So make up your mind as to where it's best paid, Sarah. You continue to give yourself to your family with potential ruin on their doorstep, or you give yourself to me, securing the second chance you've been pleading for."

"Why does it have to be this way?" she cried. Why did he want her with him?

"It's a question of trust," he answered, a relentless beat in his voice. "I don't trust your father. He betrayed the confidence I placed in him. If you trust him to come good on another chance, you have nothing to fear from this bargain and a lot to gain."

That was the crux of it. Testing her trust in the trust she was asking him to give. She saw the hard ruthlessness in his eyes and knew there was no mercy in him.

If he didn't get the performance he wanted, he would extract compensation, one way or another.

Her mind was in chaos. What if her father didn't pull himself together and apply himself to fulfilling Tareq's expectations? On the other hand, having stared ruin in the face, surely the prospect of being handed another chance would sober him up. Sarah didn't—couldn't—place much store in his caring for what might happen to her, but his love for his other children had always been much in evidence.

And the plain truth was, they didn't need her so much as they needed each other. She'd only ever been an extra, waiting in the wings to be called on. Now that Jessie was capable of managing herself, there was no real reason to stay. The best she could do for them was to give them the chance Tareq was offering.

His hand slid from her hair and travelled around her jawline to cup her chin. "Tit for tat, Sarah. I risk my horses. You risk yourself. Is it a deal?"

A two-way gamble. Put like that, his proposition was understandable. Reasonable. But it was difficult to hang on to reason, swamped as she was by the sexual current coursing from the touch of his hand, sensitising her skin and making a mash of her insides. She didn't feel safe with him.

Yet without him, Jessie and the twins wouldn't be safe. Innocent victims. As she had been. Sarah couldn't let that happen. She stared into the diamond-hard blue eyes of Tareq al-Khaima and willed him to be honourable.

"All right. I'll do it," she said decisively.

The flash of satisfaction she saw curled her stomach.

Could she trust him to keep his word?
There was no guarantee.
Only risk.

CHAPTER FOUR

TAREQ was not slow in acting on Sarah's decision. There was no time given for second thoughts. He moved straight to the telephone, leaving Sarah to listen as he set up his side of the bargain.

"Peter, call Drew Hillyard. Tell him his daughter, Sarah, is here with me. Due to her special pleading, I am inclined to change my decision and leave my horses with him."

This apparently evoked some expostulation from his trouble-shooter. Whatever was said made no difference to Tareq. He calmly resumed speaking.

"I'm sure you'll think of a way to put an effective stop to that. Just get Hillyard here, Peter. As soon as possible. We'll hear him out first, then move to break the link. From both sides."

Another pause. Sarah wondered what link they were talking about.

"Sarah has agreed to act as surety. She'll be coming with me when I fly out tonight. You'll have to stay behind and wrap this up, Peter."

Tonight! Sarah moved shakily to an armchair and sat down, dizzied by the speed at which her life was about to change. She stared out the window at the view of the city. Where would she be this time tomorrow?

"Tell Hillyard to bring his wife with him. Best to get everything settled in one hit."

The receiver clicked down.

"Sarah, have you eaten anything this morning?"

She turned blankly to the man who would direct everything she did from now on. He frowned at her, picked up the telephone again and proceeded to order a selection of croissants, muffins, and a platter of cheese and fruit. Having finished with room service, he considered her thoughtfully.

"You're not going faint on me, are you, Sarah?" he asked. "You've stood up bravely so far."

Brave words, Miss Hillyard... She wondered what Peter Larsen thought of her now. Trouble. Definitely trouble. For some reason the thought gave her satisfaction.

A spark of pride made her answer, "I'm not getting cold feet if that's what's worrying you."

"Good!" He moved purposefully to the kitchenette beyond the dining suite. "Coffee or tea?"

Surprised at his intention to serve her, she asked, "Shouldn't I be doing that?"

He laughed, a soft ripple of private amusement. "I'm being kind. Which do you prefer?"

No point in arguing. "Coffee, thank you. With milk."

She watched him make it and bring it to her, noting he seemed more relaxed. Her own tension had eased, whether from the release of having carried through her purpose, or from the weird sense of having her fate taken out of her hands, she didn't know. Maybe she was suffering some aftermath from the shock of hard decision-making. Whatever the reason, she felt oddly detached, even when Tareq came close, placing her coffee on the low table in front of her and settling on the sofa nearby.

"You said we'd be flying out tonight. Where are we

going?'' she asked, trying to get some bearings on what would be her new life.

''The U.S.''

She'd never been there. It might have been an exciting prospect under normal circumstances, but she seemed to be anaesthetised to all feeling at the moment. Shock, she decided. She'd been bombarded by the unexpected and driven to accept it. Recovery time was obviously needed.

She sipped her coffee. Tareq watched her, not with the high-powered intensity she had found so disturbing. It was more a clinical observation. It didn't touch her inner self. Since he appeared disposed to answer questions, she tried to think of what she needed to ask.

''Will I get to say goodbye to the children?'' Already they seemed distant to her. It was as though she had stepped from one world into another.

''Yes,'' he assured her. ''All going well at the meeting with your father, you and I will proceed to Werribee.''

''I drove here in a jeep,'' she remembered.

''Your stepmother can drive it home. You will come with me in my car. There'll be time for you to pack your belongings and take your leave of Jessie and the twins.''

''While you wait for me.''

''Yes.''

A hostage isn't allowed to roam free, she thought. I'm tied to him. So why aren't I feeling a sense of bondage?

Because it doesn't feel real. Not even this conversation seems real. Sooner or later reality will kick in again and then I'll feel it. In the meantime, talking filled the emptiness.

''Jessie wants to meet you,'' she prattled on. Strange irony. Was Tareq a benefactor or a curse? ''She watched for you yesterday, hoping to see you featured on television, but you weren't. She was very disappointed.''

"Then I'll make up for the disappointment by meeting her this afternoon," he said smoothly.

"You've got the wrong clothes on," she told him. "A sheikh is supposed to wear sheikh clothes."

He smiled. "I'm afraid I don't have them with me. Will the person do?"

The smile made him even more magnetically handsome. "I'm sure Jessie will be impressed." As she herself had been at twelve...impressed and flattered to be given his attention. Perhaps he was always kind to children. They made it easy. They didn't question so much.

Her mind flitted forward, away from the past and on to the future. "I guess I'm to have Peter Larsen's ticket on the plane tonight."

He shook his head. "There are no tickets, Sarah. I have my own plane."

Of course. A private luxury jet, no doubt. She was moving up in the world. Like her mother. Only to a higher strata again. That should amuse her but it didn't. "Will we be accompanied by many people?"

"I prefer to travel lightly. Only Peter came with me on this trip."

Which meant she would be alone on the plane with Tareq. Though not quite alone. There would have to be a pilot, a steward, perhaps a co-pilot for such a long flight. Whatever...there would be no getting lost in a crowd. Was she to be his closest associate?

"Peter Larsen implied he'd known you a long time."

"Since school days at Eton."

So Mr. Larsen was very upper-class English. Sarah

wondered if he knew her second stepfather. "I presume you trust him," she said a little cynically.

"Yes. He's never given me reason not to."

A question of trust…

"How long do you expect it to take…for my father to prove himself to you?"

He eyed her speculatively. "Did you watch the running of the Melbourne Cup yesterday, Sarah?"

"Yes. On television."

"Then you must have seen with your own eyes that Firefly did not run the distance he should have been trained for."

She frowned, remembering how the horse had tired. "I thought the jockey had misjudged his run."

"No, it was more than that. The horse wasn't up to the distance and he should have been."

Firefly…

A suspicion wormed into Sarah's mind.

Jessie still loved the horse…but what did her father feel about it?

"I'll have Firefly entered in the Melbourne Cup next year," Tareq went on. "If he runs as well as he should…"

"You can't expect him to win!" Sarah cried in alarm, a rush of agitation smashing the odd numbness that had claimed her. "No one can guarantee a winner in the Melbourne Cup. The favourites hardly ever win."

"I agree," Tareq answered calmly. "As long as it's a fine effort for the distance I'll be satisfied."

A year of her life. Then her fate—the fate of her family—hung on Firefly's performance. Dear God! She had to talk to her father, make sure he understood. If he had some prejudice against the horse, he had to bury it or they would never get to the other side of this bargain.

A knock on the door.

Tareq rose to answer it. The timing was fortunate. Sarah struggled to contain a surge of panic. She had to remain calm, confident. Tareq was far too perceptive. He would pounce on any hint of a problem with Firefly, and if he pursued the truth and found out what had been hushed up, he might decide he had no grounds for even the tenuous trust Sarah had pleaded for.

It was room service arriving. The ordered food was set out on the coffee table. Tareq tipped the waiter and saw him out. "Try to eat, Sarah. We have a long day ahead of us," came the sensible advice.

She had absolutely no appetite. Her stomach was in turmoil. Nevertheless, eating precluded any dangerous conversation so she started with the fruit which was relatively easy to slide down her throat. Melon, strawberries, fresh pineapple…she picked and nibbled, using up time.

Satisfied she was well occupied, Tareq moved back to the telephone on the desk and made a series of calls. Sarah didn't listen to what was spoken. Her thoughts were too loud, clamouring over each other. What if she didn't get the opportunity to be alone with her father? Would Tareq tell him what the test of his training was to be?

Suddenly there were many ifs and buts. Sarah fretted over them until it struck her that her father might actually prefer to be rid of Tareq's horses, however crazy it was in a professional sense. Although he had held on to them after Jessie's accident, being paid for their training, he might have had no heart in their doing well. Maybe even taking some dark satisfaction out of making sure they didn't.

Yet surely that was at odds with a trainer's character…the drive to win, to get the best results, to chalk up enviable records. On the other hand, it could explain her father's drinking bouts. She had put them down to stress, though perhaps she had mistaken the cause of stress…a mind divided against itself.

It seemed stupid to have had Firefly not running the distance, with his owner—a man as astute and as knowledgeable about horses as Tareq—watching his failure to perform. Yet…weren't there people who wanted to be caught, wanted whatever they were doing to end?

She should have waited to discuss the issue with her father. She should have…

Her heart jumped at another knock on the door.

Her father?

She leapt to her feet, spinning around to face…Peter Larsen…as Tareq admitted him to the suite. The two men stood murmuring to each other. With a muddle of anxiety running rampant in Sarah, the question shot from her lips.

"Did my father agree to the meeting?"

It startled both men into turning to her. Her heart kicked into a gallop. She concentrated on Peter Larsen. He was responsible for making the arrangements. His sharply inquisitive gaze told her nothing. He seemed more interested in pegging her into a newly revised slot than answering her question.

"Why wouldn't he agree, Sarah?"

It was Tareq who spoke, drawing her attention to him, and once again the power of the man came at her full bore, his eyes like electric probes, making her whole body quiver inside. How was she going to cope with this man when he could affect her like this? He'd caught her so off-guard she was hopelessly stumped for an answer. Her frantic mind finally seized on one.

"Pride. You fired him yesterday. He might be angry about me interceding on his business. I didn't think about him so much as…"

"He's here. In Peter's suite," Tareq stated, removing her uncertainty. His face took on a ruthless cast as he added, "If he doesn't agree to my terms, I'll be a very surprised man. Don't concern yourself with contingency plans, Sarah."

He was set on the bargain. He wanted it to happen. He would *make* it happen. She could see it in his eyes. And she had the prickly feeling it had nothing to do with horses anymore. It had to do with her.

"Tell the Hillyards I'm on my way, Peter," he said, nodding to the man who needed no other signal to do the sheikh's bidding. "Sarah, it's best you wait here while we settle this business with your father."

She tore her gaze from him and stared at the door closing behind Peter Larsen, wanting to snatch him back, wanting the orders altered.

"Have you changed your mind?" Tareq asked quietly.

She flashed him an anguished look. "I want to be in on the discussion with my father. I might have done wrong…"

"Then it's up to him to say so. You have done your part. The choice is now his."

Cool, clear reason. Yet she sensed the fire of purpose in Tareq and knew instinctively it wouldn't be deterred by anything. Tentacles of fear started weaving through her, clutching at her heart and mind. What had she set in motion? Where would it end?

"Speak now if you prefer not to go through with this, Sarah. I won't take it kindly if you try to back out after I've made a settlement with your father."

She took a deep, deep breath.

The equation was the same.

The future security of the children was at stake.

"As you said, it's up to my father. If he agrees, my agreement stands."

Again the flash of satisfaction in his eyes, curling her stomach.

"This may take some time. Please be at ease here. Use whatever facilities you like. Treat the suite as your own."

He left her to stew over what was transpiring between the two parties.

It was over an hour before he came back, an hour of agitated pacing, of sick turmoil, of swinging through so many emotions, Sarah felt like a limp rag when he re-entered the suite. She could tell nothing from his expression. It was guarded, controlled, yet he carried an aura of success.

"Well?" she challenged, on painful tenterhooks as to the outcome.

"I believe we've come to a clear and mutual understanding. Your father will continue training my horses. He and your stepmother would like to speak to you, Sarah. If you'll come now..."

It was done.

Really done.

The next year of her life belonged to Tareq al-Khaima. He might not be dressed in traditional clothes but Sarah had no doubt he was a sheikh through and through, born to rule, used to dictating his own terms, determined that his will be carried out.

The only question left was…what was his will where she was concerned? Her soul trembled at the thought of finding out that reality.

CHAPTER FIVE

THE stretch limousine heightened Sarah's awareness of what life with Tareq was going to be like. She sat beside him on a lushly cushioned, blue velvet seat, every luxury at hand—cocktail bar, television, radio, telephone—and tinted windows around them, forming a cocoon of privacy from the ordinary world. Even the chauffeur, having been given directions to the Hillyard farm at Werribee, was removed from them by a glass partition.

Tareq dominated her space, dominated her thoughts, dominated her every sense.

Her gaze was pulled again and again to the hands resting on his thighs; long-fingered, brown-skinned, elegantly formed yet suggesting a tensile strength capable of catching and holding anything they wanted to. The future of her family was in those hands now, and she was within very personal reach of them any time he chose to make physical contact.

Her nostrils kept picking up the subtle scent of some male cologne. She hadn't noticed it in the hotel but in the close confines of the car, it intruded enough for her to try to define it, thinking it might define the man. Like the navy suit he wore, it was classy, understated, yet tantalising in suggesting something primitive overlaid with especially tailored sophistication.

Her ears were constantly alert for any movement from him, a shift towards her, a recomposure of himself. He seemed to have mastered the art of utter stillness, which

made Sarah extremely conscious of her own little out-
breaks of nervous fidgeting.

He hadn't touched her since he'd drawn her into con-
senting to the bargain. He didn't need to. He knew she
was now tied to him by honour and integrity. She could
feel his touch on her heart and mind and soul.

In her mouth was the sweet-bitter taste of what he had
drawn from her father on her behalf, whether by threat
or persuasion or simple instruction, she didn't know.
Susan's tearful gratitude she could accept as a natural
response, but her father's halting speech had been a raw
exposure of hidden hurts, intensely embarrassing.

It had touched on feelings they had never talked
about, never acknowledged, and because nothing of that
ilk had ever been said between them before, Sarah had
difficulty in deciphering what was sincere or simply
forced out of the situation. She couldn't help thinking of
the Christmas in Ireland where she'd spilled too much
to Tareq…a kind stranger she'd never expected to meet
again…a man who was acutely, dangerously perceptive.

"Did you tell my father to say those things to me?"
she blurted out, wanting to know how pervasive Tareq's
influence had been in that last painful scene at the hotel.

Out of the corner of her eyes she saw his head turn
towards her. Sarah had to summon up her courage to
look directly at him, needing to maintain a protective
shield around herself while she held his gaze.

"What things, Sarah?" he asked, the powerful blue
eyes scanning for cracks in her hastily erected defences.

"About not letting me down again."

"You think he didn't carry any guilt over abandoning
you to your mother's whims when you were twelve?"

"Did you make him feel guilty, Tareq?"

A slight shrug. "Perhaps I tapped at his conscience in explaining why you felt you could approach me personally…the past connection between us."

"You must have laid it on thick," she accused.

He was completely unabashed. "Sometimes it's very beneficial, very sobering, for people to be faced with the consequences of the decisions they make."

There was a hard glint of ruthlessness in his eyes.

Her father had certainly been sobered up by the time she'd walked into Peter Larsen's suite. His alcoholic bender the night before had left him looking drawn and haggard, his eyes red-rimmed, but he'd spoken with convincing determination about making good on this second chance. Having accepted Tareq's terms, whatever they were, he could hardly do anything else. He'd undoubtedly been made to face that his career in training was on the line.

It was the second part of his speech she questioned. He'd moved straight on to expressing—openly expressing—his regret in failing her as a father; his realisation that he'd selfishly accepted her ongoing assistance to his family, thinking only of their need instead of seeing she was putting her own life on hold; his hope that her new position with Tareq al-Khaima would be a door to a lot of opportunities for her; and finally, his fervent vow to live up to her good faith in him and be there for her if she ever called him in need.

They had to be lines fed to him by Tareq. Under duress. Although it was possible her father had taken them to heart. Either way, it was too late for a real rapprochement between them. Tareq was taking her away.

"I didn't have much evidence of his caring for you, Sarah," Tareq remarked, reading her thoughts with disquietening ease. His mouth quirked. "And what good is a hostage without a strong value of caring? I thought it worthwhile to add an appropriate load of guilt."

Questions answered.

Sickened by his logic even as she recognised its truth, Sarah dropped her gaze and turned her face to the side window. They were out of the city and travelling through the countryside to the place she thought of as home. Except it had ceased being her home eleven years ago when her status had changed to occasional visitor. More recently she'd been the live-in family help. But she didn't belong there. She didn't belong anywhere.

Which had probably made it easy for Tareq to claim her with no one to protest, no one to fight for her. She was on her own. But that didn't mean she was a pushover for anything he wanted. Her hands curled into determined fists. If he made unreasonable demands on her she would fight him.

Without looking at him, she asked, "What are the duties of a travelling companion?"

"To travel with me." His tone was lightly amused.

Her nails dug into her palms. "Nothing else?"

"Oh, I daresay we'll come to various little accommodations."

"Like what?"

"You can unclench your hands. I've never taken an unwilling woman to bed with me."

Smarting at his knowingness, she flashed him a furious glance. "It's all very well for you, sitting in your control box."

He laughed, his eyes dancing, teasing, enjoying his control. "Are you a virgin, Sarah?"

"That's none of your business!" she cried, futilely willing the rush of hot blood to her face to recede.

"Just curious. You're so uptight…"

"There've been plenty of men interested in me."

"Was the interest returned?"

She thought of the "precious" young men her mother had lined up as "catches" for her before she'd left London. Compared to Tareq al-Khaima they were bloodless boys. She was swimming with a shark in these waters. Which raised the question of how many *willing* women he'd gobbled up along the way.

"Let's talk about you," she said defiantly.

"By all means. What do you want to know?"

"No doubt you've had quite a love-life."

"A little correction there. I don't think love has ever entered into it. Desire, certainly. Satisfaction, yes. Mutual pleasure definitely attained…"

"All right!" she cut him off, disturbed by the images running through her mind. "Let's say sex-life."

"Ah, yes. Well, I can't deny having had considerable experience."

The smile lurking on his mouth was tauntingly sensual. Sarah could feel her blood heating up again. She had no difficulty in believing he was a very sexy man when he put his mind to it. If he put his mind to it with her…but it would be madness to succumb even if she did wonder what it might be like with him. Where could it lead? He was a sheikh, tied to a culture that was very foreign to her.

"Won't it put other women off, having me tagging along with you everywhere?" she commented archly, wondering if he'd looked down the track to see the consequences of *his* decision.

"Not at all. You'd be surprised," he said cynically.

He was right. Even marriages didn't stop some people from going after what they wanted.

"What about your family? It could give them the wrong impression."

His mouth curled with some private satisfaction. "They will think what I tell them to think. Where my family is concerned, it suits me very well to have you with me, Sarah."

His ruthless streak was showing again. This time it piqued her curiosity. "Why?" she asked, wondering if he was at odds with them.

He weighed the question, his eyes regarding her speculatively. Eventually he said, "My background is similar to yours…a broken marriage, my mother returning to England, the agreement that I be educated there at Eton and Oxford. It got me out of the way for my father's second wife and the family they had together."

No wonder he had been sympathetic to the child she had been, cut adrift between two worlds and not really belonging to either. He really had understood and possibly empathised with her sense of apartness, her loneliness, the feeling of being a shuttlecock in an adult game that sought only personal gratification.

"The difference is…the complication is…I'm my father's eldest son, despite my mixed heritage," he said sardonically. "The sheikhdom had to pass to me when he died."

"Did you want it?"

A flash of ruthless possessiveness in his eyes. "I was entitled to it."

And no one was going to take *that* away from him, Sarah interpreted.

"Though the truth is...I am not in tune with my people. For years now, my uncle has ruled in my absence while I maintain a diplomatic role. It has suited us both very well. But circumstances change. My oldest half-brother will soon marry the daughter of a very powerful family. Ahmed and Aisha make a formidable coupling. If they work against me, it could stir some political instability. My uncle is pressing for me to marry a woman of his choice to cement my position."

Sarah inwardly recoiled against the concept of an arranged marriage although she knew it was done and accepted in eastern cultures. For Tareq, it would seem the most sensible decision to make.

"You don't want that?" she queried.

A flash of steely pride. "No one dictates my life anymore, Sarah."

She could well believe it!

"Naturally I will be attending my half-brother's wedding. And you'll be with me. It neatly disposes of any machinations my uncle might have in mind."

So Tareq had a purpose for her. Sarah could see it was very convenient for him to have a woman on tap who'd agreed to stay with him for a year. No possibility of a refusal to accompany him. No running away, no matter how sticky the situation.

The bargain he'd offered her suited him on many levels.

"I suppose you'll want us to pretend to be..." *lovers* teetered on her tongue and she quickly withdrew it as a possibly dangerous suggestion. "...closer than we really are in front of your family."

Amusement sparkled. "I don't think any pretence will be necessary."

Did he mean to seduce her before then? Sarah's heart flipped over. Her whole body started churning as she remembered how he'd measured her desirability. Then, when he'd offered the bargain, she'd stood like a mesmerised idiot, letting him touch her. Had that assured him he could make her *willing*?

"You'll soon get bored with me, you know," she fired at him, hating the thought he was confident of arranging everything his way. She might have agreed to being his companion but she wasn't his slave!

His amusement broke into a laugh that tap-danced all over Sarah's nervous system. "I can't remember when I've felt so challenged by a woman. But you could be right. A year is a good test."

A year...

God help her!

She turned to look out the window again, knowing more now but not exactly comforted by the knowledge. They were passing by familiar Werribee landmarks. Soon she would be saying goodbye to all this, leaving the safe little world where she had been closeted for two years.

Her heart began to ache. She would miss Jessie and the boys. Though Tareq was right. They were Susan's children, not hers. All the same, it didn't mean she couldn't love them...her half-sister and half-brothers. They were the only family she had.

Tareq had capitalised on her feeling for them.

She was risking herself for their sake and they'd probably never know. Not that it mattered. She knew. Regardless of what happened to her, something good had been achieved. Jessie and the twins would not become the flotsam of a broken family.

Like her.

Like Tareq.

Except no one in their right mind could think of Tareq al-Khaima as *flotsam*.

CHAPTER SIX

As THE limousine came to a halt in front of the house, Sarah saw Jessie zoom along the veranda in her electric wheelchair, heading for the series of ramps that would bring her down to the road. She could go almost anywhere on the property in the custom-made chair, the powered base giving it a four-wheel suspension and amazing mobility. The novelty of seeing a stretch limousine at close quarters was not about to be missed.

Jessie wasn't the only one whose curiosity and interest were aroused. The foreman's wife came to the veranda railing, watching as the chauffeur opened the passenger door. Sarah waved to her as she stepped out, determined on acting as naturally as possible in the circumstances. The startled look at Sarah's arriving in such style turned to awed wonder as Tareq emerged from the car.

"Sarah!"

Jessie's cry of surprise claimed attention. The little girl was also staring goggle-eyed at Tareq, the chair halted several metres away as she took in the man accompanying her older half-sister.

Sarah was momentarily tongue-tied, not having prepared what to say to Jessie. Tareq had dominated her thoughts during the trip here. Now the moment was upon her, she instinctively seized his arm and drew him forward with her. Since this was his doing, let him handle it.

"Jessie, remember how disappointed you were not

seeing the sheikh yesterday? Well, here he is… Sheikh Tareq al-Khaima!''

''Really?'' Incredulity was almost instantly mixed with excitement and pleasure, lighting up her face and dismissing all her woes. ''You came out to see me?''

''Sarah told me about you, Jessie,'' he answered, smiling indulgently and offering his hand. ''You'll have to forgive the suit. I don't wear robes outside my own country.''

''Oh!'' Jessie blushed. Her small hand was gently enfolded in his. ''That's all right. You look…well, sort of like a royal prince anyway,'' she said in an admiring rush. ''And the car is fantastic!''

''Would you like to see inside?'' Tareq invited.

''I'd love to!''

Sarah realised she was still hanging on to Tareq's arm. She quickly released it as they moved to make room for Jessie to manoeuvre her chair into position beside the car. It was crazy to have seized on closeness to him for some kind of reassurance. Yet he was good with Jessie. Faith…if it could be called that…in his kindness to children had been justified.

''That's a great machine you're driving,'' he remarked, watching her zip the chair around the passenger door which he'd opened for her viewing.

''It's the Rollerchair Trail Blazer,'' she proudly informed him.

He grinned. ''Well, I'd have to say it blazes, Jessie.''

She laughed. ''You mean the colours. Dad got them specially for me. I reckoned with a red seat and a yellow frame, everyone would see me coming.''

''Couldn't miss,'' he agreed. ''It's a brilliant combination. I'm afraid this car is fairly dull in comparison.''

''No, it's not,'' Jessie insisted, peering in at the plush interior.

''Would you like to have a ride in it with me? I could lift you in and strap you up and sit beside you, showing you everything while the chauffeur drives us around.''

''Yes, please,'' Jessie cried, thrilled at the prospect. ''Wait till I tell the twins about this!'' she crowed at Sarah.

Her arms went trustingly around Tareq's neck as he gently scooped her out of the electric chair, no hesitation at all, despite his being a virtual stranger. Somehow his innate strength of personality and self-assurance evoked confidence in him. Sarah, too, had accepted his trustworthiness when she'd been a child. She wished it could be the same now.

''Sarah, will you move my chair out of the way, please?''

She operated the toggle switch with the ease of long practice, reversing the chair to a safe distance. Jessie had no compunction in instructing Tareq how best to settle her on the seat of the car and he showed no discomfort with her disability, chatting away naturally while he settled her as promised.

''Perhaps you'd let the lady on the veranda know what Jessie and I are doing,'' he said to Sarah as he straightened up, hard blue eyes turning the request into a command.

Only then did she begin to understand there was purpose in his kindness. They'd come to collect her passport and possessions, and he was diverting Jessie while the real business was done. ''Of course,'' she answered, forcing a smile. ''Enjoy the ride, Jessie.''

"Aren't you coming, too?" came the slightly plaintive plea.

Tareq answered for her. "Sarah has other things to attend to, Jessie. She'll be busy for a while. I was hoping, after our drive, you'll show me what you've got in the special rooms your father had built for you. If there's anything more like your Trail Blazer…"

Jessie giggled. "It's the best. But there is some other clever stuff I can show you."

A master manipulator, Sarah thought, as she left them to head up to the house. Though it had to be conceded he was making the situation less harrowing for her, keeping Jessie happily occupied and probably setting up an understanding of why Sarah would be going with him instead of staying at the farm.

The foreman's wife stood at the top of the steps to the veranda, her gaze darting between Sarah and the limousine. Ellie Walsh and her husband had been working for the Hillyards since Sarah was a child. Ellie was in her forties, a tall spare woman with a no-nonsense attitude. She invariably wore a shirt and jeans and kept her hair cut in a short, boyish style. Practicality was her byword.

"What's going on?" she asked as Sarah started up the steps.

The limousine was moving off. Sarah smiled to relieve any worry. "Jessie has just made the acquaintance of Sheikh Tareq al-Khaima. He's treating her to a bit of high life in his car."

"The sheikh!" Shock and alarm crossed Ellie's face. "Has he come about his horses?"

It was obvious she knew the training wasn't up to par.

Probably everyone who worked here knew but none of them wanted to be unemployed.

"Everything's all right, Ellie." Sarah could only hope it would be. "The sheikh has offered me a position and I'm taking it. I'm here to pack and say goodbye."

Ellie was dumbfounded, her fears about the future frozen in the face of such unexpected news.

"Susan is on her way home. She's got the jeep and will be collecting the boys from school," Sarah went on. "I really appreciate your minding Jessie at such short notice today…"

"No problem," Ellie muttered. "You're really going with the sheikh, Sarah?"

"Yes. It's an opportunity to widen my horizons again."

Ellie shook her head, still stunned at the turn of events. "The children will miss you."

"I'll miss them, too, but…" She shrugged. "…I can't stay here forever."

"I guess not," came the weak rejoinder. "Well, I'll leave you to it. I wish you luck, Sarah." She gave a funny laugh. "Mind you don't end up in a harem."

It was a possibility for the duration of the brother's wedding, Sarah thought ironically, though she had the strong impression Tareq didn't hold much with tradition. In any event, taking a wife was not on his agenda. Squashing the issue of marriage was.

Having seen Ellie on her way, she went into the house to set about uprooting herself again. It was difficult to keep depression at bay as she dragged her million-miler suitcase out of the storage cupboard and set it on her bed, ready for another packing, another move. She'd made a personal home of the room Susan had given her and it hurt to look at one more part of her life which was now over.

Her gaze mournfully skimmed the colourful collection of soft toys she'd knitted while sitting with Jessie. They were lined up on top of her chest of drawers, waiting to go to the boys' school fete. A stack of library books was on her bedside table, some of them destined to be left unread. Photographs depicting Jessie's progress were glue-tacked to the frame of the mirror on her dressing table. No point in taking them. They belonged here.

Sarah fiercely concentrated on what had to be taken…clothes, toiletries, important documents. The sooner her packing was accomplished, the better, she told herself, and set about tackling her clothes first. Most of them were leftovers from her student days, hardly a suitable wardrobe for the high life, but Sarah shrugged off that problem. If Tareq wanted her dressed differently he could pay for it. She hadn't exactly applied for the position of his companion.

A shiver of trepidation ran down her spine. Would he think he was buying her if she let him pay for clothes? He obviously didn't have any high expectations of women, viewing those who'd been in his life as nothing more than sexual partners. *Willing* sexual partners. When he'd said he'd never felt so challenged by a woman, did he mean because she wasn't offering herself to him?

Sarah shook her head, trying to dismiss the rising anxieties. Stupid to keep worrying about the future. The decision was made. Whatever the outcome of a year with Tareq, she had to take it in her stride and let it flow past her. It was one thing she used to be good at, letting things flow past her.

It had been different with Jessie and the twins. Her

involvement with them had been so easy, natural…an uncomplicated love, given and returned. Sarah hoped it would always be the same with them. All going well, they would still be here next year when she returned with Tareq for the Melbourne Cup.

Her packing was well under way by the time Jessie returned with Tareq. She stood still, listening to the high excited voice leading her important visitor down the hall to her especially equipped domain. There was no pause outside Sarah's door. Jessie had to be still in ignorance of her half-sister's imminent departure.

Almost an hour later, Sarah took her luggage out to the veranda. The chauffeur collected it and stowed it in the limousine. Susan and the boys still hadn't arrived. Sarah waited outside until she caught sight of the jeep approaching the gate into the property, then steeling herself for the inevitable leave-taking, she walked quickly into the house and straight to Jessie's suite.

A swell of emotion broke past her guard as she knocked on the door. Tears stung her eyes and her chest was so tight, the deep breaths she forced herself to take were painful. Keep it bright, keep it simple, and make it quick, her mind dictated. It would be easier that way, easier for everybody. Having blinked back the tears, she pasted a smile on her face and opened the door.

Why her gaze went first to Tareq, she didn't know. It was Jessie she had to face, yet somehow he dominated even this parting scene…sitting in the chair she usually sat in, commanding attention simply by being in this room. He looked at ease, yet she felt the driving force behind his kindly facade and her heart quailed at what she had invited upon herself in accepting his bargain.

The electric chair hummed into life. Sarah tore her

gaze from Tareq and looked anxiously at Jessie, now turning away from the desk where she'd obviously been showing Tareq some of her sketches. She had a real gift for drawing, a talent Sarah had encouraged her to develop since it was not dependent on two active legs. One day it might lead her into a rewarding and fulfilling career.

"You can sit on my bed, Sarah," she invited, her little face still glowing with excitement. "Are you all packed, ready to go with Tareq?"

The knowledge and the ready acceptance in the question jolted Sarah. "I...yes. The chauffeur put my luggage in the car," she answered weakly, searching for and finding no sign of distress in the child. "I know it's sudden, Jessie, but..."

"Oh, you couldn't miss out, Sarah," came the eager urging. "You'll have a wonderful time with Tareq."

"You don't mind my going?" It amazed her, disturbed her that Jessie seemed to care so little about losing her.

"Gosh, Sarah! It's not as if everybody's sister gets asked to travel with a sheikh." She looked absolutely entranced with the idea. "You're so lucky!"

"Yes, aren't I?" she agreed, trying to inject some enthusiasm into her voice.

She darted a glance at Tareq as she sat on the bed, wondering if he'd brainwashed Jessie into thinking he was sweeping Sarah off on a magic carpet. The look he returned telegraphed very clearly he left nothing to chance when he wanted his purpose achieved. Sarah knew she should feel grateful he'd removed any trauma from the situation. Instead, she felt cheated, as though he'd wiped out the value of her involvement with her family.

"I'll be thinking of you all the time," Jessie went on. "Promise you'll send me postcards of wherever you go, Sarah?"

"Of course I will." Her inner stress eased a little at this evidence of wanting a continuing connection.

"I'm going to get a big map of the world and put it on my wall. Every time I get a postcard from you, I'll stick in a pin of where you are so I'll only have to look at it to know and think of you there. Isn't that a good idea?"

One of *his*? "I'll be thinking of you, too, Jessie. I hope you'll write to me."

"I'll write you very special letters, Sarah."

This declaration was accompanied by a secretive smile which she shared with Tareq. His smile in response indicated a conspiratorial arrangement. Sarah hoped Tareq wouldn't conveniently forget his part of it once they were away from here. She didn't want Jessie disillusioned by broken promises. On the other hand, she couldn't argue with the ideas he'd implanted. It seemed he had gone out of his way to ensure she remained a presence in her family, however far away she was.

"I'll look forward to hearing all your news, Jessie," Sarah said in warm encouragement. "You must write me news of the boys, too."

She giggled, delighted with the plans concocted with Tareq. "It's going to be such fun!"

The eruption of noise in the house heralded the twins' approach. They burst into Jessie's room, two hyperactive bundles of trouble with wild, curly hair and big brown eyes, determined on finding the sheikh and seeing him for themselves. Jessie performed the introductions and both boys looked their fill of the man, somewhat daunted by his powerful presence.

"Mum said you're taking Sarah with you," Tim spoke up, showing his misgivings about this arrangement.

"Sarah is ours," Tom stated belligerently.

"Sarah will always be yours," Tareq answered, smiling his assurance. "She's your sister and she loves you. Coming with me won't make any difference to how she feels about her family."

"But I don't want her to go away."

"Don't be a baby, Tom," Jessie cried in exasperation. "Sarah's a grown-up and she hasn't had any time for grown-up things with us. You've got to be fair."

Another one of Tareq's ideas?

"Do you want to go, Sarah?" Tim asked.

"I do need to do something more with my life, Tim," she answered, "though I've loved being here with you."

"Who's going to tell us bedtime stories?" Tom demanded.

"I will," Susan said from the doorway. "And I think you should thank Sarah for giving you so much of her time instead of making her feel bad about leaving you."

"We didn't mean to make you feel bad, Sarah," Tim rushed out. "We want you to be happy."

"Well, she'll be real happy with Tareq," Jessie declared, giving her younger brothers a supremely smug look. "*I* went for a ride in the stretch limousine!"

The boys instantly set up a clamour to be taken for a ride, too. Tareq good-humouredly agreed, inviting Jessie to lead them out to the car. She had a lovely time, playing Queen Bee, escorted by the sheikh who had apparently taken on the guise of fairy godfather.

"Will you be happy with him, Sarah?" Susan asked, scanning her anxiously as they trailed after the limousine party.

"I expect it will be an experience," she returned dryly.

Susan shook her head fretfully. "You've done so much for us. I don't know what to say...except thank you."

"Try to keep Dad off the bottle, Susan."

"I think Tareq has taken care of that. Your father got caught up in doing things he really hated and now he'll be free of it, thank God!"

The passionate relief in Susan's voice piqued Sarah's curiosity. She stopped walking and stayed her step-mother from following the others off the veranda. "I'm not sure I understand," she said, her eyes sharply questioning.

Susan looked intensely discomfited. "Never mind. Better that you don't. Drew needs to save some pride. He feels bad enough it was you who got Tareq to give him a fresh start. He won't let you down on this, Sarah."

"It's not just me. It's the family," Sarah retorted, frustrated by Susan's evasion. There were some things more important than pride and she tried to press them home, given this was her last opportunity to do so. "I'd hate to see you and Dad break up."

She shook her head. "I'd never leave your father. We've been through so much. He stood by me when I was hopelessly incapacitated. I'd stand by him through anything, Sarah. Don't worry about us. We'll get over this hump and turn it all around."

Faced with such faith and determination, Sarah didn't have the heart to question further. Marriage was a private business to the two people involved and nothing she said would make any difference anyway. It certainly hadn't in the past.

They remained on the veranda, watching Tareq directing the final show for the day. The limousine took off for another spin around the property, carrying three exuberant children and the man who held all their lives in his controlling hands for the next, testing year.

"I'm sorry you were so messed around by the divorce, Sarah," Susan said, apparently stirred into an awareness of where her stepdaughter was coming from in the previous conversation.

"Not your fault," Sarah replied dismissively. Sympathy had not been around when she'd needed it and hindsight sympathy only made the omission worse.

"I could have offered to keep you here with us. But I didn't," came the regretful admission.

Sarah had had a gutful of guilt from her father. She didn't want it from Susan, too. "Water under the bridge," she said curtly.

"I want you to know you'll always be welcome here. Any time. For as long as you want."

Too late, Sarah thought with rueful irony. A debt was owed now. People were uncomfortable with debts. It colored the flow of natural feelings. Though not with the children. They would never know. Nevertheless, it would lie between her and their parents, denying her the closeness she would have liked.

"Thank you," she said, acknowledging the offer which had been sincerely made, however unlikely it was to be taken up. Tareq was about to dominate her life for the next twelve months. Perhaps longer if…her heart clenched with a sense of ominous urgency as she turned to her stepmother. She'd almost forgotten the most critical thing of all!

"Please tell Dad to do his best with Firefly, Susan. It's important. Tell him from me it's terribly important if he doesn't want to let me down."

Tareq might have freed her father from his self-made stress, but Firely's performance was her passport to freedom.

"I'll tell him," Susan replied.

"You won't forget?" Sarah pressed.

"I promise."

Promises…she'd had a gutful of them, too…broken ones.

The limousine came back.

Her time here was up.

The children were happy to say goodbye…hugs and kisses and well wishes. Sarah settled on the plush seat beside Tareq. The chauffeur closed the door, the last separating act. She watched her family waving her off as the limousine moved away from them. There was no point in her waving. They couldn't see her. She was behind tinted windows, cut off from them, enclosed in Tareq's world.

"Thank you for making it easy," she said stiffly.

"Was it easy?"

She grimaced, her eyes drawn to his by the gentle probe for honesty. "Yes and no."

He nodded, understanding her ambivalence. There was both comfort and disquiet in his understanding so much. Recalling his skill at manipulating everyone today, Sarah was goaded into making one stand on principle.

"I appreciate your…graciousness…in the circumstances. But if you've made promises to Jessie, please keep them, Tareq."

The blue eyes held hers, unperturbed, unwavering. "I never make promises I don't intend to keep."

Sarah suddenly felt foolish for raising the matter. Everything he'd said today indicated he set a lot of store by trust. In his life it was probably as precious a commodity as it was in hers.

"Then you *will* let me go if Firefly runs well next year," she said, wanting him to voice that promise in undeniable terms.

She felt the power behind his eyes intensify, boring into her, flooding her veins with tingling heat, enmeshing her mind with threads of entanglement that would never let go unless he willed it.

"You will be freed...from being a hostage."

His words rang hollowly in her ears, rendered meaningless by vibrations of a much more personal connection. Sarah knew in her bones she would never be free of Tareq, even given the lifting of the hostage tie, even given he didn't want her with him beyond that time.

The impression he'd left on her twelve-year-old mind was still with her, and that had only been a week of her life. How much stronger would it be after twelve months?

"Why are you doing this to me?" It was a cry of protest, wrung from the depths of her being.

He didn't question it. He didn't pretend he didn't know what she meant. "You think you don't touch me, Sarah? What am I doing here?" His eyes glittered with a reckless pleasure in the challenge. "We shall travel this road together until I know all of it."

CHAPTER SEVEN

SARAH didn't want to get out of bed. The moment she woke she remembered what was ahead of her today—the trip to Silver Springs, being at Tareq's side amongst other people—and the now familiar tightening of nerves around her stomach made her feel sick.

Ten days she'd been with him—another three hundred and fifty-five to go—and at this rate of personal upheaval, she was not going to survive the distance. It was difficult enough, coping with the tension of her position when she and Tareq were alone together. The thought of others looking on, questioning the relationship, speculating, as they surely would, stirred an intense inner violence. She wanted to hit out at something but there was nothing to hit out at, nothing of any substance.

Tareq could not have been more gentlemanly towards her, more considerate. There was no physical touching she could object to, no unseemly words she could hang him on. It was the constant waiting and expectation of something more to come from him that had her on edge.

Worse was her growing obsession with the man, the insidious attraction she couldn't control, the tug-of-war between denial and desire, the awful, vulnerable sense of being powerless to stop what was happening to her.

Unless she reneged on their bargain and left him.

Which was impossible.

She'd given her word. And Tareq was ruthless enough to withdraw the agreement with her father if she failed to keep it. There was no escape and he knew it. He had all the time in the world to make his move on her. If he chose to.

We shall travel this road together until I know all of it.

With those relentless words beating through her mind, Sarah turned over, punching her pillow for the lack of anything else to punch. Her gaze fell on the lush tropical garden in the courtyard beyond the double glass doors of her bedroom. She'd forgotten to pull the curtains last night. Not that it mattered. The guest suite she'd been given was completely private, even to the courtyard outside. She couldn't accuse Tareq of intruding on this space, yet the knowledge it was his house and he was in it with her, was constantly intrusive.

This past week on the west coast of Florida should have been heaven, a vacation in a warm sunny climate, one of the most handsome and wealthiest men in the world intent on giving her pleasure, making no demands on her whatsoever except to relax and enjoy herself. It had turned into a hell of ever-increasing awareness. Of him. Of herself.

Her mind flitted over the procession of events, tracing the progress of her torment. The plane trip to the States hadn't been too bad. Perhaps emotional and physical exhaustion had drawn a protective curtain around her. Tareq had been solicitous of her comfort, coaxing her to eat and drink at various intervals during the flight, but she'd managed to put him at a distance from her, sleeping a lot, watching videos, reading magazines. He'd let her be, not pushing his company on her.

After they'd landed at Fort Myers, she'd focused on external things, looking at where they were going, asking questions about what they were passing. They'd driven through a fabulous estate development comprising dozens of magnificent homes and luxurious condominiums set on perfectly landscaped and beautifully maintained lawns and lakes and gardens, three golf courses, neighbourhood pools and gyms and tennis courts, a private beach and marina facing onto the Gulf of Mexico. It had surprised her to learn it was one of Tareq's property investments, another mind-boggling sample of the wealth at his disposal.

"Have you come to check on it?" Sarah had asked.

"Not particularly. I kept one of the houses facing the beach for myself. It's a convenient base for this time of year. People come to spend the winter months here."

Only very rich people, the kind who mixed in his league.

"And it's not far from Ocala. Handy for looking at the horses on the ranches around there. I've been advised there's a couple of yearlings that might interest me."

"So we're here on business."

"A short vacation first." Blue eyes smiling warm kindness. "You need it."

Kindness with a purpose…always a purpose behind everything Tareq did.

The first day…arriving at this fantastic house with its impact of glorious space; huge airy rooms, tall ceilings, lots of glass, the decor in all shades of sea colours; pale blues and greens, white tiles on the floor, rugs patterned with sea-shells, wicker furniture…a beach house, but on such a luxurious scale it seemed a misnomer to Sarah. Being given her own suite and meeting the couple who took care of everything—Rita and Sam Bates—created a comfort zone. For the first day.

The second day had actually been fun, bicycling around the estate, trying out the pool and hot tub, discovering the wonderful taste of stone crabs, a special delicacy of the area served by Rita that night. Seeing Tareq stripped to a minimal swimming costume had been slightly unnerving but not overly disturbing. She could still concentrate on other things at that point.

The third day he'd taken her on an exhilarating airboat ride over the Everglades, skimming the seemingly endless grassy marshes, seeing the fascinating bird life and alligators, amazingly a nest of baby ones. She had enjoyed it, though she'd become very conscious of Tareq watching her enjoyment, gleaning some private pleasure in it.

She had the sense he had forgotten what uncomplicated joy was like and was relearning it from her. It had made her feel good, useful, of some positive value, giving him something that had been lost from his life.

The next day there'd been a rapid escalation of good feelings. Too rapid. It reminded her of sugar candy being spun around a stick. One was so entranced with the fairy floss, the stick supporting it was lost in a cloud of pink.

Tareq had taken her to Smallwood's Store and she'd wandered around the historic trading post, fascinated by all the relics of the past which had once been sold to the pioneers of the Everglades, coming in their boats which they tied to the piers of the old wooden structure at waterside. Furs and plumes were traded here for food and cloth and all manner of household goods from lamps to treadle sewing machines, medicine, books, every kind of working tool. The place was a treasure chest of past lives and Sarah revelled in the experience of stepping back in time.

Tareq had seen it all before but he wasn't bored, wasn't the least bit impatient with her journey of discovery. He shared the knowledge he'd picked up from reading local books, fed her interest, indulged her fascination, and watched her with a warmth that kept getting under Sarah's skin.

There was something very intoxicating about approval. She'd had so little of it in her life. Yet she found herself wary of its bestowal from Tareq, not quite trusting it, looking for the purpose behind it. Was Tareq subtly plumbing her unfulfilled needs and wants to establish a deeper tie with him?

I don't think any pretence will be necessary.

Better if the woman he used for confronting his uncle was very convincingly stuck on him.

The fifth day they'd spent on the beach. The sand was gritty with broken-up shells. They lay on loungers shaded by umbrellas, swam in the relatively warm waters of the gulf, picnicked from a hamper Rita had prepared for them. It should have been a blissfully relaxing day, if only Sarah had been able to keep her eyes off Tareq.

She couldn't help it. In clothes the man was strikingly handsome. Virtually naked, for hours on end, lying beside her, walking in and out of the water, towelling himself, his physical beauty was almost mesmerisingly addictive, compelling her gaze to linger on his perfectly proportioned and powerfully muscled body. More disquietening was the desire to touch. His skin gleamed like rich, bronze satin and it was a continual strain to clamp down on the impulse to reach out and graze her fingers over it.

He caught her watching him slap oil around the calves

of his long, strong legs. ''Want some?'' The blue eyes twinkled teasingly, knowingly, shaming her with the realisation he had to be aware of his effect on the opposite sex and she was proving no different from any other woman.

''No. I'm fine, thank you,'' she'd answered stiffly.

He'd returned to his task, smiling to himself, and there was still a little curve on his lips when he lay back down on the lounger, his eyes closed to her. Was he amused that she couldn't stop herself from being attracted to him? Satisfied it was beyond her control? Or was she being hopelessly neurotic, reading a connection to her into a smile which might simply be expressing gratification in a lazy, sensuous day.

Sarah's gaze slid down over his taut stomach and fastened on the very male bulge at his crotch. She felt a point of sexual heat start burning between her own thighs and quickly turned away from him, squirming both physically and mentally from the wild desire to know what he was like as a lover, to feel that body intimately engaged with hers. She'd never actually lusted over a man before. It made her uncomfortably conscious of her own body, as well as his.

On the sixth day they'd gone fishing with Captain Bob, which had been another new and exciting experience until she'd had the misfortune to hook a very big fish on her line. She wasn't strong enough or practised enough to reel it in. Tareq had stood behind her, his arms around her waist, one hand helping to hold the rod in its holster, the other closed over hers on the handle of the reel, showing her how to play the fish on the line.

It wasn't a sexual embrace, merely a supportive one, yet it blew away all Sarah's concentration on what she was supposed to be doing. It was Tareq who eventually landed the fish. All she remembered was his breath warming her ear as he gave instructions, the strength of his fingers pressing on hers, the electric excitement coursing through her body from the contact with his, the sudden scorching hunger to feel everything he could make her feel.

When he moved away, admiring the catch netted by Captain Bob, Sarah was left trembling violently, shocked by the snaking intensity of sexual need which was still writhing through her. She dropped shakily onto the closest bench seat and stared at the fish, caught no matter how much it struggled. Like her, she thought, only Tareq was still playing her on his line.

"Let it go," she'd croaked, then fiercely challenged the quizzical look from Tareq. "I want it released."

"Your fish," he conceded, nodding to Captain Bob.

It wasn't really hers. He'd caught it. Perhaps that was why she felt such a savage surge of satisfaction, watching it swim free again, a silver flash in the water, escaping the painful confusion of being pulled into a different, alien world.

On the seventh day, Tareq had casually announced he was taking her shopping for clothes.

Defiance had leapt off her tongue. "No!" The thought of parading a range of outfits for Tareq's approval, having his eyes measuring their effectiveness, how well each garment fitted her figure…her stomach had cramped. She couldn't bear it.

Tareq had frowned at her vehemence. "I thought you would enjoy it." His frown had deepened. "There is also the matter of feeling at ease when we start mixing with others, Sarah." A quiet, gentle reasoning. "Inevitably, you will suffer considerable scrutiny as my companion. Critical scrutiny.''

Resentment at her enforced position had spilled out. ''And you'd prefer me not to look the little brown mouse at your side.''

His eyes had sparked with amusement. ''You're more a lioness than a mouse. Protecting your cubs.''

His reminder of the children made this even more a cat and mouse game to Sarah. Except Tareq wasn't a mere cat. He was a dangerous, dark, and very sleek panther, prowling around her, waiting to pounce, keeping her in almost intolerable suspense.

''It is irrelevant to me how you are dressed, Sarah,'' he'd declared. ''My main concern was to protect you from the bitchiness of other women. However, if you feel armoured enough against their barbs...''

She wasn't. She knew she'd hate being looked down upon, hate looking like a fish out of water. ''I do need some new clothes,'' she'd admitted grudgingly, then in a proud show of independence, had added, ''It's just that I want to go shopping by myself, choose them myself, and pay for them myself.''

To her intense relief he had let her do precisely that...after the embarrassment of having to accept the thirty thousand dollars he put in her credit account, a three months' advance on the salary he'd arbitrarily decided upon.

''But I don't do anything!'' she'd protested.

''That's for me to judge,'' he'd answered.

Recognising the futility of arguing, Sarah, nonetheless, had no intention of frittering away anything like that amount on clothes. Sam Bates had driven her to Naples, a shoppers' paradise with its many fashion boutiques, and she'd managed to find quite a few bargains amongst end of season stock that had been marked down.

Temporarily freed from the turmoil Tareq stirred, Sarah had enjoyed acquiring a range of clothes she felt really good in, assuring herself she didn't have to be competitive. As long as she was confident in her appearance, she'd be fine. Though she did wonder if Tareq was as uncaring about it as he said.

"Pleased with what you've bought?" he'd asked on her return to the house, eyeing the shopping bags with interest.

"Do you want to be shown?" she'd challenged.

He'd laughed, shaking his head. "I'll see soon enough."

But there'd been something—a cynical glint in his eyes?—that had made Sarah suddenly feel there'd been a purpose in letting her go shopping alone, a test in giving her so much spending power. The sense of being weighed on everything she did had her swinging from fierce belligerence—why should she care what he thought of her?—to sick panic, because she did care.

It was crazy to crave his good opinion, crazy to crave what could only be a self-destructive liaison with him. There might be physical satisfaction—even intense pleasure—in experiencing his sexual expertise, but there'd be humiliation, too, knowing she was letting down the ideals she'd clung to for so long. All the same, she hadn't known how strong carnal desire could be...its raging demands, its dreadful distraction, its power to pervert any normal thinking.

Sarah closed her eyes to the brilliant light of this new day, wishing she could shut Tareq out as easily. Maybe it would be easier with the company of other people around them, drawing his attention away from her. Looking at the horses he wanted to see had to be a diversion, too. The trip to Silver Springs might be less of an ordeal than she'd initially thought.

After all, she didn't know the people she'd be meeting. What they thought about her didn't really matter. Here today, gone tomorrow. Tareq was the unavoidable constant. Somehow she had to learn to live with the way he affected her.

A knock on the door. "Sarah?" *His* voice calling out.

Her eyes flew open. Her heart catapulted around her chest. She had to work some moisture into her mouth before answering. "Yes?" It came out high-pitched and quivery. He hadn't entered her suite all the time they were here. Was that about to change?

"There's a letter from Jessie. Do you want to come and read it?"

So much for her fevered imagination! On a wave of sheer delight, Sarah leapt out of bed, thrust her arms into her light silk wraparound to cover up her satin slip nightie, and raced to the door. She'd bought and sent postcards to Jessie and the twins but they couldn't have received them yet. It was a lovely surprise to get a letter so soon.

Her face was lit with happy anticipation as she opened the door, her smile spontaneous as she held out her hand for the expected envelope. Tareq grinned at her, his eyes taking in her dishabille and obviously savouring the lack of restraint apparent in her appearance. In sharp contrast, he was immaculately groomed and freshly clothed in body-hugging blue jeans and a white and navy Lacoste sports shirt.

Fighting a prickling sense of vulnerability, Sarah stared pointedly at his empty hands. "You said…"

"Tousled hair becomes you."

Was he checking how she looked first thing in the morning? Her teeth clenched. It was a non-effective action in stopping the rush of heat to her face. "Tareq…" she bit out.

"The letter came in on E-mail. You'll have to read it off the monitor screen in my study."

"E-mail?"

"Much quicker than the postal service."

Incredulity billowed over her confusion. "Jessie's using E-mail?"

"It's not difficult once you've learnt how. Follow me and I'll show you."

He set off, taking it for granted she would do as he dictated. Sarah hesitated, torn between having her curiosity immediately satisfied and wanting to bolt back into her bedroom and get properly dressed so she wouldn't feel at such a disadvantage. The drawcard of modern technology won over fears that seemed silly with Tareq's back already turned to her. Tying her belt firmly to prevent her gown flying apart, she trailed after him to the study which was furnished with every form of communication.

Tareq waved her to the swivel chair at his desk. The monitor screen above a computer keyboard glowed invitingly. Sarah could hardly believe her eyes as she sat down and began reading the printed script.

Dear Sarah,
I bet this surprises you. I'm writing this on my very own computer. It came the day after you left and a

tutor has been showing me how to use it. I can do drawings on it, too, and colour them any way I want. If I don't like one colour, I can use my mouse to change it to another colour. Isn't that marvellous? And so quick. Tareq said it would be a lot of fun and it is. It's the best present. Please thank him for me…

Her mind spun in shock. Her gaze jerked up to the man standing beside her. "You bought Jessie a computer? And lessons?"

He nodded. "Children take to computers very quickly. Here she is, up and running already," he said, clearly pleased with her progress.

"But why?" The extravagance of the gesture stunned her, even as she recalled the conspiratorial smiles he and Jessie had swapped, and his insistence that he kept the promises he made.

"I took you away," he answered with devastating simplicity. "This puts Jessie in easy touch and has the added benefit of keeping her well occupied. It's a great educational tool for a handicapped child."

Dear God! She had thought him ruthlessly manipulative while all the time he'd been thinking and planning how to help a crippled little girl over the absence of her big sister and give her something good to go on with.

"I'll show you how to reply once you've finished reading," he offered matter-of-factly.

She couldn't read. Her eyes were blurred with tears. She shook her head helplessly.

"Sarah?" He gently tilted her face up, his eyes questioning her distress.

"It's so kind…so generous," she choked out.

His mouth twisted into a self-deprecating grimace. "A

bit of thought, an order given, and the cost meaningless to me. Nothing compared to the two years you gave.''

"I love her." Reason enough to give anything.

"I know. After what happened to you as a child, it amazes me you didn't lose the capacity to love." He tenderly brushed his knuckles across her cheek. "I'm glad you didn't."

Her heart contracted at the sense of enticing possibilities hovering. "Did you lose your capacity to love?" she whispered, the softness of the moment prompting the impulsive question, the wish to reach into the inner man and know what he was truly made of.

Then suddenly the moment wasn't soft anymore. His hand dropped from her face, erasing the warmth. A hardness glazed his eyes. She could almost hear the armour he wore being locked into place. No cracks.

"Let's say it was whittled away very effectively," he answered sardonically. "To the point where I prefer horses to people. Horses are always beautiful. You can establish an empathy with them. And on the whole, they run true to form."

The cynical comment drove her to protest. "But you cared about Jessie."

"I always try to balance what I give and what I take, Sarah. I pride myself on playing fair."

"By whose rules?" she flared, afraid that what he might take from her could never be given back.

He laughed. "My own, of course. In the end, we have to live with ourselves so it's best to stay true to what we personally believe is right."

It was a sobering reminder of what she knew in her heart. Somehow she had to steel herself against the temptations inherent in being with Tareq al-Khaima.

There was no love on offer, only bargaining chips. If she didn't stay true to herself…yet what was true? Since she'd been with Tareq, a Sarah she hadn't known before was emerging, a stranger with needs that swamped common sense.

While Tareq—damn him!—was always in control.

"You don't need to stay. I know how to use E-mail," she said curtly, focusing her eyes on the screen again.

"Very well."

His withdrawal hurt, which was utterly stupid since she'd more or less asked for it. She tried to ignore the thud of his footsteps, concentrating fiercely on the words Jessie had written to her.

Please thank him for me…

She hadn't.

"Tareq…" She spun the chair around to face him. "Yes?"

He paused in the study doorway, half turning to look back, so supremely composed, so arrogantly confident, so totally self-contained, so frustratingly untouchable, it stirred a wilful streak in Sarah that furiously dismissed the danger of courting trouble. He touched her whenever he felt like it. She wanted to know how he'd react if she touched him, if he'd still keep his armour intact.

Her feet sped across the room. Her hands lifted to splay over his chest. She went up on tiptoe. "A thank you from Jessie," she said, and kissed his cheek.

The next instant her hands were trapped by his, preventing their removal. Her palms were forcibly pressed to his body heat, transmitters for a sensory power that charged up her arms and exploded through her body, making every cell tingle with awareness of imminent and possibly cataclysmic change. His eyes blazed, scouring her soul of the petty vengefulness that had driven her, searing it with white-hot needs her mind could not even begin to encompass.

She stared back, helplessly caught in the thrall of his power, fearful of what she had triggered so heedlessly. She felt herself begin to tremble, shaken by the whirlwind of sensation beating through her. Her heart seemed to be thumping in her ears. Her breasts were swelling, tightening. A heavy, dragging feeling in her thighs was transforming into a melting heat.

Most shocking of all, he saw…he knew…and he said, "Don't tempt the devil unless you want to play with fire, Sarah."

Harsh, challenging words. No intent to seduce. No forcing anything. Demanding an unequivocal decision from her. And her memory spewed out the words… *I've never taken an unwilling woman to bed with me.*

Living by his rules…

Dear God! What were hers? How could they be so easily lost, overwhelmed? In sheer panic she clutched at safety. The alternative was too frightening.

She swallowed hard and forced out the one weak excuse for her behaviour she had. "I was only thanking you."

"Were you?"

Her skin burned.

The searing fire in his eyes slowly retreated to a mocking simmer. "So be it then. Consider me thanked."

He carried her hands down to her sides, released them, then walked away…a man of rigid principle.

Sarah was left feeling bereft…foolish…relieved. The truth was scorched indelibly on her brain. She could and had tapped into a furnace of feeling that would swallow her up if she opened the door to it. Touching was very different to loving, powerful but extremely perilous and not to be played with. Unless she wanted to be completely consumed by Tareq al-Khaima.

Surely that would be the ultimate madness.

Or would it be the ultimate experience?

CHAPTER EIGHT

TAREQ cursed himself for being a quixotic fool. He could have taken her then. He could have spun her into a sexual thrall so fast, resistance wouldn't have occurred to her. Instead, his body was screaming against the restraint he'd imposed on it.

For what? She wanted her curiosity satisfied. She wanted to know what he'd be like as a lover. She was so transparent...

And so was her innocence, he reminded himself savagely.

He headed out to the pool, stripped off and dived in, threshing through the cool water for several lengths, using up the explosive energy that had been denied its natural outlet. When he finally paused for breath, the needling tension had gone but he was still at war with himself.

He'd thought to give Sarah a good slice of life while he had the satisfaction and pleasure of knowing her in every sense. A fair exchange, he'd reasoned. She'd get to experience all she'd been missing out on and he'd enjoy giving her pleasure, showing her the world, being her teacher.

She was different to the women who usually peopled his life and he'd wanted to savour the difference. The bitter irony was the very difference that appealed to him, defeated the purpose he'd started out with.

It was cruelly obvious her loving heart would attach

more to sexual intimacy than the physical satisfaction he had in mind. If he took advantage of her vulnerability, how would they both feel about it afterwards? She'd already suffered a miserable pile of disillusionment in her life. He had a gut-recoil to adding another heap of it.

Yet he wanted her, wanted the full experience of her. He was so damned jaded, her freshness had a compelling appeal and with her giving nature, her artless honesty, whatever he had with her would be very special. He knew it and he wanted it more than anything he'd wanted for a long, long time.

So what the hell was he to do?

The quandary was killing him.

He had to find some way around it.

CHAPTER NINE

THE calm after the storm, Sarah thought ironically, sitting through breakfast with Tareq. His usual gentlemanly manner had been resumed without the slightest suggestion of strain. Sarah worked hard at holding a natural approach to today's activities, asking about the ranch they would be visiting, the horses that interested him, the people who owned them.

She fixed their names in her mind—Jack and Miriam Wellesly-Adams—suspecting the double-barrelled surname represented an amalgamation of two very wealthy families. She'd taken her cue from Tareq, dressing casually in jeans, a black pair which had a matching battle jacket she could wear if the afternoon turned cool. Her lime green polo-necked top went well with it. Since no critical comment was forthcoming from Tareq, Sarah concluded she was suitably attired, regardless of her hostess's fashion standards.

Although dinner this evening was somewhat trickier. She and Tareq were to be overnight guests. "Classy casual," he'd advised when she'd asked him what to pack for it. How classy and how casual were left undefined. Sarah hoped her new lemon pants-suit fitted the requisites.

Cluttering her mind with superficial details kept more fretful thoughts at bay. Sarah almost managed to pretend she felt no tension at all. Logic insisted that as long as she didn't touch Tareq, he would respect whatever distance she chose to hold. Pouncing was not on his agenda. He was playing a waiting game. Though if she let herself think about that, her nerves would start screaming again.

She was glad when it was time to go. She wanted to put the confrontation in his study behind her, a long way behind her, physically as well as mentally. Once they were on the road she could immerse herself in the role of travelling companion and hopefully find lots of distractions.

Tareq surprised her.

A gleaming red Cadillac convertible was sitting outside the house and Sam Bates was loading their overnight cases in the trunk. Sarah stopped and stared. They'd been riding around in a silvery grey BMW all week. This car had certainly not been in evidence. Anyone would have to be blind not to see such a flamboyant vehicle.

"Where did that come from?" The question spilled from her lips.

"I hired it for this trip," came the matter-of-fact reply.

Sarah shook her head. It made no sense to her. Tareq spared no expense on his comfort and convenience but she didn't have him tabbed as a show-off sort of playboy. The red Cadillac convertible shouted *Look at me*! *I'm king of the road*! She tore her gaze from the glittering, extrovert attraction of the car and searched Tareq's eyes for the purpose he had to have for it.

"Why?" she asked.

He grinned, totally disarming her and sending a flock of butterflies through her stomach. "For fun," he answered and held out the keys to her. "I thought you'd enjoy driving it."

"Me? But I can't, Tareq. I've never driven on the wrong side of the road."

He laughed. "Here it's the right side. And you won't find it a problem on the highway. You just drive along in a lane as you do at home."

She was torn between caution and temptation. "What if I make a mistake?"

"I'll be right beside you with advice and instructions."

Still she hesitated. "It will be much safer if you drive."

"Safe, Sarah?" His eyes sparkled a teasing challenge. "How very boring! Haven't you ever thought it might be fun to drive such a car with the sun on your face and the wind in your hair and the wheel in your hands?"

"Of course I have."

"So be brave. Take a risk. Do it. At least once in a lifetime."

She took the keys, took the risk and did it, embracing the exhilaration of zooming along the highway at the controls of a flashy convertible because it was fantasy-fun and such an extraordinary experience might never come her way again. For a while driving demanded all her concentration, but once she was accustomed to the car and the different use of the road, her mind started niggling at Tareq's motives again.

Was this another test?

Had she grabbed too quickly at the once-in-a-lifetime thrill which he had the means to provide? Seduction could come in many guises and unlimited wealth was a powerful lure. Scorning the offer of driving this extravagant toy might have been a more principled stand than accepting it. She didn't want him to think he could buy her.

On the other hand, he could be measuring her capacity to dare against the instinct for safety. He had made it seem wimpish to refuse. Perhaps he thought she'd wimped out this morning after kissing him and was seeing if she *would* take a risk on something she found sensually attractive.

On reflection, Sarah had to dismiss that idea. He would have arranged the hiring of this car beforehand, probably yesterday. All the same, there had to be some purpose behind getting it for her to drive. She certainly didn't believe it was the whim of a moment.

"What made you think of doing this for me, Tareq?" she asked, darting a glance at him.

She saw the beginning twitch of a smile but had to return her gaze to the road. Since it was impossible to watch for any changes of expression and be a responsible driver at the same time, she tried to listen for telling nuances in his tone of voice.

"It's one of life's innocent pleasures. I wanted you to have it."

"Why?" Was it completely innocent?

"Why not? I could do it. Therefore I did."

Like the computer for Jessie. But there'd been a reason for that. Sarah felt uncomfortable being the focus of his spending power. "You said this morning you try to balance what you give and take…"

"And you wonder if I'm giving you an innocent pleasure so I can take a wicked one." Dry amusement.

Her heart fluttered. "I'd rather know the price if there is one," she rushed out, wanting the truth, needing to know how he thought of her.

''No price, Sarah.''

The flat, unequivocal statement left no ground for more questioning, yet she felt frustrated, wishing he would explain himself instead of letting her seethe in ignorance.

''Surely there can be prizes in being with me,'' he said quietly.

It sounded like an appeal. Sarah darted a glance at him. He caught it, jolting her with the intensity of feeling in his eyes; a disturbing cocktail of desire and a dark, personal damnation. She wrenched her gaze back to the road, struggling with the sense of having hit unexpected turbulence.

''You don't have to show me the prizes,'' she said, thinking they were undoubtedly balanced by penalties.

''Knowing them is part of our journey together. Only in knowing everything does a choice become clear.''

''What choice do I have in our journey?'' she tossed at him.

He laughed. ''A multitude of them. All the time you are choosing how much to give me, how much to keep to yourself, how much you will take from me.''

She flushed at the accuracy of the perception.

''It is interesting, is it not?'' he teased.

''I'm glad you find it so,'' she grated, feeling she was being directed through hoops for his entertainment.

''Come now, Sarah. Wouldn't you say it puts an exquisite edge to our involvement with each other? We are not bored, either of us. Finding the right pieces of the jigsaw and fitting them together is exciting.''

There had to be thousands and thousands of pieces of him. She imagined he would put her together in his mind

much faster. "Well, I guess once you have the full picture, boredom will set in," she said dryly.

"Or will it be satisfaction?" he mused. "A picture of
rare beauty can give endless satisfaction."

Beauty was in the eye of the beholder, Sarah thought,
wondering just how demanding Tareq's eye was. "You
may find the picture flawed."

"Flaws can have an individual charm. They can be
more endearing than perfection."

Sarah sighed. She was no closer to knowing him and
she resented his way of seeking knowledge of her. "I
don't like the feeling of being tested."

"Were you not doing the same to me when you kissed
me this morning?" he countered sardonically.

It was true in a way. Yet it had been more a driven
impulse than a calculated plan. Testing him? She pon-
dered the concept and decided it was alien to her. She
wasn't cold-blooded enough to work out the equations
and act on them as ruthlessly as Tareq did. Maybe that
was something she had to learn if she was to survive a
year with him intact.

"Be honest with me, Sarah," he urged, steel gloved
in the softly persuasive tone of voice. "Was it not an
experiment to test your touching power?"

Sarah instinctively recoiled from such cold, clinical
terms. "Not in the way you mean," she protested painfully. "I was trying to reach out to you. To whatever it
is you keep to yourself. I guess…in the light of how you
reacted…that was very silly of me."

He made no comment. His silence dragged on for so
long it grew heavy with a host of mulled-over variations
of what he left unspoken. Sarah glanced at him but he
wasn't looking at her. He appeared sunk in deep thought,

his face an expressionless mask as he brooded behind it. For a few moments she exulted in the possibility his calculations had been upset. Then she realised there was nothing to be gained by it anyway. He was probably re-working his jigsaw to accommodate a rogue piece. Or maybe he was realising she didn't fit and would never fit into the picture he wanted.

She drove on in a miserable haze of despondency. Gone was the exhilaration of driving a convertible. The car ate up the miles just as every other kind of car did, moving from point A to point B.

"We're getting close to Ocala," she said matter-of-factly. "Is the exit to Silver Springs clearly sign-posted?"

"I'll point it out to you when it comes up," he assured her, alertness instantly galvanised.

The interstate highway had not exactly been a scenic route. However, once they'd turned off it and were heading towards Silver Springs, the beautiful countryside lifted Sarah's spirits. They passed one magnificent ranch after another; all of them with expensive railing fences enclosing pastures that looked like perfectly mown green lawns, picture postcard settings for the thoroughbred horses grazing in them. Even the grass verges on either side of the road looked mown, incredibly tidy if not. Wonderful trees, pleasingly placed, provided ready shade.

Such superbly maintained properties bespoke long-held wealth, used lavishly over generations. It was strange, comparing them to Michael Kearney's estate in Ireland and her father's farm in Australia...the amazing contrasts in style and form. What she was seeing here seemed distinctly American, with just as high a priority placed on appearance as on performance. Such attention to detail was truly marvellous.

The homesteads were just as breathtaking, mansions on a huge scale, fascinating in their stunning architecture. When Tareq pointed out their destination, Sarah couldn't help gasping. The Wellesly-Adams home could have graced one of the old Southern plantations; rows and rows of wonderful white columns, two storeys high, with verandas decorated by gloriously ornate, white lace ironwork.

The house alone seemed to offer a veritable Eden to explore and Sarah confidently anticipated ready distraction from Tareq and the stress of resolving their differences. There was no warning of a serpent within who would poison any peace of mind for her.

Their host and hostess could not have been more friendly and charming in greeting their arrival. Tareq and Sarah were graciously ushered into the vast foyer, basking in Miriam and Jack Wellesly-Adams' warm welcome. Then down a staircase designed for dramatic entrances, came a female cobra, all primed to strike.

"Tareq, darling…"

She was thirty-something with the patina of long-practised polish; long, gleaming blonde hair, a dazzling mouthful of white, white teeth, a sexy, sinuous body encased in orange lycra-satin shirt and slacks, belted brilliantly with graduated gold chains, gold bangles on her arms, gold hoops in her ears, gold slippers on her feet, but no gold ring complementing her orange fingernails.

"Dionne…this is a surprise!" Tareq responded. "Is Cal with you?"

"Hadn't you heard, darling? Cal and I separated

months ago. When Dad and Mimsy said you were coming today, I couldn't resist flying down from New York to say hello.''

She fell on him…kiss, touch, feel…busy hands and pouty lips…saying hello with neon lights flashing *I'm available and I'd just love to climb into your jeans*.

Sarah hated watching her in action. Tareq had warned her nothing stopped some women and she knew it. They just waltzed in and staked their claim. But the black violence ripping through Sarah's heart had nothing to do with reason. A primitive possessiveness was raging through her. She wanted to fly at the woman, tooth and claw, and fling her away from Tareq. She wanted to scream he belonged to her!

Above the frenzy of her feelings rose a sense of shock, of dawning horror. How could she care so much! The only tie she had to Tareq was that of being his hostage, and he had no tie to her at all. This obsession with him had to stop.

Yet she couldn't stem the tide of revulsion she felt at his failure to push Dionne away from him. He did absolutely nothing to stop the woman drooling over him. He didn't care. And that hurt. It hurt so much Sarah tried telling herself his laissez-faire attitude meant nothing.

She had witnessed such licentious greetings many times at her mother's parties. People on the high society circuit took such liberties for granted. It was part of the game of keeping irons in the fire and a keen eye on the main chance. *Do I want this? Well, I'll just keep it warm in case I do.*

Her stomach cramped. If Tareq thought like that…

''And who have we here?'' Dionne trilled, snuggling herself around Tareq's arm as she judged it time to give some scant acknowledgment to his travelling companion. Her feline green eyes skated over Sarah, summing up the competition and dismissing it.

"Good heavens, darling! So young! Have you taken to escorting schoolgirls around the world?" Tinkling amusement. Flirty eyes. "No wonder you requested separate bedrooms."

"Dionne, you are embarrassing Sarah," her father chided, though he smiled indulgently at his *darling* daughter.

"Not at all," Sarah cut in, seething over the putdown. "Though perhaps Tareq…" she shot him a chilling, black-eyed blast "…might now take the time to introduce us."

The coolly delivered reprimand amused him. He unhitched himself from the clinging blonde and stepped slightly aside, using his now-freed arm to gesture from one to the other. "Sarah, this is Dionne Van Housen, Jack and Miriam's daughter, and until recently, the happy wife of a good friend of mine."

Dionne pouted playfully at him. "If Cal had made me happy, darling, I wouldn't have left him."

"That could be a comment on expectations being too high, Dionne," he said dryly. "May I introduce Sarah Hillyard, who was, indeed, a schoolgirl when I first met her, but that was eleven years ago. Happily, for me, time has moved on."

"Hillyard…Hillyard…should I know the name?" Dionne quizzed, prompting for Sarah's level of importance on the social register.

Tareq shrugged. "Unlikely. Michael Kearney was Sarah's stepfather during her teenage years. Her mother is now married to the Earl of Marchester."

Sarah burned with humiliation at being so labelled, as though her connection to the men in her mother's prize pile lifted her onto a more acceptable level. It revolted her even further that Tareq should feel the need to blow up her importance. Wasn't she good enough for him as she was?

"An earl! Doesn't that make your mother a countess?" Miriam Wellesly-Adams exclaimed, very favourably struck by this relationship with the English aristocracy.

She pounced on Sarah with the avid eagerness of milking a marvellous jackpot for all it was worth. Which neatly left Tareq to the eager come-ons of the snaky daughter all during the elaborate lunch, served in what was called the conservatory annexe.

Sarah hated every minute of it. Politeness demanded she answer her hostess's insistent and persistent questions on the English upper class, but she silently vowed never to suffer being put in such a position again. It was horribly false. Everything felt horribly false. How could a man feel the desire Tareq had shown her this morning, then toy with another woman? Where was the honesty in that?

Or maybe, since she hadn't made herself available, he simply and cynically took what was. After all, Sarah would keep. He had a whole year to play his game with her.

The luncheon dragged on. Tareq divided his time between talking horses with his host and responding to Dionne's demands for attention. The orange fingernails caressed his arm so often, Sarah began to wish they'd draw blood. It would serve Tareq right. She wanted him to feel as rawly wounded as she did.

It was almost four o'clock when they rose from the table, their host having suggested a visit to the stable yards was now timely. The offer to be transported by jeep was declined by Tareq who insisted a stroll would be more to his liking. A master of manipulation when he wanted to be, he persuaded Dionne into riding in the jeep with her parents and singled out Sarah as his walking companion.

Which suited Sarah just fine. It gave her the opportunity to lay down a few accommodations he could make for her in future. A hostage didn't have to be dragged everywhere. She was determined on loosening the tie with him. She had to for her own sanity.

As soon as the jeep was on its way, she dug her heels in and opened fire. "If you want to sleaze on with Dionne Van Housen, then count me out. I'll wait in my room until dinner."

Tareq turned to face her, one eyebrow raised in mocking amusement. "Sleaze on?"

"I find it disgusting. She's not even divorced from your *good friend*, Cal, yet, and you're letting her lech all over you."

"Since I've accepted the hospitality of her parents, what would you have me do, Sarah?"

"Oh, don't give me that excuse!" Her eyes blazed contempt for it. "You think I haven't been faced with stuff like that from my mother's high-flying crowd? It's easy enough to take a step back, offer your hand and maintain some personal dignity. The message gets across that liberties aren't welcome."

A smile twitched at his mouth. "Thank you for the lesson."

She huffed her exasperation. "You don't need lessons

in handling people. And you don't need me as a spectator for your little peccadilloes.''

He laughed. ''I'm not the least bit interested in Dionne. But it is interesting that you have such a strong reaction against her liberties with me.''

The urge to slap his self-satisfied face was so strong, Sarah swung on her heel and marched off down the road to the stable yards, the other option of going to her room driven from her mind by the need to walk off the violence sizzling through her. Him and his damned jigsaw, fitting the pieces together! She was a human being, not bits of cardboard, and she would not be moved around for his entertainment!

He strolled along beside her, reforging the link she was desperately trying to repel. ''From henceforth I shall keep other women at a distance,'' he declared. ''Better now?''

''Better if you leave me out of these social occasions,'' she shot at him. ''You don't value my company. Why bother with it?''

''If I didn't value it I wouldn't have sought your company for this walk. You have no reason to be jealous, Sarah.''

''It has nothing to do with jealousy,'' she lashed out in seething fury. ''It's a matter of pride. I do not like being escorted by a man who lets himself be a target for loose women right in my face.''

''If you were indifferent to me, Sarah, it wouldn't matter. And with some women, other priorities would keep them silent and tolerant.''

''Well, stick to them if that's what you expect,'' she raged. ''I don't want to be with you anyway. You're a snobby pig.''

"Ah! If this relates to my name-dropping, that was a ploy to cut dead any further patronising remarks."

"I don't care about patronising. People can be as patronising as they like and as far as I'm concerned it reflects badly on them, not me."

"It can still be upsetting."

"Oh, sure!" she mocked. "You're talking to a survivor of a toffee-nosed British boarding school where I was an Australian nobody. And let me tell you, Tareq al-Khaima, I don't need a name to prop me up as a person. I am *me*, no matter what I'm called, and if that's not good enough for you, then park me somewhere else when you want to mix with others."

"I'm delighted to be corrected on that point," he said quietly. "Such strength of character is so rare I wouldn't dream of parking you anywhere except beside me."

She shot him a baleful look. "Don't you ever, ever, attach me to Michael Kearney or the Earl of Marchester again. They don't turn me into something better. They diminish me."

"You're right. I'm sorry I did that to you, Sarah."

His agreement and apology stole the momentum of her fury. However, it didn't stop the sick churning of being with him and not being able to reach the heart of the man. Why did she care so much? How had he got to her so deeply? He shouldn't be able to do this to her when his caring was so insultingly shallow it didn't even begin to comprehend where she was coming from.

The all too transient pleasure of driving a convertible...

Protecting her from being patronised...

Luxuries on tap...

What good were they when her most innermost needs

craved what he was incapable of giving? He could keep his damned prizes for being with him in future! She wouldn't take any of them.

"I don't like you, Tareq," she stated bluntly, hugging in her hurt and wishing the intensity of feeling he stirred would go away.

"Perhaps, when you finish re-educating me, you'll like me better," he answered, a touch of whimsy in his voice.

It vexed her that he could take it so lightly while she was a torn up emotional mess. "Try being consistent," she muttered, shooting him a resentful glare. "Try being honest!"

He smiled at her…flooding her mind and heart and soul with the sweet, seductive warmth of approval and admiration, dazzling her with the beauty of it, the strength of it…tying her even more inexorably to him because he gave it.

CHAPTER TEN

TAREQ roamed around the sitting room of their hotel suite, pondering the situation as he waited for Sarah to finish dressing and emerge from her bedroom. This diplomatic visit to Washington had been scheduled long before he'd gone to Australia. Cancelling was out of the question. Sarah had to understand that Washington was an entirely different playground to Florida. Here, a united front had to be presented, regardless of what she felt towards him.

This dinner tonight marked the start of their public appearances and comment would flow from them. Sarah had to be brought into line with what needed to be projected... therein presenting Tareq with a tricky challenge since she had a mind of her own which was still set against him. Nevertheless, word of their togetherness would be relayed to his uncle and mixed messages would not put an effective block on the canny old man's political manoeuvrings.

It would have been so much simpler if they'd become lovers by now. Then staying at the embassy, which was his usual practice, would have established the relationship in the eyes of the staff, thereby making it very quickly known. As it was, taking up residence in the Oval Suite at the Willard-Continental was almost as good. It implied a desire for privacy in which to enjoy a new intimacy. Though he was fast coming to the conclusion there might never be physical intimacy with Sarah.

He'd really muddied his slate over that stupid business at Silver Springs. Letting Dionne Van Housen play with a flirtation had served as a distraction from his frustration, but it had cost him dearly, turning him into a lesser man in Sarah's eyes. An unlikeable man. And while he admired her high standards of integrity, they drew a line he found he couldn't cross. Not with an easy conscience.

Tareq shook his head self-mockingly. It was crazy, trying to live up to what she wanted him to be, yet he was doing it as best he could. The funny part was, it gave him a real buzz to win a smile from her, to feel warmth seeping past her guard. He liked being with her even if it was only company and conversation. He liked the purity of her thinking, the directness of her honesty. In that way, she was still the child he'd remembered.

Which put him into even more conflict.

The urge to look after her quarrelled with the constant desire to reach out and take her, make her his for as long as it worked for them. Yet as much as he told himself he'd be good for her, he couldn't quite dismiss the possibility he might end up hurting her. Badly. And hurting Sarah would be like hurting a child.

Don't make promises you don't intend to keep.

If she equated sex with a promise of love... a promise of commitment...

He couldn't lie to her.

Which left what... being honourable?

Tareq was grimacing at this unpalatable line of logic when Sarah made her entrance to the sitting room. Her appearance brought his pacing to an abrupt halt. It blotted out everything else on his mind. It shot a bolt of fire to his loins. It flipped his heart.

She looked utterly, stunningly beautiful, a picture of style and elegance, and so gut-wrenchingly sexy Tareq didn't trust himself to move. One step towards her and he'd be hauling her off to bed like a caveman.

''Will I do?'' she asked, slowly pirouetting to give him the full effect of her outfit.

A long tunic made of some soft, clinging fabric moulded every line and curve of her figure like a second skin. The high round neckline and long sleeves accentuated the effect of a total body covering stretched around her flesh to faithfully outline her femininity. It was overwhelmingly sensual yet undeniably modest. Youthful.

The green floral pattern on a background of pure white had the fresh appeal of spring, and this was highlighted by a single white silk flower, perched on one shoulder, close to the curve of her throat. No jewellery to diminish the effect.

The tunic was slit on both sides to mid-thigh, and she wore long white satin trousers underneath it, giving an Eastern flavour to the outfit, making it even more alluring.

''Well?'' she prompted, her eyes uncertain, seeking approval.

Her vulnerability pierced his heart. His plans—everything he'd thought in coming to some solution that would suit him—suddenly seemed terribly wrong. There was no clear course except… to protect her. Even from himself.

He took a deep breath, banking down the fire within. She was waiting for an answer. He should let her go…

out of his too complicated life… yet deep inside him screamed a need to keep her with him.

"Perfect!" he declared—a perfect torment of seductive innocence.

"I know it's right for me," she said artlessly. "I loved it from the moment I tried it on when I went shopping in Naples. But is it right for tonight?"

She would stand out like a spring flower amongst hothouse roses, Tareq thought, and the imagery instantly inspired the only course for him to take… if he was to keep her in his life… a bit longer anyway… long enough to make sense of everything.

"Perfect!" he repeated, smiling reassurance as he walked towards her. "You look so very lovely, I consider it an honour to be escorting you tonight."

She flushed at the compliment, pleasure warming her eyes.

He lifted one of her hands to his lips and bestowed a soft kiss of homage. Gallantry was not dead. Tareq had just resurrected it.

CHAPTER ELEVEN

London
14th December

Dear Jessie,
It hasn't snowed here yet but the weather people
are forecasting a white Christmas in England. It's
bitterly cold outside, much colder than Washington
and New York. Lucky for us, Tareq's house in
Eaton Place has good central heating. I do miss the
sun, though. I guess I was spoiled by the two
weeks we had in Florida.

SARAH STARED at the words on the computer monitor
screen and was struck by the sheer inanity of bumbling
on about the weather. It was what people did to evade
touching on anything more sensitive. It filled in space
that couldn't be filled with anything else. Certainly not
the truth. Impossible to confide the truth to a ten-year-
old child.

The acute sense of loneliness that she'd hoped to allay
by writing to Jessie became more acute. She was hopelessly in love with Tareq al-Khaima and there was no
one she could talk to about how she felt, no one she
could turn to for advice. Certainly not her mother.

The day after arriving in London she'd telephoned
Marchington Hall to ask that the clothes she'd left there
in storage be sent to her. Amongst them were her good

102

cashmere cape and some classic woollens that never went out of fashion.

"What number did you say in Eaton Place?" her mother had queried.

Sarah had repeated it and the Countess of Marchington had gloatingly pounced. "I know that address. It's Tareq al-Khaima's residence. What are you doing there, Sarah?"

There was no point in denial. Her mother was like a ferret when it came to finding out what she wanted to know about noteworthy people. "I met up with Tareq in Australia and he invited me to travel with him. I'm his guest at the moment," Sarah had rattled out, trying to make it all sound blithely innocent.

"What a clever girl you are! Do try to hang on to him, darling. He's fabulously wealthy. And so gorgeous!"

The avid note in her voice had been enough to turn Sarah off saying anything more. Everything within her recoiled from having what she felt tarnished by her mother's values. She'd swiftly ended the call, though she suspected her mother would now plot a meeting to check out the possibilities. That had to be blocked at all costs. It would be hideously embarrassing and humiliating.

Sarah gritted her teeth against a rise of bitterness and forced her mind back to the letter.

Washington...the word leapt out at her from the screen. She'd sent Jessie postcards of the White House, Arlington Cemetery, the Ford Theater where President Lincoln had been shot, the Air and Space Museum which had housed so many marvels from the first plane flown by the Wright Brothers to the Apollo space capsule carrying models of the astronauts; all the places she had visited during the day when Tareq was busy with meetings. But the nights…

It had been both daunting and exciting accompanying Tareq to the dinners and parties where his VIP status was awesomely in evidence. He was courted by politicians, lobbyists, diplomats, not to mention their wives who were very solicitous of his pleasure. No one mentioned horses or property developments. The oil markets and Middle East politics were the hot topics and Tareq handled them with an authoritative ease that demonstrated another dimension of the man.

He handled everything masterfully, from fending off fawning women to rescuing Sarah from sticky questions and ensuring she was not exposed to problems or unpleasantness by the simple but effective measure of not allowing anyone to take her from his side. Even pre-arranged places at tables were rearranged to accommodate his insistence on their not being separated.

It was stamped on every mind that Sarah Hillyard was to be respected as Sheikh Tareq al-Khaima's companion and under his protection and woe betide anyone who put a foot wrong with her or slighted her in any way. His manner to her was courteous, gentlemanly, above reproach in word and deed. In short, he treated her like a princess and subtly forced others to do the same.

It made her feel cosseted, valued, cared for as though she was precious to him. This was heightened by his air of possessiveness. Only he took her arm. Only he rested a light hand on her waist. Only he danced with her. It was heady stuff for Sarah who found it more and more difficult to keep her feet on the ground.

At first she had thought Tareq was treating her as he believed she wanted to be treated, a cynical display of his *re-education*. But there was nothing even slightly sardonic in his behaviour towards her. Then she had reasoned Washington was a hotbed of political gossip and Tareq's public performance was probably being reported to the embassy which served his country and thus back to his uncle. Perhaps she was being convincingly set up as the woman in his life so she would come as no surprise at his half-brother's wedding.

All she absolutely knew was Tareq eased off the act in private, remaining polite and considerate but holding a distance she could not cross. Some nights he parted very abruptly from her. Other nights he questioned her closely—Had she enjoyed herself? Was she interested or bored? Would she prefer not to be involved with such company?—and she had the chilling sense of more pieces being fitted into his jigsaw of her. What struck her more painfully than anything else was that once they were alone together, there was no physical touching, absolutely none.

Exhilaration…frustration. Sarah swung from one to the other like a yo-yo. She needed the daytime away from Tareq to regain some equilibrium. Yet still he shadowed her every hour. If she wasn't thinking of the evening before or the evening to come, she was thinking of what to share with him of her sight-seeing activities, how to be companionable while covering up the ever-constant desire of wanting more from him.

The same pattern had been repeated in New York, although there the meetings and dinners had been with bankers and the talk had revolved around the money markets. More new clothes had become a necessity. The between seasons outfits she had purchased in Naples simply didn't suit the New York winter and she was very conscious of not letting Tareq down in company.

They had flown to England a week ago, taking up residence in this house, and in some ways it had proved the most difficult time for her. There was nothing new about the city of London to distract her, no social engagements taking up the evenings, nothing to busy her in the house since a married couple looked after everything. And highlighting her failure to reach into Tareq's heart, was Peter Larsen, the person who knew him better than anyone.

The trusted trouble-shooter was already in London when she and Tareq had arrived. Whether he had flown directly to England from Australia, Sarah didn't know and didn't ask. Peter Larsen practised British reserve and discretion to the nth degree. He never spoke of business in front of her, despite spending most of each day at Eaton Place, either in this office which she presently occupied, or in the library where he was currently closeted with Tareq, discussing some business strategy.

He shared lunch with them, was unfailingly polite to her, and kept his own private life extremely private. The only personal thing Sarah knew about him was he owned an apartment overlooking the Thames.

She couldn't say she disliked him. He gave her no reason to. But she deeply envied the easy rapport between him and Tareq. Sometimes they talked in a kind of shorthand, their understanding so closely attuned, a look or a gesture conveyed more of a message than words.

Since the incident with Dionne Van Housen, Tareq had given Sarah no cause to be jealous of other women, but she *was* jealous of what he shared with Peter

Larsen. Their communication didn't miss a beat and the bond of trust was so strong neither ever paused to question it. Somehow it turned her into an outsider, despite being in the same room as them.

Sarah heaved a despondent sigh and dragged her attention back to the letter she had started. She had no heart for it but she tried to find something more to say.

I'm glad the parcel from New York arrived safely and the twins had such fun at school with the Statue of Liberty hats.

The symbol of freedom. Would she ever feel free of Tareq, even when the year was over? She hoped her father was making the best of a fresh start because she was surely paying for it.

The office door opened, startling Sarah out of her reverie. Peter Larsen stepped into the room, carrying a file of papers. He paused, frowning slightly as he saw her occupying the chair in front of the computer. Sarah leapt up, gesturing an apology as she sought to excuse herself.

''I was writing to Jessie. I hope you don't mind my being here while you were with Tareq.''

He shrugged. ''As I understand it, you have the freedom of the house, Miss Hillyard. Do continue your letter if you so desire.''

''I don't want to be in your way.''

''I have only to return this file to the cabinet and then I'll be leaving.'' He surprised her by asking, ''How is Jessie?''

''Fine! Looking forward to Christmas.''

He smiled. Actually smiled. ''Such a bright little girl.

She took to the computer like a duck to water. I liked her very much. Say hello to her from me.''

Sarah was quite stunned by this unexpected crack in Peter Larsen's customary reserve. ''Yes, I will,'' she answered, dazedly watching him cross the room to the filing cabinet before it occurred to her to remark, ''I didn't know you'd met her.''

He answered matter-of-factly as he took a set of keys from his trouser pocket, unlocked the cabinet and pulled out a drawer. ''I made a point of it after my last meeting with your father. Mainly to check her progress, see that the tutor was doing his job well and Jessie was happy with what she was learning.'' He glanced at Sarah, smiling again. ''She insisted on demonstrating her new skills to me so I could tell Tareq how good she was.''

A child like Jessie could bring warmth out of a stone, Sarah thought. Hoping this was an opportunity to milk Peter Larsen of more information on her family, she asked, ''How long ago was this?''

''Just before I flew out,'' he replied, inserting the file in the drawer. ''First of December.''

Sarah totted up the time he'd spent in Australia after she and Tareq had left. Four weeks. Which seemed an excessive amount.

''Was my father holding up okay?'' she asked anxiously. ''I mean…were you satisfied he was doing the right thing by the horses and everything?''

''I was satisfied your father had every good intention, Miss Hillyard.'' He gave her a sympathetic look. ''You must know that only time will bring results.''

''Yes. of course. It was just… I was worried about Firefly…and his poor performance in the Melbourne

Cup.'' She cast around for a way to ask if her father had displayed any particular attitude towards the prize horse.

"It's been taken care of, Miss Hillyard. I saw to it personally. There'll be no more trouble coming from that quarter,'' Peter Larsen quietly assured her, then proceeded to relock the cabinet.

Sarah's concerns were far from answered. Had Peter Larson taken Firefly to another trainer? But that would defeat the test of Firefly's performance at the end of the year.

"How has it been taken care of?'' she cried. "I don't see how…''

"Miss Hillyard, it's quite irrelevant how.'' There was a ruthless cast to the face Peter Larsen turned to her. "Rest assured the bookmaker who was squeezing your father has been convinced that any further attempt at dirty dealing with Tareq's horses would be very bad business. Extremely bad business.''

Sarah's mind was reeling. All her assumptions were knocked in a mushy heap and what was emerging was too repulsive to accept. Dread clutched her heart, yet she had to ask, had to look at the can of slimy worms Peter Larsen had opened up. She could barely get her voice to work. The words came out faintly, strained through a welter of emotional resistance to hearing an even more damning statement.

"Are you saying my father threw races for a bookmaker?''

The satisfaction in the light silvery eyes blanked into shock. "Tareq didn't tell you?''

Sarah felt the blood draining from her face. "It wasn't just loss of heart and…and stress…''

"But you must know,'' he argued, more to himself

than to her. "Surely Tareq asked me to leave so he could tell you in private how far your father had abused his trust…"

He was recalling the morning at the Como Hotel, the fateful morning when the bargain had been struck. It rushed back on Sarah, too. "Why did he keep it from me? If my father was crooked…taking bribes…"

Peter Larsen passed a hand across his face, muttered something vicious to himself, then recomposed his expression to impervious reserve. "I do beg your pardon, Miss Hillyard. It seemed reasonable to set your mind at rest."

"Please… I want to know…"

"You must excuse me. I have been unforgivably indiscreet."

It was true then. Had to be. It was written all over Peter Larsen as he strode from the room, tight-faced, stiff-backed, patently appalled at what he had let slip to her. He'd almost certainly go straight to Tareq and relay what he'd done. And then what?

Sarah felt sick. Tareq's words came spinning back to her…*a matter of trust*. Trust abused beyond trusting again. And Tareq knew it. Had known all along while she'd pleaded a case for lenience, for understanding, for mercy on a man who, unbeknownst to her, had criminally cheated him.

He'd sent Peter Larsen out of the hotel room right at the moment when he should have revealed the truth. If he had gone ahead and done it, as Peter had assumed, the result would have been… Sarah concentrated hard on thinking back, remembering her state of mind. The truth would have swept the mat out from under her feet, would have smashed any grounds for giving her father a second chance. She would have died of shame and given up, faced with her father's crooked dealings with a bookmaker.

But Tareq hadn't wanted that result. He had posed the bargain, pressing her to accept, using his knowledge of her, using everything at his command to get her to accept.

For what purpose?

In the light of all that had followed in these past six weeks with him, Sarah still didn't know. Tareq had her so confused, it was driving her crazy wondering what he wanted of her. She was sick to death of his testing and teasing and tantalising behaviour. She wanted answers. And she was going to get them.

Now!

CHAPTER TWELVE

SARAH didn't bother knocking. Nothing was going to stop her from having a showdown with Tareq. She opened the library door and marched in, breathing fiery determination.

Peter Larsen swung around, opening a clear view of his employer friend, seated at the splendid mahogany desk he favoured. Sarah ignored the trusted trouble-shooter, her gaze fastening directly on the sharp blue windows to Tareq al-Khaima's unfathomable soul.

"I want to talk to you. Alone. And without delay," she stated, unshakably intent on getting her own way. Tareq was not going to dominate this encounter!

He rose from his chair, languidly unfolding to his full height, insufferably confident of controlling everything. "Thank you, Peter," he said, not the slightest trace of any acrimony in his tone. "I'll see you tomorrow."

Of course there was no cause for Tareq to be upset by the indiscretion, Sarah savagely reasoned as Peter Larsen took swift leave of them. The bargain had been struck and there was no going back. Tareq was sitting pretty on whatever he was sitting on. Except he wasn't sitting anymore. He was strolling around the desk. By the time the door behind Sarah was closed, he was propped casually against the front edge of the desktop, perfectly at ease.

The urge to smash his smooth facade raged through Sarah. How many deceptions was he juggling in the super-clever mind behind that handsome face? The feeling of being a pawn in a game she was not allowed to see put a violent edge on her churning emotions.

"I wouldn't have asked you to cover up criminal activity," she hurled at him. "If I'd known my father was intentionally cheating you, I would not have come to you at all."

"But you still would have wanted what you did achieve, Sarah," came the perfectly chosen pertinent reply. "Your father given a chance to redeem himself, and the security of the children assured as far as it can be."

In other words, everything else should be considered irrelevant. Sarah dug in her heels. "And just how far have you gone to achieve that, Tareq? How far do you go to get what you want?" she demanded heatedly.

He replied with calm logic, completely unruffled. "I find that people usually listen to reason when the profit and loss are laid out to them. Irrefutable facts do have impact."

"You withheld facts from me," Sarah pointed out, her eyes flashing resentment at his cavalier way of doing what suited him with her.

"I didn't want to hurt you," he said with heart-twisting simplicity. "You were innocent, Sarah."

But she *was* hurt, hurting non-stop from his keeping things from her and his arbitrary withdrawals that drove her into a deep trough of frustration. This confrontation wasn't really about her father. It was about attitude and honesty and the direction of this journey they were supposed to be taking together.

"I'm not a child, Tareq," she protested. "I'd rather be faced with the truth than be protected from it."

The moment the words were out, Sarah was struck by

the realisation that Tareq had been treating her like a child all along, a grown-up one to some extent, but still to be indulged and protected as though she were a complete innocent.

"What good would it have done?" he asked.

"I don't need you to make judgments for me. Nor decisions," she retorted, smarting over how many things had been arranged for her—without discussion—by her self-appointed keeper. "It's so intolerably patronising!"

"Sarah…" he chided.

"Don't use that tone of voice to me," she exploded, hating the sense of being relegated to some lesser level of understanding. "What right do you think you have to take over my life as though you know best?"

That stopped him from giving his soothing little smile. His eyes glowered, some dark emotion climbing over sweet reason. "I have tried to do my best by you, Sarah," he growled. "If you don't appreciate it…"

"Why don't you try appreciating I can think for myself?" she retaliated, cutting off his self-serving argument, finding it so intensely provocative, she stormed off around the room, savagely muttering, "Doing his best for me. Doing his best. Doing his best."

It didn't matter that it was probably true. It was what a parent said to a child. Her frustration with their relationship boiled over. She glared at him—this man who held himself back from her while subtly laying siege to her heart—and the need to strip him of his formidable control clawed through her.

"You obviously see me as a little girl to be pampered and given treats," she mocked, her hands flying around in scornful gestures. "Never mind that I'm twenty-three years old and a hardened survivor. I'm probably still twelve in your mind.''

That straightened him up from the desk and whipped some tension through him. A primitive satisfaction zinged through Sarah. She wished she could rip his clothes off, get right down to the naked truth of how he felt about her. The remembered image of his almost-bare physique played through her mind, stirring a wanton excitement, a wild desire to goad him into action, any action that involved touching.

"You are being ridiculous!" he said tersely.

"Am I? You don't credit me with a woman's needs, a woman's feelings, a woman's desires. *'Don't play with fire, Sarah,'''* she mimicked. "Just stand by and watch the sophisticated grown-ups like Dionne Van Housen play with it because they understand it and you don't.''

His face darkened with an angry rush of blood and Sarah exulted in having reached and plucked a sensitive chord. It flashed through her mind she wasn't being completely fair, but she was on a wild, non-stop roller-coaster, her nerves screaming with frustration, heart pumping with rushes of adrenalin, thoughts careering down the track he had chosen for her, the track that kept her at arm's length from him.

"Then there was Washington," she plunged on, gesticulating with mocking emphasis as she interpreted his actions. "Trotting me out like a young debutante, protecting me from other men, saving me from any little awkwardness, watching over me like a father.''

His mouth compressed.

To Sarah, it denoted she'd hit the nail on the head and she heedlessly hammered it further, furious he'd denied her the maturity she knew she could lay claim to.

"You even dictated when I should go to bed, saying goodnight when it suited you. Same in New York. And here, of course, you've had the relief of adult company with Peter Larsen. It's a wonder you haven't given me dolls to play with."

"Are you quite finished with this absurd tantrum?" Tareq demanded, his eyes glittering with barely suppressed anger.

Tantrum…

The word stopped Sarah in her tracks. She shuddered in revulsion. A child threw tantrums. She had delivered a tirade of truth. Close enough to truth anyway. For Tareq to interpret it as a tantrum…

She drew in a deep breath. Her eyes stabbed him with daggers of pain as she made the only decision she could make. Then with all the passion of her womanhood, she replied, "I'm finished with you, Tareq. Since you treat me as though I haven't reached the age of consent, our bargain is null and void and I am out of here!"

Having flung down the gauntlet she turned her back on him and marched to the door.

"Wait!" he thundered.

"What for?" she flung back at him, throwing out dismissive hands. "I don't need another father. I've already had three. Between them they've done a fine job of ripping away any innocent illusions I might have had about life, so you don't have to worry about me being hurt. Henceforth I am a cynical woman of the world who doesn't believe in anybody."

She twisted the knob and pulled the door open. Before she could step out of the library an arm reached past her and slammed the door shut. Startled, she did nothing to stop the strong brown hand from dropping to the knob and activating the locking device. Her mind grasped the consequence though, and in the next instant she was whirling around to contest it, rebellion rampaging through her heart.

"I will not be your prisoner!" she yelled, her hands slamming against Tareq's broad chest in violent rejection of any more domination from him.

"Shut up!" he retorted fiercely.

The shock of it snapped her eyes up to his.

"You want raw truth?" he demanded, his voice harsh, his nostrils flaring, the windows to his soul revealing chaotic conflict. "I'm a man with a man's needs. And those needs don't come wrapped in finer feelings. How ready are you to accept that, Sarah?"

Dark turbulence enveloped her, sucking the strength from her mutiny, swirling around her thwarted desires, fanning them into a ferment of need, tearing at the feelings that had made being with him a torment, transforming them into something more intense, overwhelming, flooding her with a warm, liquid weakness, and she knew she would accept anything of him. Anything...

Somehow he saw what was happening to her, recognised it, and his arms swept her strongly against him, and the tremulousness inside her gathered a hunger for his strength. She pressed closer, her hips against his, needing, wanting, her hands sliding up over his shoulders, around his neck, her breasts pushing into soft, no hard, harder contact with the pulsing wall of his chest, pursuing the need, the want as a whirlwind of beating, throbbing sensation travelled through her.

The storm in his eyes was rent by a blaze of blue lightning, electrifying the air, tingling her skin, her lips, jolting her heart. Her mouth fell open, gasping for breath. Her mind seized on the image of his face, his beautifully sculptured face, coming nearer, nearer to hers. Her fingers raced into his hair, clutching, grasping, pulling his head nearer still. Every atom of her energy was focused on drawing him to her, reaching into him.

Then his mouth covered hers, softly at first, gently, tenderly, holding back the fire she'd seen and sensed and invited, but the heat of his lips, the caress of his tongue, the excitement of touch and taste whirled her into a passionate searching for all he would give of himself. Her whole body seemed to soar with exultation as he abandoned softness, driven to a wild exploration that eclipsed hers with its ardent, urgent hunger to know, to feel, the wanting a sweet, fierce, nearly desperate need, crying out to be satisfied more fully, more deeply.

Kissing was not enough. Kissing was an anticipatory intimacy, a tantalising promise, a binding beginning to the journey towards the togetherness she craved.

He moved her back against the door, holding her there between his thighs, the burgeoning thickness, hardness of his arousal stroking across her stomach in a rhythmic swaying as his mouth continued to devour hers, the need of a man implicit, raw, demanding to be met. His hands moved quickly, skilfully, stripping her of blouse and bra, dragging off his shirt, freeing flesh to meet flesh, heated with feverish excitement.

Then he was kissing her breasts, his tongue circling the nipples, teasing them into needful erection, and Sarah threw back her head, arching to push for more acute sensation, the need of a woman surging through her, concentrating fiercely on the hot attachment of his lips, sucking, dragging an intense stream of pleasure through her body, her flesh pulsing to his pumping mouth, his hands stroking her thighs, rolling down her trousers, fingers smoothing her stomach, thrusting through moist curls to the core of heat, cupping it, taking possession of the wet softness.

Sarah closed her eyes and gave herself up to the sweet chaos of sensation, forgetting everything, all sense, all caution, all care, wanting only to feel. She had no idea how Tareq accomplished the rest of their undressing. Her entire physical existence was turned inwards to the hunger he fed with his skilful touching, the seductive, exquisitely pleasurable invasion of hand and mouth.

Only when he picked her up and carried her did she realise she was naked, both of them naked, and the sensuality of skin against skin was another wonderful intimacy. He lay her on the soft Persian carpet in front of his desk and she feasted her eyes on him as he knelt over her, such powerful maleness poised to mate with her, and her body was crying out for him, longing to feel him there in the place that was made for him.

She lifted her arms and he came into them, kissing her mouth, slowly, tenderly, as she felt him pressing against her, beginning to fill the opening to her charged, innermost self. Her whole body quivered in waiting. She moved, urging him on, thrusting for the fullness of him inside her. His hands slid beneath her, holding, moulding her buttocks and she felt him enter, slowly pushing further, growing, and she had the amazingly voluptuous sensation of opening before him, spilling the essence of herself around his passage, muscles pulsing, drawing him in.

She heard herself cry out sharply when he stopped. But it was only a pause to negotiate a barrier neither of them wanted. A pinprick of pain and it was past, trailing in the wake of deep, deep pleasure as he sank into ecstatic union with her, and she curled her legs around him to hold him in, savouring the sense of him being captured, possessed by her, a prisoner enveloped, held in a sea of intense bliss.

His mouth took hers in a long passionate entanglement, making the possession his, and she surrendered to it, letting him do as he willed because it didn't matter. Only the togetherness mattered. And he led her on a journey she had never taken before, a wild, plunging ride of ever-increasing excitement, rising to an exhilarating peak, falling only to rise again, on and on, a tumult of sensation, tumbling endlessly, spreading out into ever-widening, powerful circles, faster, faster, drawing her into a vortex that spiralled towards a brilliance she couldn't quite reach.

Frantically she thrust at him, pulling him with her, needing his help, arching her body to drag him into it, a fierce compulsion driving her, driving him, and there was thunder in her ears, white-hot needles piercing her body, pain-pleasure screaming for release, and she needed it, needed it, him with her, riding the crest of…and there it was, an explosion of exquisite sweetness bursting through her like a supernova, and she was floating in an incredible free fall, swimming in waves of love, her heart thumping a paean of joy, her mind filling with the wonder of it, her body sinking into blissful quiescence.

She opened her eyes and Tareq was looking at her, drinking in the soft glow of her repletion, knowing he had put it there, a tender triumph in his eyes. ''This I can give you,'' he said, his voice low, throaty, husking over feelings that were inexpressible.

Gently he stroked her cheek, traced the desire-swollen fullness of her lips, kissed them, kissed her eyelids shut again. Then with a long, hissing sigh, he gathered her to him, lifting her as he moved aside to lie on the carpet, using his body to cushion hers, holding her to the warm closeness of intimate contact.

He stroked her hair, her back, languorous caresses that kept her sensually aware of both herself and him. Sarah was lost to everything else. He was her world. She rose and fell to the rhythm of his breathing. The drum of his heart echoed her own. She wanted for nothing. He had given, was still giving, more than she had ever imagined he would.

"Is it enough?" he asked, his voice oddly strained.

It stirred her sluggish mind out of its comfortable haze of pleasure. He had fulfilled her needs, but she simply did not have the experience to know if he was completely satisfied. What if she had been hopelessly inadequate in returning his lovemaking? Should she have been more active towards him instead of being so utterly enthralled by her own feelings? Did he feel shortchanged?

"Do you want more?" she asked in reply, her heart fluttering at the thought she had failed him.

His hands splayed possessively over the pit of her back. He gave a funny little laugh. "More and more and more. I would take all you would let me have, Sarah. Until there is no more."

She smiled, comprehending that he was pleased with what they'd shared and he was looking beyond the moment, further down the path they had taken today.

"Yes," she agreed, anticipating the filling in of all

that had been missing in her knowledge of him. ''I want that, too.''

He sighed, his whole body relaxing underneath hers. ''So be it then,'' he murmured. His arms enfolded her, wrapping her tightly to him as he turned them both onto their sides. His eyes locked onto hers, a glitter of purpose in their dark blue depths. ''You stay with me of your own free will,'' he stated, commanding her assent.

''Yes,'' she answered, thinking he was dismissing the hostage arrangement and making it a purely personal decision to stay with him, not for her father, not for Jessie and the twins, for herself alone, because she wanted to. ''Yes,'' she affirmed more emphatically.

The glitter flared into the all-consuming blaze of desire she had seen weeks ago when he had challenged her willingness to accept it. Now it was unleashed on her and she revelled in it, meeting his mouth, kissing him as avidly as he kissed her, sealing the new bargain between them.

She didn't realise that being lovers was all he had in mind, didn't realise the pact she'd just made had limits, didn't realise promises would not be given because too much stood in the way of their being kept.

She loved him and felt loved by him.

It was more than enough.

At this moment in time.

CHAPTER THIRTEEN

ALL morning Tareq had struggled to direct his mind onto
the business decisions to be made before the festive season closed everything down. The Persian carpet in front
of his desk was a constant distraction. The searing
memories of yesterday…last night…continually kicked
at the control he was valiantly attempting to assert over
the desire that tempted him to toss his responsibilities
aside and indulge himself in every possible pleasure with
Sarah.

He read the invitation that had come in the mail with
a certain amount of cynical amusement. It was addressed
to him and was from the Earl and Countess of
Marchester. Sarah's society-minded mother was undoubtedly intent on showing off her daughter's *conquest*
at a formal dinner on Christmas Eve.

Irrelevant to him whether they attended or not, but it
was Christmas, and mothers were mothers. He would be
visiting his own, as expected, on Christmas Day. It was
up to Sarah to decide what she wanted to do.

*I don't need you to make judgments for me. Nor de-
cisions*.

He shook his head over his own misjudgments. Sarah
was so young, yet very much a woman who knew her
own mind and with courage enough to seize what she
wanted and run with it. The passion of her, the wilful-
ness and wantonness, the intense response from her…
Tareq marvelled at it.

The invitation from her mother provided a valid excuse to seek her out, to be where he most wanted to be…with her. "This bit of mail is for Sarah," he said to Peter Larsen who was diligently scanning other correspondence. "I'll take it to her."

Peter looked up, concern drawing his eyebrows together as Tareq rose from his chair. "Is she okay? I do regret having upset her yesterday."

"Not a problem. In fact, it worked out very well."

The satisfaction underlining the remark evoked a quizzical look from Peter.

Tareq ignored it. His private life was private. And compellingly attractive. He made a swift decision. "We finish this paperwork today, Peter. Prioritise what absolutely needs to be done. I'm taking time off until we have to prepare for the trip to the homeland. The second week in January should cover the reports my uncle will expect."

"Suits me," he agreed, keeping his curiosity contained.

Having released himself from work that could wait, Tareq had an even more buoyant spring in his step as he went in search of Sarah. He found her in the sitting room, curled up on the sofa closest to the hearth where a cosy fire was alight. She was reading a book and he noted a pile of books on the table next to the sofa.

So engrossed was she in the story, his entrance had gone unnoticed, and he paused before disturbing her, remembering her scathing comment about giving her dolls to play with. He was well aware Sarah was far too intelligent to be content with a frivolous life. Nursing a child with Jessie's disabilities had obviously been rewarding and the time would come when she would crave another challenging occupation.

Time…it was always going to be the enemy for them. The thought stirred an urgent greed for all he could take now, while it was new and good and untainted by the conflicts that would inevitably part them.

She was so lovely…every aspect of her.

As though sensing his presence, she glanced up, her dark chocolate eyes sparkling with delight when she saw him. "Why are you standing there?"

"Just remembering how you looked when I took up your breakfast tray this morning."

She blushed but newly bold mischief curved her luscious mouth. "Naked and tousled is not exactly appropriate for the sitting room."

"I had no problem with it in the library." He closed the double doors behind him, ensuring uninterrupted time together.

Her eyes widened, disbelief that he would repeat their lovemaking here warring with excitement as he crossed the room to where she sat, squirming slightly at his approach, revealing a desire as strong as his, a consciousness of aroused sexuality. He saw her breasts peak, hardened nubs pushing out the soft, clingy fabric of her shirt, and though he'd only intended talking to her, the urge to touch and revel in the freedom to touch zinged through him like a strong intoxicant.

"We have an invitation to Marchington Hall," he said, holding out the embossed card to her.

She fumbled her book onto the table and took the card to read it. He lifted her curled legs and sat beside her, laying her legs across his lap, stroking them, savouring the feminine grace of their long curves. The fine black tights encasing them made them even more sensually alluring. Her ankle-length skirt was buttoned down the side, a tantalising row of little openings offering further temptation.

"A formal dinner," Sarah groaned. "It's sure to be a five-star production and my mother will make you the showpiece, Tareq. She thinks…"

The pause in her speech drew his attention and the look of confusion in her eyes reminded him quite poignantly that she was not a hardened sophisticate, and while she might want and accept their relationship, it left her very vulnerable to other, more cynical views of what they shared.

"Do you mind her seeing that we're lovers?" he asked.

"No, of course not. I'm not ashamed of what I feel," she replied strongly, another flush colouring her cheeks. "It's just… I guess I'm not used to the idea yet. And I resent her thinking I set out to hook you and get what I can out of you. As it is, she'll take one look at us and think she was right."

The boot was on the other foot, Tareq thought with a twinge of guilty conscience. He had set out to hook Sarah and get what he could from her. Though it was different now, he quickly assured himself. He wanted to give, wanted her to have everything within his power to give.

"We don't have to go, Sarah. It's your choice. I'll have no compunction whatsoever in writing a refusal."

She heaved a sigh which drooped into a rueful grimace. "I haven't seen my mother for two years. We had a huge argument over my decision to help with Jessie.

I wish I could believe she really wanted to see me, and not because I'd have you in tow."

"Maybe she does," he said, responding to the sadness he sensed in her. "Once there's a deep rift, and communication is difficult to re-establish, it's an easier situation to meet in the company of other people. Less chance of another blow-up."

It prompted an ironic smile. "You mean nothing really gets said in a crowd."

He shrugged. "There is still comfort in seeing a person you care about. At the very least, it's a check on their well-being. As you said, it's been two years."

And he didn't like to think of her being completely cut off from her mother. Even tenuous links to her family were worth keeping. There was no joy in feeling alone in the world. He wished he could promise their togetherness would last and she would never again be alone, but the realities of his life made nonsense of any such assurance.

"Perhaps we should go," she said uneasily. "It is Christmas. My mother and I don't see eye to eye on much, Tareq, but I guess it would be mean not to at least show goodwill."

"No harm in it," he agreed. "I'll send an acceptance then."

Her eyes were anxious, embarrassed. "Will you mind if she gloats over our connection?"

He laughed. "I may very well do some gloating myself. No other woman can hold a candle to you, Sarah."

It made her laugh. "I'm glad you think so but my mother won't."

"Oh, yes, she will." The hard-core protective instinct she had evoked in him all along was instantly tapped.

No one was going to slight Sarah while he was at her side. The anticipation of many pleasures buzzed through him as plans formed in his mind.

"Tomorrow we fly to Paris. I'll take you shopping. I shall drape you in splendour from head to toe, and no one will shine more brightly."

She fluttered towards him in agitated protest. "I don't want you to buy me things, Tareq."

He scooped her down on the sofa and swiftly repositioned himself to lean over her, imprisoning her legs with his. "Why would you not want to celebrate being a woman with me?" he asked, gently brushing wayward curls from her forehead, kissing the tip of her nose, flirting wickedly with his eyes, drawing his hand slowly along the inner sides of her thighs, feeling the excited quiver of her flesh under his touch. "You are an incredibly beautiful woman and I want you to know it and feel it and enjoy it."

Her breath shuddered out and her breasts rose enticingly as she dragged in more air. "People will know it's your wealth dressing me, Tareq. It will look as though…as though…" Her voice trailed off uncertainly and he knew her body was tensely poised, waiting for his hand to move higher.

"As though I cherish you," he finished for her. "I want to give you the best, Sarah. The best of everything." He fanned his fingers over the soft nest at the apex of her womanhood and slid his thumb down the cleft, stroking with all the seductive skill at his command. "I want to dress you in satins and silks and velvet…which is how you feel to me…smooth and soft and sensual…"

Her stomach contracted. Her lips parted in a little

gasp. He swept his tongue around them then kissed her, plundering her mouth of its infinitely sweet giving, revelling in her uninhibited response, feeling it flow through him, arousing the power to take her on any journey he desired.

"I find you utterly intoxicating, Sarah," he murmured, brushing her lips with his words, their breaths mingling in heated intimacy. "I see you dressed in wine red, a dark fire glowing, like the fire burning in me...for you..."

"I only need you, Tareq," she pleaded.

It put a twist in his heart. He almost lost it then, his need for her a thunder that almost obliterated all rationality. But he couldn't let her need him to the exclusion of everything else. There had to be other avenues for her, roads she could take with confidence. There would be a cost to the relationship she had chosen with him and it had to be made up. He had to supply her with the means to go on without him, though he hated the thought of losing her.

"Would you deprive me of the pleasure of giving?" he pleaded in reply, trailing kisses to her ears, pausing to erotically sensitise each lobe. "I want to hang rubies here...red-blood rubies...because you're in my blood..." He dropped his head, sucking briefly on the pulse at the base of her throat. "...And a necklace of rubies...precious jewels to show you are precious to me."

Her back arced, her distended nipples pointing provocatively. Uncaring of the fabric covering them he tugged on each inviting peak with his teeth, heating them with his mouth, exulting in her little moans of excitement, the threshing of her body in seeking more intense pleasure.

"I'd have these beautiful breasts encased in soft swirls of French lace…" He bit onto the zipper fastening of her shirt and pulled it down, nuzzled the fabric away from the soft valley, traced the line of her bra with his tongue. "It should be the finest lace…tantalising…transparent…sinfully sexy for both of us. Wouldn't you like that?"

"Yes.…" A cry…a hiss…a moan of wanting.

He lifted himself to look into her eyes; hot, melting chocolate pouring over him, into him, through him, touching him as no other woman had. "Let me express what I feel for you, Sarah. In every way I can," he pleaded. "I'll make it good for you."

"Yes…"

Her sigh of surrender relieved him of his nagging concerns and released the brake he'd forced on his own raging desires. Assured she would accept gifts that would at least give her future material security and the standing she deserved in the eyes of others, Tareq set tomorrow aside and took what he could of today, kissing her in a frenzy of passion, losing himself in the glory of her giving.

CHAPTER FOURTEEN

HER skin prickled with sensitivity as Tareq smoothed the necklace of rubies around her throat…dark red fire pulsing at her accusingly in the mirror. She had given in, cast all her principles aside in letting him do this, letting him change her into someone she barely recognised. Somehow she couldn't stop it. Her resistance melted under the desire in his eyes. She wanted to please him, wanted him to be pleased with her. Nothing else seemed to matter.

"You look magnificent," he murmured, assessing the result of his re-imaging of her in the mirror, approving what he saw. Then he bent his head to her bare shoulder, kissing it, heating the skin that leapt alive to his touch, gliding his hands down her arms in a tingling caress.

Sarah stared at her reflection, wondering who she was now, what she had become in this past week, letting him mould her to his will. In the mirror was a stunningly beautiful woman. Her wild curls had been restyled to a more dramatic shape, cut so that the fabulous ruby earrings showed to full advantage on either side of a face made up to look much more than it had before…sensual, shadowy eyes, sexy red mouth.

Her dark red gown was strapless, a fan of artful pleats covering her breasts, the gleaming satin tucking into an even deeper red velvet cummerbund that accentuated the womanly curves of her figure. The skirt billowed into a rich, luxurious fullness and rustled when she walked, making her conscious of the erotic lingerie underneath it. She felt like a courtesan, attired for her lover, yet it hadn't seemed wrong when Tareq was buying all this for her, seducing her into it with the pleasure in his eyes, with his personal involvement in everything they did.

I'll make it good for you, he'd said, but she didn't know if it was good. She only knew she had changed in becoming intimately connected to him. Their desire for each other dominated her every thought and feeling, influencing her every action, heightening her senses, drawing out needs and desires that overwhelmed any rationality.

Even now—right now—as he ran feather-light fingertips back up her arms, she felt an urgent knot of heat in her belly, wanting more of him. Her heart was thudding so violently against her rib cage, surely he must hear it. When his hands reached her shoulders he would slide them down over the swell of her breasts and…but he turned aside to pick up the velvet cape and she stood, transfixed by the strong sexuality he stirred while he draped the heavy, satin-lined garment around her shoulders.

"Time to leave," he said, his eyes glowing with pride in her…pride in his possession?

She didn't want to go to Marchington Hall tonight, didn't want her mother to see her dressed like this. Nevertheless, she couldn't bring herself to reject what Tareq had taken so much pleasure in doing for her. Without a word, she accompanied him downstairs and out to the chauffeured Rolls-Royce which would take them on the forty-five-minute journey out of London to the stately home of the Earl of Marchester.

The car provided the same sense of private luxury as

the limousines Tareq had used in Australia and America; tinted, one-way windows, a glass panel between them and the driver, a bar with a bottle of champagne and glasses ready for them, dishes of nuts and olives, radio, disc-player.

Sarah thought whimsically of her innocent awareness of Tareq on the trip out to Werribee. Here they were, almost two months later, in a similar situation—going to visit her family—and her sexual knowledge of him made her awareness intensely pervasive as the chauffeur closed them in together.

"You're very quiet," Tareq commented. He took her hand, interlacing her fingers with his, energising the flow of feeling between them. "Are you worried about this meeting with your mother?"

He was always so quick to read her mind. Sarah wished she could read his as easily. She looked at him, trying to see through to his heart. Beyond the incredibly consuming passion they shared, she didn't know what he felt for her. His eyes were soft, kind, concerned.

"I look...too glamorous for me, Tareq."

"No. This is a you that's possible, any time you want to present it. Don't ever limit yourself, Sarah. You should feel you can belong to any world you choose."

His world? Was this dressing up a preparation for her to look appropriate in a sheikh's palace? Did he need to present her like this when he returned to his homeland for his half-brother's wedding?

"Is it better for you...politically speaking...looking as I do tonight?"

He shook his head, smiling at her reasoning. "I wanted it for you, not for me, Sarah. I think you have felt like a cuckoo for too long. Your mother won't regard you as one this evening.''

He was certainly right on that score. The cuckoo had been turned into a peacock. ''She'll think you've bought me,'' was her wry comment.

''It doesn't matter. You and I both know differently. We are only going to bridge a gap with your mother, are we not? Goodwill at Christmas? And speaking of gaps…'' He lifted her hand and kissed the inner side of her wrist, making her pulse leap at the electric contact with his mouth. His eyes simmered over the sensual caress. ''I wish I could bridge the one between us right now. But for rumpling that perfect dress, I would.'' He slid her hand down to his lap. ''This I shall be feeling all night, waiting for you, wanting you.''

She couldn't resist stroking her fingers along the hardness stretched so tightly against his trousers, feeling its thickness, its power, knowing she had excited it, exciting herself with thinking of how it made her feel, this extension of him seeking her, wanting connection, sinking into her innermost depths.

She forgot where they were going and her search for meaning in what he did for her. His arousal spun her along other paths of thought. Spasms of remembered ecstasy convulsed through her. She wondered if she could touch him the way he touched her, driving her mindless with ever-mounting sensation while he kept control, giving her all the pleasure. She wanted him to feel that, too, wanted to give him the sense of being utterly loved to every extreme.

A wild compulsion swept through her, gathering momentum. Before the decision was even consciously made, she was turning towards him, reaching for his zipper, pulling it down. The action jolted him. His hand came down on hers.

"Let me!" she commanded.

His hold eased. "It would mess you up, Sarah. We can't…"

"*I* can. I don't want you to touch me, Tareq. This is just for you."

For me, too, she thought fiercely. Somehow he was always taking her over. She needed to feel she was giving him something, making him feel very specially loved, every part of him special to her, loved, adored, cherished. She worked quickly to free him, her heart pumping with bursts of adrenalin.

His thighs tensed as her fingers closed around him, drawing him fully erect for her to stroke and caress and make him realise how deeply she cared for his pleasure. He had tasted her so often, turning her into a seething mass of incredible sensation. It was her turn.

He was so big it was an exciting challenge, taking him into her mouth, learning the shape of him… delicately, tentatively at first, and then more boldly, confidently. It was incredibly erotic, thinking of her red-lipsticked mouth surrounding him, circling him, imprinting him with her possession.

It was amazing, marvellous, taking him like this. And Tareq certainly wanted it. He slid forward on the seat, giving her more access, his stomach contracting, his breathing quickening. She sensed he was enraptured, his entire body focused on the sensations plunging from her mouth. She took him deeper, revelling in his excitement, exulting in the power to tease and tantalise, drawing out the exquisite anticipation, driving him to the throbbing edge of ecstasy, but not too quickly. She wanted the feelings to build and build, giving him all the delicious tingles and tension of approaching climax.

She slid a hand between his taut thighs, squeezing gently, wanting him to erupt beyond any semblance of control, wildly and wonderfully, as she did when he kissed and caressed her most intimate place.

She heard him groan. It was so good to hear that involuntary response. Her own excitement soared as he lifted himself to her, giving himself, arching for more, wanting all she gave, craving it. She felt the straining tension of his being poised on the brink, and she took him beyond it, drinking him in, loving the sense of owning him more fully, more intimately than she ever had before.

No gap between them, she thought with deep, primitive satisfaction. This made them equals. She had made him come, taking him into that incredibly blissful state all by herself. She lifted her head and looked at him, needing to see if he felt as exalted by the experience as she did.

His eyes were dark, swimming with surges of emotion. His mouth was soft, slightly parted. She saw the effort he made to recollect himself and smiled, knowing she had taken him on a journey this time, one he had not expected nor been prepared for. She had been the leader, the one initiating action, the one who took him into the sweet valley of peace, the one who gave unstintingly, asking nothing in return. It was amazing how fulfilled that made her feel as a woman…knowing she had pleasured her man to the ultimate limit.

"Thank you," he said softly, his voice deeply furred with the feelings she had evoked. "You touch me in ways I have never felt before. I have never known anyone like you.''

A huge wave of emotion swelled through her, bringing tears to her eyes. ''There can never be anyone like you for me, either.''

He touched her cheek in a tender salute, then smiled, happiness bursting into his eyes. ''I think this calls for a glass of champagne.''

She laughed, lovingly watching him resettle on the seat and zip himself into proper formality again. She was deliriously happy, caught up in the thraldom of a love that knew no barriers.

''So now you don't have to wait,'' she bubbled, riding a high that didn't need champagne to elevate it any further.

''Oh, I'll be waiting, my sweet.'' His eyes sparkled wickedly at her as he lifted the bottle out of its ice bucket. ''Waiting to give you a slice of heaven on the return journey. With the same rules applying. You sit. I touch.''

Heaven... Sarah laughed again, excited by the prospect, loving his lust for her, exhilaratingly sure it had to encompass a love as strong as hers. And there was absolutely no reason to care what her mother thought. This designer dress meant nothing. The jewels meant nothing. What sizzled between her and Tareq was everything. They were bound together, uniquely special to each other. She was certain of it.

This conviction carried Sarah through their arrival at Marchington Hall, keeping her pleasantly detached from any sense of embarrassment over her mother's effusive greeting and the introductions that followed. There was a certain cynical amusement in hearing the unaccustomed pride in her mother's voice as she recited again and again, "My daughter, Sarah... My daughter, Sarah..." obviously brimming with pleasure in their relationship now that Sarah had the appearance of belonging to an aristocratic society, albeit through Tareq.

The cynicism turned into sadness as she reflected that her mother had never given her a sense of belonging. It was doubtful she ever would. They were poles apart in their thinking and the rift was too wide to be closed. This meeting established a token peace between them but it was empty of any real meaning.

Sarah was relieved to realise it wasn't important to her anymore. She belonged to Tareq now. She didn't need anyone else. They were together, wonderfully excitingly together. Not once did he stray from her side. Nor did he allow anyone to take her from his.

There were twenty-two guests for dinner and when they were ushered into the banquet room to take their seats for dinner, she noted all the other couples were separated, but not her and Tareq. They were seated together. As they always had been in Washington and New York.

"Did you demand that we not be parted?" she whispered as he held her chair for her.

"I stipulated it on my acceptance," he answered, his eyes warmly possessive. "The pleasure of being with you is mine."

It made her feel even more loved and wanted.

This was not the first time Sarah had dined in the banquet room at Marchington Hall with all the splendours of centuries of wealth surrounding her; a magnificent hand-painted ceiling set in ornate plasterwork, dazzling chandeliers, silk curtains luxuriously draped to pool on the highly polished parquet floor, huge gilt mirrors, marble fireplaces, paintings by masters that would have been coveted by any museum, Chippendale furniture, and on the long, mirror-like surface of the table, the finest Spode china, gleaming silver cutlery, and exquisitely cut Baccarat crystal. It *was*, however, the first time she didn't feel like a total alien here.

She had always thought such wealth obscene.

Yet what it provided *was* beautiful, a feast of riches that seduced the senses. And having put herself in Tareq's hands, Sarah had succumbed to it, accepting all he wanted her to accept. *I'll make it good for you*, he'd said, and she now decided he had. Even this. With him at her side, colouring it all with intense happiness, sharing, involved, he made her feel she could, indeed, walk into any world and belong. Somehow he had completely refocused her life.

She looked down the table to where her mother sat at the foot of it, holding court to those sitting closest to her…the countess…and Sarah could see, and finally acknowledge how brilliantly she suited the role. It still saddened her that she had virtually been locked out of her mother's life, that their values were so different, but she wondered if she had been too judgmental, too critical. What did she really know of her mother's innermost feelings?

Michael Kearney could have been as overwhelming as Tareq. In which case, it would have been devastating to lose him to another woman. The earl was certainly a good deal older, but if he made her mother feel good about herself, and she gave him what he wanted, perhaps there was more to the marriage than money and position.

Sarah knew her mother to be forty-eight though she

barely looked thirty, her gleaming blonde hair softly styled to enhance a prettiness kept young by skilful nips and tucks. She was dressed in a slim, elegant silver gown, diamonds at her throat and ears, all especially chosen, Sarah thought, to echo the lovely groups of angels set on the table as Christmas decorations.

In years gone by, she had viewed her mother's obsession with perfect detail—superficial detail—with secret contempt, turning away from it, resenting the time given to it, despising the kind of values it represented. People were more important than having things look right.

Yet there was pleasure in it, pleasure and satisfaction.

Her mother glanced down the table, caught Sarah's gaze, and smiled, delight and warm pleasure lighting her face.

Sarah couldn't help smiling back. She felt good. She felt beautiful. She felt loved. And it was Christmas Eve, a time for peace and goodwill. She was glad that her mother felt happy, even if it was brought about by superficial things that didn't really matter.

The food and wine were superb, or maybe everything just tasted better because sitting with Tareq sharpened all her senses. Occasionally he grazed her hand with his fingertips. Daringly, she scraped her nails along his thigh. He blew softly in her ear, pretending some confidential murmur. She lifted her glass of wine, her eyes promising a different toast to the one she mouthed. It was a delicious game.

She noticed the smudge of red from her lower lip on her crystal wineglass and thought of the ring of red she might have left on him, then almost squirmed in excited anticipation of what he was going to do to her on the return trip to London. *You sit. I touch.* All the possibilities of how he would touch danced through her mind.

The dinner conversation around them seemed like a lot of distant yapping, not affecting them even when out of politeness they had to respond. They shared an intense private world, their bodies humming to the same tune, their eyes secretly feasting on far more than what was set on the table.

Coffee was served in the drawing room. Knowing that Tareq would soon call for the car—the urgent hunger burning in his eyes was warning enough he wouldn't wait much longer—Sarah excused herself to take advantage of the powder room before they left.

Her mother waylaid her, hooking her arm around Sarah's. "Darling, come upstairs with me. We can repair our make-up together and have a little chat."

Sarah inwardly recoiled from the "little chat" suggestion. Any distraction from Tareq was unwelcome, especially the kind of frivolous conversation her mother indulged in. She wanted to hurry back to him. He was waiting for her.

But her mother beamed at her expectantly and Sarah's conscience was pricked by daughterly duty. It had been two years. It was Christmas. And a few minutes of inconsequential chatter shouldn't feel such an unwanted burden, shouldn't stir such tense frustration.

Just a few minutes of being civil…

No matter what her mother said, it wouldn't change anything between her and Tareq.

CHAPTER FIFTEEN

"I CAN'T get over how wonderful you look!" her mother gushed, drawing her along to the staircase. "You're absolutely glowing."

"Thank you, Mother. You look wonderful, too. It's been a lovely evening."

The arm around hers hugged more tightly, her mother leaning closer, conspiratorially. "Those rubies are fabulous. They must have cost a fortune."

Sarah cringed at the avid note in her voice. "I really have no idea what they're worth," she said flatly. "Tareq bought them."

Soft, indulgent laughter. "He's obviously besotted with you. I must say you surprised me, linking up with him. Oh, I know he's stunningly handsome and terribly sexy, but you were always such a stickler for love and marriage."

Sarah kept her mouth firmly shut, glancing up to the next floor and wishing there were fewer stairs to climb.

"I suppose he swept you off your feet and offered you the earth. And I must say he's being very generous. Those rubies are fabulous. Has he given you any other jewellery?"

Sarah gritted her teeth. She hated this. "Mother, I'm with Tareq because I love him," she bit out.

"Well, of course you do, dear." Another arm squeeze. "But you must know it won't last with him. It's not as if he'd ever marry you."

Sarah flinched. She hadn't thought that far, but if they loved each other, wasn't marriage the natural progression? She couldn't imagine life without Tareq.

''You don't understand, Mother,'' she said tersely.

''Sarah, you can't imagine he'll marry you,'' came the incredulous retort. ''Tareq al-Khaima is a sheikh. As English as he might seem to be, his own culture will eventually claim him. You have your head in the clouds if you think anything else, believe me.''

Nothing and nobody dictates to Tareq how to live his life. He had told her so himself. Sarah clung grimly to that thought as they reached the head of the stairs and turned towards the first guest suite. She was not going to argue with her mother. There was no point to it.

Her silence, however, was a goad. ''My dear, he may seem to be free-wheeling, but when it comes to marriage, he'll do what he thinks is best for his country and that won't be you.''

She was wrong. Tareq wasn't going to fall in with his uncle's wishes.

When the well-meant advice met with no response, her mother's reasonableness sharpened to exasperation. ''The hard truth is you're the latest in a long line of women who've come and gone in Tareq al-Khaima's life. He has the reputation of being very generous while they're with him. That's the way the game is played, Sarah.''

''It might have been with them. It won't be with me,'' she fiercely stated, hating the imputation and refusing to let in any doubt. So he liked buying women things. He liked being generous. It didn't mean he thought of her as he had his previous lovers.

''Oh, Sarah…'' Her mother shook her head despairingly as she opened the door to the suite and waved Sarah inside. "What makes you think you're any different?"

Because she was. Tareq had told her so. No other woman touched him the way she did. He'd never known anyone like her before. But her mother would probably scorn such avowals as nothing more than a lover's flattery, spoiling the special feeling with her horrid view of Tareq's interest in her.

"Please excuse me, Mother. I need to use the bathroom." She crossed the bedroom quickly, heading for the bathroom door.

"If he was really serious about you, Sarah, and not playing the usual game, why do you suppose he bought you those rubies?"

The hard question knifed her heart and left it quivering. She kept going, denying her mother the satisfaction of thinking she'd scored a hit. The problem was, she could shut the bathroom door on her mother but she couldn't shut out her thoughts.

Why had Tareq insisted on buying her things, pressing her to take them, seducing her into accepting them? She'd told him she didn't want them. He'd overridden her protest. Was it because he didn't like to leave her with nothing...when they parted?

No...no...she wasn't going to believe that. He had explained his motives and they were good, caring, wanting her to feel confident.

Then why had she felt like a courtesan earlier tonight?

Stop it! she screamed at herself. Remember how it had been in the car coming here. He loved her. He really truly loved her. It was stupid to let her mother—her mother, of all people—put doubts in her mind. She'd known all along her mother would think Tareq had bought her.

He was waiting for her and he loved her and the sooner she got back to him the better.

Determinedly she carried on with using the bathroom facilities, wishing she could recapture the excitement her mother had stolen with her insidious comments. All the lovely anticipation was gone. But surely it would come back once she was with Tareq again. He'd look at her and she'd know their togetherness was rock-solid. He'd draw her back into their private world and everything would be all right.

Having shored up her confidence, Sarah left the bathroom, intent on making a quick escape downstairs. Her mother was agitatedly pacing the floor, back and forth across the path to the bedroom door, frustrating an easy exit. She fastened a pained but resolute gaze on her daughter.

"Sarah…for your own good, this is one time when you must listen to me."

"Mother, please leave it. Tareq is waiting…"

"No! You can give me a few more minutes of your time. It's not asking much."

Reluctant to completely snub her mother, Sarah stood mutinously silent, mentally blocking her ears, determined on not letting anything that was said unsettle her further.

The pacing continued, accompanied by vehement gestures, emphasising the bewilderment and frustration behind the outpouring of words. "I know you don't think much of it, but I have tried to do my best by you, Sarah. You've always made it very difficult. You never forgave me for leaving your father, yet the truth was we weren't happy together. We were mismatched. He never wanted to do the things I wanted to do…''

''Mother, that's way in the past,'' Sarah cut in impatiently.

She was ignored. ''You were barely civil to Michael and you always looked at me with accusing eyes. I wanted to be happy. Maybe that was selfish of me. Whatever… The best solution seemed to be to send you to boarding school.''

Out of sight, out of mind, Sarah thought.

Her mother raved on. ''I chose that school carefully for you, Sarah, wanting you to make the social connections that would help give you a good start in life. You seemed to take pleasure in defeating my purpose.''

Sarah grimaced at the lack of understanding. ''It didn't work that way, Mother. The other girls saw no profit in knowing me.''

''You didn't try!'' came the angry retaliation. ''You didn't try anything I lined up for you. You just turned up your nose at everything. Even the eligible men I introduced you to.''

''They were wrong for me.''

''And you think Sheikh Tareq al-Khaima is right?'' A scathing whiplash. ''I don't know what goes on in your mind, Sarah. All your decisions seem to be self-defeating. Now you're blindly involving yourself with a man who could at least do something for you if you played your cards sensibly. He would probably give you…''

''Don't start on Tareq again,'' Sarah cut in, hard and fast, her stomach cramping in instant revulsion for any mercenary conversation targeting the man she loved.

Her mother would not be stopped. ''What you're

thinking is so foolish, and all you'll end up with is a broken heart.''

''So be it then,'' Sarah sliced in, determined on cutting her short.

''Just listen to yourself! So impossibly stubborn. Closing your eyes to obvious realities. I don't know how long you've been lovers, but in all that time, has he ever once said he loves you?''

Tareq hadn't actually said it in words but that didn't make any difference. He did love her. She knew it. He was waiting for her so he could show how much he loved her again and again and again!

Although a disquieting little memory did niggle...her asking Tareq if he'd lost the capacity to love...his replying it had been whittled away. And even then he'd wanted her, waiting until she was willing. Willing...

A chill crawled down her spine. Her hand crept up and tugged at the ruby necklace. It felt uncomfortable around her throat.

''So he hasn't declared his love,'' her mother concluded, having waited for an answer that hadn't come.

There was no triumph in her voice. The words were spoken in a dead tone, empty of hope and not expecting any. Sarah wanted to defy the knowingness in her mother's eyes. The sadness and sympathy shining through the knowingness made it even worse...hurting because the understanding was wrong.

Her mother sighed, then pushed another *destroy* button. ''Has he talked about the future with you?''

Defensively Sarah clutched at the known fact that Tareq certainly had a year with her in mind. There was plenty of time ahead to start looking beyond that. And it was perfectly possible she had stirred the capacity to love in him. She didn't want these doubts. They hurt. They twisted things.

"Sarah, has he actually promised you anything?" her mother pressed, relentless in forcing the issue.

I never make promises I don't intend to keep.

She frowned. It was too soon for promises anyway. They'd only been lovers for ten days. She was *not* going to think about it. Her mother was judging on things that had nothing to do with what was really going on between her and Tareq. She wouldn't listen to any more.

"No talk of love or the future and no promises made," her mother recited, hammering home what she saw as damning facts. "Now will you listen to sense?"

"No." A violent revulsion rose out of the sick churning. "Not your kind of sense, Mother. You've laid it out for me. You've done your best. I'm sorry I don't appreciate it more but I'd rather go my own way. Thank you and goodnight."

She moved quickly, deftly skirting her mother as she headed for the door.

"Sarah, I am trying to help," came the last urgent plea.

She paused, her hand on the knob, desperate to get away from the constant clawing at her heart, yet tugged into one last reply by what had probably been a genuine desire to help, regardless of its miserable outcome. She glanced back.

"I'm sorry, Mother. Please forgive my shortcomings and have a happy Christmas. I do have to go now. Tareq is waiting for me."

She left, but there was no joy in the going, no sense of happy anticipation winging her steps down the staircase. Her mind was a jangle of unresolved questions. Her chest felt so tight it was painful to breathe. Her soul screamed that she had to have faith...faith and trust. Tareq set a lot of store in trust. Absolute trust.

Then she saw him. Her feet faltered. He was at the end of the great hall, speaking to the butler. Was their car outside waiting? Waiting to enclose them in fevered intimacy again? Her heart pounded so hard all her pulse points throbbed. She wasn't just another one of his women. She wasn't!

He turned and saw her. She watched him come to the foot of the staircase, strong, purposeful, so very sure of where he was going and what he would do. *I always try to balance what I give and take, Sarah. I pride myself on playing fair.* He'd taken her gift of pleasuring him and now he was going to give it back. Playing fair. But what did the rubies mean...by the rules he'd set himself?

He held out his hand to her, his eyes drawing her down to him like a magnet, telling her she was mesmerisingly beautiful, infinitely desirable, and no other woman could hold a candle to her. The wanting to be with her—only with her—pulsed from him and squeezed her heart.

But did he love her?

Would he always love her?

The wretched doubts swirled around her like the black funnel of a tornado. There was his hand held out to her, an offering of himself, unwavering, an open invitation to the togetherness she craved, compelling her to take it. With a sense of inevitability, she laid her own hand in his.

What else could she do?
She loved him.
He was her world.

CHAPTER SIXTEEN

CHRISTMAS morning…a crisp, fine day…and two clear weeks at the estate in Surrey ahead of them. Tareq revelled in a happiness he had never expected to feel. Even driving his Jaguar—the power, the speed, at his control—added to an exhilarating sense of freedom.

For the next fortnight he wasn't going to think of who he was or the demands of the role he'd been born to. Certainly his mother wouldn't remind him. She preferred to forget *that other life* when she was married to his father. Christmas Day would be very English, the rest of their stay with her, likewise. She wouldn't dream of intruding on his relationship with Sarah. Acceptance with grace and discretion was assured.

Besides, his mother excelled in providing a cosy, comfortable atmosphere. Sarah would like Hershaw Manor. It was much more of a home than the very stately, impersonal Marchington Hall. He wanted her to feel at home. Christmas tended to tug at family strings and she could be missing what she'd shared with Jessie and the twins on the two Christmas days she'd spent in Australia. Was being with him enough for her?

"What are you thinking?" he asked, suddenly craving a reconnection with her mind. It was almost obsessive, the desire to possess all of her. She was like a compelling narcotic. He kept wanting more and more and more.

He felt her glance at him, sensed her reluctance to reveal her thoughts, and the determination to know them impelled him to reach over and take her hand, using touch to forge the intimate mood that encouraged confidences. "Tell me," he softly urged.

She sighed. "I was wondering what your mother would think of us."

He flashed her a reassuring smile. "She'll think you're very lovely and I'm very lucky to have you."

She remained pensive, distant from him. "Have you taken other women with you to Hershaw Manor, Tareq?"

He frowned, not liking the comparison she was toying with, not liking the strained note in her voice. Still, he could not lie to her. "Yes, I have." He squeezed her hand. "But none like you, Sarah."

She looked down, her gaze fastening on the physical link he was pressing. "Will your mother know that?" she asked quietly. "Or will she think I'm just another bit of...of passing trade?"

The phrase thumped into Tareq's heart, making him wince at the crass impact it carried. He'd had many pleasurable interludes with women but he hadn't *bought* them. All his previous liaisons had been mutually agreeable. As this one was. To use the word *trade*...he flinched from it.

"I've never consorted with whores," he said gruffly. "And my mother certainly wouldn't consider you one." He threw her a critical look. "Why are you thinking in such offensive terms?"

She evaded eye contact, turning her head towards the side window of the car. He saw only the hotly flushed skin of her neck and cheek.

"I'm sorry," she said in a small voice. "I didn't mean

to offend you. I was just wondering…where I'd stand in your mother's eyes. It is for two weeks…''

Vulnerable! The realisation of how she was feeling jolted him. He'd forgotten she lacked the experience and sophistication to feel at ease with his mother's knowing and accommodating the fact of their being lovers. He took his mother's acceptance for granted. How could Sarah take anything for granted, not knowing, not even having been in such a situation before? She was no longer an innocent sexually but she was still very much an innocent at heart…open to giving and open to being hurt.

Damn it! He should never have started this. All the justification in the world didn't make it right. Not for her. He couldn't balance what he'd taken. Yet if he had the chance to turn back the clock and give up what she'd given him…no, he needed this, needed to have and know these incredibly rare feelings at least once in his lifetime. And she was experiencing them, too. It might never happen again for her, either. They had to seize as much as they could while they could.

He retrieved his hand in order to change gear, slow the car, park on the verge of the road.

''What's wrong?'' she cried, swinging her head back to him in alarm at the abrupt action.

''You are,'' he said, switching off the engine.

''Tareq…please forget what I said,'' she rushed out in a fluster. ''It doesn't matter. I was being…''

He placed a gentle, silencing finger on her lips. ''I want you to know how special you are, Sarah. You see, my darling girl…'' He hoped she could see it in his eyes, feel it flowing from him. He cupped her face to hold her still, hold her tied to him while he said what he had to

impress on her. ''…I love being with you. I love everything about you. I love you so much my mother can't
fail to see it. And she will look at you in wonder because
I've never loved anyone else. So you have nothing to
fear from her. There will be no awkwardness. Only happiness, my love.''

He felt his heart turn over at the luminous look of joy
in her eyes. Never mind that they were on a public road.
He leaned over and kissed her, loving the way her mouth
seemed to melt into his, loving her passion, loving the
giving that poured into all the empty places in his heart
and refreshed his soul.

''I love you, too, Tareq,'' she whispered when they'd
drunk their fill of each other.

He smiled, knowing it couldn't be anything else but
true, coming from Sarah. ''Then that's where we stand,''
he said. ''Are you okay with it now?''

She laughed, exhilaration sparkling in her eyes. ''Yes.
Very okay, thank you.''

He laughed with her. It was so good. It was as if
everything within him was humming with happiness.
When he restarted the Jaguar, he couldn't resist a burst
of acceleration.

Two uninterrupted weeks of bliss, he thought exult-
antly, as they sped towards Hershaw Manor. After
that…he didn't want to think about it…although one
thing he had to find out was what Sarah would like to
do in the future. He felt a deep twinge of regret at the
necessity to provide some foundation for her to build on.
Realities, however, could not be pushed into the background forever.

There had to be something he could arrange by way
of settling Sarah into an occupation or career she would

find rewarding. He had the power to open doors, make useful introductions, finance anything she wanted.

People were lost without a purpose in life.

He would make absolutely sure Sarah had something of substance to work with, to carry her forward, to give her satisfaction and fulfilment as a person. She had the inner strength of a survivor but he wanted more than survival for her.

He wished he could give her everything.

CHAPTER SEVENTEEN

SARAH loved Hershaw Manor. It was as warm and welcoming as Tareq's mother. The rooms were chock-a-block with personality; pretty chintz fabrics used in most of the furnishings, patterned carpets, a huge collection of antiques from different periods, chosen for charm and character rather than style, and every possession seemed to have a memory attached to it.

There were horses in the stables for riding, dogs underfoot, as much part of the household as people, and a casual, country mood imbued the life that flowed in and out and through the lovely old building in its parkland setting.

Tareq's mother—"Do call me Penny, dear. Everyone does."—Penelope Lambert—had married again to a veterinary surgeon, and had been widowed a few years ago. In her fifties now, she still had a wonderful vivacity that lit up the beauty of her youth, especially her sparkling blue eyes and beautiful smile. Her thick wavy hair was unashamedly white, though it had once been a glorious, rich red, as evidenced in many framed photographs of her with the champion Corgis she bred.

Kindness oozed from her. It was from her Tareq had learned his kindness, Sarah thought, and wondered if his father had been ruthless. Where did inherited genes begin and end and where did conditioning take over? Impossible to tell. She remembered her impression there was always purpose in Tareq's kindness and decided it wasn't necessarily so.

Though she did have an uncertain moment or two one evening. She and Penny shared an interest in books, both of them being avid readers.

"Have you ever tried to write one?" Penny asked.

"No. Have you?"

"I dabble with the occasional article about dogs. It's fun, playing with words, getting them in the right order so they shape the picture you want to draw. Like doing a jigsaw."

Sarah was amused by the parallel. "I'd love to read what you've had published. Actually it's the publishing side of books that interests me. I imagine it could be very exciting being an editor, getting a great manuscript and helping to turn it into a book people will want to buy."

"Do you have any first-hand knowledge of the publishing business?" Tareq asked, suddenly showing a keen interest in the conversation.

"Not really. I just think the whole process would be fascinating. Not only getting the book right for print but planning the cover and the selling points."

"We don't have any investment in that area," he said thoughtfully. "I'll look into it. Publishing must be profitable."

"Don't you have enough business to control already?" she teased.

He smiled. "I was thinking more along the lines of appointing you manager."

"Oh, don't be silly! I wouldn't have a clue."

"Think of the challenge."

"You're not serious."

"I think it's a splendid idea!" Penny interjected. "Just think, Sarah. Tareq could fix it for you to learn every aspect of the business first and then you could produce a lovely line of books." Her beautiful smile lit up her face. "Of course, I'd expect free copies."

"It's only a pipedream I had," Sarah protested, embarrassed that it had been seized upon by both of them.

"Let him spoil you. That's what men are for," Penny airily declared. "I've got my dogs. You should have your books."

Tareq grinned. "Thank you, Mother."

Kindness, generosity… Tareq insisted he loved her and wanted her to be happy…but Sarah didn't see how she could pursue a career, however attractive, and be with him, too. He travelled so much. Surely he wouldn't want to leave her behind.

Or was he looking at a future when they wouldn't be together anymore?

Kindness with a purpose.

She pushed the unsettling idea into the background, blaming her own mother for raising that spectre. Tareq's motive could just as easily be precisely what he said, not wanting her to get bored or restless, doing nothing of any consequence. Though she wouldn't be doing nothing if they got married and had children.

Deciding to let the future look after itself, she immersed herself in the joy of each wonderful day at the manor. She loved being here with Tareq. He seemed softer somehow, more relaxed, more open to her in this place that had been home to him through most of his growing up years. His mother had the habit of drawing out his sense of humour, adding fun to the pleasure of getting to know him better.

They rode most mornings, walked the dogs in the afternoon, helped his mother with a huge jigsaw—she was addicted to them—which accounted for a certain pattern in Tareq's thinking—enjoyed cosy little parties with local friends, played cards, spent many hours lounging by the fire in the sitting room, idly conversing, and many more hours making love in the privacy of their bedroom.

To Sarah it was an idyllic existence. She hoped the closeness they'd forged here would be carried on when they left. But her hopes and dreams received a shattering blow the day before she and Tareq were to return to London.

She was helping Penny do some more of her giant jigsaw while Tareq was busy with telephone calls. She couldn't help grinning triumphantly as she fitted in a piece they'd all been searching for over the past week. ''There!'' she cried, and they both laughed.

Penny sat back, shaking her head in a bemused fashion. ''You remind me so much of myself with Tareq's father. The heady days of passion…so impossible to believe we couldn't overcome everything with our love.''

Sadness dulled her eyes and Sarah was prompted to ask, ''Why did it end, Penny?''

She shrugged and gave a rueful smile. ''His country claimed him. I didn't fit in there. The culture was so different. I was always viewed as *the foreigner* by those closest to him, pushed into the background. And passion fades when love doesn't overcome everything.''

''I'm sorry,'' Sarah murmured sympathetically, wondering if she would face the same problems, then quickly assuring herself times had changed. Thirty years ago, countries were much more insular than they were now.

"Oh, I don't regret having known such passion even though it didn't last. Seeing you and Tareq so wonderfully consumed by it… I'm glad for both of you. It's rather rare, you know. It's worth having, every minute of it."

Sarah smiled, her happiness brimming over.

"There was nothing like it in my second marriage," Penny went on. "It was…comforting…congenial. We had a great deal in common and sharing is nice."

Nice…such a weak, insipid word.

"It's especially nice when the only sharing you've done for years was in bed," Penny added wryly.

Sarah felt a twinge of apprehension about how much sharing there'd be with Tareq once they left here. He'd be back to business with Peter Larsen, then the trip to his homeland for the wedding. Claims on him would certainly be made there. Their time together would be quality time, Sarah decided, deep, glorious quality time.

"Sarah…" A pained look had come into Penny's eyes. "Maybe I shouldn't say this. It's really none of my business. But…I've come to care about you and…and I feel you believe everything is possible for you and Tareq…"

"Yes, I do," Sarah affirmed, trying to ignore a prickling of alarm.

Penny shook her head in some anguish of spirit. "You'll be so terribly hurt…if you're not prepared."

The prickling turned into a nasty crawl down her spine. She had been through this scene before. With her mother. Though surely it couldn't be the same. Tareq's mother had seen they loved each other. There had to be something else on her mind.

"What do you mean?" Sarah asked warily, trying to fight off the anxiety attacking her heart.

A deep breath. A look that appealed for both forgiveness and understanding. "Don't bank on this lasting, Sarah…what you have with Tareq now."

No…please don't say that. Please?

The words kept coming. "There's too much against your staying together for very long."

We're strong enough to beat any problems.

"The time will come when you'll have to let it go," came the unequivocal statement. Blue eyes—so like Tareq's—begging belief. "Just…be prepared for that time, my dear."

It was said so kindly, Sarah found she couldn't dismiss the advice as she had her own mother's, however much she wanted to. This woman knew her son, knew more about him than any outsider could ever know, except perhaps Peter Larsen whose loyalty to Tareq would forbid him giving any advice that might be against his friend's interests.

"Why…" She swallowed, then forced out the question. "Why are you so sure it can't last?"

A heavy sigh, then slowly, agonisingly, a list of cogent reasons. "This is not a simple life you're dealing with. A marriage between you and Tareq would be a disaster. A half-English sheikh is barely acceptable to his people. Taking a wife, not of his country, would destabilise Tareq's authority. As much as he might want to force his will on the situation, there are those who would work against him. And you, Sarah, would be caught in the middle of it."

Tareq had actually spelled it out to her when they were leaving Werribee. It seemed like aeons ago, but the truth hadn't changed. His uncle…pressing him to marry a suitable woman to cement his position. Not an old man entrenched in old ways but a shrewd politician spelling out a necessity. That was what Penny was telling her, and buck as Tareq had against his uncle's choice of bride for him, the reality of the situation did not allow for Sarah to step into the role. She could only be a symbol of rebellion.

And Tareq had meant to use her as precisely that, perhaps as a staying tactic while he negotiated something else. He had anticipated their becoming lovers— no need for pretence—but had he anticipated falling in love with her? Wanting her as he did now? It made a difference, didn't it?

"Love doesn't always find a way," Penny said regretfully, as though reading the anguished hope in Sarah's mind. "It wears thin under tensions and conflict and conspiracies. Then it becomes untenable. Believe me. I know. Just…be prepared to let it go, Sarah. For your sake and his."

"But Tareq loves me." The protest burst from her heart. "He won't want to let me go, Penny."

"I can't imagine he will want to. There's the pity of it. But he knows such a journey is paved with trouble. And because he does love you, Sarah, I don't think he'll want to take you with him down that road. It would be destructive…to both of you."

Was it true? Couldn't there be some way around it? Or was he already preparing to let her go? Her frantic mind circled and fastened on the career he seemed so intent on her having. She desperately wanted to reject what it might mean, yet felt driven to face what had to be faced now. Even the worst.

"Is this why he's latched onto the idea of a publishing business for me?" she asked, her heart sinking as she saw the answer in his mother's eyes.

"I think so." Her own love for her son threaded the sadness in her voice as she explained, "Tareq has always tried to balance everything, even when it was impossible. I think he needs to find a gift for what you've given him…when the inevitable can no longer be held back."

Tears blurred Sarah's eyes. Tareq's rules…by which he could live with himself…trying to be fair. "I love him," she said helplessly.

"I know." Tears shone in Penny's eyes, too. "If I were you, I'd hoard every golden moment you have with him, Sarah. Savour every special feeling. Life with anyone you love can be so short. Don't waste it. It's worth too much to waste."

No guarantee with Tareq…only risk. Sarah recalled thinking that just after she had agreed to his bargain. After she had declared the bargain null and void, he'd asked if she'd stay with him of her own free will. She'd risked her heart, without guarantees, and the answer she'd given then was still the answer she'd give now.

Yes.

She'd stay with him until the journey ended, wherever it did, whenever it did. And she wouldn't waste a second of it.

CHAPTER EIGHTEEN

SARAH sat in the private courtyard adjoining Tareq's apartment in the palace, watching the fountain endlessly recycling water in a harmonious pattern. Fountains were supposed to be refreshing and soothing. This one was not fulfilling its purpose today. She kept wondering if Tareq was fulfilling his purpose in bringing her to his country or whether his stand was being frayed by a growing bank of opposition. Either way, she felt she was living every hour on the desperate edge of time running out on them.

She'd seen so little of him since they'd arrived a week ago. It seemed that as the ruling sheikh, his presence was required elsewhere virtually from dawn to so late at night, Sarah was sometimes asleep when he joined her in bed. She instantly awoke but he didn't want to talk about the meetings that had occupied his day. He wanted to hold her close to him.

She sensed urgent need in his lovemaking. The tensions he brought to bed with him were translated into intense passion, and only when that was sated did he relax and go to sleep, comforted by the lingering warmth of their intimate togetherness. Sarah couldn't help thinking he was being strongly pressured to set her aside. The echo of her own secret desperation seemed to vibrate in every kiss, in every possessive embrace, in the compulsive hunger for every expression of love.

Sometimes she was tempted to ask him to confide the

conflicts he faced, wanting to know the worst, yet she shied from doing anything that might precipitate the end of their being together. Love kept her tied to him for as long as he didn't actively reject it. Love…and a grain of hope for a resolution that didn't involve their parting. Though it seemed less and less feasible with every day that passed.

Adding to the despair she tried to suppress was the first-hand experience of the problems Penny Lambert had outlined to her. She was not welcome here. Tareq's stepmother and her daughters had invited her to lunch with them—only once—more to scrutinise her than to ease an entry into the family circle. Although she was treated with studied courtesy, they made her feel very foreign to them. A curiosity. An alien.

Mindful of filling in the hours for her, Tareq had arranged a guide to show her through the palace, explaining the history of its architecture and art works. She'd also been taken on tours of the city and the nearby resort on the shores of the Red Sea. The people, the places…everything was stamped with a culture so foreign to her, Sarah seriously doubted she could ever fit into it, let alone be happy living here on a permanent basis, despite being domiciled with every luxury and servants on hand to do her bidding.

The wretched truth was…the situation was hopeless in any long-term sense. Maybe Tareq wanted her to recognise that herself before the axe fell. There needn't be only one purpose in bringing her here.

''Sarah…'' Tareq calling her.

Amazed at his seeking her out midmorning, she leapt up from the garden seat to be more easily seen. ''I'm out here.''

He strode through the archway to the courtyard, his sheikh's robes somehow giving him more stature, while clothing him in an unfamiliarity that subtly emphasised how little Sarah had comprehended the full nature of this man she loved. Nevertheless, there was a huge grin on his face and his obvious good humour lifted Sarah's heart.

"Come…" He beckoned expansively. "…I have a surprise for you."

A surge of happiness sped her feet towards him. The fact that Tareq was here to spend some time with her was delight enough. He glanced back over his shoulder, nodding to someone in the shadows of the salon beyond the arches. Sarah looked past him to see what the surprise might be.

A red and yellow wheelchair came zooming into the sunlight and a high excited voice cried, "It's me, Sarah!"

"Jessie!"

Hugs and kisses and emotional tears and words tumbling over each other…

"It's so wonderful to see you."

"Tareq had me flown here in his private jet."

"All this way on your own?"

"A nurse came with me. And Peter was at the airport to pick us up."

"You mean Mr. Larsen?"

"He said I can call him Peter. And I've got special rooms in the palace with all the stuff I need."

"Truly?"

"Peter showed me. I'm to stay for the wedding so I'll see all the sheikhs."

"Oh, that's marvellous, Jessie! I'm so happy to have you here with me."

"Me, too. Doesn't Tareq look terrific in his robes?"

"He looks terrific to me whatever he wears."

"Or don't wear," Tareq muttered wickedly.

They laughed, Jessie not quite understanding but bubbling with so much excitement it didn't matter what they laughed at. The next few hours skimmed by, the pleasure of catching up with each other's news enhanced by Tareq's staying with them and light-heartedly stirring more fun with his dry sense of humour.

They had a lovely lunch together. When Jessie started to flag, Sarah and Tareq accompanied her to the specially prepared suite of rooms where she happily crowed over her new domain and introduced the nurse who had been employed to look after her, a cheerful woman in her thirties who seemed to be enjoying this adventure as much as Jessie. She steered her young charge into getting ready for an afternoon nap, leaving Sarah and Tareq alone together in the sitting room while she was settling Jessie into bed.

"It was so kind of you to do this," Sarah murmured, turning to him, her eyes eloquently expressing a heart full of love.

His arms came around her in an ardent embrace. "You've been lonely here," he answered gruffly. "It was selfish of me to bring you with me, but there was need, Sarah. I hope having Jessie's company will make it easier for you."

Need…the word buzzed through her brain, stirring a maelstrom of hopes and doubts. "Have I helped? With your uncle, I mean," she rushed out, searching his eyes for answers.

"Your presence reinforces my decisions," he said enigmatically.

"Is it...difficult for you?"

His face relaxed into a wry smile. "Yes and no." He lifted a hand to her cheek and tenderly fanned her skin with his fingertips. "As much as one might be determined on change, there is an underlying tug for what has been in place, for what is so ingrained it becomes a part of natural thought."

She sensed the inner torment of a struggle that tore him in two and knew intuitively it was centred on her. "Will you explain that to me?" she pleaded, suddenly uncaring of the outcome for her, wanting him to share his pain as well as his love.

He shook his head. "The problem is mine, my darling. And it's up to me to overcome it. Can you bear with me for a while longer?"

"You know I will," she cried fervently. "As long as you want me."

The wanting blazed into his eyes and seared her mouth as he kissed her, drawing from her all she would give and demanding more, hotly and hungrily, wanting so much it felt as though he was absorbing the very essence of her being, plundering her of energy to reinforce his own for the battle he was fighting.

A loud, theatrical cough broke the torrent of passion. Dizzily, Sarah heard the nurse say, "Uh, please pardon me...it's Jessie. She's in bed but she wants to tell you something before you...um...leave about your business."

Tareq took a deep breath. "Fine. Thank you," he said with creditable aplomb.

He scooped Sarah along with him to Jessie's bedroom

and the nurse scuttled out of their way, retreating to her own adjoining quarters in a flood of embarrassment at having witnessed and interrupted the sheikh's dalliance with what should have been very private desires.

Jessie was watching for them to come in, her gaze latching onto Tareq as they walked over to her bed. "I forgot to say thank you for bringing me here."

"I wanted it, Jessie," he confided. "I'm glad you were brave enough to make the trip."

She grinned. "Wild horses wouldn't have stopped me. I'm going to brag about this for years."

"Then you must tell me everything you want to do and see while you're my guest."

She heaved a big sigh. "You've been so good to me already with the computer and all. Mummy said Sarah must have told you about Firefly and that was why you wanted to do things for me."

Sarah shook her head but her little half-sister had all her attention focused on Tareq.

"I don't want you to think it was Firefly's fault that my legs don't work anymore, Tareq," she said earnestly. "You don't have to make it up to me."

He frowned, inadvertantly sparking Jessie to say more.

"I don't blame him at all. Firefly got frightened by the sparkler. I just wanted to show him but it scared him real bad. He didn't know he was hurting me. I think he was trying to put the sparkler out."

Sarah's chest tightened as Jessie spilled out the cause of a painful train of events that had led to her father cheating Tareq. The reason to hide it was gone—her father had his second chance—yet it still might leave an impression of carelessness on Tareq. He looked deeply concerned as he sat down on the edge of the bed and took Jessie's hand, fondling it sympathetically.

"Why don't you tell me your story of what happened?" he invited, his tone softly persuasive.

Sarah resigned herself to the inevitable. It was out of her hands. In fact, everything was out of her hands. Tareq was the dominant force, as he had been from the very beginning.

Jessie took a deep breath and poured out the tragic little story. "It was my birthday, you see. I was eight. Mummy was in hospital having the cancer treatment that made her sick, but Mrs. Walsh—she's married to Daddy's foreman—made me a cake—a big cream sponge cake with strawberries and candles on it—and me and the twins had a party after school. We had sparklers and balloons and party hats and blow-out whistles."

"Sounds like great fun," Tareq popped in encouragingly.

"Oh, it was! But the twins tore off together, doing their twin thing…" She grimaced as though Tareq would understand what she meant. "…And I thought I'd take Firefly a big slice of my cake and share my birthday party with him."

"With a horse?" Tareq gently teased.

"Firefly isn't just any horse. He's the most beautiful horse in the world. He used to let me pat him 'cause he knew I loved him. And I often went and talked to him in his stall. I knew by his eyes he was listening and he'd nod at me."

"Yes, he does have very intelligent eyes," Tareq agreed.

A heavy sigh. "I knew I wasn't supposed to go into

his stall. Daddy said it wasn't allowed. But it was my birthday, and I thought if I sneaked in, nobody would see me but Firefly and he wouldn't tell. So I did. And you should have seen Firefly scoff the cake I'd brought him. He thought it was great.''

''I'm sure he did,'' Tareq warmly agreed.

''But then I lit the sparkler and…like I said…it scared him. He reared up and got all frantic. I tried to calm him down but he accidentally knocked me against the wall and…'' She shook her head and shrugged off the crippling injuries she'd sustained. ''…I don't remember anything after that until I woke up in hospital.''

''I guess it wasn't much fun in hospital.''

Jessie rolled her eyes expressively. ''The pits! Especially all the stuff with my legs. I cried heaps when it finally sunk in I was never going to walk again, but Sarah helped me get over that.''

Tareq looked up at Sarah, an oddly intense weighing look in his eyes, as though he was measuring her power to achieve miracles of healing.

''Sarah was the best at getting me through everything!'' Jessie declared.

''Yes. I'm sure she was,'' he said very softly.

''Anyway, it wasn't Firefly's fault, Tareq.''

His gaze dropped to Jessie again.

''It was me being dumb about the sparkler and disobeying Daddy. So you really don't have to do things for me. Besides, there's nothing to make up for,'' she insisted strongly, her little face determined on this point. ''Walking isn't everything, you know. I can do lots. More even than I did before 'cause I think about more things.''

He shook his head, bemused by the enormous strength in such a positive attitude.

Tears pricked Sarah's eyes and she fiercely blinked them back. Jessie didn't want her tears. She wanted approval like everyone else. "You certainly do," she said half-laughingly. "What you've been sending me on the computer is marvellous."

Jessie giggled happily. Her eyes actually flirted in a very female way as she addressed Tareq again. "Mind you, I won't say no if you think of more things for me, Tareq."

"Jessie..." His face had softened into an expression of almost awe...certainly the warmest admiration. "You give me more than you receive." He leaned over and softly kissed her forehead. "Thank you for telling me your story."

She glowed under his kindness. "I just didn't want you to have it wrong."

"I have it right. Perfectly right," he assured her, squeezing her hand again as he stood up. "Sleep well, my dear Jessie. I must go now, but your spirit goes with me."

Jessie was content to be left, having squared her conscience with Tareq's generosity.

As Sarah accompanied Tareq out of the suite she was aware of steely purpose emanating from him, pulsing from him. Although she was walking beside him, she felt she was walking alone. He was focused on something else, intensely focused.

Afraid it might relate to her father, she said, "I think Dad might have justified what he did...because of Firefly. Not that it's any excuse, but..."

"Your father doesn't matter, Sarah." He stopped and

spun her towards him, his hands grasping her upper arms, his face blazing with a look of enlightened and ruthless power. "From the mouth of a child… My God! Sarah! To put so much behind her and go forward as she has done…and you were there to help her. You were with her. I need no more. I will do no less."

He kissed her forehead as he had done Jessie's, then left her, taking the corridor that led to his administrative centre, every stride away from her firmly decisive.

CHAPTER NINETEEN

THE banquet room in the palace was a long way from the one at Marchington Hall, in every sense. The riches here were dazzling; a mirrored ceiling ornately latticed in gold, magnificent marble columns supporting wonderfully carved arches coated with gold leaf, fantastic friezes, a marble floor seemingly grained with gold, and the exotically designed table and chairs standing on gold legs. The chairs were upholstered in a gleaming silk imprinted with a shimmering peacock's tail pattern, and peacock feathers wavered from wonderful gold urns set around the room.

Sarah was glad she had chosen to wear the wine red dress Tareq had bought her in Paris, adding the long-sleeved bolero that had come with it, mindful of the modesty expected of women in this culture. The ruby necklace and earrings felt right tonight. She wanted Tareq to be proud of her in front of his family and certainly anything else she owned would have been hopelessly outshone by this room.

Besides, every woman here—his stepmother, half-sisters, cousins—was fabulously dressed, glowing like gloriously plumaged birds amongst the formal white robes worn by the men. She fitted into the company…more or less…though she was extremely conscious of not being family. She was the only one here who was not kin. Even Peter Larsen had been excluded from this pre-wedding gathering.

Sarah couldn't help wondering what it meant...Tareq putting her in the spotlight like this. He, of course, was at the head of the long table. She was seated on his right, opposite his uncle whom she had met for the first time tonight. She had half-expected to feel hostility coming from the formidable old man, yet he was showing her every courtesy, conversing with her in a respectful manner which obviously pleased Tareq.

Perhaps it was the best political move at this point, bowing to the sheikh's will. Certainly Tareq was exuding masterful authority. Sarah particularly noticed how deferential every member of his family was in addressing him or listening to what he had to say.

Had he taken some totally dominant stand with all of them or was this the normal order of things in his presence? Though what appeared on the surface need not reflect what flowed underneath, she thought soberly, remembering Penny's talk of conspiracies. All the same, in the days since Jessie's arrival, Tareq had not been quite so tense, and tonight he seemed very relaxed, happy, as though he was relieved of the burdens he'd found so testing.

The long dinner with his family proved less of an ordeal than Sarah had imagined it would be. After coffee had been served, Tareq rose from his chair to command attention, obviously intent on making a speech. Talk stopped. Heads turned to him. Sarah marvelled at the power he held, an innate charisma that simply fanned out from him, creating a magnetic field. A born leader, she thought, a man of destiny, and if that destiny could not include her, then she was still fortunate to have known his love.

A stab of pain accompanied the thought, but there was

pride, too, and when he momentarily met her gaze before beginning his speech, his vivid blue eyes burned with a fire that encompassed more than the desire to have her with him. There was a flame of exaltation, as though they had reached some glorious pinnacle together, and only with her could he stay there. It gave her a beautiful feeling, a sense of completeness, of having loved well…even if not wisely.

"For many years, our lives have travelled side by side," he started. "The sense of a family going forward is a matter of satisfaction and pride. For our family, it also carries a strong sense of responsibility to our country, an ongoing leadership that is trusted and esteemed. Our people look to us to care for them and give them a secure and stable government."

He paused to smile benevolently. "With the marriage of my brother, Ahmed, to our cousin, Aisha, the bond of unity is strengthened, and I wish them both a long, happy life and many children."

There was a smattering of applause around the table, eager murmurs of agreement trailing into silence for Tareq to continue.

"As you all know, it is the custom of our country that the firstborn son of the sheikh becomes the sheikh after him. This tradition has been practised through many generations of our family. I hold my position through right of birth, and it could be seen as my duty to marry and have a son, who would be my natural successor."

These words were not so happily received. The mood of the company subtly changed. Sarah sensed tension underneath a stirring of unrest. Several frosty glances were thrown her way. She was obviously a bone of contention, bringing disfavour on Tareq's judgment and probably raising questions over his respect for the position he had inherited.

It was a highly discomforting moment…realising that her being here was not working for Tareq, apart from the personal intimacy he still wanted. She didn't belong in this country and never would. Surely he understood that and appreciated the ramifications of flouting his people's sense of rightness.

Tareq, however did not appear perturbed by the negative vibrations coming their way. "As I am the ruling authority," he stated with arrogant disregard for any disapproval, "I have the power to change customs and law as I see fit."

More than unrest now. Grumblings, anger, open resentment at his high-handedness, glares at Sarah as though she were the instigator of the changes to come. It wasn't true, she fiercely told herself. Tareq was his own master. She was not a party to any of his decisions here.

Tareq's uncle gave him a hard, knowing look. Unbelievably, Tareq smiled at him, a whimsical, carefree little smile. It had the effect of focusing attention on him again.

"Your alarm cements the decision I have already made," he said, his confidence unshaken. Then his gaze turned to Sarah, his eyes like lasers, irresistible power boring into her, commanding her acquiescence as he held out his hand to her. "Will you stand by me, Sarah?"

Uproar.

She stared at him in disbelief. He couldn't mean to announce a marriage with her. He couldn't! He hadn't even asked her!

His uncle crashed his fist on the table, rising to his feet. "No! It cannot be done, Tareq," he growled.

"Sarah…" The repeated call to her carried unwavering purpose.

The noise around her seemed to recede into a distant wash of sound. The thunder of her heart filled her ears. Her legs trembled but she pushed up from her chair and grasped the hand held out to her, compelled beyond sense and reason to stand with him against the whole world, if that was his will.

His uncle, aggressively angry. "Tareq, I warn you…"

"Enough!" came the steely reply. A strong sweep of his arm brought the noise around the table down to a subdued mutter. "You will hear me out with the respect I am due."

His uncle sat. A mutinous silence settled. Tareq interlaced his fingers with Sarah's, gripping hard. Fear was quaking through her. Not even Tareq with his dominating will could make people accept what they didn't want to. If he was entertaining the idea of making her his consort, the journey ahead looked impossible, loaded with landmines. Yet if he wanted her with him…

"Firstly, I wish to thank you, Uncle, for your loyal support over the years, and for the important service you have given to our country on my behalf. Your advice has been invaluable and I heed it now. I also accept the truth of what you have told me."

The old man compressed his lips and shook his head.

Tareq shifted his attention to encompass his family and spoke with ringing conviction. "The ruling sheikh should give himself wholeheartedly to his people and his country, belonging to them as they belong to him. The bonds of trust and loyalty go deep. They are rooted in a shared heritage, a shared understanding, a shared life, a perception of the sheikh as being of the people and for the people he rules.''

Vehement nods around the table.

"I have lived my life in two worlds," Tareq went on. "And I shall continue to do so, at the service of my country and my family."

Instant protests. Insistence that he reconsider the position he was striking.

Tareq raised his hand and silence fell again, a brooding belligerent silence.

"I am mindful of what is needed here." He paused to lend weight to his words. Scepticism hung heavily around the table. "And I know I am not the man who can best fulfil it."

Surprise, frowns at this extraordinary admission. Suspicion of trickery.

"Therefore, with the power invested in me, I now change the customary order of succession. The official announcement of my abdication will be made public tomorrow."

Shock! Total shock!

Sarah's mind buzzed with horror. If he was doing this for her... Dear Heaven! Giving up all that was rightfully his... How could she live with such a sacrifice! But there was nothing she could do or say to change his decision. The line was already drawn. He had passed the point of no return.

"Ahmed..." Tareq's gaze fastened on the man seated at the foot of the table, his oldest half-brother, the bridegroom-to-be. Every head turned to Ahmed, who stiffened, straightening in his chair, his handsome face struggling to comprehend the enormity of what was happening. "…I pass my authority to you," Tareq declared, ripping straight to the heart of the matter. "It is you who can truly wear it. You are more our father's son than I am, and I know your sense of responsibility to our people will lead you to use your authority with their best interests at heart."

Cries of approval erupted, the shock fading as all confusion over Tareq's intentions was erased. The nerve-tearing tension eased into relief. For everyone except Sarah. Her anxiety increased with a million uncertainties about the future.

Tareq smiled at his half-brother. "It is a timely wedding gift, is it not? It will give our people much to celebrate…the marriage of their new sheikh."

"Tareq…" Ahmed rose to his feet, his hands lifting, gesturing a plea for a settlement of their differences. "…I was not expecting you to…to…"

"I know you will accept this mantle with dignity, my brother, and wear it with honour. Come…" Tareq stepped aside and waved Ahmed to the place he had vacated "…take this chair. It is yours."

His head high, shoulders straight, eyes shining, Ahmed walked directly to Tareq and embraced him. The two men exchanged kisses of respect on both cheeks.

"Aisha…this chair on the right hand of your sheikh will belong to you. Come and be seated beside your betrothed."

She, too, moved with great dignity, bowing to Tareq before standing by Ahmed. Neither of them sat. They waited, they all waited for Tareq's next pronouncement.

"Uncle, I am sure you will counsel them well in their duties. As you know, their hearts are already in the right place. On mine there is another claim."

He recaptured Sarah's hand, enfolding it now in comforting warmth. He raised his other hand in a salute of farewell. ''I leave you to welcome and celebrate our new regime. I wish you all a very good night.''

Chairs instantly scraped back. Everyone stood in respect as Tareq and Sarah made their unified exit from the banquet room. Only the sound of their footsteps on the marble floor accompanied them out, and to Sarah, they seemed to echo in a great emptiness. Tareq had cut himself off from a world that had occupied half his life. Probably more than half. How was the hole to be filled?

CHAPTER TWENTY

FREE…elation zinged through Tareq…free of the duality that had plagued him since early boyhood, free to take new paths, free to keep the companion of his heart, free to choose how to live, where to live, and with whom to live.

Maybe this was the high before the low of feeling the loss of all the privileges attached to his former status, but he doubted they were worth caring about. Jessie had it right. When one power was irretrievably gone, the incentive to find and use others pushed useless regrets into the discard bin. Besides, over and above everything else was the love he couldn't bear to lose.

It was colour.

It was meaning.

It gave him the sense of belonging he had always craved and never known…before Sarah.

Happiness surged through him as he closed his door to the rest of the palace, ensuring their absolute and intimate privacy in his apartment. His blood was singing. His soul was soaring. His eyes feasted on the woman who had braved a journey of faith with him, matching him every step of the way, despite the risks, the tests of strength, the trials and tribulations thrust upon her by the demands of who he was and what was expected of him.

No more.

The way ahead was clear now if she would share it with him.

He tore off his headdress and tossed it onto a chair. There was only one thing left to do and he whirled Sarah into his embrace, buoyantly confident of the outcome he wanted. Her hands fluttered against his chest, signalling her inner agitation.

"You think I've given up too much," he said, reading the distress and worry in her eyes.

"Tareq, you once told me love always had a price. But this…" She shook her head in anguish. "It's impossible for me to count all you've sacrificed."

"It's not a sacrifice. It's a gain, my darling." He gently smoothed the lines from her forehead. "Have you ever wondered what your life was about? What it was for?"

Her eyes remained anxious.

"I was brainwashed from childhood to accept and fulfil a role I didn't choose," he explained. "There were times I railed against it. My English half rebelled. I felt burdened with duties I was not in tune with. Yet my responsibilities did give my life purpose, and with the power I had, I could make things happen. Both factors influenced my view of what was worthwhile. Everything, I thought, was relative to that central core of purpose to achieve for my country."

"Then won't you feel a terrible gap in a future that doesn't hold that?" she fretted.

"It holds something different. Something more worthwhile to me," he replied with passionate conviction.

She trembled. "How do you know?"

"Because any purpose pales in comparison to what you give me. Your gift of love is beyond price."

Tears put a luminous sheen on the conflict still evident in her eyes. She swallowed, determined on voicing her doubts. "Tareq, you're used to having more than me in your life."

"So? I still have more. Sarah, my love, I have a vast, personal fortune. I can play with whatever market offers me a satisfying challenge. We can do it together...publishing...breeding dogs and horses..." He laughed. "The sky is the limit and the world is ours. *There's* the difference, Sarah. It will be *our* world, not one imposed on us. And we get to say who belongs in it."

She looked at him searchingly. "You're really happy about this?"

"Oh, yes. You see before you a man no longer divided." He smiled reassuringly. "However, I would like one guarantee on the future."

"Tareq, there aren't any guarantees. You may regret..."

He touched his fingertips to her lips, cutting off any looking back. A new life had begun. "I won't regret anything if you will give me one promise and keep it."

"What is it?"

He moved his hand to cup her cheek, tenderly, persuasively, possessively. "Say you will marry me."

Still the anxious caring for him, yet overlaid by a growing look of awe, of wonder. "You trust me that much?' she asked huskily, a deep well of emotion furring her voice.

"It's not trust, Sarah. It's love."

Tears hovered on her lashes. Her mouth quivered. Tareq felt his heart turn over. She was so beautiful. So vulnerable. The desire to love her, protect her, give her everything she needed and wanted, streamed through him, finding no barrier, no trace of conflict, not even a pause for second thought.

He kissed her, softly, tenderly, longingly. "Say yes, Sarah. Say yes," he urged, needing to hear it, knowing he wouldn't feel complete without her verbal commitment.

"Yes," she whispered.

Her mouth said it. Her body said it. There was no holding back. None at all. And he held nothing back. He didn't have to. They were truly one.

The foundation for their future was set, their journey together assured. It was much later that night, lying in contentment with Sarah nestled close to him, Tareq remembered the day she'd walked back into his life, and the answer he'd given her when she'd asked how long their journey was to be.

Until I know it all.

He smiled.

He'd spoken a truth not encompassed by the arrogant confidence he'd felt at the time. Impossible to know it all, even given a lifetime. He was only at the beginning of unlocking his mind and unfolding his heart to the love Sarah had brought to him. He looked ahead to the many pleasures of having her as his wife…the children they would have together…the family they would create and bond in an unbreakable sense of belonging…it was endless, their journey.

Endless.

And he loved the thought of every minute of it.

CHAPTER TWENTY-ONE

"FIREFLY sitting eighth, well positioned in the field as they come around the bend..."

Eighth...it was where he had finished in the Melbourne Cup last year. Sarah's heart was pounding as hard as the horses' hooves hitting the turf. Firefly had to do better. He had to. She desperately wanted the exonerating proof that her father was doing his best by Tareq's horses.

She was sure he was...the whole family was here to watch the big race, the twins madly excited, Susan smilingly confident, Jessie glowing with pleasure, her father eager to discuss anything and everything with Tareq. Nevertheless, only a really good performance would take away the stigma of shoddy training.

"Come on, Firefly!" Jessie yelled. Peter Larsen had hoisted her up against his shoulder to give her a clear view and she was jiggling wildly, making Peter laugh.

He was really a very nice man underneath his rather austere exterior, and still Tareq's trouble-shooter, though there was less trouble to deal with these days. Sarah wondered if the crooked bookmaker was here at Flemington and swiftly squashed the awful thought. It had nothing to do with them anymore.

"Into the straight with four hundred metres to go and Firefly is making a move..."

Was it too soon? Could he stay the distance if he went

to the front now? Doubts and fears swirled through Sarah's mind. If he flagged before the winning post...

"Come on, Firefly!" Jessie yelled, and the twins yelled to see, too.

Tareq scooped them up against his shoulders. Sarah couldn't help smiling. He was going to make a wonderful father. She touched her slightly rounded stomach. Thank heaven the morning sickness was over. She was churning enough as it was without that added nausea.

The whole crowd was yelling now. The field of horses was bunching up, the jockeys urging their mounts into a final sprint.

"Two hundred metres to go and Firefly takes the lead..."

He looked magnificent, powering ahead at full stretch, a long neck in front, then half a length, a full length... Sarah tore her gaze away from the race to look at her father. Was it all right? Could Firefly maintain this speed?

Her father caught her anxious glance and winked reassuringly. "He's a champion stayer," he said with pride.

The children were cheering him on, beside themselves with excitement. Sarah heard herself screaming, "Yes...yes...go!" as the distance to cover grew less and less and still Firefly held his lead. It was impossible, she thought, but miracles did happen. Wasn't she married to Tareq? With their very own family on the way? And she was even friends with her mother now!

The winning post was coming up...two other horses on his heels, gaining on him bit by bit, but surely Firefly would have to falter for them to catch and pass him.

And he didn't. He just kept flying, poetry in motion, and they were all screaming, even Tareq.

"And it's Firefly, the winner of this year's Melbourne Cup…"

Sarah burst into tears. Her father wrapped her in a bear hug and rocked her with his own glee. "Your old Dad wouldn't be letting you down when you're about to make him a Grandpa, now would he?" he chortled. "I'll be taking Firefly to win the Japan Cup next."

"And well you might, Drew," Tareq declared, clapping him on the back in delighted approval.

It was wonderful. Everyone was deliriously happy. A horserace shouldn't mean so much, Sarah thought, but today it did. Today, with Firefly actually winning, felt like the crowning glory of the year in her life when everything had come right for her and all the promises had been kept.

As they were going down to the winner's enclosure for the presentation of the cup, she stumbled on the stairs. Even as Tareq caught her to him, Peter, two steps ahead, whirled to save her from falling. He breathed a sigh of relief as he saw she was safe.

"That's my godchild you're carrying," he archly reminded her.

She smiled. "Don't worry, Peter. You'll have plenty of chances. We're planning on half a dozen children at least."

He raised an eyebrow. "Brave words."

"And trouble," she laughed at him.

He grinned. "I've never minded good trouble."

"Well, we can guarantee you plenty of that," Tareq informed him, as high-spirited as the rest of them.

The whole family gathered around the dais where the

official presentation was to be made. Firefly was there, too, being paraded in front of the crowd. Speeches flowed. Tareq, as the owner of the winning horse, should have had the cup presented to him, but he insisted it be given to his wife. After all, it wouldn't have been won without her, he argued. She was the miracle in his life. And always would be.

Sarah didn't have a speech prepared. She looked at her father and his family, so proud and happy and secure in their togetherness. She looked at Peter and thought of trust and loyalty and caring. She looked at Tareq and saw the love in his eyes...her husband, her partner in the journey of life...and the words came from her heart.

"This cup represents a dream fulfilled..."

Helen Brooks lives in Northamptonshire and is married with three children. As she is a committed Christian, busy housewife and mother, her spare time is at a premium but her hobbies include reading, swimming, gardening and walking her two energetic, inquisitive and very endearing young dogs. Her long-cherished aspiration to write became a reality when she put pen to paper on reaching the age of forty, and sent the result off to Mills & Boon®.

Look out for

A SPANISH AFFAIR by Helen Brooks

in Modern Romance™, July 2001

THE SULTAN'S FAVOURITE

by

HELEN BROOKS

CHAPTER ONE

'CAN I be of assistance?' As the deep, lazy voice with its faint accent sounded just behind her, Louisa swung round in surprise, her arms full of the rich, vibrant silk and her dark velvety brown eyes wide with a mixture of apprehension and annoyance. Not another intended pick-up? In the two weeks since she had been in Istanbul the sheer persistence of a certain section of the male population had astounded her.

'I beg your pardon?' Her voice was deliberately cool and remote but even as she spoke she realised her mistake, her cheeks flushing a faint pink. This man was not out of the same mould as the fancy-free youths who assumed a young female on her own was looking for a little diversion which they were only too happy to supply. He was tall, very tall, dark and exquisitely dressed in a pale grey suit and silk shirt that shouted intimidating wealth, and as his eyes locked on to hers the jolt she received was stunning.

'You seem to be having a little difficulty?' She heard him speak but for the life of her was unable to respond. He was devastatingly handsome and wickedly male, the wide, strong shoulders set at an angle that proclaimed overpowering confidence in his virility and ability to command, but it was his eyes that dried up the words in her throat and were rendering her helpless. He was so dark she would have expected his eyes to be black, maybe grey but almost certainly brown to fit in with the shining ebony hair, but the vivid tawny-

7

gold eyes flecked with an iridescent green were as mesmerising as those of a big cat and just as deadly.

The slightly ironic twist to the hard mouth suddenly informed her she was staring with her mouth half-open and still without having made any coherent reply. 'It's all right, thank you,' she said quickly, lowering her eyes in confusion as she half turned back to the small beady-eyed shopkeeper she had been bargaining with for the beautiful peach-coloured silk shawl. 'I don't need any help.'

'You do not?' The rich voice was openly disbelieving and as he shot some rapid Turkish at the attentive little trader watching them both so closely she saw the man's sharp-featured face melt into an ingratiating smile.

'*Evet effendi, evet.*' He nodded vigorously. '*Mersi, mersi.*'

'The item is yours.'

'What?' In a daze she watched an inordinate amount of lira change hands before she could move, and then as realisation washed over her in a burning wave she raised her head sharply, her soft brown eyes flashing fire. 'Now just hang on a moment! I don't know if I can afford this and ——'

'The shawl is a gift, a humble token of my admiration for your beauty.' It was an outrageous line but somehow in the exotic confines of Istanbul's famous Covered Bazaar it fitted perfectly. 'The only thing I would ask in return is to be allowed to know your name.' His voice was low and husky and touched with the faintest lilt of an accent, and Louisa felt the shiver that started somewhere in the region of her spine travel all the way to her toes. How old was he? she thought irrelevantly as she stared back into narrowed eyes watching her so intently. A touch of white at his temples and the laughter-lines cut deep into the tanned, clear skin put his age in the late thirties, maybe even forty; the taut, powerful body was giving nothing away.

'Look, this is ridiculous, Mr. . .?' With a tremendous effort she pulled herself together. 'I can't possibly accept a present from a perfect stranger and I doubt if I can afford the shawl myself. Could you just ask for your money back or something. . .?'

Her voice died away as he threw back his head in laughter. 'My name is Melik, my hot-tempered enchantress with eyes of midnight, and no, I cannot "just ask for my money back". That would be extremely rude and quite out of the question. You have to decide whether to make this shop owner the unworthy recipient of an undeserved bonus or to allow me the pleasure of a purely spontaneous action with no thought of compromise or ungentlemanly motives on my side, I assure you. You are very beautiful; I know of no one at the moment more suited to be clothed in the richness of silk, so. . .?' He smiled slowly with a trace of dark amusement lighting the feline eyes as they wandered over her hot face. 'I would be most honoured if you would accept the gift.'

'I don't believe this.' She gazed helplessly down the street packed full of shops and tiny cubby-holes rich with silk, lace, cotton and a thousand other materials made into beautiful shawls, gossamer-thin dresses, pretty blouses and every other item of clothing possible to imagine, with the traders sitting in front of their wares like patient spiders waiting to pounce.

The Bazaar was a small city in itself, over four thousand shops of varying sizes from tiny one-stalled indentations to large, impressive glass-plated establishments in the more opulent sections where the jeweller's shops stood shoulder to shoulder displaying their glittering bounty. Each section was devoted to its own trade and she had wandered through the vast maze, all under one roof, without any clear intention to buy until she had spotted the delicate, exotically patterned shawl in rich fine silk in one small shop. She wished with all her heart now that she had stayed at the apartment.

'Is it too dreadful a thing to contemplate?' She felt the laughter in the dark voice even though his face was politely grave now. 'Can you not look on it as a delightful diversion out of the normal rush of life?'

'But——' She stopped abruptly as her eyes were drawn back to his. What should she do? He had bought the shawl now, the trader had pocketed the money immediately, his eyes flashing from one to the other as his teeth exposed themselves in a knowing smile; it was a *fait accompli* and yet she couldn't, she just couldn't accept it. . .

'Come.' The decision was suddenly taken out of her hands as the tall stranger took the bag the trader was proffering in one hand, her arm in the other, and walked a few paces down the street before she pulled herself free.

'I'm not going anywhere with you.' There was real fear in her face now even as she forced her voice to remain steady. 'Just take your shawl and go away. I'll call for help——'

'I do not think the shawl is quite my colour.' He couldn't hide the laughter that was shaking his voice and as she glared up at him he made a visible effort to control his amusement. 'I apologise, little tigress—I can imagine how this must seem. If it helps at all you have my word that I am as surprised by my actions as you undoubtedly are. I do not make it a habit to buy strange women gifts of any sort but I had been watching you for some time and I wanted to make contact.' The direct honesty took her breath away, coupled as it was with the totally disarming smile that softened the cruel eyes and hard mouth. 'I would like to buy you a coffee, maybe talk a little, but the decision is yours. Say the word and I will disappear like the frost before the first breath of summer.'

'Well. . .' She glanced again at the exquisite hand-made suit and soft leather shoes. He was obviously a wealthy businessman idling away a couple of hours between engagements, and the situation had got ridiculous. A coffee wouldn't hurt and then she could say goodbye quickly and cleanly but the shawl was staying with him come hell or high water! She didn't doubt for a minute that there were plenty of female 'friends' he could give it to! 'A quick coffee, then, but I really can't accept the shawl although it was very kind of you.' She smiled carefully and coolly, her eyes guarded.

'Kind?' The sweep of his lashes made her stomach muscles tighten with a strange foreboding. 'I am not a kind man, Miss. . .?'

'Collins. Louisa Collins,' she said quickly.

'Louisa. . .' He let her name trail over his lips sensuously. 'I like this name; it suits you.'

'Thank you.' She stared at him helplessly, feeling like a schoolgirl totally out of her depth instead of a grown woman of twenty-eight perfectly in control of her own life. 'This is crazy. . .' She shook her blonde head as they began to walk.

She didn't realise she had spoken out loud until he smiled mockingly. 'Isn't it,' he agreed lightly. 'But surely one is allowed a little madness occasionally?'

As she met his eyes again, her mouth rueful, she

caught a flash of something hot and bright deep in their gold depths that suddenly caused the blood to pound through her veins madly. It had been hungry, voracious, something quite out of keeping with the persuasive talk and smiling banter, as though a carefully constructed mask had slipped for a brief moment to reveal a fierce volcanic primitive force that was supremely powerful and intrinsically cruel. What was she doing? She almost stopped as her mind raced. She shouldn't even be having coffee with this man. He was dangerous—her sixth sense had picked up something that the layers of civilisation couldn't quite hide—and he wanted her. She knew it as clearly as though he had voiced it and it wasn't false vanity. Her sixth sense also told her he wasn't a man who liked to be thwarted.

'No second thoughts, Miss Collins.' The razor-sharp mind had picked up her agitation somehow. 'I have always understood that an Englishman's word is his bond and I am sure that applies to the female of the species. Now, let us take a nice stroll to a little coffee-shop I know that is quite delightful. Have you been to Ic Bedesten?'

'Ic Bedesten?' She shook her head. 'I'm sorry, I don't understand——'

'The old bazaar.' His face was reassuringly bland now and she took herself to task firmly. He had only asked her to have coffee, for goodness' sake! He was obviously disgustingly wealthy with film-star good looks to boot; he'd have the women fighting a path to his door, and here was she thinking he was interested in her! She almost smiled. Stop imagining things, Louisa, and enjoy the moment, she told herself crossly; there haven't been too many to enjoy for some time after all. The ever-present cloud that had lifted during the last few minutes settled again as she remembered, and as the man at her side glanced at her closed face his own darkened quizzically.

'Louisa? There is something wrong?'

'Wrong?' She smiled quickly. 'Of course not, and no, I haven't been to the old bazaar, or I don't think I have! Is it different from this?'

'The old bazaar is at the centre of this maze,' he said quietly as his eyes searched her face. 'The jumble of centuries is located there — rusty swords and old camel bells, ancient tiles painted with texts in Arabic calligraphy and a million and one other secrets that have been unearthed through time and man's greed. Occasionally a treasure is found and a fortune made; I will take you there one day,' he finished in the same breath. 'It is the real bazaar, a taste of the past.'

One day? She forced her expression to reveal nothing even as mind and body protested. One day? Over her dead body! This was definitely a one-off. She didn't need any complications in her life; she was too bruised and raw for that, and this man was far too. . . uncomfortable. A coffee, a brief chat and then a parting of the ways.

Although protected from the fierce rays of the September sun by its roof, the sixty-seven streets of the bazaar were warm and humid in the Turkish heat, the highly coloured sights, exotic spiced smells and crowded streets and alleys alive with the taste of the orient, Istanbullus shopping for daily essentials alongside rich American tourists. As they reached the tiny coffee-shop set slightly back from the street Louisa found her feet were aching and she sank gratefully on to the small upholstered seat Melik indicated, smoothing back a wisp of bright golden hair that had escaped from the tight knot at the back of her head as she did so.

'Why do you try and hide such beauty?' he asked her softly as his eyes followed the gesture. 'Your hair should be your glory, is this not so?'

'I prefer to keep it under control,' she said shortly. 'It's too curly and there's too much of it.'

'You are a strange young woman, Louisa Collins,' he said after a long moment. 'If it weren't so ridiculous in one so lovely I would almost think you are frightened of life.'

'Frightened?' She eyed him angrily now, her thin brown brows drawing together in a frown. 'You're right, it is ridiculous.' She raised her chin defiantly.

'Maybe.' He smiled easily although this time it didn't touch the hard gold of his eyes. 'And maybe not. Nevertheless you do not have the look of a woman who has been kissed recently; am I right?' He stood looking down at her from his great height, his arms folded, legs slightly apart, his whole manner one of male domination, and she felt hot rage flood her chest. How dared he? How dared he question her like this? A virtual stranger probing into her life!

'I don't really think that's any of your business,' she said coldly, her cheeks scarlet. 'Do you?'

'On the contrary.' He was blatantly unaffected by her rage; she was furious to notice that there was even a slight twist to his mouth as he surveyed her angry face as though he was finding it all most amusing. 'It is quite immoral to think that a woman as beautiful as you is not enjoying the pleasures of love at night in the arms of her lover. I dislike waste in any form.'

'Oh, you——' She was still spluttering for words as he leant forward and touched her hot cheek gently with the tip of one finger, his eyes lingering for a moment on her parted lips before he brushed them lightly with his own. She leapt back in her seat as though she had been scalded, shocked to find that that light pressure had ignited a host of feelings totally alien to her that ran from the top of her head to the soles of her feet.

'Coffee.' He drew back smoothly, his tawny gaze like fire on her skin. 'I have to make a telephone call; I am already late for an appointment. I will not be long.' He indicated a partly concealed telephone booth at the back of the shop with a nonchalant wave of his hand. 'I will arrange for coffee and pastries to be sent over so you will not be disturbed, and then on my return we will continue this interesting conversation, yes?'

'I wasn't aware that we were having a conversation,' she said stiffly as she forced herself to sit perfectly still and hide the trembling that was threatening to become visible at any moment. 'And I've no intention of tolerating any more questions of a personal nature, Mr Melik.'

'Melik is my first name,' he said softly, his narrowed eyes flicking over her stony face with a piercing light that seemed to reach out to her very soul, 'and why so threatened, Louisa? I'm not going to hurt you.' His gaze lingered on the pale cream of her skin before moving to the pure gold hair so tightly confined in its pins. 'You are a very beautiful woman—many men must have told you this—added to which you have an elegance, a confidence that only comes with maturity and is far more sensual than any girlish shyness. Can we not talk as equals?'

She dragged her eyes away from his dark face, quite unable to reply. He had assumed she was a woman of

the world, cool, poised and able to take care of herself
in any romantic situation, and she had to admit that
was exactly the effect she liked to give. It was her
protection, her safeguard in the male-dominated world
she had chosen to work in, but it went far deeper than
that. But she would not, she *could not* explain herself
to him! Let him think what he liked; she wouldn't ever
see him again after today anyway, and maybe it was
better if he saw her as a composed career woman with
a cool head on her shoulders and a mind to match.

'As equals?' It took every ounce of her will to smile
quietly into the eagle-eyed handsome face watching
her so closely. 'I wouldn't have thought a Turkish man
would encourage such presumption from a mere
woman!'

'You have been reading too many novels, Louisa,'
he said silkily, the inflexion he gave her name causing
that now familiar shiver to travel down her spine. 'The
days of the harems are long since gone but even in
those times there was more power wielded in one pair
of tiny hands weighed down with rings and bracelets
than in the hand holding the sword. Make no mistake,
just because my countrymen have always appreciated a
woman's beauty, it does not mean that they have
ignored her intelligence and wisdom.'

'Really?' She eyed him with scornful disbelief and
his mouth tightened.

'Really,' he said coldly. 'Turkish men treat their
womenfolk with great respect; in fact a woman travelling alone in my country is safer than in many other
countries including your own.'

'So you're saying you're interested in a woman's
mind first?' She realised her mistake immediately. The
hard eyes softened into a smile and the sensual mouth

twisted slightly as his gaze wandered over her flushed face.

'I would not like to be guilty of such deception,' he said gravely, 'especially where you are concerned. Nevertheless you are a person as a whole, mind, soul and body, as I am. This I would respect.'

As a smiling waiter appeared at their elbows Melik spoke swiftly in fluent Turkish before turning to her again, his expression slightly preoccupied. 'I really must make that telephone call, if you will excuse me? This is the first time I have played the — how you say? Hookey? — in a long, long time.' He smiled warmly. 'But I could not resist such temptation. My mind, soul *and* body responded to the call.'

She leant back in the small seat as she looked up at him, her eyes steady even as her heartbeat raced. He was so good-looking, so sure of himself even when he was mocking her like now. What would it be like to be loved by a man like this? The thought shocked her; she could only view it as a betrayal of Oliver, and she lowered her eyes quickly as a small pulse beat agitatedly in her throat. 'That's fine. Please, make the call.'

As he walked away, his big, lean body towering over the other occupants of the small, deliciously scented coffee-shop, she felt herself begin to shake as the urge to escape became paramount. He was too much, she thought desperately. Too big, too aggressively masculine, too savage, the very antithesis of Oliver, in fact. He belonged to a different age, a golden age of all-powerful sultans majestic and terrible in their cruelty and infinitely skilful in the arts of love. A warm ache followed the trembling into her lower stomach. She didn't like him, she didn't like him at all, and she liked still less the flickers of fear that were sending shivers all over her body. Or was it fear? That thought galvanised her feet into action as she cast a quick glance across the room.

She was just beginning to get herself together again and she couldn't risk having the peace of mind, fought for at such cost over the last few months, casually destroyed by this insufferable, dominantly male stranger with his probing questions and strange cat-like eyes. 'I won't allow it,' she muttered desperately to herself as her eyes fastened on his hard profile across the room. He was talking with intense concentration into the receiver and she seized the opportunity like a tiny caged bird who saw the door swinging open. She was out in the street almost without being aware of it and then she was running, blindly and with the breath rasping in her throat, until the mad headlong flight was stopped when she crashed into a huge pile of intricately weaved baskets outside one of the shops several streets away.

The shopkeeper was immediately to hand, waving aside her apologies with smiles and bows and offering her the inevitable cup of tea with which the traders tempted all prospective buyers into their shops.

'Please.' She almost clutched hold of the small man's tunic as she spoke. 'I need to get out of here quickly; which way do I go?' If she saw him again now she would die of embarrassment; whatever had possessed her to leave like that?

'*Efendim.*' The little man bowed as he spoke, his eyes concerned as they took in her white face. 'You are in trouble, you need help?'

'I just need to get out of here.' She gestured wildly. 'Which way is quickest?'

It seemed hours before she stepped out of the bazaar

into the hot September air but in reality was only several minutes, but it wasn't until she was safe in a taxi speeding crazily along the busy streets of the huge city that she dared to relax, the breath leaving her body in a long deep sigh as she leant back against the plastic-covered seat.

She was mad! She should have stayed! What if she ran into him again? What would she say? Her thoughts continued to tumble crazily over one another until at last, as always, the magic of Istanbul, that most romantic of cities, soothed her. Three thousand years ago a small fishing village on the headland between the mouth of the Golden Horn and the Sea of Marmara, kept cool in the blinding heat of summer by welcome sea breezes, and now a beautiful city bursting at the seams with exotic domed mosques, sultans' palaces and Eastern bazaars, its appeal was timeless. The whole bustling labyrinth was a fascinating mixture of East and West, old and new, a rich and colourful legacy from its past position as the capital of three world empires.

'You like Istanbul, eh? Is good, maybe?' The taxi driver turned round with a toothless beam, having noticed her rapt contemplation of the whirling scene outside his window, and like all the taxi drivers she had met so far seemed quite oblivious to the fast and furious traffic surging along all around them.

'Very good,' she agreed quickly, sagging with relief as he turned back to the wheel.

When she had first arrived two weeks ago, heartsore and more than a little apprehensive, the busy port city had overwelmed her with its contrasts, Byzantine brilliance and Ottoman opulence blending with poor shabby houses and back-street alleys, the sirens of ships often competing with the ancient timeless sound of muezzins calling the faithful to prayer. But she loved it now. She hugged her knees as she gazed out of the gleaming window. It had reached something deep inside her, touching a passion for the past that she had never known existed. And the Turkish people must be the most friendly and genuine race on the planet, she reflected soberly; it was true what Melik had said. . . The thought of him brought her bolt upright again. Well, that little interlude was over now and best forgotten! She hadn't handled it very well, on reflection, but it had been his fault! She hadn't wanted a tête-à-tête with anyone, least of all a dashing golden-eyed Turk who had had more than his fair share of cheek!

She relaxed again slowly as the taxi neared the end of its race to her apartment block. That was it; it had been nothing more than a brief amusing interval in her undeniably busy life. Amusing? Somehow the word didn't quite fit the emotions that were still keeping the blood hot in her cheeks and the butterflies dancing crazily everywhere else. And she'd keep it to herself! She nodded slowly, unaware of the taxi driver's appreciative glance on her soft, creamy skin, flushed cheeks and bright eyes. She somehow couldn't share this episode with anyone and she would never see him again anyway. It was best forgotten and locked away and she wouldn't, she *wouldn't* think about him any more.

CHAPTER TWO

'Oh, wow! *Who* is that? He's absolutely gorgeous!' As Louisa followed Sandra's eyes across the crowded office her own widened with horror. It couldn't be! She must be mistaken. She shut her eyes tightly for a moment as she took a long deep breath to calm her racing heart. It wasn't Melik, just someone who looked like him, and she had interposed the devastating features she had dreamt about every night for a week on this other man's face.

She opened her eyes again cautiously but the man standing in the doorway talking to her boss had moved slightly and his face was turned from her. All that was visible was a slight glimpse of one tanned cheek, jet-black straight hair gleaming with health in the harsh artificial light overhead, and the tall, broad-shouldered body that dwarfed little Mr Ashton into a tiny gnome.

'Dephni?' Sandra leant over backwards from the large desk she shared with Louisa and whispered an aside to the little Turkish girl next to her without taking her eyes off the remote figure in the doorway. 'That man, the one with Mr Ashton, who is he?'

As Dephni's large liquid eyes glanced across the room they dropped immediately back to the work at her fingertips as she shook her head slightly. 'I speak with you later, Sandra.'

Sandra made a face at Louisa as she turned back into her seat, adequately expressing her opinion of the other girl's reticence. 'Well, he's a dreamboat anyway,'

21

she muttered longingly as, leaning on her elbows, she let her eyes take their fill. 'A real-life, Technicolor dreamboat. . .'

'Sandra, you'll be in hot water again.' Louisa's voice was low and full of meaning as she caught her friend's eye and indicated Mrs Jones, Mr Ashton's dragon of a secretary, who was following the two men into Mr Ashton's private office after a cursory glance at the rest of the office. Damn! She'd missed the opportunity to have a good look at his face, listening to Sandra's ramblings, but it couldn't be him, not here, not in the office.

'How can you think of work with such a vision only yards away?' Sandra whispered dramatically, rolling her big blue eyes heavenwards. 'I mean he's gorgeous, *really* gorgeous!'

'Because that's what we were brought over from England to do,' Louisa returned drily, blessing the fact that her inner agitation wasn't showing on her face. She looked down at her hands resting on the desk and was annoyed to see that they were trembling slightly. This was ridiculous! It wasn't even him and she didn't *want* it to be either, did she? No, she didn't! Of course she didn't.

'Twelve months in Turkey and getting paid for it.' Sandra was still muttering away at her elbow. 'There's always a catch, though, even in paradise, and Mrs Jones is certainly it in this case. She's determined herself as a cross between a guardian angel and a chaperon and she's spoiling all our fun. I haven't even had a goodnight kiss in the three weeks we've been here; she's driving me mad. It's all work, work, work. The woman's obsessed with it.'

'Sandra. . .' Louisa's voice was flat. Her thoughts

were racing and she really couldn't take Sandra grumbling in her ear at this precise moment in time.

'Oh, it's all right for you!' Sandra flicked her head sulkily. 'Mrs Jones knows you don't want to meet anyone, so she doesn't bother with you. She knows you'll be content to die an old maid——' She stopped abruptly, her eyes stricken. 'Oh, I'm sorry, Lou, I didn't mean that really. I'm such a pig.'

'Yes, you are.' Louisa smiled brightly to hide the hurt the other girl's words had caused. 'But I'll put it down to frustration this time.' As Sandra smiled gratefully and lowered her head to her work, Louisa tried to concentrate on her bulging file of data, but it was impossible—her mind was flitting all over the place.

Thursday, September the tenth. The tiny date window on Oliver's gold watch, slightly incongruous on her small, delicate wrist but which she wore with fierce pride, reminded her yet again of the fact she had been struggling with all week along with the acutely disturbing dreams that seemed to mock her daytime reflections. This would have been her honeymoon. . . As hot tears pricked the back of her eyes she cautioned herself sternly. Don't think of it, not now, not here. Later.

'Miss Collins?' She hadn't been aware of Mrs Jones crossing the office but now the other woman's voice brought her head snapping upwards. It was the general opinion among the staff of Lectron Technics that the managing director's secretary was the real power behind the throne and it was well known that she had personally hand-picked the chosen few for the Turkish project. Although formidable, the middle-aged lady was both perceptive and extremely intelligent, and now, as the iron-grey eyes met Louisa's nervous gaze, they were not unfriendly. 'Could you spare a moment, please? In Mr Ashton's office?'

For a crazy moment Louisa thought about refusing but then common sense prevailed over blind panic. It wasn't him! Of course it wasn't him and she couldn't decline the order disguised as a request anyway.

The slashed rays of sunlight filtering through the blinds at the windows turned Louisa's head into blazing gold as she followed Mrs Jones across the room, her pencil-slim skirt and neat white blouse unable to hide the tiny waist, full breasts and long legs that had more than one pair of male eyes following their progress in predatory interest.

'If I could just explain, my dear?' Once inside the small ante-room where Mrs Jones had her desk the older woman put a restraining hand on Louisa's arm, turning her round to face the wall so that they both had their backs to the general workforce. 'The gentleman with Mr Ashton that Sandra noticed?' Louisa grimaced inwardly; those sharp grey eyes didn't miss a thing! 'It's Mr Haman—*the* Mr Haman,' she added with slight emphasis.

Louisa tried to look suitably impressed, which wasn't difficult as her stomach churned at the mention of the great man's name. This, then, was the Turkish-French millionaire that Lectron were entering into partnership with? The demanding, obstreperous individual who had the future of countless jobs hanging on his precarious whims and fancies? This was one man she would prefer not to meet. She had heard——

'Now I don't know what you've heard, Miss Collins,' Mrs Jones continued quietly, 'but no doubt it's all been grossly exaggerated—you know what the office grapevine is like at the best of times. Our agent, Mr Pasha, speaks very highly of him.'

Louisa nodded politely without replying. Mrs Jones knew as well as she did from the correspondence she had dealt with since the project was first envisaged that Mr Haman had been the very devil of a man to deal with. After the prices had been negotiated by careful tender over long, tedious months and finally agreed, he had been adamant that he have the final say in sources and funding despite the English reservations that if the Turkish source should run into difficulties they would be left high and dry. Once committed the English funding was irrevocable and delays of a few days could cost the firm dearly.

Mr Haman had swept all objections aside, insisting that he had access to credit and grants that would suffice in all emergencies despite the red-tape bureaucracy that was forever rearing its head. Most of the items that Lectron would be dealing with were on the Turkish restricted list for which permission must be sought, and although the specialist agent, Zengi Pasha, had been invaluable, Lectron were still seeing bogeymen behind every door. It had all made for tense relations and to date Mr Haman had not proved a patient or sympathetic observer of any hesitation or nervousness on Lectron's part.

'When we enter I will introduce you and then you will sit quietly in the seat indicated while Mr Ashton explains what is required of you. There will be no need for you to make any comment or venture an opinion. Is that understood?'

Louisa stared in astonishment at the other woman's face, noticing for the first time the tell-tale stain of pink colouring the strong cheekbones and the faint tic

beating under one eye. She was nervous! The thought
was so mind-boggling that Louisa's mouth opened
slightly in wonder. In the six years she had worked for
Lectron since leaving college with a fairly mediocre
degree she had never, ever seen Mrs Jones other than
perfectly poised and in charge.

Had Mr Haman wrought the miracle? In that case
she was even more sure she didn't want to meet him!
If he could cause the esteemed Mrs Jones to develop
an attack of the vapours, how was he going to affect
her?

'Miss Collins? Do you understand? This is important.' There was a shrill note in the normally rather
masculine voice that emphasised over-tight nerves.

'I'm sorry, Mrs Jones,' Louisa answered automatically, still staring at the secretary's long face. 'Yes, of
course I understand. I won't say anything at all unless
directly spoken to.' And I'll curtsy first, she thought
wryly.

'Fine, fine, I knew you'd understand.' Mrs Jones
looked anxiously at the closed door. 'You're a very
reliable girl, Miss Collins, very reliable.' The severe
mouth allowed itself a faint twist that was meant to
serve as a smile. 'Come along.'

Louisa had only been admitted to the inner sanctum
that the rest of the office irreverently called the 'holy
of holies' once, and then Mrs Jones had whisked her in
and out at the speed of light although she had gained
an impression of beautifully worked Turkish carpets
covering the polished wood floor, shiny antique furniture and an overall feeling of luxury quite at odds with
the spartan comfort in the main office.

The building itself was magnificent, one of the old
palaces dotted throughout Istanbul that had been

crumbling gracefully away until restored by a hopeful entrepreneur into a somewhat regal office building of which Lectron occupied the second floor along with Mr Haman's employees.

'Ah, Mrs Jones and Miss. . .' Mr Ashton let his reedy voice fade away as Mrs Jones made the necessary introductions, but Louisa neither heard nor felt anything beyond a racing buzzing in her ears and a surge of blinding adrenalin had her heart leaping out of her chest as her gaze met the tawny-gold eyes that had haunted her for long restless nights.

Close to, Melik Haman seemed even larger than she remembered, the tanned, hard-planed face cruel and sardonic as he savoured her horror and confusion, his eyes narrowed slits of light that gleamed with deadly brightness.

This was it, then! It was the first coherent thought to surface out of the panic. She'd be straight back to England post-haste and very possibly straight out of a job there too! Strangely the realisation brought her head up and her shoulders back and as she stared back at him, her eyes turned into dark ebony full of defiance. Go on, then, they spoke into the cat-like gaze fixing her to the spot, have your revenge, get the fun over with. Her chin rose a fraction higher.

'Miss. . .Collins, I think the name was?' It was the same deep, rich, cool voice as before but with a hard edge to it that hadn't been there previously.

She nodded slowly, her eyes fixed on his like a rabbit before a snake.

'Yes. . .I like that name.' He turned to Mr Ashton with a cold smile. 'For some reason it appealed to me when you read me the list of possible assistants.'

'Good, good.' Mr Ashton was almost rubbing his

hands in gratification. 'Anything we can do, Melik, anything at all. You only have to ask. I can't apologise enough but you understand the circumstances?'

'Calm yourself, John.' The ruthless gaze switched back to Louisa and she just stopped herself flinching in time. 'Are you acquainted with the circumstances?'

'What?' She stared at him blankly as her mind went into hyper-drive. He wasn't going to denounce her, then? Insist on her immediate dismissal? For a moment heady relief swamped all other sensation and then an icy trickle shivered down her spine. Why not? He would be furious at the trick she had, almost unwittingly, played on him, and it wasn't in this man's nature to be forgiving. She knew that as surely as she drew breath.

'I thought it would be better for you to explain,' Mrs Jones interposed hastily with a swift glance at Mr Ashton. 'But I can —'

'Would you like me to explain the position we find ourselves in, Miss Collins?' He cut across Mrs Jones's voice as though she hadn't spoken and the older woman immediately fell silent. In other circumstances Louisa would have felt like giving such courage recognition but just at this moment in time she was struggling to remain upright.

'Take a seat, Miss Collins.' He had seen the trembling in her legs, she just knew it, and although she would have given the world to refuse his magnanimous gesture she knew if she didn't sit down soon she would collapse in an undignified heap on the expensive carpets. 'It would appear Lectron have a little problem.' The phrasing was pointed and she could almost see Mr Ashton subside a little further into his enormous chair. 'I was promised an English assistant at this point in the proceedings,' Melik continued smoothly, his dark face expressionless. 'A Beryl Swinton, Mrs Jones's deputy?'

Louisa opened her mouth to speak and then closed it again. She knew her voice would come out as a breathless squeak and she just wouldn't give him the satisfaction. She nodded instead as though it were all known to her.

'Unfortunately Mr Ashton informs me that the lady has been rushed into hospital in England, appendix. . .' He let his voice fade away to savour the growing alarm in Louisa's huge brown eyes and, after a long moment when no one spoke, rose in one fluid animal-like movement to stand in front of the deep arched window, the late afternoon sunlight picking up a dark sheen of blue on the strong, virile black hair.

When the gold gaze turned back to her the beautiful eyes were remote and very cold. 'How can we surmount this problem, Miss Collins?' He smiled humourlessly. 'This lady was designated to work closely with me, you understand, and I do not like delays; indeed, there have even been those who have called me an impatient man.' The sardonic face was a closed mask and she had no idea of what he was thinking. 'I need a member of the English team who knows all the part numbers, the numbering systems, the method of working, who understands that there are high quality standards that *must* be maintained, and who will interface with me and transpose my requirements into the English style of working with no hesitation and implicit obedience. Mrs Jones assures me that you are such an individual. Is she right?'

For the last few minutes she had been mentally preparing herself for the death-blow when it came but, even so, hearing it put into words was beyond her wildest fears. Even in normal circumstances to work closely with this man would be like riding a giant roller-coaster that was out of control, breathtakingly terrifying and utterly exhausting. But in view of what had gone before. . . She turned to Mrs Jones quickly.

'But Sandra?' She was gabbling but she couldn't help it. 'Or Peter or Michael? Any of those could do it, I'm sure. I don't see —— '

'Miss Collins!' Mrs Jones's scandalised expression confirmed she had overstepped the mark by several hundred yards.

'You do not want the post, Miss Collins?' Melik's voice was smoothly reasonable. 'Too much responsibility perhaps?' He'd trapped her! As she turned from Mr Ashton's and Mrs Jones's barely concealed annoyance to face the heavy-lidded gaze a full realisation of the impossible position he'd put her in washed over Louisa in a hot wave. If she refused the opportunity after it had been offered to her she could forget promotion where Lectron was concerned, besides which the firm had been good to her, she had to admit it. Apart from the excellent monthly salary and steady promotions over the last six years the powers-that-be had given her two months' leave without question when Oliver —— She caught her breath painfully. And then this Turkish trip. The rest of the firm had been green with envy at the favoured few. Yes, she owed them, and what was Melik Haman after all? Just a man like any other. She wouldn't let him intimidate her; Oliver would have expected her to stand her ground.

'Sandra is excellent at her work but there are other requirements to this assignment, Miss Collins,' Mrs Jones said crisply into the silence. Louisa knew immediately what she meant. Sandra would be all out for a romantic interlude, which could prove embarrassing, whereas she. . . She could be relied upon to give no thought to a dalliance in that area and all her loyalties would be exclusively Lectron's. But the overwhelming factor in Mr Ashton's and Mrs Jones's eyes was that Melik Haman had decided on her. Nothing else mattered. It was as simple as that.

'Well, Miss Collins?' Melik's voice was silky smooth and perfectly pitched but she knew from the narrowing of the hooded eyes that he had sensed her capitulation. He could smell it, she was sure of it, like a big black panther that had settled on its prey and was sizing up its advantage. 'You feel it would be too much for you?'

'On the contrary, Mr Haman.' She smiled carefully as she answered, pleased her voice was steady and cool when her heart was pounding so violently that she was sure it must be visible. 'I would be pleased to accept such an interesting post and I'll do my best not to let you down in any way.'

'Oh, you will not let me down, Miss Collins.' As the hard, glittering eyes swept over her upturned face again they lingered on the wide, soft mouth for a moment before meeting her gaze. 'I do not allow such things to happen.' It was said with such arrogance and regal disregard for her own feelings of human frailty that for a moment she was speechless, and then she responded as she had responded to all the challenges, good and bad, in her twenty-eight years of life — head-on, with chin held high and spirit fighting.

Why, you're just a bully, Melik Haman, she thought furiously as sheer anger replaced all other emotion and turned her eyes into black chips. A nasty, arrogant, spoilt bully who thinks he's holding all the aces and hasn't hesitated to use them.

Something of what she was feeling must have been clear to the others because she found herself ushered into the main office by a determined and red-faced Mrs Jones before she could say another word and with her feet hardly touching the ground.

'I'll explain everything later, Miss Collins.' Mrs Jones patted her arm in what could almost have been termed a maternal gesture. 'You'll get on with him all right after a time, you're a good girl.' She had disappeared back into the inner sanctum before Louisa could reply, and as she stood, somewhat dazed by the force of her emotions and the suddenness of it all, Sandra noticed her arrival and called urgently from her place at her desk.

As she reached her friend's side she was aware that even little Dephni, normally the most studious of the Lectron employees, had raised interested eyes to her face and Sandra was positively exploding with curiosity. 'Dephni says that's Melik Haman, the all-wise and powerful one,' Sandra said with a lack of respect that caused the little Turkish girl to look at her with horror. 'What did he want? He can have anything, anything at all from me. . .' She rolled her eyes at Dephni with such lewdness that Louisa could have smiled if the circumstances had been different. The small Turkish girl had been brought up strictly by fervent Muslim parents and was in turns fascinated and appalled by Sandra's mischief-making.

'I'm to work with him for a time, that's all,' Louisa said quietly. 'Apparently Beryl was going to come out but she's in hospital with appendix trouble.'

'That's all!' Sandra's shriek caused more than a few heads to turn in their direction and as she lowered her voice a few octaves her eyes were frankly envious.

'You lucky dog! You lucky, *lucky* dog. So many goodies wrapped up in one neat parcel!'

'It's just a job, Sandra.' Louisa sat down at her desk. 'It might not even work out,' she finished flatly.

'Just a job? How can you say that?' Sandra leant forward conspiratorially. 'Come on, Lou, you've got to admit he's something else. You can't tell me he doesn't make the old heart beat just a bit faster!'

Louisa thought again of the cold, hard arrogance, the strong, overpoweringly male body and cruel, handsome face, and unbeknown to her an expression of distaste curled her lip. Oliver had been slim, fair and with a boyish charm that had made him almost pretty, his warm, caring personality shining out of mild blue eyes that had rarely darkened in anger. He had been good to her, so good. . .

'I can see that you find him attractive, Sandra,' Louisa said slowly, her eyes looking inward and missing the dawning horror colouring her friend's face, 'but I can honestly say that if Melik Haman were the last man on earth I wouldn't want him. He does nothing for me, absolutely nothing.'

'Well, now that we have established that, Miss Collins, perhaps you would join me for a meal to formalise arrangements?' The deep, silky voice behind her froze her mind and body and for a moment she knew what it was to be totally paralysed with shock. As she slowly turned and raised her eyes upwards she saw his face was quite expressionless, his eyes frosted gold and his mouth unsmiling.

She thought about bluffing things out for a split second and then realised the futility of such action. She had been terribly rude and in front of two of his employees to boot; Sandra and Dephni were sitting in a frozen tableau as though someone had waved a wand and stopped the passage of time, and from the look on Dephni's face when the ice melted she would burst into tears.

'I'm sorry, Mr Haman,' she said quietly as the colour staining her cheeks rose up into the dark gold of her hair, 'you weren't meant to hear that. It was in reply to something that had been said—something complimentary,' she added hastily.

'Quite so.' The tawny gaze flicked over Sandra's and Dephni's stunned faces and for a moment she thought she saw a faint smile touch the cold mouth. 'Shall we go?'

'Go?' Louisa stared at him stupidly. What was he going to do? Incarcerate her in a dungeon somewhere?

'For lunch.' The dark voice was smoothly patient. 'I suggested to Mr Ashton that the final arrangements would be best concluded in an informal atmosphere to put you at your ease.'

'You did?' She glanced behind him at the firmly closed door of Mr Ashton's office. 'Where is he?'

'Otherwise engaged.' The narrowed eyes dared her to complain. 'And now if you're ready? We do have quite a lot to discuss. . .don't we, Miss Collins?' It was really a statement, not a question, and there was a wealth of meaning in the apparently innocent words.

Sandra handed her her shoulder-bag without speaking and Louisa took it in the same way. This was awful, terrible, and she had the uncomfortable feeling she had brought it all on herself. What on earth was he going to say to her when they were alone?

As Melik took her elbow in a firm grip and raised her to her feet she was conscious of his closeness, the clean male smell that emanated from his tanned skin, a mixture of delicious aftershave and sun-warmed flesh, but most of all the heat that his fingers induced. They were making the barest contact with her skin as they walked towards the door, his touch guiding rather than possessive, yet it seemed as though the contact was burning her and she could feel the fire spreading out in ripples over her skin. She didn't dare look at him as they left the office and began to walk down the massive stone steps towards the foyer, but she had never been so aware of another human being in her life.

'Calm down, Miss Louisa Collins.' The murmur in her ear was just audible to the two of them alone, and almost in the same breath Melik smiled and nodded to two young office girls walking up the stairs which had the effect of one of them losing her grip on the big box of files she was carrying, and almost falling to her knees in an effort to retrieve them before they cascaded away. Louisa had the sudden feeling that the little incident was indicative of the effect Melik normally had on women.

'You're enjoying this, aren't you?' she hissed quietly without looking to right or left and the answering chuckle at her side made her grate her teeth in impotent anger.

'You'll never know how much, my little tigress,' the hateful voice replied. 'The moment when you walked into that office was everything I had hoped for and more.'

'You're a, a. . .' She was spluttering with rage again and as she turned to him to vent her anger she found the feline eyes were looking straight at her, a hardness in their depths that suggested he was not quite so amused with the situation as he would like her to believe.

'Don't try and label me, Louisa.' They had reached the foyer now and she was painfully conscious of the little stir Melik's arrival caused, especially among the female population, although he seemed totally unaware of the veiled and not so veiled glances in his direction.

His ego must be jumbo size, she thought balefully as she glared at one particular well endowed redhead whose bust size had suddenly grown a few inches as she moved her body into the best possible stance for attracting Melik's attention. How could these women be so obvious?

'We are going to eat lunch now, Louisa.' He came to a halt just before the revolving doors and lifted her chin to raise her face to his as he looked down at her grimly. 'You will be well behaved and submissive as befits a newly hired secretary being taken out for a meal by her boss.' She was vitally conscious of his great height as he towered over her, the light musky perfume that drifted off his skin sending her senses into hyperdrive. 'Do you understand me?'

He gave her no chance to reply, ushering her out into the hot, busy, noisy street whereupon a chauffeur-driven Mercedes appeared like magic at their side and she found herself installed in its air-conditioned depths without being aware of how she got there.

'That is better. It is more restful when you are quiet.' His voice was lazy as he stretched out his long legs at her side after issuing orders in rapid Turkish to the uniformed driver. She glared at him but didn't answer, letting her heart slow down in time with her breathing as she took a few long hidden breaths.

The car was magnificent. In spite of her misgivings Louisa found the drive through the crowded, colourful streets with the vast cupola of St Sophia dominating the skyline as it had for the last one thousand, four hundred years luxuriously comfortable. She normally travelled in dolmuşes, one of Istanbul's shared taxis, with Sandra and a few other English personnel on the daily journey to and from work, but although cheaper than conventional taxis the vast majority of dolmuşes were American 55 Chevys and the like and when crowded to capacity did not make for a restful or relaxing homecoming in the hot, fume-laden air. The sign on most of the dashboards, 'Masallah', which roughly translated meant 'May God protect you', she always found particularly apt after a journey on the crazily crowded streets, where the drivers always seemed to see someone they knew, hanging out of the window to shout greetings and waving as they careered madly past.

'I am trying to work out if you are real.' The cool, deep voice was thoughtful.

'If I'm real?' She stared at him in surprise. They had been travelling for a few minutes in an uncomfortable silence that Louisa had found herself unable to break. She had been aware of his eyes on her for the last few moments but had kept her face turned to the window, her profile calm even as her heart thudded in her chest.

'Are you as totally unaware of your beauty as you seem?' he asked slowly. 'You do not touch your hair, glance in a mirror to check your make-up. . .' He eyed her musingly. 'Have I found that rare pearl? A beautiful woman without vanity?'

'I don't have the faintest idea what you are talking about,' she said stiffly as fire flooded into her cheeks.

'And this.' He touched the hot, silky skin lightly. 'You are. . .how old?'

'Twenty-eight.' Her voice was flat.

'Twenty-eight and yet you still blush so prettily,' he drawled mockingly. 'It's most attractive, but then, maybe you know this? Maybe it is all a clever strategy to attract even as you rebuff?'

'Don't flatter yourself.' Her voice was icy and as she turned to face him her eyes were flashing sparks.

'I rarely do.' His voice was dry. 'I find there are many people who are only too ready to perform that service for me. But not you.' Now his gaze sharpened. 'I have to give you that, not you.'

'Maybe I think you are conceited enough already?' She expected him to be insulted, angry, but the gold eyes crinkled with laughter.

'The male ego is a fragile piece of equipment, my little tigress; have pity.'

'I don't think yours is at risk,' she said cynically. 'Not with your wealth and. . .passable good looks.'

He bowed his head ironically. 'Careful, Louisa, don't be too enthusiastic. And you are quite right—mine is not at risk from your opinion or anyone else's, but not on account of my physical appearance or solvency.'

'No?' She raised her eyebrows disbelievingly.

'No.' His voice was quiet now and deep, his eyes sombre. 'I am thirty-seven years of age and due to the many circumstances of my life which I will not bore you with today I have the dubious blessing of knowing myself—my weaknesses, my strengths, the good, the bad. . .' His gaze wandered up to her hair and then back to the wide brown eyes. 'I say a dubious blessing because once a man or woman has reached that stage in life, and some never do, it can be a dangerous awareness. The human spirit needs a little uncertainty, a little vulnerability to keep it soft, open, alive.'

'And yours hasn't got that?' she asked almost in a

whisper, sensing this compelling man was speaking of things he normally didn't reveal.

He gazed for a long moment into the soft velvet darkness of her eyes and then, before she had time to react, his lips were on hers, not in a fleeting sigh but in a hard, hungry kiss that sent her senses spinning into another world where touch and sensation were the only things that mattered.

She was free again even as the strange feeling of every bone melting in her body registered on her stunned mind, and as he sank back into his seat it was as though a great beautiful cat had leashed its claws for a moment's respite, each muscle tensed and hard in anticipation.

'I had thought not.' His mouth twisted as he smiled to himself. 'But maybe. . .' The flecked eyes settled on her face and became withdrawn, remote. 'Who really knows themself, after all?' he said lightly. 'Do you?'

'Me?' She stared at him in confusion. 'I think I do. . . No, I don't. . . Oh, I don't know.' Her lips were burning from the brief contact with his hard, firm mouth and she suddenly felt a stab of blazing anger that she was reduced to a quivering wreck whereas he. . . He was cool and controlled and seemed to be finding the whole situation slightly amusing. And why shouldn't he? she thought with sickening honesty. He was immensely wealthy, dangerously powerful and she doubted if the word 'failure' had ever featured in his vocabulary, be it in regard to women or the business world in which he lived. She had sparked his jaded palate by the moves she had made, in all innocence, to avoid him. And that had placed her in a dangerous and vulnerable position. She looked again at the breathtakingly attractive face and hard, lean body and drew a deep, shuddering breath. She was going to have to be on her guard every moment around this man, *every single moment*.

CHAPTER THREE

'LOUISA?' She was brought out of her frightening reverie abruptly as Melik's cool voice claimed her attention.

'Oh, I'm sorry?' She realised too late he had spoken and she hadn't heard a word.

'I don't usually have to repeat myself when I am in female company,' he said silkily, 'but I am beginning to realise that "usual" is not a word that applies to you.'

'No?' She stared him full in the face, her eyes stormy.

'No. I haven't had a woman bolt on me before either,' he drawled mockingly. His expression was unchanging but despite the cool amusement Louisa could sense something, something dark and hard under the smiling mask. 'You are somewhat refreshing.'

'I'm so glad you approve,' she said tightly, and now he laughed outright, his flecked eyes narrowing.

'I didn't say I approved,' he corrected softly. 'In fact you put me to a great deal of time and trouble trying to find you and all the time you were safely caught in my net without my even knowing. Fate was laughing at both of us, my little tigress.'

'Please stop calling me that,' she snapped ungraciously as she tried to master her body's betrayal at his closeness. 'And I am most certainly *not* yours!'

'Then whose?' The reply had been whip-sharp. 'Was there — *is* there a man foolish enough in England to let you go for twelve months?'

'That's none of your business,' she said hotly.

'Yes, it is.' The hard ruthlessness he had displayed in the office was suddenly very much in evidence. 'We are going to be working very closely together over the next few weeks and you know as well as I do that they are crucial to this project's success. I do not need someone swooning over love-letters from England or making long telephone calls of a personal nature, so again I ask. . .' He paused coldly. 'Is there anyone in England?'

She stared at him helplessly, hating his questions, hating *him*, hating the vibrant life that was evident in every line of his lean, hard, uncaring body. How do you answer something like this? she asked herself desperately as her mind raced wildly. Yes, there was someone in England. . . The memories flashed in fleetingly. Oliver, the day she had first met him when he had capsized the small boat he was punting down the river by standing up to wave to her, a cheeky grin on his young face. When he had emerged from the brown water, dripping wet and disgustingly muddy, to collapse in a laughing heap on the bank, she had offered to run him back to his flat in her car for some dry clothes, and that had been the beginning. . .

He had been gentle and kind and protective, all the qualities she had looked for in her father and never found. Not that her father had been physically unkind, it was just that he had been so wrapped up in her mother, and she in him, that anyone else had merely stayed on the perimeter of their lives, even their own daughter. And she had grown to accept that she was unlovable, unwanted, her physical appearance counting for nothing to her in the face of their unintentional cruelty.

But Oliver had loved her. If that love had sometimes been a little dogmatic, a little dull, it hadn't mattered. He had been completely, wholly hers, she had known that from the first meeting, and the settling down of their relationship, the routine, the comfortableness. . . well, that happened to everyone, didn't it? That was life, the real world.

After twelve months they had set their engagement for the New Year, their wedding for the end of August, and a long September honeymoon somewhere hot. And then, three weeks before Christmas, Oliver had begun to feel tired, deathly tired, and a rare and virulent blood disorder was diagnosed. And within two months she had been left all alone again, unable really to take in that she would never see him again.

The last few weeks of his life she had been with him almost every minute; Lectron had given her the leave without quibbling and she would be eternally grateful for that precious time when she had been able to comfort, to reassure, to lie. . .

He had died believing he was going to get well and she felt no guilt about that. He wouldn't have been able to cope with the truth. But it had made it doubly hard for her.

And when he had left her a little bit of her soul had gone with him. She had weathered the feeling of loneliness since she was a little girl, her insecurity and lack of confidence making her outwardly self-sufficient and inwardly wary of any show of affection, but through Oliver new doors had beckoned, the promise of a life where there would be children, her own home, and most importantly of all where *she* would be the pivot of someone's life, loved and being able to give love. And when that had been so cruelly snatched away

she had made the decision that never again would she
open herself up to such devastating pain. And she
wouldn't, ever. . .

She raised her head and looked straight into the
tawny green-flecked eyes, unaware that the play of
emotions across her face had caused the man watching
her so intently to catch his breath and wonder. . . 'No,'
she said dully, her face wooden now, 'there is no one
in England.'

The restaurant was close to the Topkapi Palace, the
seat of the Ottoman sultans for three hundred years
where power politics had mingled with the intrigues of
the harem, and it was to this tiny walled city in
miniature that Melik referred as they sat down at their
table, his expression as bland and carefully friendly as
it had been since their conversation in the car.

'You haven't been there yet?' he asked incredulously
as she shook her head to his question. 'And you have
been three weeks in Istanbul?' He shook his head
slowly. 'I do not believe it.'

'There's hardly been any free time at all,' she said
defensively, 'and Mrs Jones keeps everyone's nose to
the grindstone.'

'Nose to the grindstone?' His smile, the first she had
seen of genuine, unaffected amusement uncoloured by
cynicism or sensual overtones, brought her heart
thumping into her throat. It transformed the handsome, intimidating face so completely that it made her
bruised heart ache. 'This grindstone must be most
uncomfortable,' he said seriously, his eyes laughing at
her. 'In that case I feel you deserve an afternoon
sightseeing, and where better to start than with the

most fascinating palace of them all? We will eat and then stroll.'

'I can't do that!' She looked at him aghast. 'The office——'

'I own the office,' he reminded her coolly, 'and believe me, Louisa, when we start work tomorrow you will feel you have earnt every minute of this respite. You are going to put in more hours, and more blood, sweat and tears over the next few weeks than even the formidable Mrs Jones could ask.'

'But——'

'For goodness' sake, woman, you do not want to see the palace?' His voice was tight with irritation at her discomfiture, his accent suddenly very marked.

'Of course I do,' she answered back in the same tone, 'but not with——' She stopped abruptly as the glittering gold gaze dared her to continue.

'Not with me?' he finished icily. 'Well, that is a cross you will have to bear.' He settled back in his seat as he spoke, the immaculate suit and beautiful silk shirt and tie he wore so casually bringing the waiters hovering around like bees sensing a honey-pot.

The restaurant had a first-class, international flavour and was situated just outside the Topkapi Palace walls on Sogukcesme Sok. Melik had commented that the whole street was reminiscent of New Orleans but not having been there she merely nodded quietly, her eyes widening at the prices on the menu.

It was as they finished the first course of *cacik*, a delicious mixture of yoghurt and chopped cucumbers, and the waiter had begun to fill a small side-table with an array of temptingly aromatic dishes for the main course, that Melik dropped his minor bombshell—a punishment, she felt immediately, for her earlier rejection of his company.

'You will not mind the travelling, I hope?' He smiled slowly as he gave her a long, calculating look that made her instantly alert.

'Travelling?' With a tremendous effort she kept her voice steady. 'Exactly what do you mean?'

'It's obvious, surely?' Melik's voice and face had assumed an innocent, open quality that caused Louisa's toes to curl in her high, open-toed sandals.

'I'm sorry.' She smiled as coolly as she could. 'You'll have to be more explicit.'

'I travel all over the country, Louisa; I actually have homes in the Black Sea region and the south-west, and then of course there are my frequent trips abroad, although I would not expect you to accompany me on those.' He smiled with gentle reasonableness. 'But you would find my château in France a particular delight.'

'Doubtless.' She eyed him coldly.

'I would, of course, need my English assistant with me at all times. I am not prepared to lose valuable time making unnecessary telephone calls and dictating letters into one of those infernal machines without seeing instant results. You understand?'

'Perfectly.' She glared at him angrily as the silent waiter replenished their half-full glasses of *misbag*, a white wine that tasted fruitily of the raisin grapes it was made from.

'Good.' He smiled smoothly. 'And now please enjoy your food. Have you tried the *cerkez tavugu* before?'

'Probably.' Her eyes were icy. 'I could answer that question in more detail if I knew what it was.'

'Chicken served in a thick sauce made from walnuts,' he said cheerily, quite unperturbed by her rage. 'It's delicious, trust me.' Her face answered him with such frankness that he was shaking with silent laughter as he served her a small portion from each of the side-dishes, explaining each mouthwatering spoonful as he did so. 'Puréed spinach, broad beans marinated in olive oil, fried aubergine slices with yoghurt, mussels stuffed with rice, pine nuts and currants, and, of course, pilaf rice. OK?'

She nodded slowly, aware that he had been careful to choose dishes that were not highly spiced and secretly grateful for his consideration. 'Thank you, it looks lovely,' she said quietly.

'Thank you, it looks lovely, *Melik*.' The gold eyes were broodingly intent. 'You have been very correct so far but I am sure you can relax just a little?'

'You are my boss,' she said quickly. 'It wouldn't be right to —'

'Melik,' he said with a silky thread of steel running through his rich voice. 'In the office, out of it, wherever. . . Understand?'

'If you say so.' The blood was so hot in her cheeks that they actually hurt.

'Oh, I do.' In contrast he was relaxed, cool, and seemed to be thoroughly enjoying the meal. 'Now eat up and don't sulk; I find that the least attractive failing in the female sex.'

'I never sulk,' she said hotly, 'never.'

'Is that so?' He leant forward suddenly, his face a breath away as his eyes travelled slumberously over her flashing eyes and angry mouth. 'And the other little tricks and fancies that a woman uses to get her own way? They are learnt from babyhood, especially when the female in question has more than her fair share of beauty like you. I would imagine that you had the men in your household twisted round your delightful little finger.'

'There was only my father,' she said tightly as the pain bit deep, 'and you are quite wrong.' She tried with all her might to stop even a shred of anguish filtering through in her voice but the hard face sharpened suddenly, his eyes narrowing and then widening as he shook his head.

'I seem to have hit a nerve; I apologise, I have no wish to hurt you.'

'You couldn't.' Her smile was brittle and she finished the glass of wine in one gulp without being aware of it, spearing a piece of chicken on her fork and tasting it quickly. 'Delicious; do you know how it's cooked?' The diversion was obvious but he was too much of a gentleman to ignore it, and the rest of the meal was conducted with banal conversation, the pace slow and unhurried as in most Turkish eating places.

She hated this man! Louisa's thoughts were quite at odds with her outward appearance. Hated, loathed, detested. . .there weren't enough adjectives in any language to describe how she felt about him. How dared he make his sweeping statements that were so cruel, so ——? She forced her mind to stop its destructive cycle. He had asked for her to work with him, as a penance, a punishment, and so be it. Her eyes were cloudy and dark. But if he expected anything else he was in for a shock! And she was going to make that clear, crystal-clear, at the first opportunity!

As they finished the desert of *baklava*, a deliciously flaky pastry bulging with nuts in syrup, Louisa felt her stomach muscles begin to tense. She hadn't really tasted any of the meal—the weight of her thoughts had turned it to sawdust in her mouth—and now she had to spend the afternoon with him? It was monstrous. . .

'I have distressed you with my clumsy talk.' As her hand was taken in his she flinched back automatically, her eyes shooting up to his face.

'I'm perfectly all right,' she said stiffly.

His eyes had hardened at her withdrawal and now she saw he made a visible effort before speaking again. 'Louisa, you are very beautiful and I am appreciative of such loveliness,' he said slowly. 'Can we not try to establish a relationship of harmony——?'

She interrupted him before he had time to finish, her eyes blazing with outrage. He thought a few soft words, a convenient carefully worded apology and she would fall into his arms in happy surrender? He was appreciative of loveliness? Well, bully for him! He had said himself the days of the harem were over and there was no way, even for a minute, she was going to let him think she would be content to be one of the many who no doubt frequented his bed!

'I never mix business with pleasure, Mr Haman,' she said tightly, 'and I'm sure you would be the first to applaud such sentiments. I am good at my job and I will do my best to fulfil the duties I have been given, and of course I'm sure we'll work well together. That is all that's necessary, isn't it?'

He held her glance for a long, still moment and then nodded curtly. 'Quite.'

She felt an overwhelming misery swamp her for a few seconds at his hard voice and cold eyes, but pushed the weakness aside determinedly. It would be suicide to let him get under her skin.

As they emerged from the pleasant, air-conditioned restaurant into the busy street he took her arm in that proprietorial gesture she was beginning to know. In spite of her churning feelings she felt a moment of guilty pleasure at being held close to his side as several female heads swivelled round for a second and third look, but then the feel of his hard-muscled body next to hers caused the blood to sing through her veins and she took a deep, calming breath as they began to walk towards the Topkapi Palace. The response of her body to his shocked her; she had never imagined such strong physical attraction was possible. Oliver had never seemed particularly interested in that side of their relationship, content to wait until they got married to consummate their love, and before him she had never really had a serious boyfriend, just a few brief encounters where no more than a few hugs and kisses were involved. Oliver had surprised her with his easy contentment and lack of ardour, but it was only now that she realised, as the big, lean body at her side sent the strangest sensations flowing down into her limbs, that she had felt all along there was something wrong, that there ought to be more. The thought was a painful betrayal.

She wondered what this strange, passionate man at her side would say if she told him she had never had a lover. Laugh his head off, no doubt, her mind told her tersely. Twenty-eight years old and still a virgin? He wouldn't believe it.

'Do you have a flat in England, Louisa?' The tone was pleasantly conversational but she stiffened instinctively before forcing herself to relax. He was right; they were going to spend a great deal of time together over the next weeks and months, so it was ridiculous not to communicate naturally.

'I did have.' She smiled brightly. 'But it was rented

and the other three girls couldn't carry my share for a year and I couldn't afford to subsidise from here so they got someone else when I left.' He nodded. The answer seemed to please him although she couldn't imagine why.

'And your family?'

This time she was prepared. 'My parents live in Sussex and I am an only child,' she said quietly. 'I left home for college at eighteen and haven't lived with them since.' She continued quickly before he could speak. 'And you? Do your parents live close by?'

'My father died several years ago, a heart attack.' He looked down at her slowly. 'He was Turkish and my mother is French so she decided to go back to France to live with her sister who was also widowed at about the same time. They are happily established in a château a few miles from mine where they argue all day long about anything and everything.' There was a look on his face that touched a chord deep inside her; in spite of his words it was clear that he loved his mother very much. 'They are a pair of quite dreadfully irascible old ladies but they keep each other young.'

'Have you any brothers or sisters?' she asked with a curiosity that surprised her.

'No.' He smiled softly. 'I was what you may call a late arrival. I understand my parents had given up hope of ever having a child and then I arrived.'

'You must have been spoilt.' She was quite unaware of the note of raw envy in her voice and unconscious of the perceptive glance he shot at her from under heavy brows.

'Undoubtedly, but then Turkish children often are, although only, in my opinion, in the very best way.

Children are precious here; I wish it were so in more countries.'

'Yes.' She bit her lip till it hurt. Why was any conversation with this man guaranteed to hurt?

The Topkapi Palace was everything she had imagined and much, much more. Behind the Imperial Gate the four courts stretched majestically rich with the treasures of a bright lost age when money had been no object to the favoured few, and the sultans had had absolute and unquestioning power.

Although the First Court with its beautiful concert hall, the Second with a museum holding exquisitely delicate Chinese and Japanese porcelain and the others with the four-roomed Treasury holding regal pre-eminence were breathtakingly lovely, it was the Harem that drew Louisa's complete fascination.

The secluded quarters of the wives and concubines of the Sultan, shaded by cypresses and plane trees, fired her imagination vividly, and as they walked through the gates where only the Sultan himself had been allowed to ride on horseback, even his viziers being forced to walk, she felt a strange feeling trickle down her spine that was magnified as she glanced up to find Melik's brilliant gold gaze tight on her face. 'Just less than a hundred years ago a beautiful English girl with pale, honey-coloured skin and hair the colour of corn would not have been free to walk through these gates of her own free will.' His eyes lingered for a moment on the tiny curling whisps that had escaped the severe knot and wandered closer to her face, and then he moved almost sharply, pulling her tighter into his side and looking straight ahead. 'You would have been brought here by the chief eunuchs, probably in chains and with your hair falling in glorious abandonment about your bare shoulders, terrified, frightened and all alone. They would have dragged you to the quarters of the Black Eunuch, who held the highest office of all, being the adviser and confidant of the Sultan, and his black eyes would have lit up at the sight of such a prize for his master.'

She wanted to stop the sensual pictures he was painting in her mind but her power of speech, indeed her very thoughts, were subjugated in fascinated compliance.

'He would have ordered that you be treated as a queen, the very best of perfumes, lotions being used to anoint your body for painstakingly long weeks until your hair and skin were the texture of pure silk and your body was ripe for surrender. Then you would be clothed in veils, each one transparent and soft, allowing a brief glimpse of the beauty beneath, and he would take you to his master, throwing you at the Sultan's feet before kneeling with his head touching the floor as he paid homage to the all-powerful and mighty one. And then. . .'

His voice died away and Louisa felt her eyes being raised to his as though she were drugged. 'And then?'

'The Sultan would smile at such a treasure, such a priceless treasure, and the Black Eunuch would know that he had succeeded, that his position was more secure than it had ever been because he would have been the one to give his master the ultimate prize, the favourite.'

The slow warm ache that had taken hold of her limbs, turning them to water, made Louisa glad of Melik's arm holding her so tightly, even as the burning tawny gaze seemed to sear into her brain.

'The Eunuch would leave and at a glance from their

master's commanding face the other slaves would melt away until at last it was just you and him. He would ask to see the beauty that he could only glimpse at and you would refuse, shrinking back against the floor as he left his jewel-studded throne to stand over you, magnificent and dark in his flowing robes of purple and black, the jewels flashing on his brown hands. He would be gentle where you expected force, considerate where you feared violence and ravishment, lifting you to your feet as he slowly unwound the floating veils from your trembling body until at last you would stand naked and shaking before him. He would coax you, use all the skills and vast sensual knowledge he possessed until you were compliant and submissive, trembling now not with fear but with a strange excitement that — '

'Stop it!' She swung away from him so violently that she nearly knocked a tiny Japanese man who was unfortunate enough to be passing at the time clear off his feet. 'That's enough; I don't want to hear any more.' She couldn't believe she was letting a man, a virtual stranger, affect her like this. What on earth was the matter with her? It must be the heat and this whole sensual experience of a place. The very air seemed to breathe a fleshly, voluptuous intimacy that made her flesh tingle.

Oliver. She summoned up the name as an unconscious talisman for protection. She must think of Oliver. It didn't occur to her until many weeks later that that instant was the first time she had ever forced herself to think of him.

She didn't fully appreciate the beauty of the Harem, recently lovingly restored, as she tried desperately to bring her wandering senses and aroused feelings under control. The vivid picture that Melik had so skilfully painted was there in the forefront of her mind and every tile, every room, was a vivid reminder. It horrified her, thrilled her, to her shame, and made her aware of dark emotions buried deep within her that she had never known existed and dared not acknowledge.

The principal royal apartments were quite magnificent and as they wandered through the audience chamber, bedroom, prince's quarters and the Pasha's mother's bedroom, where a personal slave girl had slept over the canopy of her four-poster bed, the full enormity of the Sultan's absolute power and authority washed over her again.

'The Sultan had up to two hundred concubines to attend to his needs,' Melik whispered softly in her ear as she paused in the exotic atmosphere to take in a particularly beautiful silk curtain hiding yet another quiet, slumberous room. 'A most fortunate man, wouldn't you say?'

She turned round quickly, her eyes sparking as they took in the lazy, confident smile and arrogantly male body. 'You agree with such a chauvinistic concept, then?' she asked tightly. 'I might have known.'

'You seem to have answered the question you asked me yourself,' he said coolly as his eyes fastened on her jutting chin and temper-flushed cheeks.

'You'd answer differently?' She stared at his handsome face aggressively. 'Well, would you?'

'Louisa, Louisa. . .' The unspoken amusement colouring his voice was more irritating than he would ever know, she thought furiously. 'All this contention, hostility, why?' The feline eyes narrowed thoughtfully.

'Why do you feel the need to oppose me so strongly, to be suspicious of everything I say?'

'I wasn't aware I did,' she said tightly. 'Maybe you mistake normal healthy disagreement for something else?'

'Maybe.' He was smiling openly now and she would have given the world to hit him, hard. 'One thing is for sure — the minute you were brought through the gates the Harem would never have been the same again.'

She glared at him without answering and his light chuckle brought the blood rushing to her cheeks. The nerve of the man! He was constantly provoking her with everything he said, every little comment, and all that talk about the Harem before. . . He had made love to her! Without even touching her he had made love to her. It was. . .it was *immoral*.

'Here's the car.' They had continued the tour in silence and once outside the palace grounds she saw the regal Mercedes with a stab of relief. 'You enjoyed your taste of culture?'

'Yes, thank you.' As Melik opened the door for her she almost collapsed inside the car. Enjoyed it? Well, that was one way of putting it.

'Good.' He settled back as before, strong legs outstretched in relaxed ease and one arm resting on the back of the seat, which brought physical contact precariously close. His whole body language spoke of perfect contentment and peace with his surroundings whereas she. . . She was going mad, she thought grimly as the powerful car drew out into the honking, chaotic traffic.

'The Blue Mosque next, I think, another day.'

'Another day?' Her head snapped round to his immediately.

'It should not be missed,' he continued silkily. 'One cannot describe the vast beauty of its interior, the two hundred windows, exquisite coloured stencilling, the sheer majesty of the place. No visit to Istanbul is complete without seeing the Blue Mosque; it is disgraceful you haven't been yet. I——'

'I think I'm going to be too busy over the next few weeks to go sightseeing,' she said stiffly, cutting into his deep voice determinedly. 'Besides which I think it would be most unwise to associate on a social level with you or anyone else at the office. People talk. . .' Her voice dwindled away as something dangerous leapt into the gold slits watching her so closely.

'Do they?' he asked coldly. 'And what do these people say when they talk?'

'You know what I mean,' she snapped quickly. 'It's all right for you; your reputation——' She stopped abruptly, aware that what she had been about to say was neither tactful nor polite.

'My reputation?' Now he was really angry; she saw it in the dark flare of red on the high cheekbones and the flaring of the straight nose. 'Yes? Please continue.'

'Well, it's different for a man,' she said tightly, throwing caution to the wind. 'It's all hail and well met, isn't it? Back-slapping and "you're a fine stud" type of thing. No one would think any the worse of you if they thought that we. . .that you. . .' The ice in his eyes was making her flounder. 'Whereas I would be put in quite a different category.'

'A fine stud?' The note in his voice would have been comical if the look on his face hadn't been so terrifying. 'Believe me, if anyone, male or female, ever made the mistake of referring to me as a stud, fine or otherwise, they would live to regret it.' He eyed her furiously. 'I can't believe that in this day and age you still hold such outdated views.'

'Outdated views?' Now it was her turn to look amazed. 'What sort of cloud-cuckoo-land are you living in anyway? Maybe the jet-set hold different values from everyone else, as the tabloids would have us believe, but I can assure you that in the normal everyday world in which *I* inhabit a girl getting over-friendly with her boss is not the best reference I know.'

'Jet-set?' The flared nostrils twitched. 'Now who is labelling whom?'

'I'm not arguing with you, Mr Haman,' she said faintly as the knowledge that she was losing ground began to dawn on her. 'The meal was lovely and I very much appreciated your kind invitation to show me a little of what Istanbul holds, but that's as far as it's going. OK?'

'The hell it's OK!' They had just passed a magnificent mosque, gold and silver in the evening sunlight, and as a small dusty square surrounded by ancient houses and quaint shops lit a spark of recognition in her she realised she was nearly home. 'What do you think I am, anyway? Some kind of rapacious animal, for crying out loud?'

'Not at all.' As the car drew up with a flourish outside the apartment block she felt a rush of relief that was indescribable.

'Well, everything you've done and said so far is making you a liar, Miss Collins.' The light had died swiftly and now she could only just see his face in the dancing shadows inside the car. 'And I am very tempted to give you exactly what you expect from me to teach you the lesson you deserve.'

'You just try it and——'

He moved sinuously against her in one fluid cat-like movement that had her caught under his body as securely as if she were in the chains he had spoken of earlier, her hands caught in his iron grasp and his mouth locked on to hers in a kiss that brought shocking tension to every part of her body. The hard contours of his male shape were pressed into her soft curves in a perfect male-female jigsaw that had the blood flowing hot in her veins as she recognised the arousal he was making no effort to hide, and after a few moments, as a rush of searingly hot pleasure had her horrified at her body's betrayal, she felt the potency of his desire melting her resistance.

This was how a man could make you feel, then? Lost in an excitement that had no reason to it, no control?

He was neither rough nor violent, his mouth warm and sensual as it did its devastating work of cutting through her defences and turning her soft and melting beneath his skilful lovemaking until at last he released her hands, knowing she was his captive, that the trembling, fluttering female shape beneath his was wholly subjugated.

Her throat was his now, thrown back and defenceless as she lay half swooning in his arms, and as he lightly touched his lips to the frantic pulse beating there she moaned softly, unable to think, to care. . . This was everything she had dreamed about as a young starry-eyed girl when she had read her first romance, and so much more besides. It couldn't be real. *He* couldn't be real. A glimmer of uneasiness penetrated the stupor his lovemaking had caused, making itself felt now that his hands and mouth had stopped their devastating work. She opened dazed eyes to see his face an inch from her own, and strangely it didn't hold the cynical satisfaction she had expected.

'And *I* was teaching *you* the lesson?' His voice was faintly incredulous. 'How many people live under your skin, Louisa?'

The searing embarrassment turned her skin scarlet as she struggled upwards and out of his hold, backing into a corner of the car as though she were a tiny animal trying to hide. The dark little street in which the apartment block was situated was deserted but she felt as though the very walls had eyes, and although the linen screen in front of the glass that separated the driver from the passengers was very firmly anchored in place she felt exposed, vulnerable and horribly mortified.

'Don't look like that.' As Melik reached out for her she shrank still further from him and immediately his hand dropped back. 'What happened between us. . .' He shook his head slowly. 'It was as much a surprise to me as it was to you, I promise. I didn't expect —' He stopped abruptly.

'Please let me go.' She was opening the door as she spoke, fumbling with the handle, and as he made to follow her she knew her voice was rising but couldn't control the pain any longer. 'Leave me alone.' She stared at him wild-eyed, unaware that her hair had come loose in the close embrace and was framing her head and shoulders in a halo of shining golden curls that brought a burning darkness into the eyes watching her. 'You must leave me alone. I can't have this, I can't stand it. . .' Her voice broke on a sob and then she was gone, running into the building as though the devil himself were after her and not stopping until she

THE SULTAN'S FAVOURITE 61

burst into the flat, desperately relieved to find she was alone as Sandra had not returned yet.

He must think she was mad! After long, strained, painful minutes of staring into nothing she had forced herself to fix a cup of coffee in the tiny kitchen, more to give her hands something to do and stop the shaking in her limbs than anything else, and now, as the hot liquid calmed her mind, she found herself red with humiliation. Mad, deranged. . . She shut her eyes tightly in embarrassment. First of all running like a startled rabbit in the Bazaar and now this. Why couldn't she have handled it all differently, smoothly, coolly, maintaining a sedate distance at the same time as giving no offence? Because she wasn't the sort of woman he thought she was. The thought came with a sickening jolt. He was looking for a pleasant diversion for a short time with a willing partner who knew the score and wanted it as much as he did. That was the way men like him worked. Rich, handsome, spoilt, masterful men who had the world at their fingertips. And she couldn't handle it.

She rocked to and fro on the high stool in front of the minute breakfast-bar. She would tell Mrs Jones she had to go back to England tomorrow. Strangely the thought brought no comfort, only fresh pain. She would go home, find a new job, a new flat, and try to pick up the pieces of her life which the last twelve months had smashed into tiny fragments. Sudden tears were hot and gritty behind her closed eyelids and she moaned softly into the silence. In all the agonising time with Oliver and the harrowingly painful months after he had died she had never, ever felt such savagely overwhelming hopelessness, and that realisation, along with the events of the day, seemed the final betrayal to her memory of him. It was the key that unlocked the flood of tears that had her eventually crawling into bed, weary and heartsore, to fall into a deep, dreamless sleep until morning.

CHAPTER FOUR

'THAT last set of part numbers? Have those been checked, Louisa?'

'Yes, and the shipment received this morning too. Do you want me to fax the part number of that new processor chip through to England tonight?'

'Please.' Melik nodded abstractedly and Louisa smiled to herself quietly. The last two months had been a revelation on how much work one man could consume by the hour, and she had nearly missed the excitement, the utter absorption of working with such a razor-sharp, blindingly intelligent mind.

When she had arrived at the office that morning two months ago after her visit to the Topkapi Palace with Melik the day before she had been determined to leave Turkey as soon as possible. And he had been waiting for her, whisking her into his office before she'd even had a chance to open her mouth and sitting her in a chair as he had begun to talk at her. And it had been talking *at* her, she remembered with a wry smile.

'Where's the letter?' He had eyed her intimidatingly. 'The resignation letter?'

'In my bag.' She had been too raw and tired to resist.

'Rip it up.' He had uncoiled from his position on the side of the desk and begun to pace the floor, talking in quiet clipped tones as he'd outlined his plans for the next few weeks. 'Total business, Louisa, I promise, nothing else.' He'd glanced once at her swollen, mauve-stained eyes before continuing the pacing. 'I apologise for last night; I take utter and absolute blame, of course. For what it's worth I have never instigated an office liaison in my life before, I would like you to believe that.' She hadn't nodded or replied, her great eyes fixed on his dark face as he'd prowled round the small room. 'I want you to stay; it would mean the loss of your job here and possibly at Lectron in England if you left and it is not necessary. We can work well together; I need someone who is prepared to put in long hours almost constantly and frankly from what I've seen of the rest of the contingent you stick out like a sore thumb.' She hadn't, even then, feeling as empty as she did, liked the simile. 'We have got off to a bad start but it is not irretrievable and now I feel we both know where we stand. Well?' The piercing eyes had suddenly fixed on her face. 'Are you going to run or stay here and do the job that Lectron is expecting of you?'

She had recognised the clever psychology even then, although she was going to become more familiar with it in the weeks ahead, when she watched, amazed, as he manipulated situations and people to his will with very little effort, but his words had hit a raw spot. Lectron *had* supported her unhesitatingly when she had needed it, even if one could argue that she had always been the model employee and excellent at her job, and she hadn't liked the idea of letting them down.

'I'll stay.' Her voice had been wooden. 'At least for the time being.'

The somewhat one-sided conversation with Melik in absolute control had set the tone for the following weeks. Their working relationship had been one of cool efficiency interlaced with hectic and exhausting panics at least once a day, and gradually Louisa had come to accept that he had forgotten the brief and strange passion he had had for her and now regarded her as a necessary part of the office equipment without which the project couldn't function properly, and yet. . .

She glanced under her eyelashes at him now as he straightened from his sitting position behind the huge desk and stretched wearily. There were times, just now and then, when she caught him looking at her in a certain way, a dark intensity colouring the golden eyes bronze, but immediately he registered her glance a shutter would snap down over the beautiful eyes and he would become the remote professional again, cool, calm and very much in command. And she would be left thinking it was all in her imagination.

He was a vitally complex man, that much she had learnt. Fiercely proud, unbearably authoritative, ruthless to the point of cruelty at times when faced with any inefficiency or laziness, and yet he was harder on himself than anyone, working far into the night when everyone else had gone and arriving long before dawn if the situation commanded it.

He was as proud of his French heritage as of his Turkish, fluent in six languages, undeniably cosmopolitan in his outlook and morals, and yet. . . She remembered the day he had told her he could trace his Turkish ancestry back to Suleyman the Magnificent, the greatest of all the Ottoman sultans. He had been all Turkish then. And his women! She shut her eyes for a moment. If all the rumours and whispered office hearsay were true he had his own version of the harem in modern-day Turkey, although where he found the time she would never know!

'Are you tired?' His voice brought her eyes snapping

open to see him leaning back in his big leather chair, hands behind his head, his shirt stretched tight over the broad masculine chest. Her breathing quickened before she had time to control it.

'A little.' She smiled carefully and forced her eyes to move to a point just over his left shoulder. 'It's been a long day.'

'One of many.' He smiled slowly. 'And tonight I think we can afford to indulge ourselves a little with a reward for hard endeavour. Yes?'

'A reward?' she asked cautiously. The only reward she wanted was to relax for an hour in a hot bath with maybe a glass of wine and a good book, followed by eight hours of uninterrupted sleep. It took that long to prepare the armour in mind and body for the close proximity with him each day.

'You'll need your jacket.' He nodded at the light wool thigh-length coat on the antique coat-rack in a corner of the room. 'The nights are getting cooler.' She eyed him without replying. This time last month the weather had been a comfortable seventy degrees most days but with the onset of November the temperature had fallen and now, three weeks through the month, a cooler fifty-seven had been recorded. Not bad by English standards but after the fierce, unrelenting heat of the summer months the change here was striking.

'Melik, I don't think this is a good idea.' She faced him squarely without reaching for her jacket.

'You don't eat?' he asked with simulated surprise, glancing down her slim shape consideringly. 'Well, I do and I'm starving.'

'You know what I mean——'

'Don't argue, Louisa.' The tone was soft and quiet and shut off her voice more effectively than any force.

'We are going for a bite to eat, that is all, OK?' She opened her mouth to speak and he silenced her with an upraised hand. 'Say, Yes, Melik,' he ordered softly.

'But——'

'Yes, Melik.' There was a faint thread of steel in the silky tones now and she knew defeat when she heard it.

'OK, but I can't be late; Sandra will send out a search party,' she said lightly as she turned for her coat, aiming for a cool, friendly approach to offset the sudden tension.

As she followed him out of the deserted building into the noisy, crowded street her eyes automatically skimmed along the kerb for Melik's distinctive Mercedes, her hand holding the English newspaper that one of the office staff always fetched each day from Divan Yolu, the main street in the Sultanahmet district.

'No car tonight.' As her eyes fastened on his face she saw he was smiling quietly. 'We can reach our destination by foot.'

'Can we?' As a thought occurred to her she frowned slightly, her eyes opening wider. 'Did you know we were going to do this, then?'

'It had crossed my mind.' His dark face was enigmatically distant and as she stared up at him he shook his head gently. 'You have the most transparent face of any female I know. Don't you ever try to hide your thoughts when they might be a little. . .uncomfortable for the recipient?'

'No.' She regarded him unsmilingly. 'Should I?'

'Perhaps not.' He shook his head again. 'It's just that your particular brand of honesty takes a little getting used to. I'm used to more co-operation from my women.'

'I don't doubt it,' she said tartly, 'but as I am not one of your women that comment is a little out of place.'

'*Touché*, child.' The sudden smile lit up the flecked eyes and she had to force herself not to smile back. He knew how devastating that smile was, she just knew it!

'I rather like this high horse of which you English speak,' he said softly, touching her flushed face with a thoughtful finger before taking her arm and putting it through his, drawing her comfortably into his side. 'Now, if we are going to negotiate the crowded pavements you will need a little protection.' As they walked along the uneven busy pavement she was glad he was concentrating on steering their path through the jumble of human bodies; it gave her time to get used to the feel of his hard, lean body next to hers and compose her face accordingly.

As they passed two small children splashing each other from one of the numerous fountains that could be found in every street and alley, in every courtyard, square and park, a particularly energetic splash sent a cascade of water showering over Melik's immaculate trousers in diamond droplets. Their apologies were immediate and profuse, and as she watched him bend down to reassure the infants, his eyes soft and his mouth smiling, she felt a sudden hard lurch to her heart that was almost painful. She had noticed this before, this gentleness with anything small and timid; even little Dephni in the office who held him in such awe always received a consideration that was lacking in his dealings with the more worldly-wise of his staff, and it produced feelings in her she would rather not acknowledge.

'Are you going to ask me where we are going?' As

they continued walking he glanced down at her after taking her arm in his again, turning off as he spoke into a long, narrow cobbled street that led downwards, away from the main throng.

'I suppose so.' She looked up at him and it was a mistake. His black hair had been ruffled by the salty wind and suddenly it was a much younger Melik who smiled down at her, younger and devastatingly attractive. The memory of that night in his car was, without warning, there in front of her and as she stumbled his arm tightened, drawing her even closer into his side.

'Steady.' He frowned down at their feet. 'These damn cobbles look picturesque enough but there are more broken ankles per square yard. . .'

He had felt so good. . . Her body seemed to have a life of its own, refusing her brain's command to ignore feelings that were best buried.

'Now, for dinner I can offer you giant mussels charcoal-grilled while you watch, the biggest peaches you'll ever see, from Bursa, nuts from the Black Sea. . .' As he had been talking they had arrived on the waterfront, somewhere she had always meant to visit but had not had the time for. She had heard of the culinary delights on its shores from the Turkish contingent in the office, and now she saw that they had not exaggerated the magic of the place. The quay was alive with rich colour and exotic smells, visitors and locals alike represented in the teeming, busy throng that swelled and moved like a flowing tide.

'Oh, it looks——' Her voice was cut off abruptly as she felt his fingers loosening the clip at the back of her head just a moment too late to stop her hair flying loose in a soft curling cloud around her face and shoulders, the tiny golden curls and soft waves gleam-

ing in the light from the bright stalls and shops. 'Melik!'
she protested weakly, her voice faltering as she looked
up into the darkness of his eyes which wandered slowly
over her hair and skin as if he were a thirsty man who
had just been given his first taste of pure clean water.
'What did you do that for?'

'Because I wanted to,' he said thickly, 'and I have
been more patient than you will ever know.'

'Melik —— '

'No more words.' He cut off her protest abruptly by
the simple expedient of placing his lips on hers for a
fleeting second, the light touch sending ripples of
awareness flooding into her limbs. 'We are going to
eat.' He pointed to a glowing brazier a few feet away
on which mussels, cubes of swordfish and other seafood
lay gently sizzling in mouthwatering splendour. 'Or
maybe shish kebab, corn-on-the-cob. . .?'

'Melik —— '

'And do not say you are not hungry. You eat too
little and work too hard. Has no one ever taken you in
hand?'

It hurt. It shouldn't, because he had said it in total
innocence, but nevertheless it hurt. He always hurt
her. And she couldn't understand why. Couldn't
understand why the remarks that would mean nothing
from anyone else always seemed to find the vulnerable
spot when spoken by him.

'You ought to be pleased because I work hard,' she
said huskily. 'As my employer —— '

'Oh, no.' He placed a finger on her lips, his eyes
flashing. 'Tonight you are not keeping the barriers in
place, my Louisa. I will not allow it.' There was a touch
of the old arrogance in his tone and it made it easier to
harden herself, to take a mental step backwards. She

had to remember, *had* to remember that he was rich and powerful, that he was used to many different women, that his lifestyle was fast and furious and little incidents like this would mean nothing to him. Whereas she —— Her mind stopped and she didn't pursue the thought. Some people were meant to walk through life alone, she told herself fiercely as she watched him talking to a bearded stall-holder in long, flowing robes, pointing out some mussels for the heaped plates he was holding, and it was futile to fight against one's fate. She had already done that once with Oliver, and with catastrophic results.

All around the hot, spicy smells of the East were mingling with the vibrant, colourful waterfront, the occasional veiled woman clothed from head to foot in sombre black at variance with the gaily dressed tourists and majority of Turkish locals in casual jeans and jumpers. It was a melting-pot of a place and in other circumstances, in another world, she would have loved every minute, but now. . . She glanced across at Melik again to see that he was on his way back to her, the plates of food steaming gently. Now everything was too poignant, too strained, her nerves stretched as tight as piano strings.

'Here.' As he reached her side he flicked his head to a small wooden bench at the side of a wall. 'Eat and enjoy.' The smile he gave her was warm and soft and as he placed the plate of food in her hands his gaze lingered for a long moment on her face. 'It's eating with your fingers, I'm afraid.'

'I like that,' she said lightly. 'I think I'm quite uncivilised at heart.'

'Really?' As he joined her on the bench she was acutely aware of hard-muscled thighs under the thin material of his suit, even more so when he crossed one knee over the other and bit into a shish kebab with hard white teeth. 'Mmm, that's good.' He eyed her out of the corner of his eye. 'So you are a savage like me? Maybe there is hope for me yet, then.' As his teeth tore at the meat again her eyes followed in fascinated interest; he suddenly seemed quite unlike the awe-inspiring, ruthless businessman of the daytime hours who wielded such total and absolute power. She blinked as the golden gaze flicked over her face again. But she had to remember that like any dangerous animal he was at his most lethal when seemingly indolent and relaxed. She couldn't afford to be caught off guard again.

'Do you like it?' He waved a lazy hand at the moving scene in front of them. 'The plan is to turn all this area into parkland eventually; most of the old waterfront is gone already.'

'You disapprove?' she asked quietly as she began to eat, finding the hot, spicy food incredibly good.

'Unfortunately the bulldozer is not a discerning machine,' Melik said wryly. 'Admittedly the whole area was crumbling and less than enchanting but there are many facets in this ancient part of Istanbul worth saving and restoring. I think that maybe this is being recognised slowly. I hope the recognition has not come too late. With a city such as this one must tread carefully or improvements become a death-knell to the past.'

'You love this country, don't you?'

His dark face was alive with emotion. 'Of course, it is in my blood,' he answered proudly. 'Where else is there such a choice of beauty, such rich history? Nine thousand years of historical remains, troglodyte settlements and underground cities, relics from the dawn of civilisation at every corner.'

'You make it sound fascinating.' They seemed to be getting on safer ground and she relaxed a little more, eating a juicy cube of swordfish with its taste of the ocean and far-away places as the strong sea breeze fanned her hair into a golden cloud across her shoulders.

'I shall do more than that, my little tigress,' he said softly, and she tensed immediately; this was the first time he had called her by the old name since the night in his car and the easy use of it was confirmation of her worst fears. He had been biding his time after all, like the big dark-natured cat he reminded her of, biding his time and waiting. . .'I shall not be content until I have shown you the rolling hills and sunflower fields of Thrace, the snow-capped peaks of the mighty Taurus mountains, the white sands and translucent waters of the Mediterranean with its shores of pine forests, orange groves and banana plantations—all that and much, much more. You will grow to love this land as I do, love it and never want to leave.'

'I will?' She tried to laugh to break the mood of intimacy that he had woven but the sound stuck in her throat. 'I hardly think the few months I've got left here will be enough time for all that.'

'You think I will let you leave?' He took one of her hands in his, turning the palm over slowly and stroking the tiny pulse at the base of her wrist with persuasive fingers before raising her hand to his lips and kissing the soft interior of her palm with a slowly lingering caress. His mouth burnt, a hundred sensations leaping shockingly along her nerve-endings and causing her to wrench her hand from his grasp, her cheeks hot and her eyes bright.

'Don't.' She eyed him angrily. This was all part of the usual seduction scene, was it? The deep, rich, throaty voice and glittering flecked eyes that promised so much?

'Why not?' He eyed her flushed face and shaking hands with hard, speculative eyes. 'Is it because you want it too much?'

'No, I don't, of course I don't,' she protested immediately. 'I'm not into cheap affairs, Melik, so look for someone else to have a little diversion with if that's what you want.'

'A cheap affair?' For a moment she thought he was going to hit her as his face turned as black as thunder and his eyes blazed an icy light that stopped her heart from beating. 'Is that how you view a relationship between a man and a woman? As something cheap, something. . .unclean?' His gaze flashed over the English newspaper lying on the bench beside her and as he raised his eyes back to her face she saw a hard, biting contempt darken them still further. 'You are happy to live your life by watching the experiences of others? Of reading about life and love through the pages of your newspaper? Is that it?'

'That's unfair!' Anger was pumping welcome adrenalin into her system now to combat the trembling his rage had produced. 'Just because I don't fall gratefully into your arms the minute you beckon like all your other women, you needn't try and twist things.'

'All my other women?' He shut his eyes for a brief moment, his countenance black. 'I have many other women, is that it? I do not believe I am allowing this conversation to continue! And where do I keep all these other women, Louisa? Pray let the fairy-tale carry on; I am quite fascinated.'

'I don't suppose you exactly keep them anywhere,' she said icily, furious at the sarcasm. 'But you can't tell me they aren't around anyway; I'm not stupid, Melik.'

'That is a statement open to debate,' he ground out through gritted teeth. 'And where have you been hearing these so delightful stories about the big bad wolf and all the Little Red Riding Hoods? No, do not tell me, let me guess. The office staff?' He nodded slowly as she kept her head still and stiff in front of him. 'I might have guessed; that is it, isn't it? And you dare to say you are not stupid?'

'You aren't seriously trying to tell me you live the life of a monk?' she said furiously as the last thread of her self-control was broken by the insult.

'Oh, so now you are asking *me* to tell *you* something?' he spat furiously. 'How kind, how reasonable of you. What is it that you want to hear? Grovelling assurances that I am as pure as the driven snow? Protestations that I have never had a woman in my bed? Well, as you so rightly guessed, I cannot oblige with such untruths. Of course I have had women, Louisa; I am a thirty-seven-year-old man with a healthy body and appetites to match.'

If he had suddenly reached out and punched her in the stomach it would have been preferable to the pain that coursed through her body at the softly snarled words. But she had known, hadn't she? She caught at her shattered nerves desperately. She had known! What was so bad about hearing him put it into words?

'However, the difference between two people who find each other attractive enjoying a satisfying relationship for a time and the sort of picture you have painted is enormous,' he continued icily. 'I have never pretended in the past that my feelings were those of undying love as written about by the poets and suchlike. I have always been totally honest.'

'And they were content with that?' she asked incredulously. 'They didn't want more?'

'Of course they were content with the situation,' he said tightly, 'or I would not have done them the injustice of getting involved in the first place. Not every woman wants slippers by the fire or even a permanent hearth in which to have a fire! And for the record there have not been droves beating a path to my door. I abhor promiscuity whether it be in the male or female of the species.'

'I find that hard to believe.' She was totally out of her depth and floundering badly, but there was no way she was going to let him know that, she thought painfully, forcing a scornful note into her voice to block the trembling she was frightened he would hear.

'Doubtless.' It was clear from his taut body that her attitude was not going a long way to diffuse the situation. 'But as I do not have to justify myself to you or anyone else it really doesn't matter, does it?' He was being deliberately cruel and she steeled herself for more of the same but he rose swiftly, pulling her up and placing their half-full plates of now cold food on the bench. 'Why the ivory tower, Louisa?'

A young Turkish family out for the evening, the children dark and pretty and beautifully dressed, passed them, smiling and nodding, as Melik inclined his head.

'I said, why the ivory tower?'

'I heard you.'

'And you do not intend to reply,' he stated flatly,

slipping his arm through hers as they began to climb the steep cobbled path away from the noise and colour of the busy waterfront, the silvery moonlight filtering down between ancient houses on either side of the narrow, silent street. 'Well, you will tell me one day, Louisa, that I promise you. In fact, you will tell me all I want to know when the last defence is broken down and——'

'And I become just like any other woman?' she interrupted bitterly, incensed at his autocratic manner and the way he made her feel even when he was being at his most arrogant, like now.

It was this alien country, she told herself desperately, the seductive aura of the East that pervaded every nook and cranny and worked its lethally sensual magic in a land where for centuries it had been the normal way of life for one man to expect total and complete submission from the women he took for his own, a primal possessiveness in his bearing that had been accepted and considered natural.

The major face-lift of the last sixty years had changed some things, she thought helplessly, but still the insidiously voluptuous beauty of this diverse land had an ageless magic that lingered to beckon and entice and enthral. She had never burned to feel a man's hands on her body, his mouth pressed to hers before, never——

'Just like any other woman?' he said coldly, his tight voice jerking her eyes back to his face. 'I think you insult your sisterhood with such. . .sexist talk. No man or woman is like another in the way you suggest; we are all different. I am surprised you do not think this.'

'Of course I think it,' she shot back hotly, aware that he had done it again, turned things around until she was on the defensive and having to explain herself. 'I happen to believe men and woman are equal, that neither one should expect to dominate the other.'

'I agree.' She stared at him wide-eyed. He agreed? Never! 'Apart from just one place, that is. In the bedroom.'

'The bedroom?' she said slowly, hating the weakness in her voice.

'You have not found this so?' His face was in shadow, the tawny eyes veiled and closed against her, but she still felt as though the golden gaze was boring into her brain, seeking out that hidden part of her that even Oliver had not known existed.

'I don't want to discuss this any further.' She jerked herself from his grasp as the blood pounded through her ears. 'I think it would be better if I arranged for someone else to work with you. Most of the ground work is done now; someone else could easily——'

He swore, softly and fluently in his own tongue, his eyes blazing now as they raked her face. 'Did I get too close for a moment?' His voice was icy in stark contrast to his face. 'What is his name, Louisa, the name of the man who has left you so empty and frightened of life? What the hell did he do to you anyway?'

'Just leave me alone!' She glared at him even as the shaking that had taken hold of her limbs transferred itself to her voice. 'I work for you, that's all; what do you think gives you the right——?'

'*Gives* me the right?' His voice was contemptuous and cold. 'You think I wait for life to *give* me the right? We're here once and once only, Louisa; you have to reach out and take what you want. . .' As he pulled her into his arms she began to struggle, her breathing quick and ragged, but it was as ineffectual as beating her fists against rock, his body immovable. She made to turn her head away but he was too quick, taking her lips in a hot, fierce kiss that explored her mouth with savage concentration.

She tried to fight him but even as her struggles ceased she knew it had been her own weakness she was frightened of, and so she should have been, she thought, panic-stricken, because it was happening again, that sweet, melting warmness that caused desire to flicker and then burn in a thudding flood.

His mouth was gentler now, even leisurely, his hands moving up underneath her coat to mould her shoulders further into him as he tasted her sweetness slowly, savouring each movement of his flickering tongue. He was drawing little shocks of sensation from every part of her body and he knew it; he knew the effect he had on her. Even as she felt the trembling that was shaking her limbs communicate itself to him she melted still further into his hard shape, accepting his mastery, his instinctive knowledge of how to conquer all her inhibitions, utterly vanquished beneath his expertise.

'And you would deny us this, my sweet, savage tigress?' he whispered huskily, his hands roaming over her body under the light coat and igniting shivers of fire wherever they touched. Her hands moved flutteringly up into his hair, almost of their own volition, and as he felt her fingers at the back of his neck he groaned softly and deeply against her mouth, the movement of his body against hers as he pressed her back against the wall in the shadowed darkness shockingly indicative of his arousal.

She had to stop this, had to. . . Her brain knew it but her body was helplessly caught in a drugged dreamlike state that was all the more thrilling because of its newness, the unknown shivers of passion and desire rendering her defenceless and abandoned in his arms. 'You are so beautiful, so sweet. . .' The whisper was faint against her ear and she responded blindly, a tangible ache that she had no will to resist engulfing her in its powerful need. 'You *will* be mine. . .'

The four small words brought her out of the fantasy he had woven with appalling suddenness and as she pushed against his chest his arms tightened briefly and then relaxed. 'What is it?' He moved back a pace as he spoke and she heard his breathing was harsh and unsteady although his face was hidden from her in the shadows. 'Don't be frightened; I would not harm a hair of your head.' Even through her distress she recognised the enormous self-control that was the master of his desire as well as her own, and although she was grateful that he had immediately responded to her withdrawal a tiny perverse part of her was angry that he could dismiss her so easily.

'Please take me back to the apartment.' She had to force the words through dry, shaking lips, her distress obvious, but he didn't try to dissuade her, simply taking her hand and beginning to walk up the dark street without saying a word for long moments as he fought to control his breathing.

'I will not allow you to bury yourself alive, do you understand this, Louisa?' His voice was low and deep but with a curious lack of expression that made his words all the more chilling. 'I do not know what has transpired in your life to make you the woman you now are, but I will know, one day.' He turned her round at the top of the alley as they came into the bright, noisy thoroughfare and she saw his eyes were slits of light, piercingly intent. 'Believe me, Louisa, I *will* know.'

CHAPTER FIVE

THE sharp knock at the apartment door early the next morning, as Louisa and Sandra were having breakfast still in their nighties, brought an immediate frown to Sandra's smooth brow. 'Oh, for goodness' sake, that woman gets earlier and earlier,' she hissed tightly at Louisa as she rose from the table with an angry flourish. 'I'm fed up with sharing a dolmuş with the old bat anyway; I'm going to tell her to go on if she's so desperate to get to the office and we'll follow when we're ready.'

'Sandra. . .' Louisa's voice rose warningly in the air just as Sandra reached the front door, but she grimaced defiantly before whisking open the front door with a swift display of irritation that died an immediate death before Melik's cool stare.

'Good morning.' He was the first one to find his voice, but then he would be, wouldn't he? Louisa thought nastily as she hastily reached for her robe on the back of the chair and pulled it over her thin cotton nightie with more haste than aplomb. *He* wasn't half naked. And what did he want?

'Oh, I'm sorry.' The sheer satin of Sandra's nightie left nothing to the imagination and she backed away from Melik as though he were the devil himself, her cheeky poise quite deserting her for once. 'I thought you were Mrs Jones, Mr Haman, but of course you're not. . .'

'No, I am not,' he agreed gravely, the sombre face

81

unable to hide the wicked dart of delighted amusement that burnt briefly in the glittering eyes.

'No. . .' Sandra backed right to the door of her bedroom and with a muttered, 'Excuse me,' disappeared into its sanctuary like a startled rabbit.

'I'd have called more often if I'd known,' he said drily. 'Am I allowed in?'

'Of course.' Louisa forced herself to move from behind the comforting bulk of the table even though the thigh-length robe revealed far more of her flesh than she would have liked. 'Would you like a coffee?' Play it cool, Louisa, cool. . .

'I'd love one.'

She was painfully aware of his eyes on her hair, which always curled in riotous, unrestrained curls around her face and shoulders after her morning shower before she trained it back into the severe style she wore for the office, but he said nothing, walking across the room in slow, measured steps and sitting down on the seat Sandra had vacated, his dark, brooding presence suddenly filling the whole flat.

'What can I do for you?' She turned with the coffee-mug as she spoke in time to see him shut his eyes for a brief moment, their flecked gaze brilliant when they opened a second later.

'I'm trying very hard to be professional this morning, Louisa,' he said flatly, 'but at the moment I'm losing ground fast. Before I show you exactly what you can do for me perhaps you ought to go and change into something. . .less comfortable? I'll sip my coffee like a good boy while I wait.'

She opened her mouth to speak and then shut it again quickly. He was absolutely right: she had been about to suggest the same thing herself.

When she re-emerged ten minutes later in a linen skirt and neat blue blouse, her hair sedately brushed into tight order, not a wisp escaping from the severe knot, both her mind and her body were under control again. She was English, practical, cool and down-to-earth, more suited to a walk in the rain in sensible brogues than a flight into fantasy in this hot, beautiful, wild land with its ancient customs and dark, untamed men, and she had better remember it. Last night had been a mistake, a grave mistake. She would not let him repeat it.

'There are a few problems that have arisen on my estate on the Black Sea coast.' He spoke immediately she entered the room, his voice cool and contained. 'I feel we have reached a plateau as far as the work here is concerned and can safely leave for a few days without a major catastrophe rearing its head. You agree?'

'Yes.' She looked at him warily. Why had that 'we' been slipped in there? He didn't seriously think ——

'My plane is waiting and I would like to leave this morning. Can you pack a case and be ready in half an hour?'

'Me?' She stared at him in horror. 'You don't expect me to come, surely?'

'Of course.' His voice was as cold as ice now and his face quite expressionless.

'But why?' She became aware that her voice was too shrill and lowered it hurriedly. Sandra was still in her room no doubt with her ear pressed to the keyhole! 'I can carry on with things here and ——'

'I thought I had made the position perfectly clear when you first accepted the job?' he said tightly.

'But that proviso was if it was necessary ——'

'I will decide what is necessary and what is not,' he

said coldly. 'Be ready in half an hour. My car will return for you then. Mrs Jones is fully acquainted with the details and you will be communicating with her every day by telephone. Do you understand?'

'No, I do not!' She would have liked to scream at him to dent the iron-hard composure but contented herself with a splinter-sharp reply. 'If I am reading you correctly you expect me to pack a bag and accompany you to goodness knows where at the drop of a hat. Is that about it?'

'Consider yourself a first-class reader, Louisa,' he said coolly. 'At the beginning of this assignment the facts were made very clear to you; please do not tax my patience or my time now by choosing to be difficult.'

She was still staring at him open-mouthed, amazed at the sheer audacity of the man, when he left, his handsome face expressionless and the big body confident and relaxed.

'What was all that about?' Sandra emerged at once from the bedroom in a cloud of perfume and goggle-eyed curiosity, turning on the flat's small radio as she did so, which immediately filled the small room with the wailing tones of Turkish music, the whining tune reminiscent of an Eastern chant.

'Sandra! Do you have to?' Louisa felt immediately ashamed of her snappishness but her friend just smiled knowingly, shaking her head as she cut off the unmelodious sound.

'He's getting to you, I knew he would. I could see it coming.'

'Don't be ridiculous.' Louisa drew herself up stiffly and prepared to march into her bedroom. 'He's got some business to attend to somewhere else and I've got to go with him. I'm going to pack.'

'Business?' Sandra's throaty chuckle was meant to annoy and annoy it did. 'That's not the first time I've heard it called that either. I've seen the way he looks at you!'

She was ready and waiting when Melik's chauffeur arrived thirty minutes later, waiting and gently simmering like hot, angry jam on the top of a stove.

'There has been a slight change of plan,' the stony-faced man told her impassively as he carried her case down to the waiting Mercedes. 'You will be meeting Mr Haman at the Galata Bridge.'

'Will I?' She hadn't known where she was going to meet him anyway so the news didn't mean anything to her.

As the Mercedes plunged into the four-lane highway, congested as always with a mixture of cars, buses, disreputable trucks and the odd horse-driven cart, she sank back into the luxurious seat and wondered if it was just her who was mad or the rest of the world. Mrs Jones had been as po-faced as normal when she had arrived to collect Sandra for the office, her whole attitude proclaiming that Louisa should count herself very lucky even to be considered for such a prestigious post, and her heavy eyebrows raising up into the steel-grey hair when Louisa had expressed her nervousness.

'Mr Haman is an extremely wealthy and well known businessman, Miss Collins,' she had said with scornful hauteur, her face rigid. 'He has offices in different countries all over the world; this Turkish project is just a drop in the ocean to him. Do you seriously think we can, for one moment, refuse to co-operate with him in any way?'

Sandra hadn't helped either when she had left, taking Louisa aside for a brief moment as she whispered in her ear, 'Co-operate with him? I'd eat him alive!' Her wink over Mrs Jones's shoulder as she had left had been lewd and lascivious, adding to the pounding of Louisa's heart. She should have refused to go, *she should have*!

They arrived at Galata Bridge, on the Karakoy side, at half-past nine, and she saw Melik immediately, her heart leaping into her mouth at the sight of his tall, broad figure as he scanned the moving traffic impatiently. As his eyes met hers through the window of the car she thought, for just a brief moment, that she saw an expression of profound relief on the hard features, but then as the car stopped and he helped her to alight she saw that his eyes were cool and distant, his mouth straight.

'Thank you for being prompt,' he said tightly, nodding to his chauffeur as he disappeared back into the traffic.

'Oh, my case is in there,' she said urgently, forgetting her antagonism for a moment at the prospect of losing all her clothes in one fell swoop.

'Calm yourself, Louisa. Osman will be meeting us soon,' he said shortly, 'but in the meantime I thought you might like to combine business with pleasure for once.' The twist to his mouth told her that he had not forgotten her earlier comment on the subject. 'We are travelling to my home on the Black Sea coast and a trip down the Bosporus takes us in the right direction. I thought at least you might appreciate the improving of your mind?'

Why did he have to make even the simplest comment loaded with hidden meaning that she was powerless to respond to? she asked herself irritably, although the excursion he was suggesting was one that she had promised herself ever since arriving in Istanbul. The nineteen-mile Bosporus, the winding strait separating Europe and Asia, had enough of the past and present scattered along its shores to satisfy even the most discerning traveller. Grand hotels, ancient wooden houses known as *yali*, splendid marble palaces and tiny picturesque fishing villages—they were all there in vibrant, colourful, roaming beauty which made the Bosporus the most scenic waterway of the world.

'Well?' Her eyes had been drawn to the seven hills dominating the skyline; the domed roofs of the Topkapi Palace, the regal silhouette of St Sophia, the breathtakingly majestic Süleymaniye Mosque, the Tower of Beyazit all visible and heart-stoppingly beautiful, and now as his voice called her back to him she turned wide eyes to meet his cool gold gaze. 'Are you prepared to endure my company for a few hours?' There was something in his voice, a throb of emotion, that she couldn't quite place but that somehow melted her resistance as effectively as a flame on ice.

'It's very kind of you to think of this, Melik,' she said softly, suddenly shy. 'Thank you.'

He stared at her for a long moment, his gaze piercing on her face, before smiling slowly and taking her arm as he pointed to a long, sleek, white-painted boat that was already half-full. 'Your transport awaits.'

She was glad the morning was so clear and bright as they set off a little while later; November fog had been evident in the last week and it would have spoilt the fantastic view up the Golden Horn where the hillsides were packed with ancient and modern buildings, pencil-slim minarets and towers galore.

'Comfortable?' As she dragged her eyes away from the Dolmabahçe Palace spread comfortably along the shore, the shafts of sunlight from the clear blue sky overhead turning it into picture-postcard handsomeness, she met Melik's warm gaze. He was sitting with his arm casually draped round her shoulders and although she had stiffened at first, her body instinctively freezing at the physical contact, the unfurling scene in front of her had soon claimed total absorption.

'It's so beautiful.' Palaces, majestic gardens, splendid hotels and luxurious waterside villas had given way to tiny villages, the delightful, two-storey wooden houses with carved beams wonderfully picturesque.

For the rest of her life she was to remember that trip down the Bosporus, with Melik warm and companionable at her side while he explained the different sights that crowded in on her entranced gaze before she could draw breath, as a time unreal and breathtakingly magical. The past and present, intrinsically linked by the mixture of ancient and modern, was suddenly enough for the moment; there was no future, no tomorrows, no rejection, no goodbyes. . .

'You see there?' Melik leant over her slightly to point ahead and as the faint scent of him surrounded her in its intoxicatingly sensual attraction her heart pounded violently. His hard thigh was pressed against her softness, his arm was tight against her shoulders now as he held her against him, and she was vitally conscious of the leashed power of the big body, the hard masculine limbs and strong, broad chest. Would he ever marry? The thought popped unbidden into her mind and once there flourished. Did men like him ever *really* marry or did they just join their name to a suitable partner for business or social reasons, a family, the linking of estates? She forced the train of thought to stop abruptly and concentrated on what he was saying, his clean breath warm against her cheek.

'You see at the narrowest point the two castles?' he was asking softly. 'They played a key role in the Turkish conquest of Constantinople.'

'They did?' She found the nearness of his hard square jaw, faintly dusky with the swift growth of his beard, far more fascinating than the two mighty castles in spite of their history.

'The first castle on the Asian side was built in 1395,' Melik continued, 'to enforfce the control of maritime traffic to and from the Black Sea. Then Mehmet the Conqueror, at the young age of twenty-one, had the Rumeli Hisari fortress built on the European side so total domination was accomplished by the Turkish forces. The whole thing from start to finish took just nineteen weeks to complete, with an army of workers and a thousand skilled masons working day and night. Turks, even at that tender age, can be quite ruthless when they want something,' he added expressionlessly. 'It is not natural for the word "failure" to feature in our vocabulary.'

As the golden gaze turned down to her she saw there was a heat in the beautiful eyes, a banked-down glow, that caused the blood to pound through her veins. 'And no?' she asked softly. 'Does the word "no" have any effect on the Turks?'

He smiled slowly, his handsome face magnificently male. 'Only if we allow it.'

'I think I've figured that out for myself,' she said after a long still moment, her back straight now.

'Have you?' His gaze lingered on her mouth for a second before turning to the castles. 'I don't think so, not yet, but you will. The inner courtyard in the Rumeli castle is used for open-air theatre now,' he continued blandly as though all they had been discussing were architecture and history, 'and they have concerts and folklore shows there too. Have you been to a folklore evening yet?'

She shook her head silently.

'The fierce Mrs Jones again?'

She didn't return his smile; it was taking all her will to calm her racing heart into submission. 'That and work,' she said shortly.

'Of course.' He shook his black head slowly. 'I have not left you with sufficient time for such pleasure, have I, working you day and night? I will make amends, I promise.'

'I don't want you to make amends,' she said urgently, aware that she had played straight into his hands, and what large, capable hands too! 'I've done the job I was paid to do, that's all.'

'I disagree.' It was the end of the conversation as far as he was concerned.

As they slowly travelled past beautiful little water-side villages, sleepy and quiet in the mild November sun, the odd elderly Turk sitting meditatively with his hubble-bubble pipe amid green fishing boats and col-ourful little blue and yellow houses, the tranquillity of it all was overpoweringly poignant. Soon it would end, Louisa thought helplessly, and she would be plunged back into the turmoil and confusion that seemed to have been with her ever since she had first laid eyes on this big, dangerous man. And she could do nothing about it. Nothing at all. The thought was not comforting.

When they docked it was to find the chauffeur

waiting impassively at the end of the quay, the powerful car parked broodingly in the afternoon sun. 'The end of the Bosporus is a closed military zone,' Melik informed her quietly as he seated her in the Mercedes's comfortable seat, 'and as we do not wish to tangle with the authorities we will now resume our journey by car, yes?'

'It was a lovely trip, Melik.' She touched his arm hesitantly as he sat with his face in profile to her, looking out of the window. 'Thank you.'

'My pleasure.' He turned, his eyes soft. 'If a trip down the Bosporus is all it takes to hear you say my name so prettily then we will do it every day. You rarely do, you know. . .say my name.'

'Do I?' She blushed hotly, knowing full well she found it difficult. It seemed too intimate somehow, too friendly, especially when everyone else in the office apart from Mr Ashton addressed him formally. And he wasn't a man it was easy to be informal with. Apart from the knowledge that he was immensely wealthy and dangerously powerful the very maleness of him, the overwhelming physical attraction she felt for him, kept her tongue tied very often in a way it had never been before. And she did find him so physically devastating. The thought was something of a shock and she realised she had never faced it before.

'You know damn well you do,' he said shortly. 'And that's another thing that's going to change in the next few days. You can hardly stay in my house, eating my food, sleeping in. . .one of my beds without using my Christian name, can you?' He smiled wickedly at her red cheeks. 'Can you?'

'Of course not,' she snapped quickly. He was infuriating, absolutely and utterly infuriating; he never missed an opportunity to get under her skin! 'But I do understand I'm still working so don't worry I'll take advantage.'

He eyed her long and seriously until at last, much to her chagrin, she was forced to look away from the piercingly intent tawny eyes. 'I am sure there is Turkish blood flowing somewhere in that delectable body,' he said at last with a deep sigh as he folded his arms across his chest and settled further down in the seat, shutting his eyes and allowing his big body to relax. 'You sure don't give up, do you?'

She didn't, couldn't reply, and they travelled for a few miles in silence before he spoke again. 'We will be stopping shortly for a late lunch. I normally travel home from Istanbul by air as the roads are not conducive to fast motoring, although the coastal road we are on now is adequate. However, I thought you might like to see a little of the countryside.'

'Thank you.' There was nothing else she could say.

They stopped for lunch a short time later at a caravanserai, an old stone inn where once ancient traders rested and ate a meal free of charge, which had been converted to a modern-day motel.

The meal was excellent and Louisa found that the trip down the Bosporus in the fresh, salty air had given her a ravenous appetite. They feasted on *lahmacun*, Turkish pizza, although the delicious concoction tasted like no pizza Louisa had tried before. A thin, crisp dough had been topped with ground lamb, onions, cheese and spices and when served with ice-cold, frothy *ayra*, a fortifying drink of beaten yoghurt, spring water and a dash of salt, the *lahmacun*, served hot and steaming out of the wood-burning oven, was mouth-wateringly good.

'That was out of this world,' Louisa murmured with replete satisfaction as she finished her last mouthful, leaning back in her seat with a little sigh of contentment. 'Absolutely out of this world.' She raised her eyes to find Melik's amused gaze warm on her face. 'Well, it was,' she repeated a little indignantly as he eyed her smilingly.

'I agree.' He let his gaze wander over her body in a frank approval that brought the blood surging into her cheeks. 'I was just wondering how one so tiny could fit so much food into such a slender shape.'

'I think if I stayed too long in your country I wouldn't have a slender shape,' she countered quickly.

'That would not matter.' Now the amusement had left his face and his eyes were deadly serious as they held hers with their golden light. 'Slim, plump, old, young, you would still be beautiful, little tigress.'

'I doubt it.' She tried to laugh, to break the intimate mood; the look in his eyes was unnerving. 'You men are very good at saying things like that!'

'You think I am merely saying what you would like to hear? That I am flattering you?'

She stared at him warily. That was exactly what she thought but from the look on his face he wouldn't like hearing her say so, and she had to spend at least a few days locked away with him in this home of his wherever it was. 'I think you are being pleasant,' she hedged carefully, 'that's all.'

'Oh, Louisa. . .' He shook his head slowly, his eyes narrowed and gleaming in the tanned darkness of his face. 'How am I ever going to get through to you, my cautious English rose? You are twenty-eight years of age and yet there are times when I could almost think that you are as innocent and untouched as a virginal fifteen-year-old, if it were not impossible with that hair and those eyes. When are you going to come out of your shell and start living again, tasting life and love again? Whatever happened, whether it be a man or something else, it is not worth such a sacrificial offering of a life. Don't you see?'

'Melik, I don't want to discuss——'

'I'm not interested in what you *do not* want,' he said softly, his eyes glittering. 'I have held you in my arms, I have felt your heart beating under mine; you cannot hide what you feel, Louisa.'

'You are saying you feel I am physically attracted to you?' she said flatly, summoning all her strength to project an image of cool distaste when her heart was pounding so violently it was making her feel sick. 'Well, so what if I am? I'm sure it's not a first with you and there must be lots of women only too happy to oblige mutual lust by jumping immediately into bed at the first sign of sexual compatibility. Unfortunately I am not one of them. I've met a lot of men I've found attractive,' she lied expressionlessly, 'but it doesn't mean I've gone to bed with all of them.'

He stared at her for a full minute, his face curiously enigmatic. She had expected offended pride, rage, hot and cutting words, but when he spoke his voice was reflective, thoughtful even. 'You are being offensive and uncharacteristically cruel. Now why?' He leant across the tiny wooden table and took her chin in his hand, forcing her eyes up to meet his as he looked long and hard in their deep brown depths. 'This intrigues me. You intrigue me.'

'Do I indeed!' She jerked away sharply, her skin tingling at his touch and her nerves jumping. 'Well, I'm sorry but I can't return the compliment.'

'Now you are being childish,' he remarked crushingly. 'My culture rates good manners highly, not just in a social sense but as a means of expressing care and affection for whoever it may be, stranger or friend. I have noticed that your gentleness is an intrinsic part of your nature, it has not had to be learnt, and you are fighting this now with me. Does what you feel frighten you so much?'

He was intuitive, she had to give him that, she thought angrily, but just at this moment in time she would have given all she possessed to wipe the superior awareness from that good-looking face. His eyes were warm and perceptive as they searched hers but she didn't trust that expression of concern, the all-too-obvious examining of her emotions. A man like him wanted a woman like her, a virtual nobody in his world, for one reason and one reason only. Dress it up how you like, she thought bitterly, but it was the law of the jungle. Like the big cat he reminded her of he would not be satisfied with one woman for long and as the lion gathered his lionesses around him in harem-like submission, so he would expect the freedom to wander where he would.

'Doesn't the thought that you might be wrong about things ever come into your mind?' she asked as coolly as her burning cheeks would allow. 'You may have grown up thinking you were the mighty and all-powerful one, no doubt aided and abetted by your parents, but frankly I find such an attitude distasteful in the extreme. You think you will always get what you want just because you want it, don't you? *Don't* you?'

'Yes.' His eyes had hardened and narrowed as her voice had progressed but his voice was quite without apology, clipped and sharp. 'That is exactly what I think.'

'Well, not in this case,' she said cuttingly. 'I'm a person, Melik, not a walking doll on two legs, and I place a higher value on myself than obviously you do.'

She had hit him on the raw at last. She saw it in the way his eyes suddenly blazed a cold fire that made her skin prickle and the hairs on the back of her neck rise in protest. He was angry, furiously, smoulderingly angry, and she was immensely glad of the other diners as he glared at her, his eyes flashing.

'You deserve to be whipped for that,' he snarled savagely. 'Whipped to within an inch of your life.'

'Oh, so now we're back to the old days all of a sudden, are we?' she countered bitingly although inside her stomach had turned to melted jelly and her legs felt as though they had just been run over by a steamroller. 'As soon as you meet with a little resistance, a woman who doesn't see things your way, it's back to the sultan approach with force and whips? Charming, absolutely charming.'

The oath that spat from his lips made her very glad her knowledge of Turkish was so limited, and then she was up and out of her seat as he grasped her arm and virtually dragged her out to the car, throwing her into the back seat with a glowering nod at the driver who seemed to shrink down in his seat a good few inches as they started off.

'You are the most impossible woman I have ever had the misfortune to meet,' he said tightly after several electric minutes had ticked by, the atmosphere so hot that she wouldn't have been surprised if the expensive upholstery had begun to melt. 'Argumentative, difficult, exasperating and ridiculously independent.'

She didn't reply; there was nothing on reflection she could add to what he had already said, and in spite of his tone and the set, cold face as he stared straight ahead at the chauffeur's dark head through the tinted-glass panel she didn't altogether disagree with his summing-up. There were other aspects to her personality he could have mentioned but if she was honest he had only seen what she had been prepared to let him see so far, and in the main she felt the words he had used were quite mild. She didn't have much to arm herself with as far as this man was concerned; she was painfully aware that he seemed to touch a spot in her that was quite raw and unprotected, and she had to make use of every weapon to hand.

He could destroy her so easily. She risked a careful glance under her lashes and found he had shut his eyes, his face still like stone. He made her feel vulnerable, frightened, helpless, excited, so many things that she couldn't even acknowledge what half of them were, but underlying them all was a deep and powerful emotion that she didn't recognise and couldn't understand — but it scared her to death.

The resentment, hurt and pain she had always felt with her parents, the loneliness, the gnawing loneliness that had seemed ten times worse since Oliver had gone, the heartache and agonising desperation when he had died, all these were as nothing compared to how Melik could make her suffer if she were foolish enough to let him into her mind and body. She knew it. She didn't know how or why but she just knew it.

CHAPTER SIX

THE rest of the journey was painfully beautiful in marked contrast to Louisa's thoughts: lushly forested mountains plunging dangerously into crystal-clear unpolluted seas, ripe hazelnut groves, tea terraces, sprawling tobacco plantations green and rich in the afternoon sun, tiny sandy beaches as well as seashores of black pebbles from which the sea got its name, all fitted between craggy projections of rock that were as mighty as they were dangerous. . . So much wild *and* tamed beauty and so unexpected. The noise and frantic bustle of Istanbul seemed another lifetime away.

She had read somewhere that according to legend the Black Sea shores were the land of the Amazons, that fierce tribe of female warriors who had competed with men and reigned supreme, and as they went on into the dusky evening she found herself reaching out to the long-dead Amazons, asking for some of their strength for the days that lay ahead.

It was almost dark when they reached their destination, the sky a soft indigo-blue velvet canopy under which Melik's tea plantation stretched endlessly along a vast mountain slope.

'Tea?' She had stared at him in amazement when he had explained what the estate entailed. 'I didn't know you were into tea.'

'I am probably "into" many activities of which you know nothing,' he had returned drily, his cool face betraying the fact that he had not quite forgiven her for her earlier defiance. 'However, this is the ancestral home of the Hamans, as it happens; I was born here.'

'Were you?' She stared at the handsome closed face in fascination as the big car purred through massive gates after climbing steadily for twenty minutes or more.

He nodded slowly as they scrunched along on a beautifully laid road in marked contrast to the rough lanes they had been travelling on a few miles before. 'My mother was booked into the finest hospital in Turkey, so I understand — my father was desperate nothing should go wrong — but they were here seeing to some estate problems when she was eight months pregnant and I decided I had waited long enough to see the world, and was born within an hour of announcing my arrival was imminent. She was still clutching a leaf of tea in her hand when it was all over, or so she says,' he finished quietly.

'Why tea? Why did your family decide to grow tea?'

'Why not?' He turned to fix her with his tawny gaze, his expression indicating slight surprise at her curiosity. 'The main export crops are cotton, tobacco, fruit and nuts but my grandfather changed to tea for reasons of his own and now, since 1945, Turkey grows all its own tea in this area; we're self-sufficient.' He smiled slowly. 'I've no complaints; we did well out of it all. The men in my family all seemed to marry well, bringing more wealth into the Haman fortunes, and now the business interests are vast — vast and time-consuming,' he added ruefully. 'This estate is a relaxing hobby in comparison.'

'Oh.' She smiled flatly. His words only confirmed her earlier thoughts. He would marry for convenience and marry well. It would be expected. The small dart of pain that cut off her breath for a second was unexpected and unwelcome.

Either side of the road alder, lime and elm trees grew wide and tall, a mass of rhododendrons, arbutus and yellow azalea in bloom in the sheltered regions underneath, and then as they turned a sharp corner the house was there in front of her and within a second they were in front of the huge pillars guarding the arched doorway.

She realised, as she gazed at the magnificent huge old house, that she had been mentally preparing herself for something like this for the last fifty miles or so, but nevertheless it still took her breath away.

The house had been painted in traditional white, with massive full-length windows on the second and third floors opening on to intricately wrought iron balconies from which a profusion of vividly coloured winding flowers hung down in gay contrast to the white-painted walls. The sloping roof was red-tiled, the mass of red and green ivy that clung in gay abandon to the walls reaching almost to its stately contours, and the whole effect was one of stunning colour, graciousness and cool, tranquil peace.

'I don't know how you can ever bear to leave this place,' she said softly as she stared transfixed out of the car window, unaware of Melik's eyes warm and satisfied on her face as he took in her rapt appreciation of his home.

By the time he had walked round the car to open her door his face was set in the hard, chiselled lines she knew so well, calm, controlled and giving nothing away. 'It is beautiful, isn't it?' he agreed quietly as he took her arm and led her across the wide pebbled drive towards the front door. 'I am a most fortunate man.'

A single star had just made its appearance in the soft dusky sky, the air was perfumed with a thousand heavy scents from which she could just pick out honeysuckle and jasmine and as the chauffeur drove the car round the side of the house, disappearing from view, Melik suddenly stopped, his expression veiled and strange.

'Welcome to my home, Louisa.' He had taken her in his arms before she knew what he was doing and before she had time to resist, his mouth hot and sweet on hers as he took her mouth in a long, fierce kiss. And then she was free again, swaying slightly as she stared up into his dark face.

'Do you always welcome your employees like that?' she asked shakily as she took a step backwards.

'Not always.' His voice was dry. 'But maybe, if they all taste as good as you, I should start a precedent.'

'I don't think that would be a good idea.' She tried to match her voice and manner to his, to dismiss the kiss as unimportant although it was hard with the feel of his mouth still on hers and the smell of him in her nostrils. 'You're likely to have a host of angry husbands and boyfriends turning up on your doorstep.'

'But you do not have a husband Louisa, do you?' he stated silkily. 'Or a boyfriend either, for that matter. So, in your case. . .'

As he took a step towards her she stepped back again, her eyes flashing. 'Oh, no, once was a welcome, twice would be verging on the ingratiating, don't you think?'

'Not ingratiating, my little tigress.' Now there was a thread of steel in the velvet voice. 'I am a cruel and vicious sultan, remember; whips and chains are far more my style, as you so rightly pointed out, and now that you are in my domain I have you at my mercy. Isn't that the way you see it?'

'Hardly.' She eyed him with far more scorn than she was feeling inside. 'This is the twentieth century, remember.'

'Ah, yes, I had forgotten.' He smiled a smile reminiscent of a cat with a very large bowl of cream. 'In that case all I can do is to ask you to grace my humble home with your beauty and charm.'

'And sarcasm is the lowest form of wit,' she muttered darkly as the front doors were flung wide and a horde of servants, or so it seemed, appeared in the doorway.

'They are eager to meet you; come and be introduced,' Melik said quietly in her ear as he led her through the large arched doorway, picked out in tiny tiles in varying shades of blue and green in a fan-type pattern, and into the large, airy hall. She just had time to notice that a handsome Turkish carpet was covering most of the huge hall's shining wooden floor and take in a highly decorated and magnificent vase standing a full six feet in a quiet alcove, before Melik drew her further into his side as he introduced her to his staff, who bobbed a polite curtsy at their names.

'What are they doing that for?' she whispered to Melik, highly embarrassed. 'Don't they know I'm employed by you too?'

'It's different.' He eyed her unsmilingly. 'Trust me.'

The 'horde' shrunk into Safiye, the somewhat rotund housekeeper, her husband, Tegrul, who was Melik's estate manager and who inclined his head politely towards Louisa before disappearing through a side-door into the back of the house, and Cybiele and Kathi, the two maids who were small and dark and remarkably alike.

She mentioned this fact later to Melik at dinner, as they sat alone at the huge, beautifully engraved dining-table, a work of art in itself with gold and silver leaf worked beautifully into exquisite patterns of Eastern splendour. The whole house was the same, vast, beautiful and terrifyingly intimidating.

'Cybiele and Kathi?' He nodded slowly. 'They are twins, I understand, but not identical. Their family was killed in the political unrest of the 1970s and my father found them through a friend who ran an orphanage in the capital when they were just three months old. Safiye and Tegrul are unable to have children and so, after a mass of red tape, the babies were brought here in 1973 to the mutual satisfaction of all concerned.'

'Why did he do that?' she asked in amazement. 'I mean, Safiye and Tegrul are just employees——'

'You do not understand.' He leant forward, his eyes intense and his body powerful in the dim light from the beautiful old oil lamps scattered strategically round the glowing room. 'Tegrul's family has always served my family; they have been loyal and faithful and trustworthy. They were my father's responsibility as they are now mine. It was right that he, as their protector, should do all in his power to bring them happiness. It is a matter of honour.'

'I see.' She was way out of her depth here, she thought helplessly. 'Do you consider all your employees your responsibility, then?'

'Here on my estate, yes.' He settled back in his chair, the big bulk of him suiting the magnificent room and sumptuous furnishings, very much the master of his own empire.

He actually *looked* like a sultan, she thought suddenly, especially in the open-necked, full-sleeved embroidered shirt he was wearing over loose white cotton trousers. The cool Western businessman had vanished as though he had been a figment of her imagination. Here he was all Turkish, dark, proud and very unapproachable, and terrifyingly attractive.

'The members of my household and those of the workers on the estate are under my protection and care,' he continued quietly, his eyes iridescent in the flickering light. 'It is my duty to watch over them, provide for their needs; it is a matter of trust. In return I expect total loyalty and unquestioning obedience.'

'You consider them your slaves?' she asked faintly as his tanned skin and black hair melted into the shadows until only the green-gold eyes seemed alive.

'My slaves?' He leant forward abruptly, bringing his face into startling vision, and she saw he was frowning, his black brows heavy over icy cold eyes. 'Are you trying to annoy me, Louisa?'

She was saved a reply by the arrival of Cybiele and Kathi with a huge loaded trolley containing a vast quantity of covered dishes which, after removing the soup dishes, they proceeded to place in the centre of the table before moving to stand quietly behind Melik's chair. 'Would you like to indicate which dishes you prefer?' he asked quietly.

'I. . .I don't know,' she answered vaguely as she glanced with something akin to horror at the massive choice.

He spoke in rapid Turkish to the two small girls and within seconds her plate was full of wonderfully aromatic food, half of which was totally new to her. It all proved delicious.

Dessert was nothing more adventurous than peeled fresh almonds mounded on a bed of ice and sliced

apricots, peaches, cherries and grapes marinated in a
light wine and served with a dash of brandy and thick
fresh cream.

'Would you care for more wine?' Melik had been the
perfect host, courteous although more than a little
distant, and now as he refilled her enormous crystal
wine glass with the light sparkling pink wine she raised
her eyes to his enquiringly.

'It's lovely, what's it called?'

'Harem.' He eyed her wickedly, his face perfectly
serious. 'I thought you would like it. I have it delivered
especially from Thrace.'

'Oh.' She smiled weakly. 'Well, it's lovely. . .'

The sultry perfumes of musk and jasmine were heavy
in the room from tiny solid blocks placed in lacy pottery
jars on the marble fireplace that ran along half the
length of one wall, the air was thick and warm and
lazy, the deceptively light wine in the enormous glasses
was making her head whirl a little, and suddenly Louisa
felt she had to escape.

'Could I. . .could I have some air?' She half rose as
she spoke. 'I feel a little faint, the long ride. . .'

'Of course.' He was at her side immediately, taking
her arm as he gestured for the maids to clear the table
as they reappeared right on cue. 'The courtyard is
through here.' He indicated the open latticed doors at
the end of the room. 'The gardens are beyond that but
I would suggest you allow me to show you those
tomorrow.'

Of course! It just had to be, didn't it? Louisa thought
with an overwhelming sense of helplessness as she
walked through the arched doorway into a beautifully
intimate little courtyard surrounded by flowering
almond trees rich with heavy, intoxicating blossom and

tiny rustling fountains sparkling magically in the moon-light—an *Arabian Nights* scene of total sensuality guaranteed to melt even the most determined female heart. Was this his *fait accompli*? The place where he brought those women who were foolish enough to resist his advances, if there were any?

'Why so tense?' His shirt had fallen open to reveal the hair-roughened, muscled flesh she had just known was beneath, and Louisa found she was quite incapable of tearing her eyes away from his body. This may be planned, she thought desperately, and it may be a practised technique, but it was a prize formula.

'I have dreamed of seeing you here.' He hadn't touched her since they had walked through the doors but every nerve in her body was as sensitised as though they had been making love for hours. 'Clothed in silk, your hair flowing free. . .'

'Whereas I'm in sensible cotton.' She forced a bright smile to her lips as she gestured at the pretty sleeveless evening dress that she had bought as a safeguard for any situation, formal or informal.

'Half of my fantasy can be realised.' He removed the clip from her hair with practised ease before she could protest. 'And incidentally I forbid you to wear these things while you are here.' He flung the slides disdain-fully to the floor. 'They displease me.'

He even sounded different, she thought despairingly, his accent so pronounced that his words seemed to flow and ebb in a soft, silky tide that was seductively rich. 'Well, I'm *so* sorry,' she began sarcastically. 'If I'd only known——'

She was enclosed in his embrace before she could finish, his lips tasting her half-open mouth as his hands ran over her bare arms, his naked chest prickly against the soft swell of her breasts in the low-cut evening dress. The smell of him encompassed her, sensual, dark and altogether satisfying. 'You're mine, you *are* mine. . .' The kisses were tender and sweet and coaxing and with a mindless groan she knew she was lost. Force she could have resisted, violence she would have fought, but this. . . This was heavenly.

His mouth moved down to her throat, kissing the pulse beating so frantically, and then further downwards, brushing her silky skin with warm, teasing kisses that brought tiny little whimpers of delight from her half-open mouth. She wanted to resist, wanted to say no, but it was so unbearably sweet. . .

'I *can* make you forget.' His voice was low and fierce with triumph as he raised his head to look into the dazed blackness of her eyes. 'Whatever has happened, however bad it may be, I can make you forget. I will brand you, brand you as mine, until the past will be a dream that no longer belongs to you and the future will have only one name — mine!'

'Melik. . .'

'You have had no past, do you understand me? I will be the first, the only one, a new beginning. I will not *allow* it to be any other way.'

Maybe it was possible, she thought dazedly, as the last weeks and months in his powerful ruthless presence took their toll. If he wanted her, really wanted *her*, the complete person he had talked about once before, perhaps they had a chance? Knowing him as she did now, having seen his energy and the vehement force of his spirit, she knew he was strong enough to lay all the ghosts that hung round her, dismissing them with the authority that was natural to him. And maybe he wouldn't reject her the way her parents had, leave her like Oliver? Maybe. . .

'I will utterly possess you.' As his lovemaking reached new heights she felt she would faint with the pleasure he was inducing. 'Everything that you are will belong to me; I will be your world as you will be mine.'

His lips left a trail of fire as they burnt over the silky skin beneath his mouth and his hands were knowing as they played over the womanly curves beneath his fingertips. 'Talk to me, Louisa, tell me I am right — that I am speaking the desires of your heart.'

The tinkling of the tiny bell at one side of the curved archway that led from the house hardly registered on her whirling senses but he raised his head at the sound, his breathing harsh and ragged as he fought for control. 'There are guests. . .' He took a few long deep breaths as he looked down into her upturned face. 'Someone has opened the front door; we must have visitors.'

'Visitors?' She was trembling but she couldn't help it; but for his arms still supporting her she would have sunk to the floor.

'Here.' He adjusted her clothing with deft, quick fingers and then pushed her gently on to a smooth curved wooden seat at the side of an enormous tub of trailing, conical-shaped flowers whose heavy, sweet fragrance was reminiscent of roses and lilac. 'I will endeavour —— '

What he would have endeavoured she would never know as at that moment Safiye appeared in the doorway after a discreet cough to announce her presence, speaking rapidly to Melik in Turkish, a few seconds before another voice, a young female voice, cut in behind her.

'*Melik*. . .' The voice was throaty and low and blatantly inviting. '*Nasilsiniz*?'

'I am fine, thank you, Lala,' Melik said smoothly. 'May I introduce Louisa? She knows only a little Turkish so if we could speak in English. . .?'

As Melik moved to one side she stood up hastily, and then wished with all her heart she had remained seated as the jolt in her stomach communicated itself to her legs. The young woman in front of her who had just slipped her hand through Melik's arm in one of those gestures that a man thought was perfectly innocent and another woman knew was a stamp of possession was quite strikingly beautiful. Tall, slim and voluptuous, she had smooth, silky brown skin exquisitely offset by heavy, shining jet-black hair that hung to her waist in sleek waves and exotic sloe eyes under beautifully shaped brows that were now raised in polite enquiry as they swept over Louisa's flushed face. Louisa felt her heart sink.

'Louisa?' Lala smiled just enough to show pearly white teeth between full, sensual lips. 'I do not think I have heard this name before?'

The request for an explanation was obvious but as Melik ignored it Louisa assumed she should. 'It's nice to meet you.' She smiled warmly. 'How do you do?'

'Louisa is staying with me for a few days,' Melik interposed smoothly as he took Louisa's arm in his and walked, still with Lala glued to his other side, under the archway and through the dining-room to the large living-room beyond. 'We are working on a project together.'

'You are?' As Lala sank down on to one of the low silk-upholstered divans that were scattered, Eastern fashion, around the carpeted floor she smiled up at

Louisa coldly. 'But how nice. You must tell me about it.'

'Lala and her parents are our nearest neighbours.' Melik walked over to the well stocked drinks cabinet on the far side of the room. 'We are old friends, are we not?'

'But of course.' The slanted eyes flashed over Melik hungrily and then turned back to Louisa, the soft brown becoming jet-hard. 'You are English, I understand? You are here for a short time only?' The full mouth was hostile and tight.

'We all have a twelve-month work permit,' Louisa said quietly, trying to curb the instinctive reaction of dislike she felt at the other girl's veiled aggressiveness. 'I leave around the middle of August next year.'

'Or not as the case may be.' Melik's voice was silky soft as he dropped his little stone into the already widening ripples. 'I know Lala will be drinking raki, a practice her parents heartily disapprove of. Louisa, you would like. . .?'

'Just a soft drink, please,' Louisa said quickly; the wine at dinner had been far too potent. 'Lemonade if you have it?' She wasn't fond of raki, a distillation of grape mash flavoured with aniseed, in spite of it being the national drink popularly known as 'lion's milk'. And Melik knew Lala's preferences, did he? She tried to control the trembling deep inside that was a combination of his lovemaking and the sudden arrival of this *femme fatale* who was clearly staking her claim.

'And Melik has brought you here for the wedding. How nice.' Whatever Lala thought about her arrival here, 'nice' in no way described it, Louisa thought painfully as she felt the full force of the ebony eyes a second before they switched to neutral. And what was this about a wedding? 'It's rather sweet, Melik, isn't it?' The beautiful face gave a practised smile that would melt the hardest male heart. 'One of your workers and one of ours meeting in the fields as they worked and love blooming among the tea terraces.'

'Quite.' Melik clearly wanted to change the subject but Lala turned to Louisa with another twist to her lips that now her face was turned away from the object of her devotion didn't even try to resemble a smile. 'And they were so charming about it all, waiting until the autumn when most of the crops have been harvested so that we could all really enjoy it. We're just one big family really, aren't we, Melik?'

And I'm the outsider—yes, I do get the picture, Louisa thought slowly, faintly amazed at the other girl's uncalled-for antagonism and her ability to project it while keeping Melik completely in the dark. Had she been involved romantically with him? Her heart thudded violently and then lurched on. *Was* she involved romantically with him? She certainly seemed to think she had some sort of proprietorial claim to him anyway. The sickening butterflies that had been fluttering madly in her stomach since the lovely Turkish girl had arrived suddenly went wild. Surely he wouldn't bring her, Louisa, here if that were the case, knowing they would be bound to meet? But then he might. She really knew nothing about him after all, and to think that a few minutes ago she had been considering. . .

'You must bring Louisa over to dinner while she is here,' Lala continued sweetly, earning a warm glance from Melik in the process which made Louisa's toes curl. 'I'm sure Mother and Father would love to meet her.'

'Thank you.' Louisa forced herself to smile as

Melik's eyes switched to her face. 'You live close by, then?'

'Close by for these parts; the estates do tend to sprawl somewhat.' Lala's voice was cultured and beautifully correct; she was obviously extremely well educated, Louisa thought miserably. 'Our respective families have been entwined for generations, haven't they, darling?' She flashed Melik a smouldering-hot smile. 'Melik grew up with my brothers; they were a dreadful pack of scoundrels.'

'Steady now, steady.' Melik laughed softly, his face more relaxed and easy than Louisa had ever seen it. 'Don't blacken my name on hearsay when I am trying to make a good impression on Louisa. You were too young to know anything about it anyway.'

Lala pouted prettily and Louisa's nostrils flared in distaste. What a coquette! But she was very good at it.

'Not that young! I am twenty-four now and perfectly grown-up but I still remember it was you who would allow me to tag along or ride with you on your horse.' Lala shifted slightly in her seat so that the tight, clinging sleeveless top she wore over baggy blue jeans moved in all the right places and the long gold hoops in her ears caught a flash of light that illuminated the golden skin. 'You've always been there for me, haven't you. . .?' She sent a long, lingering glance of complicity Melik's way.

'Well, you were a plucky little kid.' Melik smiled slowly. 'Plucky and very determined.'

She really couldn't take much more of this without being sick! Louisa moved abruptly in her seat and then gasped as ice-cold lemonade fizzed into her lap. Great! Just great.

'Oh, dear.' Lala's slanted eyes smiled in satisfaction.

'Now you will have to go and change, but do not worry, I will keep Melik occupied for you. We have loads to discuss about the wedding; Father has given me a list for you to look over,' she continued, turning to Melik as though Louisa had already left the room. 'He asked me to tell you that the priest is coming tomorrow.'

'Yes, I know.' Melik's voice was preoccupied and his gaze on Louisa as she arose, shaking her wet skirt slightly. 'I'll have another drink ready for when you return.'

'Don't bother.' He would never know the effort it cost her to force the bright, untroubled smile to her face as she gazed down at them both, Lala having moved to sit on the arm of Melik's chair under the pretence of showing him the long typewritten list, her long, silky black hair entwining itself over his arm as she bent slightly towards him. 'I'm very tired; it was a long journey; I thought I'd go straight to bed if that's all right.'

'Of course.' His voice was cool now and his eyes cold. 'I'll see you tomorrow morning, then.'

'Yes.' She increased the smile to hundred-watt proportions as she allowed her gaze to settle on Lala's smooth, feline features. 'Goodnight.' It would have been polite to add that she had been pleased to meet her but the hypocrisy was too much.

Not so for Lala, it would appear. 'Goodnight.' The brunette's smile was radiant now but the almond eyes looked straight through Louisa. 'It is so nice to have met you.'

Louisa left the room with head held high and legs steady but she paused in the massive empty hall, her gaze flickering over the huge feathery palms, exquisite vase and life-size statue of a young maiden with slim arms uplifted to her long, flowing hair in one shadowed corner. Even she could recognise that it was ancient and wildly expensive, and the whole house was full of treasures like this. It was another world of opulence and wealth beyond her wildest dreams and she had to admit that Lala, or someone like her, would fit in beautifully, whereas she. . . She caught herself sharply. She had been mad out there in the courtyard for just a few brief, crazy moments but it wouldn't happen again. She bit down on her lower lip until she could taste blood. She had burnt her fingers with this man several times now and here, in his own little empire, he would be even more dangerous, as this evening had proved. How many Lalas were there anyway?

He would be interested in nothing more lasting than a brief affair, a little entertainment; she had known it all along deep in her heart. How could she have forgotten? How could she? As she thought of their lovemaking, the caresses she had allowed. . . No, not allowed. Her mind refused to accept anything less than the bitter truth. Encouraged, wanted, enjoyed. . .

Well, never again. She nodded to herself slowly as she walked up the massive open winding staircase, which was regal and majestic in polished wood. Never again. And if she forgot, if she was so criminally foolish as to forget, the searing pain in her heart that was burning her chest would remind her.

'I will brand you, brand you as mine. . .' His words beat a rhythm in her head as she reached the lovely airy room on the second floor that was hers. Yes, he would brand her all right if she allowed it, and the brand would sear her skin, eating through her flesh day by day, week by week, until at last, when he left her, it would be a great ugly hole that would destroy her very sanity. . .

CHAPTER SEVEN

'READY?' Melik smiled at her over the traditional breakfast-table laid with white cheese, black olives, hard-boiled eggs, pots of golden honey and tubs of cherry and plum jam and huge mounds of fresh Turkish bread, still warm from the oven. 'The imam, the Muslim priest, will be leaving the bride's house soon and I would like to visit before the day begins in earnest.'

Louisa drained her small glass of tea before she answered, her face bland. She had grown to like the Turkish tea now, much lighter-coloured than the strong English brew she was used to, but when drunk neat without milk and just a little sugar to taste she had found it could be remarkably refreshing. 'I thought I came here to work while you attended to business? The first I heard of this wedding was last night when Lala——'

'I said I had business at my home and the wedding is business of a sort,' Melik said smoothly, his eyes narrowing at the look on her face. 'Obviously while I am here other business matters will crop up, as you will discover by the intrusion of that wonderful instrument the telephone.'

'But——'

'What business I choose to deal with in the confines of my own estate is not your concern, surely?' Now his eyes were ice-cold.

'Absolutely right.' She met him glare for glare. 'But

115

a wedding is a social occasion and there is no way I have to join in that, is there? So if you'll excuse me I'll work here until——'

'The hell you will.' His voice was quiet and even and controlled. 'I take it this unconcealed antagonism is my answer to the questions I proposed last night before Lala entered "where angels fear to tread"?'

'I wasn't aware of any questions and I'm sure Lala is no angel,' she said coldly, regretting the last part of the remark as soon as the words left her lips but unable to draw them back.

'You weren't aware. . .' He let his voice die away as he rose slowly, his big, lean body magnificent in black jeans that hugged his hips in a way guaranteed to make any female heart between the ages of nine and ninety beat a little faster, the black denim shirt he wore open at the neck to reveal his muscular tanned throat. 'I see. Well, you will accompany me to the wedding festival, all of it, whether you like it or not,' he said icily, his eyes flashing sparks of green fire. 'It would be considered a grave insult if you did not. And I told you I want your hair loose,' he added autocratically.

'I want it tidy.' She eyed him defiantly although her legs were trembling under the sanctuary of the table.

'This is ridiculous.' As his expression changed and a gentler look warmed his face she tensed painfully. 'I do not wish to fight with you, Louisa.'

'Then let me go back to Istanbul,' she said flatly. 'I can't see that I am needed here and——'

'Enough!' She had pushed him too far; she could see it in the way his teeth had ground together, a muscle jumping at the side of his mouth. 'You will be ready to leave in twenty minutes.'

'And my hair?' She didn't know what little devil was

goading her this morning but it had long black hair and sensual almond-shaped eyes that had been laughing at her all through the long, restless night.

'Do what you want with your hair,' he snarled softly. 'Cut it all off, shave your head if you like, I am past caring. Just be down here in twenty minutes in modest clothing with your mouth shut. Is that understood?'

'Perfectly.'

'Right.'

The village where the bride's parents' house was situated was just a few miles away, but as they travelled down the steep unmade road just opposite the huge gates to Melik's estate she began to feel as though she had stepped back in time, a feeling that was intensified as Melik's Range Rover bumped into the tiny market town.

Peasant women, dressed in brightly printed baggy trousers and cotton scarves, their weather-roughened faces bronzed and lined by constant exposure to the sun, sat squatting beside their roughly constructed stalls holding eggs, fruit, goat's cheese and a mass of assorted fresh vegetables.

A group of old men were sitting in companionable harmony in the small café whose doors were wide open, puffing contentedly on their hubble-bubble pipes as they enjoyed a game of backgammon, two young children wandered by leading an elderly sheep on a piece of string and a host of pigeons were ambling about the cobbles, pecking at this and that as their heads nodded busily. It was a scene that hadn't altered for centuries and was all the more poignant after the mad whirl of Istanbul.

'The priest will have left by now,' Melik said tightly as they drew up outside a small flat-roofed house about

which several fat and contented chickens were searching for food. 'The family expect me to come today and
they know I have a guest. You need do and say very
little except smile and nod. They speak no English.'
He glanced at her face fleetingly. 'And don't look so
nervous; they are just ordinary peasant folk, for goodness' sake, the salt of the earth. The festivities start
tomorrow.'

The tiny house was spotlessly clean and packed full
with relatives when they entered although it was
immediately clear to Louisa, in spite of her lack of
Turkish, that Melik even outshone the bride. They
seemed ridiculously pleased that he had made the effort
to visit and the women, the palms of their hands and
their fingertips reddened with henna to bring good
luck, immediately enveloped her in the inevitable
hospitality that characterised this friendly race.

It was late morning when they left and by then
Louisa was quite exhausted with smiling, the muscles
of her face aching with the effort.

'They liked you.' Melik's voice was expressionless as
the powerful engine urged the Range Rover up the
incline away from the village.

'Did they?' She felt a small glow of pleasure that
eased the ache in her heart for a few seconds. There
had been something unbearably painful in seeing him
with his own kind, assured, comfortable, totally at ease
be it in the confines of a small peasant house or in the
cut and thrust of the modern Western world in which
he normally lived. She wanted. . . She didn't know
what she wanted!

Melik was cool and aloof for the rest of the day and
evening, working alone in his study most of the afternoon after giving Louisa some data to compile into

neat notes and phone through to Mrs Jones. She felt desolate and abandoned and miserable but forced herself to work slowly, checking her work several times as her mind wandered. Dinner was a subdued affair with Melik very distant and correct and Louisa feeling as though a knife was twisting in her insides every time she glanced up and caught the hooded eyes.

The next day dawned cool but dry, a light wind lowering the temperature a good few degrees as the day progressed. They were due to join the celebrations in the afternoon and Louisa would have given the world not to go. She was still trying to think of an excuse when Melik walked through to the small room at the back of the house where she was working on some notes for Lectron.

'Ready?' He didn't smile and her stomach jolted as she glanced up. He was dressed simply but smartly in loose black cotton trousers and matching shirt, a heavy jacket in a dark jade-green causing the green flecks in his eyes to shine out with more colour than usual.

'Do you really want me to come?' she asked hesitantly as she half rose to her feet. 'I'm not being awkward,' she added hastily as his eyes frosted, 'but I don't know anyone and I shan't understand what's going on. . .'

He eyed her intently for a few long minutes and then relaxed visibly, walking across to sit on the side of the long, low desk on which she had been working, which brought his hard-muscled body within inches of her eyeline.

'Yesterday the priest came to the bride's house to perform a short ceremony that included prayer and an explanation of the marriage vows,' he said quietly, his eyes tight on hers. 'Today there are parties, a separate one for the men and another for the women, and don't worry ——' he had noticed the panic in her large brown eyes '— Safiye and her daughters will be there with you and Lala too, I should imagine.'

The thought was curiously uncomforting.

'We will dance and eat, and most of the men will imbibe vast quantities of raki that may well cause a few problems later on.' His voice was wry. 'Especially as the custom for guns to be brought out and fired at the night sky needs a steady hand and a sober mind. The bride's female relatives will wash her and dress her in veils and numerous layers of colourful cloth in time for the groom's friends to arrive at the house and ask for her hand, which is refused until a gift is given to her family. Understand so far?' She nodded slowly, her senses absorbing the intoxicatingly delicious smell of him and the way his muscled thighs stretched the black cloth over his hips.

'The groom climbs on to the roof of the house and breaks an earthenware jug which signifies the scaring away of evil spirits at such an important time. That is the point where many a bride's wedding night has had to be delayed through broken bones,' he added drily, a dark amusement in his eyes, 'and finally, flushed and excited and lovely in her wedding finery, the bride is led to her new home and the bedroom where she awaits her husband. And then —— But perhaps you can imagine from there?' he asked mockingly as she flushed a deep rich scarlet at the dark glitter in his gaze. He smiled slowly at her nod. 'You will be fine; you will enjoy it, I promise.' He reached out and stroked her cheek for a brief moment, his eyes strangely guarded. 'Safiye will take care of you until I am with you again.'

In other circumstances, in another age, that sentence

could have meant something so different, she thought shakily as she followed him out to the Range Rover slowly. But this was here and now and it meant nothing beyond the polite consideration any Turkish host would feel for a visitor in his home. And she had to master this feeling that had been growing on her lately, the longing to have someone on whom she could lean, someone to protect her, someone to show her what it really meant to be a woman, to love her — She caught herself angrily. Someone? Why lie to herself? It was Melik who haunted her dreams, but only because of this strange physical attraction they had for each other which would die the death of all such fleeting emotions. It was shallow, insubstantial, it *was*.

Amazingly, wonderfully, the next few hours proved surprisingly enjoyable. Safiye and her daughters remained glued to her side like obedient sentries, the Turkish women in the village opened up their hearts to her and made her welcome in a way that brought a lump to her throat, and the wonderful food, spread over a huge old wooden table that had been scrubbed to pristine cleanliness before being spread with a beautifully woven cloth hand-embroidered with butter-flies, flowers and woodland scenes, was incredibly good. The party was in the open air and from the sounds at the other end of the village so was the men's. The bride was beautiful, from the top of her carefully oiled hair covered with a veil and tiny tinkling coins to the bottom of her henna-covered feet, and when later they had led her to the tiny cottage she was to occupy with her new husband at the very edge of the village Louisa felt a twist to her heart that had the tears pricking at the back of her eyes. Would Melik's even-tual bride keep to the old ways?

Lala hadn't joined the party until almost the last minute just before the groom's friends came to the bride's house, and Louisa tried to push the unworthy thought aside that the beautiful Turkish girl had been waiting until the men were in evidence again before she made an appearance.

'Hello, Louisa.' The perfectly pitched voice was as cold as ice, the slanted eyes openly hostile. 'You came, then?'

'Yes.' Louisa stared at her warily, sensing that Lala wouldn't hold back on what she was clearly longing to say now that Melik wasn't present. She had also chosen an opportune moment to speak alone with Louisa without the threat of being overheard. In all the excitement of the traditional bargaining in front of them no one was listening to their conversation.

'I wondered if you would.' Lala smoothed what must have been a wildly expensive silk dress over her shapely hips. 'You are an executive in this English firm that Melik is involved with? A manager maybe?' The black eyes were tight and narrowed.

'Not exactly.' Louisa's hackles rose at the imperious tone.

'No?' Lala moved even closer until the heavy, clinging musky scent she wore seemed to permeate Louisa's skin. 'What, then?' she asked arrogantly. 'A personal assistant, secretary?'

'I'm just involved in the project,' Louisa said carefully, 'that's all.' She looked around for Safiye and her daughters but they were totally engrossed in the groom's friends' laughing chatter with the bride's parents, the rest of the men beginning to come down the main road in a noisy, shouting, dancing crowd. Damn! She didn't want an argument, however obscure, with this unpleasant, disagreeable young woman. In fact she didn't want any contact with her at all if she could help it.

'That is all?' The biting contempt in Lala's voice was too vitriolic to ignore and suddenly Louisa forgot all about appeasement as her quick temper rose to the bait. 'You think I am a foolish woman, is that it?' The slanted eyes narrowed still further into black slits. 'Well, I have, as you say, been around quite a bit and I know the score. Melik has never brought a woman to his home before; why you?'

'Why don't you ask *him*?' Louisa said coldly. 'And I don't doubt for a minute that you've done the rounds, Lala.'

'I shall ask.' Lala shook her head slightly so that the long gold earrings made up of hundreds of tiny little balls on thin gold threads jangled in the night air. 'That is *exactly* what I intend to do.' She glared at Louisa as though she hated her.

'Good.' Louisa stared at her coolly, her mouth straight. 'He'll be here shortly so if you'll excuse me. . .' She moved the few steps that brought her to Safiye's side determinedly. If Lala thought she was going to engage in a verbal cat fight she had another think coming! She wouldn't lower herself to Lala's standards.

When Melik joined them a few minutes later Lala was already clinging like a limpet to his arm where she remained with sweet-faced determination. Louisa was conscious of herself talking, laughing, behaving normally, while all the time it was as if she were a spectator watching a play, a painfully bad play. She couldn't have put a name to the feeling that was burning her up inside but she recognised anger as one of the ingredi-

ents, that and a hot cutting humiliation when she
thought of how near she had been to succumbing
completely, yielding totally to Melik's will after some
clever lovemaking that he had no doubt practised
countless times before and which clearly meant absolutely nothing to him.

'Am I being invited for a nightcap?' Lala's voice was
laughingly provocative as, the bride safely hidden away
with her new husband, the festivities began to break
up and everyone returned to his or her own home.

'Of course.' Just for a moment Louisa thought she
caught a thread of irritation in Melik's politely cool
voice but dismissed it immediately as imagination. 'Do
you have transport?'

'My jeep is parked behind the square.' The sloe eyes
fluttered as they rested on Melik's darkly bronzed face
in the dancing shadows of skittering moonlight. 'Would
you drive for me? It's so dark and it's beginning to
rain. . .'

It was. How convenient, Louisa thought caustically.
What would the excuse have been to get Melik all to
herself if the weather had stayed fine? It was too dark?
She was too tired?

'No problem; Tegrul can drive the Range Rover; it
was packed a bit tight with the six of us earlier anyway.
Louisa, you will come with us?' It was an order couched
in a question and suddenly everything in Louisa
rebelled. Did he seriously think she was going to travel
in the back of Lala's jeep, where she would undoubtedly be put like a sack of potatoes, listening to the two
of them billing and cooing while pretending to enjoy
being the proverbial green gooseberry? Well, thanks
but no, thanks! This was way beyond the call of duty.

'Don't worry.' She forced a cold smile to her face,

knowing that outright defiance in front of Lala and the Turkish villagers drifting around would cause a scene that would be embarrassing for everyone concerned. 'Safiye was in the middle of explaining a few of the meanings behind such a traditional wedding so I'll go with them. See you at the house.'

She gave Melik no time to react, walking over to Tegrul and Safiye who were standing beside the Range Rover and telling Tegrul that Melik wanted him for a moment. 'Tegrul's driving us back,' she explained shortly to Safiye. 'He needs the keys.' As she turned slightly she met an angry gold gaze for one blinding moment which she returned with scathing thoroughness before Tegrul joined them again and they climbed into the Range Rover. She didn't look back once.

On reaching the house she flew up to her room as though she had wings on her feet, locking the door hastily before running a warm shower in the *en suite* and, after discarding her clothes in a heap on the floor, stepping under the cascading flow of water with her eyes shut and her head pounding. She hated him! She really hated him. Letting Lala hang over him with such a total display of wantonness. 'Overbearing, conceited swine. . .' She stared viciously at the streaming shower door as she opened hot eyes. 'He thinks he's God's gift to womankind! Well, not *this* woman!'

She heard the banging on the bedroom door long before she stepped out of the shower but ignored it for as long as she could, and then, when she felt as though the wood was going to give way, she hastily wrapped her hair in a short hand-towel before pulling on her full-length towelling robe and knotting the belt tightly round her waist with fingers that shook.

'Yes?' Seizing a moment in between blows, she kept

her voice cold and strong with superhuman effort. 'Is there someone there?'

'Is there. . .?' She heard Melik's furiously incredulous voice die away with a fleeting stab of satisfaction. 'Open this damn door, *now*!'

'Why?' She could hear the sound of his angry panting behind the door and for a moment her heart pounded with fear.

'Louisa, I have no intention of standing here and talking through wood. Open the door.'

'No.' She heard herself defy him with mounting horror. 'I've just had a shower and I'm getting ready for bed. I've no —'

As the door burst open and Melik cannoned into the room she literally froze with fear, her eyes huge as she took in his glowering face and blazing eyes that were piercing in his rage. 'Melik —'

'Don't you "Melik" me,' he ground out savagely through clenched teeth. 'I should think everyone in this whole area, let alone my household, has heard me banging on that door.'

'Where's Lala?'

'Where the hell do you think she is?' he snarled softly. 'Downstairs waiting for you to join us for a drink.' His body was almost rigid with the control he was forcing on himself. 'I don't know what you're playing at but I want you dressed and downstairs within five seconds.'

'No.' A tiny separate piece of her mind was looking on with absolute amazement but something stronger than herself and him was driving her on. 'I'm not coming down, Melik.'

'You're not. . .' For the second time in as many minutes his voice faded away in incredulous fury, and she saw him close his eyes for a brief moment as he took a long deep breath, lowering his head before raising it again to look straight into her terrified eyes. 'Why?' It was one word but all the more frightening in the icy cold way it was delivered.

'Because I don't want to.' She would never, ever give him the satisfaction of even suspecting for a minute that she was jealous, because she wasn't, she *wasn't*.

'You don't want to,' he repeated flatly. 'I really don't believe I am having this conversation.' He raked back a lock of hair that had fallen across his brow as he had forced the door open and glared at her again, the cool, suave businessman whom she had known for so long and who was completely in control of himself and everything else having totally vanished. 'Am I permitted to know the reason for this sudden aversion to my drawing-room?' he asked scathingly.

'It's not a crime to want to go to bed, is it?' she said weakly. 'I really don't think ——'

'Louisa, no one has ever made me as angry as I feel right now,' he said slowly as his hard jawline tightened into pure granite, 'and although I'm trying, for both our sakes, to remain calm and reasonable you are making it damnably hard.' As he had been speaking the towel had begun to slide off the soft, silky curls beneath it and as it fell on to her shoulders and the mass of riotously golden hair sprung round her face his eyes darkened still further. 'Now are you going to get dressed by yourself or do I have to do it for you?'

'You just try it!' She took a step backwards, clutching the ends of the belt to her as she spoke. 'If you lay one finger on me I'll scream this place down.'

'And who do you think would come running to your

rescue?' he asked icily, his eyes flashing at her dogged rebelliousness.

'Tegrul, Safiye. . .' She raised her head proudly. 'Someone.'

'Someone.' He smiled slowly, a cruel snarl of a smile that had no amusement whatsoever in its depths. 'It would be more than their lives are worth and they know it.' He straightened, his shoulders big and broad against the dim lamp that was lighting the room and his hair as black as midnight. 'Now, Lala is waiting down there, no doubt wondering what the hell is going on, and you are going to come down and behave like a normal, well behaved young woman however difficult such an unusual piece of play-acting may be for you. Do you understand me?'

'I'm not.' She took another step backwards as she spoke, her eyes huge in the whiteness of her face. 'You can't make me.'

'Louisa, *making* you would be the least of my problems,' he said throatily. 'I haven't the faintest idea what this is all about but it stops now.'

'You're such a bully,' she whispered faintly as the realisation that he might, he just might, force her to go downstairs like a whipped puppy and face Lala for what was left of the evening dawned on her consciousness. 'I hate you, I really do.'

The flash of something—for a crazy moment she thought it was pain—that seared across his face seemed to shatter the last of his self-control. As he reached out for her she found she was frozen with fear, her mind and body numb as he lifted her up and carried her across the room to where her clothes lay scattered on the floor.

'Put them on.'

'Never.'

He threw her on to the bed with such force that she bounced upwards, the robe jerking open before she grabbed the sides in a vain attempt to cover her nakedness from his gaze.

'Damn you. . .' As he joined her on the bed she was aware of two things — his face torn with conflicting emotions of rage and desire and her own traitorous body that leapt into immediate life as he moved over her, his lips hot on her face.

'You won't be content until you break me, will you?'

It was more the passionate response of her body to his than anything that had gone before that had her fighting him like the small tigress he had accused her so often of being. She knew, if she let it, that the weakening, liquefying effect his lovemaking aroused would soon turn her body compliant and submissive beneath his, that his vastly superior experience would overcome all her resistance until she was quivering and shaking under his caresses. . .like before. *And it couldn't happen again.*

'Louisa. . .' He groaned her name against her flesh, his overwhelming hunger evident in every hard, aroused line of his body, his lips rough and demanding as they burnt over her skin like fire. And to her dismay, to her utter shame, she found that his passion was igniting a desire in her that terrified her.

She wanted him, she wanted his hands on her body, she wanted him to be the first one to possess her utterly, the only one. She wanted it because she *loved* him. The thought froze her beneath him but, caught up in his own need, he didn't notice for a moment. That was why the sight of Lala touching him, holding him, inviting him to take her with every glance, every movement, had hurt so badly. It wasn't physical desire only that had bonded her to this man from the first moment she had laid eyes on him. There had been something, even then, that had reached far beyond the mere outward form.

And the other women. . .that he had had in the past, that he *would have* in the future. . .that was what had been eating her up for the last few weeks until she had turned into a creature she hardly recognised. And there was nothing she could do about it, nothing at all, because the bottom line was that he didn't want her, not all of her, not in the way she cared for him. That was one thing she *had* known all along. The years of being alone, of childhood rejection and betrayal, had prepared her for that knowledge at least.

As the tears seeped hot and fierce beneath her closed eyelids she felt his body stiffen, his hands and mouth still for a long moment before he moved off her in one swift movement.

'Louisa?' She felt he was standing by the bed but couldn't open her eyes, couldn't move. 'Don't cry.' He said something harsh and violent under his breath in his own language, his voice strained and tight as he drove his fist into his hand.

And then he was gone, the door shutting behind him with a softness that was deafening. And she was alone. More alone than she had ever been in her life.

movement had but slowly......
only ....
....
.... thoughts ....

CHAPTER EIGHT

'LOUISA?' She had crawled into bed after he had gone, burying down into the covers like a small animal trying to hide, lying in still misery for long, painful minutes, but now the voice outside the door had her jolting bolt upright, her hands across her mouth.

'I have sent Lala home but I must talk with you. You have my word that I will not touch you.' The hard male voice faltered and then continued. 'You have nothing to fear, I promise you.'

She sat frozen and breathless before answering, her mind stunned. 'Come in.'

He didn't turn on the light, for which she was thankful, moving across to the side of the bed slowly in the muted darkness. 'There is nothing I can say to absolve my actions of their outrage, nothing at all, and to ask you to forgive such a betrayal of hospitality would be the final insult.' She listened to his voice, cold and steady now, with a faint feeling of disbelief. Was that all he was concerned about? That he had in some way offended one of the many social laws in which this country was steeped?

'I need to be here for a few days and I also need you to deal with the business side of things with Lectron. If you feel that you cannot stay, that you want to return immediately to Istanbul, it can be arranged.' She bit her lip tightly in the darkness. He was so cold, so remote. 'The decision must be yours. All I can say is that if you decide to stay such an occurrence will not

happen again. On that you have my word. Think it
over and let me have your decision in the morning,
unless you are decided now?'

The air was heavy and silent for a few moments and
then she forced herself to speak, her voice amazingly
normal in view of the churning inside. 'I'll see you in
the morning.'

'Very well.' There was another tense silence, as
though he wanted to say more, and then she heard him
moving across the room and the door snapped quietly
into place. He had only been visible as a big dark
shadow but even so, in spite of being unable to see the
expression on his face, she had longed to reach out to
him. She was weak. The thought stung a little but not
enough to hurt. All her senses, all her emotions were
tied up in the devastating fact she had just learnt about
herself. She loved him. He was the last man on earth
she would have chosen to love but choice had got very
little to do with it. It was crazy, emotional suicide, but
she knew as the long, sleepless night dragged on that
she would walk through live coals if it could make him
feel even a fraction of what she felt for him.

When the first cold light of day began to filter into
her room it was to the accompaniment of hard, driving
rain against the window, which in a strange way was
more comforting than sunshine. She padded across to
the large full-length window and pulled aside the soft,
filmy curtains and wooden shutters to peer out into the
grey sky. It was almost torrential, the stone floor of the
balcony an inch deep and the bedraggled pots of plants
looking as though they would be swept away any
moment.

What was she going to say to him? As the pale pearly
light washed over her strained face and tangled hair

she shook herself irritably, her expression one of bitter self-contempt. She *knew* what she was going to say to him; she had known it since the last visit to her room when he had given her a way of staying on here with him without losing face. It was madness, the worst form of self-torture, but. . .she wanted to be near to him even if it was unbearably painful. She leant her forehead against the cold, hard glass. The affection and warm gratitude she had felt for Oliver was nothing like this agonisingly fierce emotion that was making her feel physically ill. Suddenly the knowledge didn't seem like a betrayal to his memory any more. She had loved him in a brotherly, gentle way, a comfortable, almost sexless affection perhaps, but she *had* still loved him and he had been content with that. If she had married him their life together would have been one of nine-to-five routine with maybe cocoa and a good book at night and the traditional two point four children in due course. And she would have been content. Not exactly happy, not fulfilled, but content.

And Melik? Her heart pounded into her throat. It was crazy even to consider what it would be like if he loved her, because he never would, but life with him would be. . .paradise. Paradise and hell. Paradise when he was with her, loving her, reassuring her, and hell when he was away. Because he wouldn't lie. She knew that. If he had other women she would either have to leave or look the other way and either choice would be impossible, loving him as she did. So it was better he didn't love her. The ethereal reflection in the glass mocked her. *It was, it was.*

'Louisa?' He rose swiftly as she walked into the breakfast-room two hours later, outwardly perfectly composed if a little white but inwardly in such turmoil that the sight of him nearly caused her to break down. The memories were so vivid, so strong, she could still feel the taste of him as he had held her in his arms. . .

'I want to say something and then it's over.' She stood in front of her chair and looked straight into the hard, tawny eyes, noticing as she did so that his face was a little grey, his mouth strained.

'Over?' For a moment she thought he had gone a shade paler but it was the strange half-light from the appalling weather outside as the wind drove the splintering needles of rain with such force against the windows that they shook.

'Yes, over, I don't want it mentioned again.' She stared at him steadily, the effort it took making her legs tremble. 'Last night was a mistake, on both our parts.' She took a deep breath as his face remained curiously still. 'When I looked back over it all I realised I might have been a bit unreasonable — ' She held up her hand as he went to speak. 'No, let me finish, please. We were both tired, overwrought, and it was a one-off. Yes?'

'Louisa — '

'And the only way I can stay here and finish the job you've asked me to do is to pretend it never happened, to go back twenty-four hours if you like.'

'Pretend it never happened?' There was a muscle working in his jaw that spoke volumes. 'You think I can pretend it never happened? That I didn't hold you in my arms, kiss — ?'

'It's either that or I leave today.' The silence went on and on, but she couldn't, she just couldn't have a post-mortem on all the buts and wherefores when her heart was so raw and this new knowledge still had the power to terrify her half to death. 'I don't blame you,

I don't blame myself; it was just one of those things but I want to wipe it out of my memory.'

'I see.' He had the look of a man who had been punched hard in the stomach. 'I frightened you that badly? You found my touch so repugnant?'

There was nothing she could say without making a fool of herself and bursting into tears, and after a pregnant silence broken only by the hurtling raindrops he nodded slowly, his eyes bleak. 'So be it. We will continue as before. I have a pile of papers waiting for my attention so if you'll excuse me. . .?' And he left abruptly, his shoulders tight and his head facing straight ahead.

Twenty-four hours later a minor catastrophe occurred with the English side of the partnership which demanded long hours, countless phone calls and major restructuring with one of the components, but amazingly, at the end of four days of working almost sixteen hours a day, Louisa found their relationship, at least on a superficial level, was healed. They were able to talk comfortably, smile, and even exchange a wry comment or two, although she felt, at least, that the undercurrents were fiercely tense.

She was still thinking along these lines on the evening of the fifth day when Melik appeared in the doorway of her small room, strewn with papers, and smiled lazily as he glanced round at the disarray. 'You were such a tidy little thing when I first took you on,' he said ruefully as the tawny gaze swept over a heap of reports spread across the spare desk in flowing disorder. 'I'm a bad influence, am I not?'

You just don't know, she thought painfully with dark humour as she smiled brightly, her voice light. 'Not at all.'

'I think so.' He paused, and as she still looked up at him spoke a little abruptly. 'There is a dancer I would like you to see at a little restaurant I know, a rather special place.'

'I don't think ——'

'She rarely dances now,' he continued as though she hadn't interrupted, 'but when she does it is quite magical. She is an old friend and knows I am here for a few days. It would be impolite not to go.'

'I see.' Her pulses had leapt into crazy life at this, their first conversation for days about anything other than work, and every treacherous bone in her body was reaching out to the chance of being with him even though she would regret it, perhaps bitterly. But she had the rest of her life to dwell on such things and more and more, as the hours and days had gone by, she had begun to wonder if maybe, somehow, she had misunderstood about Lala, maybe projected her own doubts and fears into a situation that was quite inno-cent, at least on Melik's part. She had never felt so miserable and confused in all her life, one minute firmly convinced that all was deep blackness and the next sensing a little chink of light at the end of the tunnel.

She had done some hard thinking, faced some tough issues over the last few lonely nights as she'd lain sleepless and heartsore in her bed, and slowly, reluc-tantly, had come to the conclusion that she had never given him the chance to show her what he was really like; she had been too busy holding him firmly at arm's length. Dared she *take* a chance?

'I've arranged for my plane to pick us up at seven o'clock,' he continued expressionlessly. 'Is that enough time for you to get ready?'

'I haven't said I'll come yet!' All the finer feelings and tender heart-searchings fled in the face of his presumption. 'I thought we'd——'

'And it will be evening dress.' She opened her mouth to argue further but something in the warm, smoky gaze stopped her. He was looking at her in a way he hadn't done for days and it stopped her heart beating. 'Now you have precisely. . .' he checked the gold watch on his wrist with casual authority '. . .an hour and twenty minutes to get ready. OK?'

It wasn't but she nodded anyway.

Exactly one hour and nineteen minutes later she took one last long look in the full-length mirror in critical appraisal, seeing only the beautiful close-fitting and low-cut evening dress in dark jade silk that had cost her a month's salary some time ago, the small dark green studs in her ears of exactly the same hue and the carefully upswept hair that she had allowed to fall in tiny tendrils round her neck and face. The huge, heavily lashed velvet brown eyes, tiny straight nose and wide, full lips she glanced over in perfunctory indifference; her beauty had never brought her happiness and she had learnt long ago to place no value on its superficial appeal.

A minute later as she walked down the long, winding staircase and Melik moved out to watch her, his golden eyes stunned with appreciation, she felt, for the first time in her life, a faint stirring of pleasure that she wasn't ugly.

'You look very lovely.' His voice was low and soft and tender and her nerves curled with delight as he reached out a hand and touched the nape of her neck where a small cluster of golden curls gleamed in the light. 'Do I take it that this is some sort of compromise?' he asked mockingly as he allowed a tiny ringlet to trail over his bronzed finger. 'A halfway house?'

'If you like.' She smiled lightly.

'Oh, I do like,' he said lazily, his eyes glittering hotly. 'I like very much indeed.'

So did she but she wasn't going to tell him that, she thought faintly, as the sight of the big, lean body in full evening dress did crazy things to her equilibrium. He looked very big and very dark and strangely, in spite of the traditional dress, more savage and untamed than she had ever seen him. The powerful set of his shoulders, the long, muscled legs and wide, strong chest were all magnificently accentuated by the austere dark suit and snow-white shirt, and the quiver that began in her lower stomach moved swiftly to the rest of her body.

'Shall we?' As he took her arm she almost jerked away, every nerve so sensitised that even the casual hand on her elbow sent ripples down her back, but she controlled the gesture just in time, smiling coolly and stopping to pull on the light wool coat she had over her arm.

'I don't think so.' He took the coat from her hands and slung it on a nearby table, his eyes bright and glittering. 'Here.'

She had noticed the large package at one side of the stairs but had thought little of it, but now, as he handed her the parcel, she raised enquiring, apprehensive eyes to his. 'What is it?'

'I can assure you it will not bite so you can open it without fear,' he said drily as she held the gift almost at arm's length. His eyes softened as she still stared at him warily. 'You are as refreshing as a sea breeze, my little tigress,' he drawled slowly after a long moment

had lingered on the air. 'Most women of my acquaintance would have had that parcel unwrapped in two
seconds flat with a pretty thank-you and a hope for
more.'

'Would they?' Although the words had been faintly
mocking there had been something in the stunningly
handsome face that had told her he was not displeased.

As she tore the layers of tissue and the soft, silky
peach material draped itself over her arms she looked
up quickly, her cheeks scarlet. 'It's the shawl.'

'Indeed it is.' He was watching her carefully, his
proud, intelligent face expressionless. 'And if it
interests you at all I have never had to wait so long and
with such fear and trepidation to give a woman a gift
before.' He took the rich, glowing material from her
hands as she stood silent and still in front of him and
draped it carefully around her shoulders, his touch
sensual and warm.

'It's beautiful, Melik, and it's not that I'm unappre-
ciative——'

He turned her round, placing a finger on her lips as
he directed the full power of his golden gaze on her
face. 'I did not think that for a moment,' he said softly.
'I know exactly what you are, my English rose — warm,
lovely, fierce, proud, sensitive. I have said before, you
are Turkish under that white skin and golden hair. I
just have to find the key to unlock the door that you
have closed so tightly but in this I am learning patience.
It is not a lesson that comes easy but I am learning it. I
will not frighten you again.'

'You didn't——' She stopped abruptly, her head
whirling as he placed his lips on hers for a fleeting
moment, his mouth warm and firm.

'I am tenacious, Louisa, tenacious and very stubborn, but I do not consider these faults.' His eyes glowed in the darkness of his skin. 'I hold fast to what is mine and I take what I want as long as it does not belong to someone else.'

The Mercedes was waiting as they walked out into the cold, clear air, the storms of the previous days having cleared the last remnants of summer from the atmosphere and replaced it with a crispness that was invigorating and clean.

'Osman will drive us to my airfield where the plane is waiting.' His voice was as cool and as matter-of-fact as if he had just announced that they were popping across to the local supermarket for a basket of provisions. As he helped her into the car and the chauffeur shut the door, his face as impassive as always, Melik reached out and took her hand in his, tracing a circle in one soft palm as he looked deep into her eyes. 'You look breathtakingly beautiful and I am proud to be your escort,' he said softly, his accent very pronounced. 'Enjoy this evening, Louisa; it is my wish that you do so.'

'Thank you. . .' It didn't seem real; none of it seemed real — the short drive to a huge cleared area of land where Melik's small light plane was housed, and then, with Osman at the controls, the brief flight across dark wooded country, the sky a dark midnight-blue blanket wrapped around them and the moon a bright silver ball in the heavens. She tried to concentrate, to take in what was happening, but with Melik warm and solid at her side and his masculine scent of musk on hard male skin it was nearly impossible.

They arrived at a massive, brightly lit enclosure surrounded by a row of tiny blinking lights where a car was waiting to whisk them to the restaurant and as she

settled into the back of the stately Bentley she felt
utterly bemused at the effortless power of such wealth.
It all happened so easily, everything like clockwork,
and he had been used to this all his life. She darted a
quick glance at his dark face under her eyelashes.
When money was no object the impossible became
effortlessly simple, the unattainable child's play. It was
all so smooth and straightforward for him and if it
wasn't he threw some money into the system and it
became so. Was that why he had decided he wanted
her? She shifted slightly in her seat as she stared out
into the dark night. Because he was being thwarted of
a possession for once in his life and the challenge
appealed? No. She gave her head a mental shake. That
would suggest he was petulant, childish, and there was
nothing small in this man's make-up. She had to believe
that, needed to.

'There it is, the House of the Crescent Moon.' They
had driven along a tree-lined avenue for some distance
and now the lights that had been in the distance
materialised into a huge, fairy-castle type structure of
mellow old stone and tall turrets and pillars. The
floodlit courtyard filled with expensive cars was surrounded by tiny sparkling fountains with a mass of dark
green vegetation beyond in the shadowed darkness that
wafted exotic scents into the cool night.

'It's gorgeous.' Louisa looked up at Melik to see the
tawny eyes were fixed tight on her face. 'It doesn't look
real.'

'Oh, it's real,' he assured her softly. 'The story goes
that it was a Genoese fortress fallen sadly into a state
of disrepair before the family who owned it, a wealthy
Turkish businessman who lived in Istanbul and his
seven daughters, decided to transform it into an exclu-

sive hotel and move here. They have the occasional
floor show but only the very best is allowed; their
reputation is of the highest calibre.'

The huge, high-ceilinged room that they were ushered into after stepping through the massive nail-
studded arched doors into a gracious lobby was spec-
tacularly beautiful, and as they were shown to their
candlelit table she saw that the discreetly scattered
tables and chairs were grouped round a large, slightly
raised platform on which a group of musicians with
long black hair and brilliantly coloured flowing robes
were playing soft Eastern music under the subdued
glow of the spotlights.

As they were seated Melik spoke in rapid Turkish to
the waiter hovering deferentially at his elbow, who
immediately disappeared into the semi-gloom with a
smile and a nod. 'A bottle of champagne while we
decide what to eat,' Melik explained in answer to her
raised eyebrows, handing her the elaborate menu and
settling back in his seat comfortably.

The waiter returned almost immediately with a bottle
of vintage champagne in an ice-bucket and a big smile.
Bollinger. No wonder he was smiling. This evening
must be costing Melik a small fortune. Was this the
final assault on her defences? An attack to storm the
bastion of her heart with no holds barred and using
every weapon at his disposal — and he had a few. . .

She pushed the unworthy and disturbing thoughts
aside and sipped the ice-cold champagne that tasted of
every fragrant summer she had known. 'It's delicious.'
She smiled carefully. And if this was the grand seduction scene? Would she mind? A few days ago she
would have been so sure of her answer but now. . .
Now she wasn't sure of anything.

As she glanced round the room she saw that the clientele matched the décor — rich, elegant and very, very exclusive.

'Would you like me to order?' The menu had been in Turkish, French and English but she had found the English as indecipherable as the other languages.

'Yes, please.' She raised grateful eyes to his face.

'How about *Mantarli borek* for starters?' he asked quietly. 'It's a little pie of flaky pastry stuffed with mushrooms and cheese.'

'That sounds lovely.'

It was, and when washed down with the clean, fragrant wine doubly so. The grilled swordfish steaks accompanied by a spicy salad and savoury rice were equally delicious.

'The rich resources of the Black Sea yield a tasty bounty, do they not?' Melik smiled warmly and as she went to reply, her eyes sparkling with the pleasure his company and the good food had induced, Louisa saw his face freeze with disbelief as he glanced over her shoulder.

'*Hayir*, I do not believe it.'

'What's wrong?'

As she half turned and met Lala's cool, slanted gaze from the table across the other side of the large room her own face froze. Lala? The subdued lighting made it difficult to be sure. Melik lifted a hand in brief salute to which Lala replied with a bright little smile and wave. 'What a coincidence.' He turned back to Louisa with a slow shake of his head and she took a grain of comfort from the fact that he didn't look overly delighted to see the luscious brunette. 'This place is not usually so crowded.' The joke fell flat as she stared at him in amazement. He didn't really believe it *was* a coincidence, did he? Here they were in the middle of nowhere, at the sort of place that she would imagine it wouldn't be untoward to see dukes and duchesses, and lo and behold there was little Lala sitting comfortably in the corner like a big black spider. And she had noticed the wary narrowing of the beautiful eyes when she had first turned round and then the quick flash of relief that had shimmered across Lala's face when Melik had acknowledged her. Somehow she had found out they were going to be here tonight and with all her will-power and considerable wealth behind her the lovely brunette had decided they would not be alone.

'Did Safiye book the table?' Louisa asked quietly as Melik refilled their glasses with the sparkling liquid.

'Yes.' He glanced at her in surprise. 'Why do you ask?'

So that was it. She had heard Safiye talking to Lala on the phone that morning and had assumed the Turkish woman had phoned regarding estate business as she did occasionally, the two plantations being side by side, but although that might have been the excuse she would bet her bottom dollar that Lala had been checking up on Melik, knowing Louisa was still in residence.

Louisa shrugged gracefully. It was no use suggesting that Lala had engineered this episode on purpose. She would deny it and Melik would believe the Turkish girl; he had known her all his life after all. But why did men have to be so *blind*? 'No reason.'

As she expected Lala took about thirty seconds to make her way over to their table, her long, slim body encased in a dress of black silk that was remarkable for the lack of material holding it together, the plunging, strapless top, cut-away sides and huge slits either side of the pencil-slim skirt making her olive skin gleam and shine with sleek sinuousness as she weaved to their side.

'How amazing. . .' She stood just to one side of Melik who had risen at her approach, the slanted black eyes opened wide in surprised innocence and her long neck graceful and poised and seeming almost too slender for the weight of hair that was coiled in a gleaming mass on top of her head and threaded with tiny silver pearls. 'I just couldn't believe my eyes a moment ago. . .' She put a hand to her hair in a feminine little gesture that accentuated the silky swell of her breasts in the low-cut dress, and raised her eyes to Melik beseechingly. 'You must come and join us; it's Father's birthday next week and this is my surprise to him and Mother, a spur-of-the-moment thing.'

Surprise, surprise, Louisa thought balefully. How transparent, how utterly transparent.

'Perhaps later.' Melik smiled down at her indulgently and Louisa felt such a hot stab of undiluted anger that it surprised her into keeping silent.

'Please do.' Lala put the tips of her fingers on his arm, her hand tiny against his muscled bulk and a diamond bracelet that would have paid Louisa's salary for a year flashing on her slim wrist. 'Mother and Father would love it and they haven't met Louisa yet.' She flashed a hard smile at Louisa as she spoke. 'And I suppose you'll be leaving us soon?' It was said with such gentleness, such sweetness, that for a second the only emotion Louisa felt was one of sickness at such hypocrisy, and then she found the strength from somewhere to look the other girl straight in the face, their eyes meeting and locking in a tight scrutiny that was all the more deadly for its silence.

'What makes you suppose that?' Louisa forced herself to smile lightly and take a sip of wine before she continued, pleased to see that her hands were perfectly steady as they held the fine crystal goblet. 'I don't think anything is certain and life has a way of surprising us, doesn't it?'

As she finished speaking there was an announcement in Turkish by one of the musicians and even before he had finished a low ripple of excitement drifted from table to table. 'I will see you later, then?' Lala brought her other hand up to Melik's hard face in a fleeting caress before she left, her rapier-sharp gaze cutting into Louisa one last time as she glided away, the dark eyes malevolent and alive with bitter resentment. It was out-and-out war now, Louisa acknowledged flatly. Well, so be it.

Immediately after the musician had finished speaking a low throbbing had begun to vibrate round the room, and as the spotlight died she noticed several of the men were extinguishing the candles on their tables until soon the whole room was steeped in a velvet blackness, the only thin ray of light filtering from one dusky red lamp over the middle of the stage. The throbbing became louder and although the musicians couldn't be seen she felt as though they were one with their music as they called forth an almost unbearably poignant sound, no one instrument dominating another but flute, drum, zither and pipe combining in an Eastern melody that pulsed electrifyingly round the darkened room.

Lala's spite, the whole difficult situation, suddenly faded away like the extinguished candles and Louisa found she was leaning forward in quivering excitement, her eyes glued to the tiny red glow and her whole body tensed and expectant. The rhythm dipped and swayed, taking the listeners with it, and then as in one flash the light was gone in another it was brighter than before and this time a woman stood in its full glare, her arms raised and her head thrown back, exposing the taut line of her throat and the mass of burnished bronze hair that hung in abandonment almost to her hips.

As she began to move, slowly and with a fluid grace that made her more animal than human, the music almost seemed to be talking to her, leading her into sensual paths of desire that turned her limbs boneless and heightened the impression of a sleek, voluptuous cat, a beautiful golden creature of the night. The thin silk that just covered her breasts crept over her rounded shoulders and down her arms, stopping at her wrists to leave her slim, fine-boned hands free, and her lower body was a mass of weaving, transparent golden veils which she gradually discarded, one by one, until her long legs could be seen in all their pulsing perfection.

She was incredibly supple, moving every muscle, every piece of her flesh in dreamy harmony with the music that gradually began to quicken, to become more urgent. The full, rounded body was plump by Western standards but so liquid, so shockingly erotic, that it was almost painful to watch her.

'Do you understand the story her movements are portraying?' Melik whispered softly by her side, his voice husky and low.

'I think so.' She tore her eyes away from the dancer and turned to him, her pulses racing.

'It is a search for love, for fulfilment.' As she turned back to the writhing figure in the golden light she could feel his eyes burning into her face in the darkness. 'An abandoning of self and reaching out to all that beckons, all that entices. . .'

The music had become more intense now, almost savage, tempting the fluid body on and on as she swayed her hips in an unmistakably sensual invitation that caused the tiny golden coins and tassels edging the diaphanous silk to glitter and dance in the fierce light, all the more intense for the blackness surrounding it.

As the sinuous figure coiled its way among the tables on the other side of the room the spotlight followed her, and Louisa was shocked to see most of the men tucking banknotes into the full cleavage and down into the rounded hips.

'Melik?' Her eyes were wide as she turned back to him. 'What are they doing?'

'It's just the Turkish way of showing appreciation,' he whispered seriously, his straight face belying the leaping amusement in his eyes. 'It's quite in order, I assure you.'

'It is?'

The dancer came nearer and nearer, the music following her in a passionate throbbing that had Louisa feeling quite faint. It was so primitive, so unashamed that all the normal conceptions of what was acceptable seemed totally out of place.

There was a fascination in the dancer's gleaming body, almost an innocence at the total satisfaction with her own sexuality, that was more evocative than any-thing Louisa had seen before.

She didn't pause at their table although as she passed the heavily made-up eyes smiled at Melik and as Louisa turned to look at him she saw him nod slowly, his eyes tender and his mouth curved in an appreciative smile.

And then, as the music reached an unbearable

crescendo that caused the instruments to wail and strain, the dancer froze in the same position in which she had started, her arms uplifted and open now in an attitude of complete surrender and her face alive with the joy of giving, and a second later the stage was plunged into blackness and the spotlight died.

The darkness, the total silence, was breathtakingly shocking after the intensity of emotion and whirling colour that had gone before, and Louisa felt herself sinking back into her seat with her mind spinning and her senses only half in the real world. The floor show had been more than just a dance, more than a spectacle for culture-starved businessmen and their wives; it had been an insidious persuasion to abandonment, to fleshly love. And Melik had known what it would be like. . .*He had known.*

CHAPTER NINE

THE rest of the entertainment — a snake-charmer complete with deadly-eyed cobras, two young and scantily dressed women who proved to be the most amazing acrobats Louisa had ever seen, contorting their lithe figures into impossible positions, and a soulful-eyed guitarist with a beard and long plaited hair — although excellent, were a definite anticlimax. Added to which with all the candles re-lighted and the stage lit up like a Christmas tree Louisa was painfully conscious of Lala's tight scrutiny from the other side of the room, and it had the effect of making her flesh creep.

'You enjoyed Casia?' Melik asked as the snake-charmer's wailing tune caused one of the cobras to rear out of its basket. 'She is seductive, is she not?'

'Very.' Louisa looked at him carefully. 'How do you know her?'

'I am an old friend of her husband.' It wasn't the reply she was expecting and she gaped at him for a moment in surprise before shutting her mouth with a little snap.

He laughed softly, his eyes mocking and bright. 'I am sorry to disappoint this fertile imagination of yours; no doubt you had the lady designated as one of my many mistresses?'

It was exactly what she had done but she didn't intend to give him the satisfaction of either denying or confirming his suspicions.

'Doesn't he mind her. . .dancing like that?' There

150

was no censure in her voice, just pure amazement that a Turk, jealous and fiercely proud as a friend of Melik's was bound to be, would allow his wife to enact such an intimate, sensual and suggestive performance that could not fail to raise the temperature of any normal man between the ages of puberty and death.

'He doesn't know.' Melik's voice was soft and even. 'He died when they had only been married three years, leaving her with three children under the age of two — a boy of eighteen months and twin girls who were only a week old when their father was killed in a stupid accident that shouldn't have happened.'

'Oh, Melik. . .' She stared at him aghast, aware from the pain in his voice and the stiffness of his features that his friend's death was still hurting.

'It was an automobile accident,' he continued quietly. 'Just one of those things. I offered to help Casia financially, in fact several people did, but she chose to support herself and her children in the way you have seen her do tonight.

'Now Satuk junior has just passed for university and his sisters are determined to follow him shortly.'

'University?' Her eyes opened wider. The dancer had not looked a day over twenty-one. 'How old is Casia?'

'Not quite the question a lady should ask, but she is thirty-eight; amazing, isn't it?'

'And how!' Louisa breathed. 'And she hasn't married again, got involved with anyone?'

'Not really.' Melik's eyes were quite still now as he held her gaze. 'She loved him, you see, *really* loved him, as he did her. She knows that that sort of emotion only happens once and why should she settle for second best just to make life easier?'

'Do *you* believe that — I mean about it only happening once?' She found she was holding her breath as she waited for his reply.

'I used to believe it probably didn't happen at all until something happened to change my mind,' he said slowly, his eyes locked on her face in such a way that he seemed quite oblivious to his surroundings. 'And then, for the first time, I could understand Casia and her preference for a memory to an inferior replacement.'

'What happened?' she asked breathlessly. 'What changed your mind?' The world stopped, her heart stopped as she waited for his reply.

'Melik, and this must be Louisa? Lala has told us of your visit.' The deep gruff voice at their side brought their heads swivelling round as though they were one to see Lala's father standing in benign contemplation by their table. 'She insists we have been most remiss in not having you for dinner,' he continued heartily as Melik's eyes froze him to the spot, 'and won't rest now until you come over and have a glass of wine with us.'

Louisa raised her eyes past the portly figure of Lala's father to Lala herself, still sitting across the room, and just for a moment, as their eyes met, she saw concentrated poison oozing out of the sloe eyes with such malevolence that it turned her blood to water.

The rest of the evening was stone-cold misery. Somehow, when they joined Lala and her parents, the Turkish girl contrived to seat Melik at her side with Louisa placed firmly in between the aged parents who kept her busy in conversation the whole night, albeit innocently, leaving Melik to Lala's tender devices. And the devices were *very* tender. By the time Melik asked Louisa to dance when the last note of the solemn-faced guitarist had died away and the small stage had been cleared, she could have hit him. Couldn't he *see* what Lala was doing? Was he blind to the fact that she was positively devouring him with her eyes, her constant touching, or did he like it? The thought was painful. Two women interested in him and clearly at odds — did that give his male ego some sort of super-boost? He'd been playing with her. All along he'd been playing with her.

She was stiff and icy-faced in his arms, excusing herself immediately the music ended and making her way to the small cloakroom in the lobby on legs that were controlled by sheer will-power. It was with a feeling of inevitable doom that she saw Lala's small cat-like face in the mirror behind her a few seconds later.

'You are enjoying your stay in Melik's beautiful home?' Lala sat down on the tiny upholstered stool next to hers and fiddled with her immaculate hair with long, red-tipped talons.

Louisa took a long deep breath. What now? This clearly wasn't going to be a sociable little chat. 'Yes, thank you.' She continued renewing her lipstick as she had been doing when Lala entered.

'Yes, he is a good. . .host.' Lala slanted her gaze at Louisa's stiff profile. 'But then he is good at many things, is he not?' She stroked a hand down her arm dreamily. 'So many things. . .'

'If you have got something to say, Lala, say it.' Louisa swung round on her seat, her eyes blazing and her face white.

'Me?' Lala opened her eyes as wide as they would go. 'But I am making the conversation, Louisa, as my finishing school taught me. We were instructed to be gracious to those less socially acceptable than ourselves.'

'Were you?' Louisa's lip curled back in distaste as she looked down into the spoilt, cruel, beautiful face below her, and she stood up abruptly. 'It was most fortunate you were not instructed to keep silent in the presence of those who were better people than yourself or you would have lost the use of your tongue within months, wouldn't you?' Her eyes were withering as they swept over the other girl's face. 'You are without doubt, Lala, one of the most unpleasant, pathetic females I know, and undoubtedly rotten to the core.'

'You dare to talk to me like this?' Lala had sprung up as though there were springs on her feet, her high cheekbones scarlet with outrage.

'But of course,' Louisa said icily, her eyes dark with contempt. 'I was making the conversation, Lala, as *my* finishing school taught me, the finishing school of life. It taught me that people like you are ten-a-penny and just as cheap. You are worthless, quite, quite worthless.'

She was just opening the door into the lobby when the other girl's voice made her freeze for a split-second as it hissed into the stark silence left by her words. 'And you think you are so clever, that you are the one? When you lie in his arms at night and breathe in his body you think that it will last? That you can satisfy a man like him with your milk-white skin and your pale, cold heart? Well, he is mine, do you hear that? What we have shared, what we *will* share when he is tired of you and you have been sent away to your cold land across the seas, is beyond anything you could know. I tell you ——'

Louisa walked through the door and let it swing shut

on the viciously vindictive tirade but as she walked back to Melik and the others she felt physically ill. He had slept with her, *obviously* he had slept with her, and Lala, at least, was convinced it was not over. She hated him. Oh, she did.

'Louisa?' Melik rose immediately she reached the table, his eyes concerned. 'What is it? You are not well?'

'No, I'm not, I'm sorry. . .' She turned to Lala's parents with a wan smile. 'I seem to have developed the most dreadful headache. . .'

'It's the lights.' Lala's father touched her arm sympathetically. 'All this flashing and goodness knows what.'

'We will go.' Melik made their goodbyes swiftly and within minutes they were outside in the fresh, crisp air, mercifully without seeing Lala again. 'You need medication?' He looked at her anxiously. 'Shall I get —— ?'

'I just want to be left alone.' Her control suddenly snapped and she glared at him furiously, the hot tears pricking at the back of her eyes in stark contrast to her angry face. 'Especially by you! You never leave me *alone*.'

'I apologise.' He had turned white at the attack, his hand dropping like a stone from her arm.

The journey home was a nightmare she thought would never end. Lala's poison had got into her veins and her very bones throbbed with the words she was desperately trying to shut out of her consciousness, added to which the look on Melik's face, as they had got into the car outside the hotel, had cut her to the quick, leaving a big raw wound that was slowly seeping blood.

But it couldn't be real, could it? There was Lala and

goodness knew how many others; that expression of
stunned hurt and pain—it wasn't real, was it? *Was it?*
Oh, how would she know? She didn't know anything
any more and she loved him too much, hated him too
much, to try and make sense of it all.

Once back in her room she lay in numb misery all
night, drifting off to sleep as dawn touched the night
sky and the first birds began to call tentatively into the
still, clear air. By the time she had showered and
ventured downstairs later in the morning Melik was
already working in his study with the door firmly shut
and a pile of papers had been placed on the desk in her
room with written instructions in his clear, flowing
hand as to how he expected her to deal with them.
And so the pattern for the next few days was set. Work
all day, dinner at night with the atmosphere so thick it
was suffocating, and then a long, endless night of
tossing and turning in between cat-naps.

She bitterly regretted her words to him outside the
restaurant now but there was no way she could undo
the damage they had caused. Too late she realised she
had played right into Lala's manipulative little hands.
He was furious with her for what he considered
unreasonable and unexplainable behaviour and he had
had enough. That much was clear. No doubt Lala
would be quick to provide comfort. The thought made
her grind her teeth in impotent rage at her mishandling
of the whole miserable episode. Why did I let Lala get
to me? she asked herself flatly on the morning of the
seventh day as she sat gazing out of her bedroom
window before going downstairs for breakfast. Why
didn't I talk to him or something, anything. . .?

Because she had been frightened of what she might
hear. She shut her eyes against the knowledge of her

own weakness. If he had confirmed that Lala was more than a friend it might have opened a Pandora's box that she just couldn't face. But perhaps it would have been preferable to this? It was killing her to see him each day, hear his voice, and have him treat her with such careful, cold politeness. She clenched her hands into fists against the pain in her heart that was twisting her nerves into shreds.

Well, it's too late now anyway, she thought grimly as she rose and made her way to the door. He had made it clear that he was finished with her, she was just another employee now, and as soon as his business here was completed it would be back to Istanbul and he would probably request a replacement assistant. The bolt of anguish was ravaging.

As she made her way downstairs their conversation at the restaurant before Lala's father interrupted them was there in piercing clarity as it had been since it had been spoken. What had he been going to say? Had she imagined it all? She wouldn't be surprised. Her mouth twisted bitterly. She had felt more than once in the last few days that she was going crazy.

'Thank you, Safiye.' Louisa smiled warmly at the small housekeeper as she came bustling in with a covered dish that she placed in front of Louisa with a little nod. The little Turkish woman had decided that Louisa wasn't eating enough and had made it her mission in life to remedy the situation. Louisa appreciated the concern but, feeling as she did at the moment, the constant churning in her stomach made eating a necessity rather than a pleasure. However, the *menemen*, a delicious concoction of eggs, peppers, tomatoes and cheese served with small buttery buns called *pogacu* and various kinds of cheese *borek*—layered

pastry leaves cooked in the oven—was very tempting
and the last thing she wanted to do was to offend the
housekeeper, who had shown her nothing but kindness.

'She is worried about you.' As Safiye left the room
Melik glanced up from his own breakfast. 'As I am.
You are not eating enough and you are too pale.'

'I'm. . .I'm fine.' It was the first personal remark he
had made in days and, accompanied by the concern
which had darkened the handsome, austere face and
narrowed the golden eyes, it was almost too much for
her over-sensitised emotions. 'Really.'

'No, you are not.' His eyes moved over her face
slowly. 'Perhaps I should not have brought you here
but I thought——' He stopped abruptly. 'We will be
returning to Istanbul the day after tomorrow.'

The sickening jolt in her stomach allowed her to nod
only. She wouldn't have trusted her voice. This was it,
then, just like that.

'I want to make a detour, however, so we will
actually leave here tomorrow morning, stay overnight
in reserved accommodation and fly to Istanbul the
following day. This is acceptable to you?' She nodded
dully. 'You are not going to ask me the nature of the
business? Enquire about the. . .suitability of the
accommodation?' There was a note in his voice she
couldn't quite place but she merely shook her head
flatly, pushing the rest of the food around on her plate
with her fork. She couldn't eat another bite. 'I see.'
From the sharpening of the beautiful eyes it was clear
he didn't but he said no more, pushing his own plate
aside with a muttered oath and stalking to his study
without another glance at her bent head.

It was much later, after dinner, when she was alone
in her room and preparing for bed after packing her

belongings and leaving the case by the door for collection by Osman first thing in the morning, that she heard the sharp tones of the doorbell. Some intuitive shiver, a little shudder down her spine, made her walk carefully to the door and open it a fraction, peering out into the darkened landing as she listened intently.

'Melik, darling. . .' Lala's voice was clear and warm and seductively throaty. 'Father told me you are leaving tomorrow; you were going to disappear back into the big bad world without telling me?'

'What are you doing here, Lala?' Louisa heard the sound of footsteps on the beautifully laid wooden floor and surmised that Melik was leading Lala into his study where a small fire had been lit earlier that evening to offset the winter chill. 'It's late.'

'I just had to see you and you know me, darling, when I want something or someone. . .' The low, suggestive, sexy laughter had been carefully cultivated for maximum effect and as it coiled up the stairs Louisa shut her door firmly, her breath a burning tight ball in her throat.

She had been so gullible! As she leant back against the carved oak door she shut her eyes tight for a moment, her heart thudding. So credulous, so stupid. . . *But it was her fault.* She opened her eyes to stare unseeing into the dimly lit room. She had begun to believe what she wanted to believe, *he* had made no promises, told no lies, assured her of nothing; in fact he had been painfully honest about his past life. She collapsed on the wide, soft bed, her head whirling. He had never uttered a word of love, anything to make her think she was any different from any other female he desired. If she had chosen to read more into the odd veiled comment, the occasional fleeting glance, well. . .that was her mistake. He had talked of possession, of branding her as his, of fierce desire, but never, ever love. . .

It was very late when she heard Lala's jeep roar off into the night and she felt very cold. Cold and curiously numb.

CHAPTER TEN

'You still haven't asked.'

'I'm sorry?' She came out of the blackness of her thoughts to find Melik's eyes tight on her face.

He indicated the lush green mountainous terrain beneath the small aircraft with a wave of his hand. 'Where we are going. You are not in the least bit curious?'

'Should I be?' she asked flatly. 'I suppose it's estate business——'

'No, it is not estate business,' he said softly. 'It is Melik and Louisa business.'

'Now look here——' She had thought nothing could permeate the aura of misery that had settled on her the night before like a big dark cloud but he had accomplished it with just a few quiet words and a warm smile. How *dared* he smile like that at her, when he and Lala had been huddled together half the night. . .? How *dared* he?

'No, I will look nowhere.' His face had changed at the glare on hers but his voice was still quiet, beautifully controlled. 'I am taking you to see a ceremony, a very special ceremony that only happens once a year, that is all. I am not abducting you for dire purposes or locking you away in a dark fortress somewhere, although I would be lying if I didn't admit the thought had occurred to me more than once lately. However——' he took a long deep breath '—there is an old Turkish proverb that I have found most comforting in the last few weeks. A rough translation would be that the prize is all the more precious when it has been gained on the blood of the winner. Do you follow me?'

'I haven't the faintest idea what you are talking about,' she said in all honesty, her face still scarlet with anger.

'No?' His eyes wandered over her hot face lingeringly. 'Such an unkind little tigress not even to notice when the sharp claws draw blood, but it will make the taming of you all the sweeter, my pet.'

'I am not your pet!' The low, fierce retort was filled with such enmity that his brow wrinkled against it. 'And you are beyond belief, Melik Haman; I ——'

'Look down there.' He had completely ignored her words with such regal disdain that she didn't know whether to hit him or scream. 'We are flying over the Göreme region now; I will take you there one day. It is the strange country of the Christian troglodytes; do you remember me mentioning them?'

She nodded her head tightly, her eyes blazing.

'This whole region is a uniquely spectacular volcanic maze of giant cones and chimneys of yellow tufa that are above the general level of land,' he continued urbanely, quite unmoved by her rage, 'and in some of the fields of red and yellow volcanic earth the peasant land-owners have small plots of vines and fruit trees with some of the bigger cones being cut to form waterproof storerooms for their crops.'

'Look, Melik ——'

'The ones directly below are several storeys high,' he said evenly, 'and still inhabited today. I understand modern porches and steps have been added in the most sohisticated ones. And in Kaymakli and Derinkuyu, which we shall be reaching shortly, there are vast underground cities where at the dawn of Christianity the early Christians sheltered from persecution.'

'I'm not interested in underground cities,' she said sharply, her voice shaking with rage. 'What I want to know is ——'

'You aren't interested?' His voice was mockingly shocked. 'And I thought I was the savage? You mean to say the fact that there are churches, palaces, whole villages intricately planned and descending to a hundred and twenty metres below the ground surface does not even flood your mind with just a little wonder? How sad. . .' He eyed her wickedly. 'I am in the company of a philistine. The human moles that inhabited the underground catacombs would not thank you for such cool uninterest, my superior little English rose.'

'I'm warning you, Melik ——' She stopped abruptly as he placed a finger on her lips, his eyes dancing.

'I like to make you mad, Louisa; you were born for such sport.' He settled back in his seat comfortably without taking his eyes off her face. 'This cold icicle that has been wandering round my house for the last few days, that is not you.'

'You know nothing about me, Melik, nothing at all,' she said hotly as the sense of outrage and unfairness swamped all other emotion.

'This is perhaps a little true.' He eyed her consideringly. 'But I know all I need to know is here ——' he touched his chest lightly ' — in my heart. The rest?' He shrugged slowly. 'The rest can be told if you wish it; if not. . .'

'That is very magnanimous of you,' she said scathingly as the image of Lala flashed on to the screen of her mind. 'Do you mean to say you accept all your women at face value? Isn't that a little dangerous?'

'I have survived, as you see,' he said with irritating composure. 'But as to all these other women. . .' The golden eyes narrowed. 'I am neither a fool nor a careless man, Louisa, as I thought you knew. I was born into great wealth and with such blessing comes a heightened sense of one's own worth. I have known exactly what most of the women I have been involved with wanted and let us say the appeal of my body was somewhat outshone by the size of my bank balance.'

'But if you knew that. . .' She faltered to a halt. 'I mean, why get involved with them, then?'

He shrugged lightly. 'I am a man, not a monk. If that answer displeases you I can tell you in all honesty it is the first time I have wished it could be different. But I cannot lie to you. My only plea for mitigation would be. . .' He hesitated.

'Yes?'

'I realise now I was searching for something that I wanted without being sure if it even existed. Does that make sense?'

'No.' She stared at him in confusion.

'And then I found it,' he said softly. 'The pearl beyond price. But the shell is still tightly hiding the full beauty from coming forth, but shells were made to be broken. . .'

'We shall be landing in just under ten minutes, sir.' Osman's expressionless voice sounded over their heads. 'There will be a car to meet you and I will be here at the same time tomorrow.'

The interruption seemed to signal the end of further conversation and as Melik settled back in his seat his face was enigmatic and still, his big body relaxed as the plane flew on in the clear blue sky. When they left its warm protection a short time later the first thing Louisa noticed was the remarkable change in temperature. After leaving the wet, temperate region of the Black Sea the sharp cold of the Anatolian plateau was striking.

It was as though they were in a different country, Louisa thought as the hired car sped them onwards, surveying the plain of Konya that fanned out from the foothills of the Taurus Mountains into vast bleakness. 'In ancient Neolithic times the wild bull and leopard wandered these grasslands,' Melik said softly in her ear, 'and Konya itself is a very old city, an oasis of commerce in this massive wilderness.'

'And the celebration?' She was vitally conscious of his hard thigh next to hers in the close confines of the car, the big bulk of him next to her causing a trembling in her stomach that she had learnt weeks ago was impossible to control.

'Ah, the whirling dervishes,' he said thoughtfully. 'It is a ceremony to commemorate the death of Mevlana, who founded the order. You would have approved of him, I think.'

'Would I?' She looked at him in surprise. 'Why?'

'His basic philosophy consisted of equality for the sexes — ' he shot her a wry glance ' — the pursuit of righteousness and communion with God, which especially in those times, the 1200s, was quite radical. He was married to one woman all his life and preached passionately that such faithfulness was right, that all women as well as men should be free.'

'Did he?' She was warming to Mevlana already.

The city itself was very Islamic and very beautiful, and their hotel was situated in the area of the main

square, Hukumet Meydani, both gracious and comfortable. 'Your key.' As Melik handed her the small metal
object she caught the cynical gleam in his eyes. 'Did
you expect a key of your very own?'

She knew what he was asking and kept her face
bland. 'Of course. How else would I lock my door?'

He laughed softly, his eyes glittering. 'Of course,
how else?' Dressed as he was in casual trousers and a
thick black leather jacket, he looked overwhelmingly
attractive, and as her heart thudded a little quicker he
stroked her hot cheek with a thoughtful finger. 'How
long, my tigress? How long before there is only one
key?' It wasn't really a question and she made no
attempt to answer it.

It was with some trepidation that she got ready later
that afternoon for dinner with Melik before the
ceremony began. They had spent the day sightseeing
and she had found the ancient city, a prosperous route
and market centre for the last two thousand years,
absorbing. The Alaeddin Mosque, one of the oldest in
Turkey, with its wooden roofing supported by forty-
two Roman columns and intricately carved pulpit and
altar, was beautiful as would befit a building holding
the mortal remains of eight sultans, and the other
Seljuk monuments to architecture equally so, but it
was the Mevlana Mausoleum, the old monastery where
the order of dervishes was founded, that really gripped
her interest.

Dominated by a conical, turquoise-blue dome, it was
a landmark in the city, and the museum hall where the
ritual dances used to take place contained priceless
seven-hundred-year-old carpets, manuscripts, musical
instruments, dervish garments and prayer rugs, and
even, allegedly, part of Mahomet's beard. As she stood

there, Melik's arm resting lightly round her waist and the aura of the East stronger than she had ever known it, Louisa was vitally aware, with a painful clarity that gripped at her throat, that soon all this would just be a memory and she would be gone. Gone from this land of arid plains and lush forests, dramatic mountains and peaceful lakes, this land of exquisitely beautiful ancient mosques and sultans' palaces, tiny fishing villages and small country towns where life had remained the same for thousands of years; and gone from this man. This ruthless, cold man who could be as gentle as a kitten and as fierce as a wild animal almost in the same breath.

'Louisa?' The knock at her door brought her eyes snapping to the mirror as she checked her hair and light make-up. The smart but casual pale blue wool dress would carry her with equal sureness into a poor café or sophisticated restaurant, and the matching coat was not only functional but extremely warm, which, as the ceremony was held in front of the old monastery, she felt was more than necessary.

'You look gorgeous.' As she opened the door he moved her back into the room, taking her in his arms before she could guess his intention and straining her to him in an agony of a kiss that not only bruised her lips but tore at her heart. Had he kissed Lala like this last night before she had left? Had Lala drunk in the feel and smell of him, the intoxicating thrill of being held next to the heart of a man who was all male and unashamedly dangerous? 'Louisa. . .' As she felt her head begin to swim she was horrified to find she wanted to kiss him back, wanted the penetrating invasion of his mouth, the hard jut of his body, the overwhelming warmth of his lovemaking. . .

'Don't!' She jerked backwards and he made no attempt to stop her, turning and walking past her to hold back the flimsy curtains and stare down into the street below for long minutes, his back rigid and straight and his head stiff as though he was fighting for control.

'I'm sorry.' As he turned she saw he was his old cynical self again, his eyes hooded and his mouth sardonic. 'But that perfume you have on is the very devil.'

She met the veiled eyes and managed a small smile. 'It should be. It costs me a week's wages. It's called Enticement.'

'It works.'

He walked across the room and picked up a small package he had slipped on the table by the door as he had entered. 'Here.'

'What is it?'

'Not again.' He closed his eyes briefly. 'I really must give you lessons on how to accept gifts gracefully, when I have the time, along with a few other instructions on a topic dearer to my heart.' He eyed her wickedly and she found she had unwrapped the tiny parcel without knowing it.

'Oh, how pretty.' The perfect magnolia bloom was encased in a small transparent box that opened from the top, and as Melik lifted the corsage from its tissue the heady perfume emanating from the pure white petals filled the room.

'Let me.' He fixed the exquisite flower to her dress, just above her breast, and although the touch of his hand was making her limp she forced herself to stand perfectly still until he had finished. 'The white flower signifies innocence, virginity,' he continued softly as he gazed down into the brown darkness of her eyes, 'and this is how I see you, Louisa. I do not care about what has happened in your past,' he went on quietly as she went to speak, 'or how this thing that has hurt you may have involved another man. No, that is not quite true.' A small muscle clenched in his jaw for a moment. 'I care — hell, I care; it's ripped me apart night after night thinking that he may have hurt you, abused you —'

'Melik —' She was horrified by the savage pain in his eyes but as she spoke he took a deep, shuddering breath, forcing back the control with iron determination.

'But I want you to know that he can't touch you if you don't let him, not here, inside, where it counts.' He touched her heart gently. 'This flower is how I see you, Louisa, pure, beautiful and without blemish.'

'Melik, please. . .' She shut her eyes as the tears she had been holding back for minutes squeezed underneath her lids. 'Please don't.'

'No tears.' He touched her face softly. 'And no confessions. Be it a man or something else, I care only as much as it has hurt you. And now we go.'

The rest of the evening was bittersweet. They dined at the hotel and as they left the air was frosty and bitterly cold to their warm faces. As Melik pulled her closely into the crook of her arm Louisa knew, with a surety that stopped her heart, that this would have to be the end. Once in Istanbul she would fly back to England immediately, because if she stayed any longer within his orbit she would become anything he wanted her to become, do anything he wanted her to do, forget her scruples, her innate desperation for a relationship that excluded a third or fourth or fifth party, and he was from a different culture, a different world — he probably didn't even comprehend why she would want to be the only one; Lala showed that.

The ceremony was eerie and beautiful and strange and the religious dance, accompanied by musicians wearing tall red tarbushes, was intricately fascinating. Accompanied by the ethereal sound of reed flutes, the whirling men in their long white robes and long hats symbolising their own gravestones told their story of the shedding of all earthly ties in their quest for union with God.

'Each dancer is holding his right palm towards heaven to receive a blessing and his left palm down to distribute it upon the earth,' Melik whispered in her ear as they stood in the crowd in awestruck silence.

'How do you know? Have you been before?' she whispered back and he nodded slowly, his eyes fixed on the figures as they spun on bare heels with sublime speed and ease, the spotlights turning their robes different monochrome colours as the skirts billowed outwards. Whom had he brought that time? She hated the dart of jealousy that bit at her mind with viciously sharp teeth. Had it been Lala?

'I brought my mother a few years ago,' he said quietly. 'Amazingly, in spite of living most of her life in this country, she had never come before.' He flashed her a quick smile. 'Crazy, eh?'

So she had been wrong. Her thoughts ran on and then shuddered to a halt. But a future with this man, however short it might be, would hold the same piercing thoughts. Not about the past, she could accept and forget that, but every time he left, every time he waved goodbye, she would wonder who he was going to.

'The big circle they are standing in demonstrates

wheels within wheels,' Melik continued softly, quite oblivious to her inward turmoil. 'The movements of the stars in the cosmos and the soul's search for truth.' The dancers were making her feel dizzy; she couldn't believe that they could remain upright, let alone whirl at such breathtaking speed and with such superhuman control. On and on they went, the shroud-like skirts forming a cone and the men's faces transfixed as though they had fallen into a trance.

As the scent from the blossom fixed to her dress mingled with the enormity of the obvious dedication of the dancers Louisa began to feel that the whole evening wasn't quite real, but even as the poignant ceremony drew to an end and a man began chanting passages from the Koran she knew she had come to a decision. She would tell him tonight she had to leave, return to England. She owed him that honesty at least after the gentleness he had portrayed with the flower and his care for her feelings, however much pain he had given her.

'Melik?' As they wandered back to the hotel, part of a vast crowd, she knew the moment had come. She couldn't tell him when they were alone, she just couldn't.

'Yes?'

'I'm going back to England when we return to Istanbul.'

'You are joking.' The tone was flat but she went on.

'I need to get away.' He had stiffened at her side but she couldn't stop now.

'From me?'

'Partly.' She tried to make her voice firm.

'May I ask why?' His voice was cold now, cold and formal.

'Because I can't be what you want me to be; I'm not made like you, it's as simple as that.' She glanced at his face and then looked away quickly, shaken by the darkness moulding the strong features into a devil's mask.

'Meaning?'

He wasn't going to make this easy, she thought painfully. 'I know you want a relationship with me,' she said slowly, 'but that sort of thing, it wouldn't be enough for me. I'd want more and I know you wouldn't.'

'You know?' His voice was deceptively soft. 'What do you think I would want of you exactly, Louisa?'

'We both know that; I don't need to spell it out,' she said tightly. 'You can have affairs without it meaning too much to you; you *told* me that, like with Lala.'

'Lala?' He stopped dead and turned her to him, his eyes golden shafts of light in the dark brown of his face. 'What has Lala got to do with anything?'

'Well, she's — ' She stopped abruptly, taken aback by the fury in his face. 'I mean — '

'You think Lala is my mistress?' he hissed slowly. 'You think I would insult you by asking you to my home and then parading another woman in front of you, not to mention the betrayal of friendship such a relationship would entail with her parents? That is the sort of man you think I am?'

'But she said — ' She stopped abruptly. What had Lala said, now? She had never actually stated bald facts; it had been all suggestion and innuendo.

'Lala is a spoilt child who plays at being grown-up,' Melik said with icy coldness. 'She is the troublesome little sister I never had. That is all.'

'It might be all to you but it certainly isn't like that

with her,' Louisa said quickly as the piercingly sharp flood of relief that had flooded her body for a few seconds at his words died at the blackness of his face. 'She said——'

'I do not care what she said,' Melik said furiously, giving her a little shake that earned a few interested glances from passers-by. 'You could have asked me about it, couldn't you? Talked to me? Treated me as a human being for once? But no, I am not such a thing in your eyes, am I? Exactly how do you see me, Louisa, as an animal, an object or worse?'

'Melik——'

'I have had enough.' He took a step backwards from her as though she were suddenly unclean. 'It is not just Lala, is it? You think I am some sort of over-sexed savage who has women in every place. Yes?' Her face was scarlet now; she had never seen him like this before and it frightened her. 'Never has anyone dared to say such things before. You think I am incapable of normal commitment in spite of all I have tried to tell you, the way I feel——' He stopped abruptly as a spasm of pain cut through the steel in his eyes. 'You *should* go home to England, Louisa.' he drew himself up very straight, his big body iron-hard. 'This is exactly what you should do.'

How they reached the hotel she never did know; the journey forever remained a blank in her mind. Her whole being was consumed with the sickening dread that she had just made the biggest mistake of her life. He saw her to her room with icy politeness, careful not to touch her or even brush against her. 'Goodnight.' He inclined his dark head with arctic courtesy and as he began to walk away she thought her heart would break.

'Melik?'

He paused for a moment, his back rigid, and then walked on, his broad shoulders set and his head high.

That was it. As she closed the door and sank down on the bed her mind searched frantically for a way to undo the damage. . .but there was none. She closed her eyes helplessly. And he didn't even know she loved him.

The journey to Istanbul was tense and painful and by the time Louisa reached her flat, Melik seeing her to the door and depositing her case just inside, declining the offer of coffee with a stiff, 'No, thank you,' she felt like a wet rag. She hadn't closed her eyes the night before, sitting by the low arched windowsill that had looked out on to the road underneath and waiting for the first glow of dawn to break the black sky. When the first wailing call from the mosque minaret loud-speakers had summoned the faithful to prayer she had risen slowly, showering and washing her hair with leaden, sluggish movements as though she were weak and frail after recovering from a major operation, before getting dressed and resuming her seat by the window as the big city had come to life.

'I would suggest you have a light lunch and rest this afternoon,' he had said distantly as Osman drove them to her flat. 'The office will wait.'

'I'll see.' She had been staring out of the window into the muggy December day and hadn't turned her eyes to his, missing the swift piercing glance of concern he had given her white face. 'I might come in just to sort my desk; it's bound to be piled high.'

'Call the office and I'll send Osman if you decide to do that.'

She had nodded slowly, her eyes lifeless, while the mad whirl of Istanbul traffic had screeched noisily beyond the car's quiet interior, making Melik's peaceful, gracious home seem a million miles away.

After fixing herself a quick omelette she pushed it around on the plate for a few minutes before tipping the congealed mass into the bin, forcing herself to drink two strong cups of coffee as she brushed her hair into shining order, securing it firmly in the clips Melik hated so much. She needed to look her most efficient when she approached Mrs Jones about a return ticket this afternoon. It wouldn't be a pleasant interview. She shook her head in slight surprise as she suddenly realised that the thought didn't have the power to bother her an iota. She didn't care about Mrs Jones, about Lectron, about her job; all she cared about was — She stopped her mind from continuing. She had made her decision, burnt her boats; *there was no looking back*.

The statement mocked her as she drove to the office by dolmuş in the early afternoon drizzle that had settled on the city. No looking back? She was going to spend the rest of her life regretting she had ever set foot in this beautiful wild land.

'Miss Collins.' Mrs Jones's smile was of the hundred-watt variety and Louisa blinked a little at the older woman's enthusiasm. 'Mr Haman said we wouldn't be seeing you until tomorrow.' There was something in the older woman's attitude that Louisa couldn't quite pin down, but she was too friendly, too effusive. . .

'I wanted to talk to you, Mrs Jones,' Louisa said quietly, 'and I also thought I should put my desk in order.'

'Talk to me?' Again there was that fleeting sense of

disquiet but Louisa brushed it aside; she was imagining
the apprehension in Mrs Jones's hard grey eyes. 'Well,
this might be a good moment, Miss Collins; everyone
has gone to lunch.'

Louisa nodded slowly. She might as well get it over
with.

As she followed Mrs Jones into Mr Ashton's outer
office where the secretary had her desk she mentally
prepared her opening sentence. I'm afraid that due to
unforeseen circumstances I shall have to return to
England before Christmas, Mrs Jones. . .

'Now.' Mrs Jones indicated a seat in front of her
desk as she sat down. 'I gather you've picked up on the
credit problem? Well, it was only a matter of time.'

'I'm sorry?' Louisa stared at her in surprise.

'Lectron's little money-flow difficulty.' Mrs Jones
smiled conspiratorially. 'I was meaning to have a word
with you before Mr Haman whisked you away so
suddenly. It's all in hand, my dear; there is nothing to
be concerned about.'

'I'm sorry, Mrs Jones, but I don't have the faintest
idea what you mean,' Louisa said helplessly. 'Is there
some sort of financial problem?'

'You mean you haven't. . .?' Mrs Jones surveyed
her carefully. 'Well, you soon would have.'

'Would have what?' It was becoming more like *Alice
in Wonderland* every moment, Louisa thought dazedly.

'Would have realised that Lectron is short of a
considerable amount of money,' Mrs Jones said
quietly. 'But, as I say, it's all in hand. This little. . .
complication was foreseen before we arrived here and
measures have been taken.'

'Measures?' Louisa stared at the older woman's face
blankly. 'What measures?'

'You must understand, Miss Collins.' Mrs Jones gave her the million-dollar smile again. 'It's all to Mr Haman's advantage in the long run. He might be covering. . .more than he envisaged now but the future of this project is worth it. He will make a great deal of money long term.'

'Yes. . .' There was still something here she didn't understand, Louisa thought uncertainly, something not quite right. 'Well, if he's happy with that I suppose all's well.'

'Ah. . .now I didn't say that, did I?' The smile dimmed a little. 'In fact I would prefer you not to bring the matter to Mr Haman's attention. There is no need.'

'He doesn't know?' Now things were beginning to make sense. 'You mean Lectron is trying to pull a fast one?'

'"Pull a fast one"?' Mrs Jones's thin mouth showed her distaste for the crudity of the expression. 'Not at all, Miss Collins; we are just. . .manipulating the facts a little.'

'Cheating him.' Louisa's voice was flat.

'Don't be so ridiculous, girl!' As the steel-grey eyes narrowed Mrs Jones reverted to type. 'Do you think Lectron could miss the chance to establish themselves out here in Turkey just because of the short-sightedness of certain banks?'

'You are talking about fraud, Mrs Jones.'

'How dare you?' Mrs Jones stood up and moved round her desk to stand in front of Louisa, the angular face fairly quivering with indignation. 'Why do you think you were chosen to replace Beryl, you stupid girl? We thought we could rely on your discretion; you have always been a model employee ——'

'As I shall continue to be for however long I work

for Lectron, Mrs Jones.' Louisa glared up at the red face angrily. 'But that does not include lying and deceiving Mr Haman. Just the opposite, in fact.'

'I'm just asking you to keep quiet.' Mrs Jones's voice was threatening now and very cold. 'If you don't Mr Haman would never believe you didn't know exactly what was going on from the very beginning and you will find yourself minus a job here and also in England. References can be. . .delicate things, Miss Collins.'

'Get lost, Mrs Jones.' It was said with such quietness that for a second the import of the softly spoken words didn't register on the older woman's face. 'If you think for one minute I'm letting Melik carry more than his fair share you're wrong.' She too had risen to glare straight into Mrs Jones's tight face. 'He is worth a hundred of any of you; there isn't a deceitful bone in his body, and if you think you can pull the wool over his eyes and ask me to keep quiet then you're wrong. I won't do it.'

'You'll regret it; I'll see to it that your job——'

'And you know exactly what you can do with your precious job, don't you?' As she pushed past Mrs Jones's square body she stopped dead to see Melik in front of her, the dark face stunned and incredulous as his eyes flashed from her to Mrs Jones, who sank down into the chair Louisa had vacated with a little whimper when she caught sight of the big figure in the doorway.

'I'll deal with you later.' The deep voice was deadly and Mrs Jones sank further into the upholstery, her face ashen.

'Melik——' As Louisa went to speak she found herself whisked at great speed out of the main office, which was beginning to fill with staff, and down the stairs outside, her feet barely able to touch the floor.

'Melik——'

'Quiet; not now.'

She tried to glance up at him, to see his face, but they were flying along the pavement outside so fast that it was all she could do to get her breath, and then suddenly, thankfully, they were in one of the tiny squares dotted about Istanbul where a few pigeons were being fed by two old men and a group of children and the wailing rhythm of a Turkish pop song drifted lazily from an open window in one of the houses surrounding the square. 'Sit down.'

As he pushed her on to a small wooden bench and sat down beside her she glanced at his expressionless face anxiously. Did he think she had been in on the scheme to cheat him? How much had he heard? Did he even know what they had been talking about? And oh—her stomach knotted tightly—he did look *good*.

'It's truth time.' He turned to face her and she saw that his eyes were brilliantly iridescent, the flecks of green standing out in striking contrast to the dark, tawny surround. 'Why did you say all that to Mrs Jones?'

'Because I didn't know what was going on,' she said faintly. 'I——'

'I don't mean that!' He flicked his hand savagely. 'I know you wouldn't be involved in anything underhand; that is not in question. I mean about me, being worth a hundred of them. . .' There was something in his face that tore at her heart and melted all her pride, her carefully built-up self-protection, leaving her wide open, vulnerable. He had said it was truth time. Well, so be it.

'Because you are,' she said simply.

'Louisa——' He stopped abruptly, his hand reaching

out to touch her and then freezing in mid-air to fall
back to his side. 'Hell, I don't know what to say to
you.' There was a deep pleading in the proud face, a
brokenness, that she had never imagined seeing there.
'I don't know what you want.'

'I want you.' As she said it, finally, *finally* said it,
everything fell into place. She loved him. She couldn't
exist without him. If it meant sharing him. . .well, she
would face that when it happened and go from there;
at the very least she would have precious memories to
cling on to.

'You don't know what you're saying.' It wasn't the
response she expected and she stared at him in surprise.
'Dammit, woman, you don't even *like* me.'

'I love you, Melik.' If he wanted it all, the last ounce
of pride, it was his. 'I always have.'

'Louisa.' He pulled her to him with such violence
that the pigeons scattered in a great whirling cloud and
the old men hurried the children off into a secluded
corner of the square where they tut-tutted at the fallen
standards of the young. He didn't kiss her, merely
holding her close to the pounding fury of his heart with
such savage intensity that she really did feel he was
crushing her bones.

'Melik ——' At the first wriggle she was free. 'I want
to explain ——'

'No!' His voice was violent. 'I don't want to hear. I
just want to sit here and for you to tell me that you
love me again and again and again until I can take it
in. If you knew what you've put me through ——'

'I have to tell you.' She placed a small hand on his
chest and the shudder that racked his body trembled
through hers.

'It's not necessary.' He touched her face and then

pulled her to him again, kissing her desperately, frantically, as though he would never have his fill of her lips, his body rigid with the control he was exercising. 'If we were anywhere but here. . .' He eyed her hotly. 'I want you, now.'

'Listen.' She moved a body's breadth away and began to talk, baring her heart, her soul, and he listened, quietly and without interrupting, although as she mentioned Oliver his face stiffened for a second before relaxing again, a compassion washing over the austere features that caught at her breath. She told him about the childhood years, the loneliness, the desperate feeling of being unloved, unlovable, and the damage it had caused to a sensitive, highly responsive nature that had gradually closed in on itself for protection. And her face told him much more than she realised as she felt her way through the years until she stopped, bruised and shaken by some of the deeply buried memories she had brought to the surface.

'I could kill them.' His voice was low and painful. 'They are your parents but I could kill them. Have they any idea, now, what they did to you? What they are still doing?'

'Not still doing.' As she touched her hand to his face he caught it and pressed her fingers tightly to his mouth. 'Not now I've met you.'

'And Oliver?' The beautiful eyes stroked probingly over her face. 'You have peace now about Oliver?'

'Yes.' She met his gaze squarely. 'I felt guilty that what I felt for him was so lukewarm beside you but I know now that that was another time, another place, and he was happy with things the way they were. He wasn't a. . .physical man,' she said haltingly.

'Not a physical man?' He frowned slowly. 'You

mean——?' He gazed at her, a dawning incredulity in his eyes. 'You don't mean——'

'We never made love.' It was good that she could give him this one gift, very good. 'I've never made love with anyone.'

'But——' He shook his head wonderingly, unable to speak. 'I cannot believe, looking as you do. . . When I think of how I rushed you, frightened you. . .' A darkness came into his face. 'You should have said, my love; forgive me.'

'There is nothing to forgive, Melik, and you didn't frighten me.' A small smile touched her mouth at the almost comical tragedy in his. 'I liked it.'

'You did?' The thickening of his voice sent hot colour flooding into her cheeks. 'Oh, Louisa. . .I love you, more than life, more than I had ever imagined it was possible to love. You will marry me, *soon*?'

'Marry you?' She stared at him in amazement. 'You want to *marry* me?'

'Of course.' He raised his head proudly. 'What did you think I was offering you?'

'Well, I don't know, this country. . . Your customs are different here; I wasn't sure. . .'

'Louisa, I have never wanted to marry anyone before and if you refused me I never would again. When you become my wife, if you accept me, our hearts will become one, beat as one. I shall never want another; can you believe that?'

'I want to.' She touched the hard contours of his face tenderly. 'But you must understand, Melik, I find it hard to think anyone can love me, let alone someone like you.'

'Someone like me?' The incredulity was back in his face. 'But I am not worthy to be dust under your feet, my love; how can you ever think——?' He stopped abruptly. 'But I will spend the rest of my life convincing you, Louisa. You remember that first day at the office, when I took you out for lunch and we visited the Topkapi Palace, the Harem?'

'Yes.'

'And I told you the story of the favourite, the one woman who could tame the wild heart of the Sultan until she was the only one he desired, the one he gave absolute sovereign power to, the jewel of his life?'

'Melik——'

'You are the one, Louisa. You are my heart, my blood, my life. There will never be anyone else; you are my destiny.'

'Your destiny?' She stared in wonder at the passionate warmth in his face.

'And the future is ours, my sweet tigress, all ours. . .'

Mary Lyons was born in Toronto, Canada, moving to live permanently in England when she was six, although she still proudly maintains her Canadian citizenship. Having married and raised four children, her life nowadays is relatively peaceful—unlike her earlier years when she worked as a radio announcer, reviewed books and, for a time, lived in a turbulent area of the Middle East. She still enjoys a bit of excitement, combining romance with action, humour and suspense in her books whenever possible.

ESCAPE FROM
THE HAREM
by
Mary Lyons

CHAPTER ONE

'OH Leonie, honey, I really can't decide...' Mrs Kaminsky gave a helpless shrug as she looked around the large, draughty warehouse. 'I never imagined—I mean, honest to God, honey,' she added plaintively, 'I've never seen so many damn rugs in all my born days!'

'Yes, it can be confusing.' Leonie gave the petite American woman a brief, sympathetic smile before turning to consult some papers on a clipboard, which rested on a pile of carpets beside her tall figure.

A shaft of autumn sunlight streaming down from the high, dusty window illuminated the fiery glow of her reddish-gold, long curly hair, piled loosely up in a knot on top of her head. Her wide sapphire-blue eyes, heavily fringed with dark feathery eyelashes, gazed pensively at the notes she had made earlier in the day. This was the third warehouse that she and Mrs Kaminsky had visited that morning, and they were getting nowhere. Her client was obviously wilting at the knees, and becoming increasingly bewildered by the enormous variety of rugs and carpets available on display.

'My husband told me that London is the centre of the world market for Oriental rugs and carpets, but he never said anything about having to trudge around all these nasty old buildings,' Mrs Kaminsky moaned, clutching her pale mink coat about her slim figure. 'It sure seems a weird way to do business—and mighty tough on the feet!' she added wearily, seating herself on a pile of glowing silk Isfahan carpets.

Leonie smiled patiently, before attempting to explain the position yet again. 'It's my task, as an Oriental carpet broker, to take you around the various warehouses and help you to buy the best and most suitable rug at the keenest price. The stock you see here has come from all quarters of the globe, and because my firm, Kashan's, doesn't have expensive store premises to maintain, and only charge a small buying commission, you get a completely unbiased opinion on the merchandise for sale. That means that you save a *lot* of money and we personally guarantee the quality of the item you choose.'

The American woman gave a heavy sigh. 'Okay, honey, I get the point—dollarwise. But why can't I just have a few rugs sent to the hotel? That way I could take my time deciding which one I want?'

'I know it's not an ideal situation,' Leonie agreed. 'But everything you see here is being held under a customs and excise bond. Which means that when you've picked a rug you like, we can ship it straight over to your home in Palm Springs, and thus avoid you having to pay customs duty—a sum which would have to be charged if the rug left this warehouse.'

'I guess you're right, but I'm feeling ab-sol-lutely pooped—and in no shape to traipse around any more of these damn, dusty buildings!'

'I'm sure we'll find just what you're looking for,' Leonie said brightly, trying to sound more optimistic than she felt and resisting the temptation to look at her watch. If she didn't come up with the answer to Mrs Kaminsky's problem soon, she was going to be late for her lunch date.

'You told me that you were looking for a rug to go in your main living-room. Can you tell me about the room's colour-scheme—walls and curtains, etc?'

'Well, it's just been redecorated in shades of gold and white by a simply *divine* young man I found. My husband complained that it cost the earth, but I think it looks great—really classy, if you know what I mean?'

As Mrs Kaminsky waved her hands enthusiastically in

the air, Leonie's eyes were drawn to a large turquoise and diamond ring on the older woman's finger.

'Of course!' Leonie clicked her teeth, annoyed with herself for not having thought of the answer to the problem before now. Smiling at the assistant, who had been waiting patiently for the last ten minutes, she pointed down to the end of the large, cavernous warehouse.

'Sorry to take so long, George. Can we look through that pile of large Qum rugs?' she said, before turning to her client. 'I know you've been thinking in terms of deep blues and dark reds, but I'm going to suggest that maybe you might decide to choose something more in harmony with your colour-scheme.'

Leading the way past the piles of rugs and carpets heaped one on top of the other, Leonie thought, as she had so often, that it was like walking through a treasure vault of precious gems; the incandescent glow of the jewelled silks almost dazzling beneath the strong arc lights set high in the ceiling.

'It was your ring which gave me the idea,' she explained to Mrs Kaminsky as the assistant began to turn over a fresh pile of carpets. 'These come from the holy city of Qum, in Iran. The political climate in that country is not too good at the moment, and so these pieces are becoming increasingly rare,'

Leonie bent down to stroke the soft, turquoise-coloured silk which formed a background to a garden of paradise design in gleaming tones of white, cream and gold.

'Now, *that's* more like it, honey!' the American woman enthused. 'I just love that shade of blue.'

'It's unique to all the pieces made in Qum. You'll never find that colour in any other Persian rug...'

'*A telephone call for Miss Elliot,*' a disembodied voice from a loudspeaker high on the wall cut into Leonie's words. '*Will Miss Leonie Elliot please come to reception.*'

'I can't think who...?' Leonie stood up, looking startled. 'I'm sorry, I'd better go and take the call. Don't hurry. Take plenty of time and look at all the various designs,' she instructed the older woman. 'I won't be long.'

Hurriedly threading her way across the floor and down the stairs towards the warehouse office, Leonie had a sudden moment of panic as she realised that it might be her mother on the phone, calling about Jade. Although the little girl was only four, her irrepressible high spirits had already resulted in a broken arm from falling out of a tree, and a severe burn on her leg due to experimenting with a forbidden box of matches.

Smiling briefly at the receptionist, she picked up the phone, sighing with relief to hear the voice of her secretary.

'Leonie?'

'Yes, Gwen, what's the problem?'

'Nothing dramatic,' Gwen said. 'But we've had an urgent request for a valuation. The client has to go abroad in two days' time, and is frantic at having to leave a valuable Heriz carpet uninsured. Can you manage to see the carpet at six o'clock tonight?'

Leonie grimaced. 'I was hoping to get home early for once. Any chance of my doing the valuation tomorrow morning?'

'I'm afraid not. It's the only time that the client has free, and both Henry and Philip are fully booked this afternoon. I'm still trying to sort out Mr Dimitri's diary. Goodness knows where I'm going to fit everyone in.'

'Yes, I know it's a problem,' Leonie agreed. The bad car accident which had kept her employer, Dimitri Kashan, away from the office for the last four weeks had meant an increased work-load for the other members of the firm. 'Okay, Gwen, I'll see to it—just as long as it is only an insurance valuation, and not someone wishing to arrange a sale. I simply wouldn't have enough time for that.'

'I've already made that point clear to the client,' her secretary assured her before rattling off an address in Mayfair. 'Just ring the doorbell and ask for Sheikh Samir, okay?'

'An Arab? You never said . . .' Leonie's voice trailed away as she realised that Gwen had put down the phone.

Thanking the receptionist and walking slowly out of the office, Leonie tried to banish a strange feeling of apprehension. How could there be any problem? Especially since she already had many clients from the oil-rich Arab states, who considered the purchase of oriental rugs and carpets to be a better investment than stocks and shares. Although, of course, the fact that she could speak Arabic was another reason why many of them preferred to deal with her firm.

Totally absorbed in her thoughts, it wasn't until Leonie felt a hand grasping her arm, that she realised she wasn't alone in the dusty corridor.

'Ah ha—at last! I've been hunting high and low for you, ever since my secretary said you were in the building.'

Leonie looked up, startled to see Jeff Powell's handsome face beaming down at her. 'I'm sorry . . .' She shook her head in confusion.

'What for? I only wish I could persuade you to leave Kashan's and join the wholesale trade,' he grinned. 'Maybe if you worked here, at Powell's, I wouldn't have such difficulty trying to convince you of my manifold charms! How about having dinner with me tonight?'

'I'm afraid I can't, I'm going to be tied up with business,' she murmured, moving aside as he tried to slip an arm about her waist.

'What a pity.' Jeff's mouth tightened slightly as he gazed at the girl standing beside him. Not only was she damn good at her job, but with her unusual colouring of large blue eyes set over a pale alabaster, almost translucent skin, surrounded by the fiery brilliance of her hair, she was a startlingly beautiful woman. A regular visitor to his warehouse during the last few years, she had steadfastly refused to respond to his advances. This had at first aroused disbelief and then, when he realised that she was impervious to his charm, he had become intrigued.

Without being vain, he was well aware of the fact that women found his blond good looks attractive, and being comparatively rich and successful, he had never had any trouble in finding girl-friends. He knew, from gossip within the trade, that there was a broken marriage in Leonie's background, and that she had a young daughter to support. However, she was only twenty-four, and he was certain that she must have had many relationships with other men; she was far too sexually attractive not to have done so. Why, then, did she insist on keeping him at a distance?

'What are you looking for, today?' he asked.

Leonie smiled. 'My client and I must have viewed practically every carpet in London! However, I think she's going to settle for a Qum rug—always provided your price isn't too steep.'

'You know that I'll always be happy to quote you a special price,' he said softly, moving closer to her slim frame.

'Yes, well . . . Oh my goodness—just look at the time!' Leonie murmured, hurriedly glancing down at her watch as she edged adroitly away. 'I must fly! Poor Mrs Kaminsky will wonder where I've got to,' she added over her shoulder as she hurried off down the corridor.

Jeff Powell stood looking after her disappearing figure for some moments, before giving a helpless shrug and returning to his office. Over an hour later he was still finding it difficult to concentrate on the business in hand, the vision of Leonie's lovely face coming between him and his work.

For her part, Leonie had no such problems. She was well used to dealing with the amorously-inclined Jeff Powells of this world, who more often than not regarded her as a challenge to their masculinity. She had, therefore, completely dismissed the handsome warehouse owner from her mind by the time she rejoined Mrs Kaminsky, who was happily enthusing over her choice of carpet.

It took some time to sort out the paperwork concerning the export of the carpet and Leonie was, as she had feared, already half an hour late for her lunch appointment when the taxi in which she was travelling turned into Jermyn Street. Entering the restaurant, she made her way over to the table where her old school friend, Sally, was waiting.

'I'm sorry to be so late, but it's just been one of those days,' Leonie said, sinking thankfully down on to a comfortable, velvet-covered chair. 'First of all the car wouldn't start this morning, then it was a matter of trundling from one warehouse to another, and just when I was about to leave the office, I had to take a long phone call from New York which ... *Good God*! Do I spy a bottle of champagne?'

Sally laughed at the startled expression in her friend's wide blue eyes as a waiter placed the silver ice-bucket stand, containing a bottle of Dom Perignon, beside their table.

'*If* I can get a word in edgeways, I'd remind you that today is my birthday.'

'Oh, no! I completely forgot,' Leonie groaned.

'And I'm also celebrating a promotion at work. I'll have you know that you are in the privileged position of having lunch with Armstrong, Lord and Marshall's newest account executive!'

'Oh, Sally—how marvellous! I'm so pleased for you,' Leonie said, leaning back in her seat and beaming with delight. She knew that her friend had been hoping for this promotion within one of London's top advertising agencies, and it was good to know that all her hard work and talent had been recognised at last. 'Will you get a large rise in salary to maintain you in your new, exalted position?' she teased.

'I sincerely hope so—if only to pay for this lunch!' Sally retorted with a grin as the waiter opened the bottle and poured the champagne.

'Well, Happy Birthday, and congratulations,' Leonie said, raising her glass in a toast. 'Mmm, it's delicious—a real corpse reviver!' she added, savouring the cool dry taste of the sparkling liquid.

'You certainly don't look like a corpse,' Sally said, gazing with envy at the beautiful girl sitting beside her. 'What's the problem? Nothing wrong with Jade, I hope?'

'No, thank goodness. After her last escapade, she's been as good as gold. She now knows that climbing trees can lead to a fall—and a broken arm!' Leonie smiled as she remembered the indignant expression on her small daughter's face, when she realised she would have to wear a heavy plaster cast for some weeks. 'In fact, Jade's been angelic lately. Mainly, I suspect, because she's determined to be a bridesmaid at my mother's wedding!'

'It's only two weeks until the big day, isn't it? How are all the preparations going?'

'Fairly smoothly—so far! But Mother began panicking a month ago, about having to leave Jade and me alone in England, and I can't seem to persuade her to stop worrying.'

An American, Leonie's father had been a senior executive with an oil company based in Tehran. The Shah's departure and the rise of the Ayatollahs had left Iran in a ferment, and John Elliot had opted to take early retirement, deciding to live in England where Leonie, aged fourteen, was still at boarding school. The fact that his wife was English and had many relatives in the country was also a deciding factor in his decision, and it was tragic that he should have died so shortly after moving into their new home in London.

Over the past ten years, Leonie's mother had settled down to a reasonably contented widowhood when, quite suddenly out of the blue, a friend of her father's over on a visit from the United States had decided to round off his holiday by calling to see Mrs Elliot. That had been three months ago, and with what seemed the speed of light, Clifford T. Brownlow and her mother had decided to get married. Leonie thoroughly approved of her prospective stepfather, and of his desire to take her mother back to his home in Florida after the wedding. The only problem had been Mrs Elliot's increasing concern about Leonie and Jade's future.

'It wouldn't be so bad if you had a nice, reliable nanny,' her mother had said a few weeks ago. 'I know you've contacted all the agencies, darling, but if you can't find someone, what are you going to do?'

'I'll manage somehow,' Leonie murmured soothingly. 'There's no need to worry.'

'Well, I can't help worrying. I've been pleased to do what I can, looking after Jade while you've been at work—but even you must realise that it hasn't been an ideal situation. Whether you'll admit it or not,' Mrs Elliot added firmly, 'the plain truth is that Jade is a bright, intelligent little girl who needs a father.'

'Oh, Mother!' Leonie groaned. 'Don't let's go through it all again! My marriage was over almost before it began, for heaven's sake. I know your views on the sanctity of marriage, but all I want is a divorce!'

Mrs Elliot sighed heavily. 'I don't approve of your getting a divorce, of course, but I thought that Badyr had agreed . . .'

'The letter to my solicitor from Dhoman was quite specific. It said that he "might be prepared to consider such a course of action"—but only if I'd agree to meet him and discuss the matter.' Leonie shrugged. 'There's no way I can possibly agree to that. Badyr doesn't know about Jade, and I daren't take the risk of his finding out about her.'

'I've always said that it was quite wrong of you not to tell Badyr about his child,' her mother said stubbornly. 'He has a legal right to know about his daughter, and your fears that he would take her away from you are quite ridiculous.'

Leonie had suppressed a sharp retort. There was little point in resurrecting all the old arguments as to why she had not informed Badyr about Jade. He had been under arrest in Dhoman when his daughter was born, and couldn't have received the message in any case. By the time his despotic old father had been despatched into exile, she had heard and read about too many cases of Arab fathers snatching their children and disappearing without trace, to be able to feel that she could take the risk.

At the thought of Jade's possible abduction, Leonie could feel her stomach contract with panic. There was absolutely no doubt in her mind that she had made the right decision—however morally wrong it might be— not to have told her husband about their daughter. All she had to do was to wait for another year, and then she could get a divorce with or without Badyr's consent. Not that she had any intention of marrying again—far from it! That one, brief experience, had been quite enough to put her off matrimony for life.

'Hey! What are you trying to do—jab that steak to death?'

'What . . .?' Leonie looked up, startled out of her bitter, introspective thoughts by Sally's laughing comment. 'I was just . . . er . . . well, I was just thinking that I must make a greater effort to find a nanny to look after Jade while I'm at work. God knows what will happen to the business if I don't.'

'When I last saw you, your employer had just been carted off to hospital. Has it caused a lot of extra work?

'And how!' Leonie gave a mock groan. 'Business is

booming at the moment—which is obviously good for the firm, and since Dimitri has placed me in overall charge during his absence, I've found myself run off my feet. However, if I'm to be honest,' she added with a grin, 'I have to admit that I'm loving every chaotic moment!'

Sally laughed and then looked thoughtfully down at the table as she fiddled with the stem of her glass. 'I can see that you are frightfully busy, but I would be grateful if—well, if you could find the time to do me a favour.'

'Yes, of course I will, if I can.'

'Well, it isn't for me, exactly . . .' Her friend paused and then took the plunge. 'I realise I may be treading on painful memories, but the fact is that one of the girls sharing my apartment has gone and got herself engaged to a Prince from Saudi Arabia.'

'Oh Lord!'

'Yes, my sentiments exactly! However, I wondered if you could have a talk to her. The other two girls and I have tried to warn her about the pitfalls, but she simply won't listen. She may be in love with the man, of course, but we suspect that it's much more likely that she's simply dazzled out of her mind by his fast sports car, dining at the Ritz practically every night, and the expensive, fabulous jewellery he's been throwing in her direction.'

Leonie sighed heavily. 'It's so difficult, isn't it? How on earth do you explain to someone—especially if they think that they're madly in love—the differences between East and West; the drastic culture-shock she's likely to experience? I know that I refused to listen to any advice at the time, however well intentioned.'

'I read somewhere that Saudi Arabia has by far the strictest regime, as far as women are concerned. Is that right?' Sally asked.

'Yes. Most of the Gulf states are fairly liberal, but all women living in Saudi Arabia—of whatever nationality—must conform to very strict rules. For instance:

she won't be able to work, or drive a car.' Leonie ticked the items off on her fingers. 'Neither can she leave her house, even for a simple thing like going to the shops—not unless she is accompanied by a male relative. In effect, it means that your friend will be a prisoner in her home for very long periods of time. What's more, she'll probably see very little of her husband. He's more than likely to dump his new wife with his mother, and then spend most of his time with his male friends. So, unless she can speak Arabic, she will find herself living a silent, lonely life among complete strangers.'

'My God!' Sally shuddered. 'It sounds horrific!'

'Well, yes, it is—if you've been brought up to a life of freedom in the Western hemisphere. However, I suppose that if you and I had been born in Arabia, and raised strictly according to the Moslem faith, we would think it was a perfectly normal and generally happy way of life.'

'Did you find ... I mean, was your existence in Dhoman as bad as that?' Sally looked at her with concern.

'Good gracious no!' Leonie smiled bitterly. 'Living in Saudi Arabia would have been a picnic compared to the medieval harem in which I found myself!'

'But I thought ... surely, now that your husband is a king, or whatever ...'

'Sultan,' Leonie corrected her. 'His Majesty, Sultan Badyr ibn Raschid Al Hamad, to be precise! He ousted his old father from the throne some years ago—and I hope he's enjoying himself,' she added grimly. 'Because, believe me, a more backward, hopelessly archaic country would be hard to find! God knows, I was only there for a short time, but as far as I'm concerned it was the worst three months of my entire life!'

Although they had been friends for years, Sally had been abroad when Leonie had got married and knew very little about her husband, or the life she had led in the South Arabian Kingdom of Dhoman. She was only aware that the experience had left her friend withdrawn and silent on the subject: Leonie having always made it very clear that she didn't want to talk about her brief marriage.

'I had no idea . . .! I mean, I wouldn't have brought up the subject if I'd known . . .' Sally muttered, wishing that she had kept her mouth shut.

'There's no need to worry, and I'll certainly do what I can to persuade your friend to take a long hard look at the life in front of her! As far as my marriage is concerned,' Leonie said crisply, 'it ended nearly five years ago and now, when I look back, I can appreciate some of the good things about the country and the people—even if I couldn't see it at the time.'

She paused as she tried to find words to express the complex ideology of the East. 'It's so totally alien to everything we in the West have been brought up to believe in—it's a completely different way of life. For instance, an Arab husband would be astounded and deeply offended if you accused him of being cruel to his wife by keeping her incarcerated inside her home. The men are taught to cherish and protect their women, and what you and I would definitely think of as a jail sentence, they regard as warm, loving care.' She shrugged. 'I suppose it's only fair to say that they do have a tremendous feeling of close family unity, a solidarity and fierce pride, not only in their immediate family, but also in their country.'

'I still think that the life sounds simply awful! What we need is another glass of champagne,' Sally said firmly, catching the eye of a passing waiter. 'And while I'm on the subject, I've got some friends coming in for a drink early this evening, why don't you call by on your way back from work?'

Leonie shook her head regretfully. 'I'd love to, but I have an appointment to value a carpet at six o'clock. Besides, I always try to be home reasonably early, so

that I can bath Jade—it's the one part of the day when
we can spend some time together.'

'There's no doubt about the fact that motherhood
suits you,' Sally assured her with a grin. 'If I could have
a guarantee that I'd look as good as you do, I might be
tempted to get married and have a baby!'

'Is Robert Armstrong still trying to persuade you to
name the day?' Leonie queried, referring to her friend's
long-standing relationship with her boss.

'Well . . .' Sally blushed. 'I'm getting to the point
when I think I might give him the shock of his life, and
agree to marry him!'

'Goodness! What's brought on this change of heart?'

'Reaching twenty-five!' Sally moaned, staring
gloomily down at the bubbles in her glass.

'You poor old, middle-aged hag!' Leonie laughed as
she rose to leave. 'I'll see you and your parents at
Mum's wedding of course, but in the meantime, I
should snap up Robert while the going's good. You
know that you are both crazy about each other—so say
"yes" and be happy, hmm?' She bent down to kiss her
friend's cheek. 'I'd like to stay longer and help you to
drown your sorrows, but I've got a million things to do
back at the office.'

She hadn't been exaggerating, Leonie told herself
some hours later as she paid off a taxi and looked at the
impressive exterior of the large town house. The
telephone had never stopped ringing all afternoon, and
it had been a scramble to get here on time for her six
o'clock appointment.

'I believe Sheikh Samir is expecting me,' she said as
the door was opened by a portly butler, dressed in a
black coat and striped trousers. With a deep bow he
silently conducted her across the black and white
marble hall and up a wide staircase to the first floor of
the large building. Knocking discreetly on a large pair
of doors, he pushed them open and then stood aside to
allow her to enter the room.

My goodness—it's the size of a ballroom! Leonie thought, hardly given time to take in the proportions of the enormous room as a short, dark-haired young man came forward to greet her.

'Sheikh Samir?'

'I am delighted to make your acquaintance, Miss—er—Elliot,' he murmured, bowing his head over her hand and then gesturing towards the large carpet lying beneath a brilliantly lit chandelier.

Leonie knew of no precise formula for analysing the 'quality' of a rug, but by any criteria the deep, glowing pool at her feet had to be one of the finest antique carpets she had ever seen. Totally immersed, she bent down to examine it closer, delighting in the exquisite workmanship and in the subtle tones of the jewelled silk colours, all in perfect harmony. A breathtakingly beautiful carpet, with its pile length, fringes and borders all as good as new—it was a masterpiece!

'This is obviously an extremely valuable rug,' she said as she rose to her feet, unable to tear her eyes away from such perfection. 'Forgive me for being blunt, Sheikh Samir, but I must point out that you have been taking a considerable risk in not insuring such a piece before now, and I must urge you to contact an insurance broker first thing tomorrow morning. I will, of course, measure it in a moment and give you a firm valuation, but I can tell you straight away that a rug in this condition would fetch at least a thousand pounds a square foot.'

Leonie forced herself to turn away from the carpet, anxious to impress upon the Sheikh just what a precious object he owned. But to her bewilderment, he seemed to have vanished into thin air. Puzzled, she looked about her, before a movement in a dark corner of the room attracted her attention.

Still amazed at the discovery of such a superb example of the rug-makers' art, Leonie frowned, peering into the grey shadows which lay beyond the brilliant pool of light over the carpet. A sudden shiver of fright ran down her spine, her eyes widening with shock at the sight of the tall figure walking slowly towards her.

'B-Badyr . . .?'

Her incredulous, hoarse whisper reverberated about the enormous room, echoing in her ears as she closed her dazed eyes for a moment. It couldn't be! It simply wasn't possible! What on earth was her husband doing here? And in London, of all places?

CHAPTER TWO

'WELL, well. What a pleasure it is to see you again, my dear Leonie. It has been a long time, has it not?'

Oh, dear God! There was no mistaking that deep, faintly accented and coolly ironic tone of voice. Leonie put out a hand to grab the top of a nearby chair for support, her whole body shaking with tension as if in the grip of a raging fever. Fighting to control her ragged breathing, she gazed with stupefaction at the man she hadn't seen for almost five years.

It was . . . yes, of course it was Badyr. And yet, as her eyes swept over the man who had now come to a halt on the other side of the carpet, it seemed as if she were looking at a complete stranger.

Leonie stared blankly at his tall figure. Her dazed vision filled with the sight of broad shoulders tapering to slim hips elegantly attired in an expensively tailored dark suit, the impeccable fit emphasising the lean tautness of the body that she remembered so well. No, it wasn't his tall frame that was so unfamiliar. Forcing herself to raise her eyes from his immaculate white shirt, contrasting sharply against the brown column of his neck, she felt the colour drain from her face for a second time.

What on earth had happened to Badyr? There seemed to be nothing she could do to hide her shock and confusion as she gazed at the black patch covering his left eye, from which a deep scar carved its way down over his tanned cheek to the line of his jaw. The raven's-wing blackness of his hair, lying thick and smooth against his well-shaped head before curling over the collar of his suit, was the only instantly recognisable feature that she could recall. It was almost impossible

21

to reconcile the memory of her husband's lazy charm,
his handsome appearance and warm personality, with
the harsh, rugged features and physically dangerous
aura projected so strongly by this ... this man, whose
one, glittering dark eye was subjecting her to a slow,
silent appraisal that almost scorched her skin.

'W-what are you d-doing here ...?' she stuttered,
trying to pull her distraught mind together.

'Such a warm welcome after all these years!' Badyr
murmured sardonically. 'Perhaps I felt it was about
time that we should meet to discuss various matters,
hmm?'

'There's nothing ... nothing for us to discuss—other
than a divorce, of course,' she retorted, clasping her
hands together to hide their trembling agitation.

'I can think of one or two other items,' he drawled.
'However, if you particularly wish to talk about the
termination of our marriage, then I am prepared to
hear what you have to say.'

Leonie gasped, anger and resentment sweeping
through her body at his casual condescension, the
patronising note in his voice. How dare he treat her like
this? It wasn't her fault that she had been forced to flee
from Dhoman all those years ago. Never once, in all
that time, had he even bothered to contact her. And
now, suddenly appearing from nowhere like a genie
from a bottle ... Her stomach lurched, apprehension
and a dawning realisation of the truth welling up like
sickness inside her.

'Sheikh Samir ...?' she whispered.

'My aide-de-camp.'

'And ... and the carpet?'

Badyr gave a negligent shrug, moving with lithe grace
to lean against the edge of a table. 'It was merely a
convenient bait to draw you within my orbit—nothing
more.'

Leonie shook her head in confusion, waving away his
words with a gesure of irritation. 'That carpet is

priceless, for heaven's sake! I simply don't understand what's going on. It . . . it doesn't make sense!'

'On the contrary, it makes excellent sense.' The sensual curve of his mouth twisted in a wry smile. 'For over a year, your solicitor has been repeatedly told that I wished to talk to you personally, face to face, and each time I was informed that you would not agree to such a meeting. I therefore decided to take matters into my own hands—and here you are! What a fortunate man I am,' he added with cynical amusement, 'to have the opportunity of at last being able to see my—er—darling wife.'

I'm not your darling wife! she wanted to scream, feeling that she had somehow strayed into a nightmare. With a nervous, unconscious movement, she raised her hand to smooth away a stray tendril, which had fallen down from the heavy knot of hair on top of her head. Her heart thudded in her chest as she felt his gaze linger on the curve of her breasts, thrown into prominence by her action. Leonie's cheeks grew hot and flushed beneath his analytical scrutiny.

When he spoke again, the tone of his voice was subtly different. It contained a new, personal warmth which sent shivers feathering down her spine. 'You are thinner than I remembered, Leonie. It doesn't suit you.'

'We're not here to discuss my figure,' she snapped nervously. 'And . . . and why are we meeting in this building, anyway?'

'It would, of course, have been more convenient for us to have met in my suite at Claridges. However, since I wished to minimise the chances of your discovering my intentions,' he added with a mocking grin, 'I think that this place has served its purpose admirably.'

Had he flown over from Dhoman especially to see her? It seemed as though he was going to let her have a divorce, but if so, why had he gone to such trouble, when all he had to do was to send a letter of agreement to her solicitor? Stiff with tension, she glanced warily at him through her eyelashes as he stood up and looked slowly around the enormous room.

'A charming building, is it not?' he murmured blandly. 'I have appointed one of my sheikhs to be the new Dhomani Ambassador, and he presents his credentials to the Court of St James next week. I think he will be very comfortable here, don't you?'

Leonie gritted her teeth, shaking with suppressed anger and frustration at the underlying note of laughter in his voice. It was clear that Badyr was amusing himself at her expense, undoubtedly taking his revenge for her adamant refusal to meet him. As the ruling Sultan of Dhoman, and probably every bit as autocratic a dictator as his old father before him, the comfort of his Ambassador was likely to be a long way down his list of priorities!

Suddenly, Leonie decided that she had had enough of this confrontation. If he wanted to discuss their divorce, he could do it with her lawyer. The shock of seeing him again, especially the dramatic change in his appearance effected by the black eye-patch and the deep scar running down his cheek, had initially unnerved her. However, she was beginning to recover her equilibrium. There was no reason on earth why she should have to stand here while Badyr played whatever cat-and-mouse game he had in mind.

'I don't wish to see you again, and I suggest that any further communications between us are dealt with by our respective solicitors,' she said as firmly as she could, turning to walk over to the door.

'Not so fast, my dear Leonie!' He moved swiftly to catch hold of her arm. 'Just where do you think you are going, hmm?'

She glared up at the harsh, indomitable expression on Badyr's face, conscious of her erratic heartbeat at his close proximity.

'Take your hands off me!' she snapped, trying to break free of his grip.

'There was a time when you hungered for my touch,' he murmured softly. 'Or have you forgotten?'

'I . . . I've forgotten everything,' she retorted quickly, inwardly cursing the husky, breathless note in her voice.

'Really?' His lips curved into a sardonic smile. 'Let us see, hmm?'

'No . . .!' She found herself jerked swiftly into his arms, her exclamation of horrified denial stifled as his mouth possessed hers in a hard, determined fashion. Struggling against the arms which tightened about her like bands of steel, frantically trying to push him away, she was aware of a treacherous warmth invading her limbs beneath the kiss that burned and demanded her submission.

Gradually and imperceptibly the cruel, ruthless pressure eased, his lips becoming warm and persuasive as they softly coaxed and teased away all resistance. Her pulse seemed to be racing out of control, her slim figure shaking with long-suppressed emotions and lost beneath a sudden tidal wave of desire; totally unable to prevent herself from passionately responding to the sensual, erotic mastery of his tongue as he savoured the inner sweetness of her mouth. With a low, husky moan, Leonie's arms tightened about his neck, her fingers burying themselves convulsively in his thick black hair. The evocative, musky scent of his cologne filled her nostrils, a raging excitement seizing her body at the fierce possession of Badyr's embrace and the evidence, in the hard muscled thighs pressed so closely to hers, of his own arousal.

Drowning in a pool of dark passion, she shivered as his mouth trailed slowly down the long column of her neck, to seek the scented hollows at the base of her throat. It was some moments before her eyelids fluttered open, the light from the chandelier almost dazzling her. Through that blinding brilliance she saw Badyr looking down at her, his mouth twisted in a slight, ironic smile.

'It would appear that you have not entirely forgotten *everything*, my dear Leonie, hmm?'

Leonie felt sick with self-disgust, a flush of deep crimson covering her face as she realised just how easily she had succumbed to Badyr's embrace. He had always been able to arouse her, even when she had been a miserably unhappy prisoner of the harem in Dhoman. The physical attraction between them had been the strongest, most potent part of their relationship; a bond, it would seem, as yet unbroken by the separate lives they had led during the last five years.

She fought against acknowledging the fact. Furious with herself, and him, she quickly broke away from the loose grip of his encircling arms.

'If you think that ... that kiss solved anything, or meant a thing to me, you are sadly mistaken!' she ground out savagely.

Turning away from Badyr's piercing gaze, she attempted to control her nervously shaking hands as she tucked her white silk blouse back inside the waistband of her navy blue skirt. God knows what her hair looked like, she thought helplessly, and she didn't suppose she had a shred of make-up left on her face. But this was hardly the time or the place to worry about such unimportant details. She must ... she simply must leave this house as quickly as she possibly could.

Ignoring her words, Badyr walked over to pull an embroidered bell-rope hanging down the side of a wall. 'I suggest that we now leave. I have ordered dinner to be served in my suite at the hotel, where we can continue our—er—discussion in more comfortable surroundings.'

'There is nothing to discuss—nothing that our two lawyers can't sort out between them. I'm leaving now,' she added firmly. 'And there is no reason why we should have to meet ever again.'

'I'm afraid, my dear Leonie, that it isn't that simple. I have some personal matters that I wish to discuss with you, and if you adamantly refuse to join me for dinner, then I will simply have to accompany you to your home.'

'No . . .!'

'Why not? I would be interested to see your house.' He smiled lazily at the girl who was staring at him in consternation. 'You are living with your mother, I understand.'

'It . . . er . . . it wouldn't be . . . er . . . at all convenient for you to call at my home,' she muttered quickly. She could feel beads of perspiration breaking out on her forehead at the thought of his finding out about Jade.

'What a pity. I have many fond memories of your charming mother, and would have enjoyed meeting her again.'

'No . . . well, I'm afraid that she . . . she's in bad health at the moment,' Leonie improvised swiftly. 'She's . . . er . . . she's had the flu, and . . . um . . . still hasn't recovered.'

'Really? Then I must surely pray for her swift recovery.'

Leonie's head jerked up at the deep, sardonic note of amusement in his voice. It might be her imagination, but for a moment it had seemed as if his shoulders had been shaking with inner laughter. *The damn man!* He might not realise it, but he had somehow managed to completely outmanoeuvre her. If she didn't go and have dinner with him, he was quite capable of turning up at her home, despite any excuse she might be able to think of.

As she hesitated, desperately trying to think of a way out of her dilemma, there was a knock on the door and Sheikh Samir entered the room.

'The chauffeur awaits your pleasure, Majesty,' he murmured, being careful not to look in her direction as he bowed deeply to Badyr.

'Well, Leonie,' Badyr purred dangerously. 'Which is

it to be? Dinner at my hotel, or do I instruct the
chauffeur to take us both back to your house, hmm?'

Locking the door of the palatial bathroom firmly
behind her, Leonie gave a heavy sigh as she slipped off
the jacket of her navy blue suit, and went over to sit
down on a stool in front of the marble-topped dressing-
table.

There never had been any choice, had there? Not
really. There had been no alternative to having dinner
here in the hotel with Badyr, since she couldn't possibly
risk his finding out about Jade. She had taken such
pains over the last five years, first to hide her pregnancy
and then her daughter, that she couldn't possibly allow
him to discover the truth.

Resting her chin in the palms of her hands, she stared
gloomily into the mirror. What a mess! And she looked
a mess too, she told herself, glumly taking out the
tortoiseshell combs which held her hair in place on top
of her head. Shaking the thick mass of curly red-gold
hair free, she opened her purse, relieved to see that it
held her brush and comb as well as her make-up bag.

Leonie's lips twisted in a wry, ironic smile as she
looked around at the pale beige marble walls, the gold
taps and what seemed an enormous collection of
brilliantly lit mirrors reflecting every inch of the huge,
luxurious bathroom. What it was to be the reigning
Sultan of an oil-rich, desert state! Not that she wanted
any part of it. She had experienced life locked inside a
gilded cage, and she knew only too well that wealth,
position and privilege meant nothing without freedom.
During her incarceration in Dhoman, she had learnt
for the first time just what a precious commodity
freedom was—something she hadn't realised until it had
been taken away.

Leonie took a deep dreath and attempted to pull
herself together. There was no point in being so gloomy
and introspective about her past life. That was now well

behind her, thank goodness, and after she and Badyr
had raked over the cold ashes of their marriage tonight,
she would be free of Dhoman and all it stood for.

Drawing a brush through the heavy thickness of her
curly hair, she noticed for the first time the delicately
engraved, jewelled flask placed beneath the dressing-
table mirror. Putting out a hand to admire the
craftsmanship of the object designed in the shape of a
khanjar, the curved ceremonial dagger worn by
Dhomani men, her eyes widened as she realised it was
made from solid gold. Removing the stopper and
inhaling the rich aroma of frankincense, sandalwood,
musk and other spices, Leonie instantly recognised the
scent of *Amouage*, the mind-bogglingly expensive
cologne used by Badyr.

Suddenly, all the conflicting emotions she had felt in
his arms earlier that evening rose up to torment her.
There seemed little she could do to banish the
throbbing, sick excitement in the pit of her stomach as
she remembered the way he had crushed her so tightly
against his hard chest. The sensual touch of his lips and
. . . With a soft moan, Leonie leapt to her feet and
rushed over to splash her face with cold water, roughly
towelling it dry as she tried to expunge the visions from
her mind.

It had just been an unfortunate accident, that was all,
she assured herself hurriedly. It would never, ever,
happen again—of course it wouldn't! Badyr had only
been proving to his own satisfaction, if not hers, that he
was still an attractive man. A fact which, despite that
patch and scar on his face, she was quite prepared to
admit. But so what? Her fingers trembled as she swept
up her hair and jabbed the combs into her scalp. She
couldn't care less whom he kissed or made love to—just
as long as it wasn't her—right? The word 'wrong'
seemed to be hovering at the back of her mind, but she
ruthlessly crushed such a nonsensical thought and
quickly finished making up her face.

Giving herself a swift appraisal in the mirror, she was satisfied that the severe cut of her navy blue suit, and the v-necked white silk blouse, looked businesslike and efficient. The perfect outfit in which to discuss a divorce, she told herself, briskly walking over to unlock the door.

Unfortunately, it didn't seem as if Badyr took quite the same view. 'You look ravishing, as always!' he murmured, handing her a glass of champagne as she entered the large sitting-room.

'Aren't you going to have a drink?' she asked nervously, ignoring his compliment and warily noting the warm, intimate atmosphere conveyed by the deep piled carpet and the discreet lighting.

'In my present position, I feel that I must set a good example and follow the precepts laid down by my religion,' he said with a wry smile.

'If you are such a good Moslem,' Leonie said, swiftly tossing the Dutch courage down her throat, 'why don't you just say, "I divorce you" three times, and fly home to Dhoman? Our lawyers can deal with any paperwork, and then we'll both be happy.'

'No, I would not be happy, Leonie. That is not what I want,' he said.

'Okay,' she sighed. 'What *do* you want? What are you doing over here in London? And why, when our marriage is dead and buried, should I have been practically blackmailed into coming to this hotel?'

'Why do you not sit down and make yourself comfortable?' He waved towards one of the several deep-seated sofas that decorated the room.

'I prefer to stand,' she retorted mutinously.

Badyr shrugged, walking slowly over to seat himself in a wide leather armchair. 'You have asked me why I am here, in London,' he said softly, brushing an invisible speck of dust off his sleeve. 'It is really very simple, my dear Leonie. Don't you think that it is time that my daughter and I became acquainted with each other, hmm?'

Leonie gasped in horror, the breath driven from her lungs as if she had received a hard blow to the solar plexus. 'Your . . . your d-daughter?' she whispered, the blood draining from her face.

'Sit down,' he commanded sharply as she swayed with shock. 'Did you really think that you could keep it a secret from me?' he added quietly as her legs gave way and she sank down into a chair. 'I may have been under house arrest at the time, but I can assure you that I was well aware of what was happening in the rest of the country,' he said drily. 'I imagine that I knew of your pregnancy almost as soon as you did.'

'But . . . but why did you never get in touch with me? I never had a word from you, not from the moment you were arrested and taken away!' she protested.

'I couldn't risk it. You must remember how it was, Leonie. My father was firmly in the grip of senile dementia, and if he had found out about your pregnancy none of us would have been safe.'

'But surely . . .'

'I am speaking the truth, believe me,' Badyr assured her. 'He would have kept you under close supervision and then, if you had produced a son, my life wouldn't have been worth a damn! I had no idea what would happen to you, either. Which was why I had to arrange your immediate departure from Dhoman. At least there are proper hospitals in the West,' he added bitterly. 'As you know, the only medical care in the country at that time was the small surgery run by some Americans.'

'I—I had no idea that it was you who arranged my escape.' Leonie lay back in her chair, resting her head against the cushions. Her brain felt as if it had been battered into insensibility, totally stunned by the shocks she had sustained that day. 'But after the coup—after your father was deposed—why didn't you get in touch with me then?'

Badyr sighed. 'One of the main reasons for the coup was to take the reins of the country into my own hands.

Ignored by my father, the Marxist rebels had already gained control of the western part of Dhoman, and were being heavily supplied with men and weapons from both Russia and China. My agents told me that you had reverted to your maiden name, and I decided that you and the child would be safest if there was no contact between us. If certain "friends" of the rebels had known of your existence, there was a very real possibility of your both being kidnapped. I had no intention of submitting to that sort of blackmail,' he added grimly.

'The plain fact, my dear Leonie, is that for the last four years I have been fully occupied. Every ounce of my time and energy has been spent trying to drag my country away from its medieval condition, and into the twentieth century. Moreover, as Commander in Chief of the forces under my command, I had a nasty, brutal war to fight. I could not, therefore, afford to be distracted by the soft charms of either my wife or my daughter!'

He paused, the seconds slipping by as he regarded the trembling figure of the beautiful girl seated across the room. Her wide, sapphire-blue eyes stared blankly back at him from a face which seemed to be drained of all colour.

Leonie shifted uneasily under the intensity of his gaze, her head throbbing as she tried to grapple with the fact that Badyr had always known about Jade. No matter how hard she tried, Leonie couldn't seem to think constructively. Her mind seemed to have become numb, her brain an empty void.

Badyr rose and went over to lean against the marble fireplace. 'Now that I have at last defeated the rebels— thanks mainly to the British troops kindly lent to me by the British Government—Dhoman is now at peace.' He smiled wryly. 'Of course, there is still a lifetime of work to be done in the country, building roads, hospitals and schools for instance, but I can at last afford to sit back and relax somewhat.'

'Is that how you came by the . . . er . . . scar? In the war, I mean,' she muttered.

He gave a wry laugh. 'Alas, nothing so heroic! Having decided that my father really must be deposed, for the sake of Dhoman if not for anything else, I and my supporters arranged for a bloodless coup to take place. It was, of course, up to me to tell my father that his days as a ruler were over—not one of the most pleasant duties I have had to perform!' He came over to pour her another glass of champagne.

'Unfortunately, my father did not greet the decision with—er—enthusiasm, and I was careless enough to allow him to draw his ceremonial sword on me. I hate to think what my old instructor at Sandhurst would have said about letting myself be surprised like that!' He smiled and ruefully shook his head. 'However, I could not possibly bring myself to shoot the man who had given me birth, and so I attempted to talk him out of taking any foolish action. Whereupon, he promptly aimed a blow at my head! Of course, my father was quickly disarmed by the men under my command; the only lasting result of the fracas was that I needed twenty stitches in my face—and I suffer from a case of permanent double vision from the blow to my temple.'

Leonie winced, expecting some dreadful revelation as he raised his hand and removed the black patch. To her surprise, both the eyes gleaming at her from beneath their heavy lids appeared to be perfectly normal.

'You see?' Badyr gave her a wry smile. 'I merely wear this patch to correct my double vision. I have seen many eye specialists, and they tell me that there is nothing they can do.' He paused. 'Do you find my appearance so very terrible, Leonie?'

'No, no, not at all,' she muttered. What on earth were they doing—sitting here and calmly discussing his eye-patch, for heaven's sake? He had always been physically very attractive, and now with that patch and

B

scar he seemed doubly so. Leonie knew that most women of her acquaintance would find such a dangerous, pirate-like image almost irresistible! And undoubtedly there had been many women in the last five years, she told herself sourly, before striving to banish such errant thoughts from her mind. Far more to the point was her concern about Jade.

'We must now talk about my daughter,' Badyr said, echoing her own thoughts with uncanny clairvoyance.

There was a long silence which seemed to reverberate around the room, Leonie stared determinedly down at the glass tightly clasped in her hands, which were shaking as if she had the palsy.

'I don't see that there is very much to discuss,' she murmured at last. 'You will want to see her, of course, but . . .' She faltered as Badyr gave a harsh bark of sardonic laughter.

'Oh, yes, Leonie. I fully intend to see Jade! Earlier in our conversation you asked me what it was that I wanted. Well, I must tell you that I want my daughter. I have come over here to London, with the express intention of taking her back to live with me in Dhoman.'

'You . . . you can't take Jade away from me—*you can't!*' she whispered, almost fainting at the wave of blind panic which ran like quicksilver through her trembling body.

'I do not intend to, of course. But if the necessity arose . . .? Yes, I can see no difficulty. The courts might well award me care and custody,' Badyr drawled smoothly. 'But if that action should fail, I would merely remove her from this country.'

'*No!*'

'No? Can you guarantee to guard her for every moment of every day? I think not!'

'You monster! I won't let you take her away from me!' she cried, jumping to her feet. 'Jade has never even

seen you, for heaven's sake. She would be terrified!'
Leonie gazed at him with horror, unable to say any
more for the hard lump obstructing her throat.

'Calm down, Leonie!' Badyr rose to his feet, walking
swiftly over to place his hands firmly on her shoulders.
'I have already said that I do not intend to take Jade
away from you.'

'Then why did you mention the courts and threaten
to abduct her?' she gasped, her whole body racked with
pain.

'I wanted you to understand that I am very serious
about the return of my daughter.'

'*Serious?* I am hardly likely to find your words
amusing, am I?' she cried, unable to prevent the helpless
tears from coursing down her cheeks.

'Come, there is no need to weep,' Badyr murmured
softly, taking her trembling body into his arms. 'Yes, I
want my daughter—but I also want you,' he added,
removing a handkerchief from his pocket and gently
wiping her eyes.

'Me? You want me to return to Dhoman?' She gave a
shrill, hysterical laugh as she abruptly broke away from
his embrace. '*You must be mad!*'

He shook his head. 'No, I am very sane. I wish to live
with my wife and daughter by my side. Is that so
strange?'

'Never, under any circumstances, could I possibly
face going to live in Dhoman again. Once was enough!'

'In that case, my dear Leonie, you must be prepared
to lose your child.'

The chilling finality of his words hit her like a blow.
'For God's sake, Badyr, you can't mean it? What have I
ever done to deserve such a terrible punishment? You
can't be so . . . s-so c-cruel!' Tears of utter desolation
streamed down her cheeks as she clutched frantically at
his arm. 'Don't do this to me . . . please don't take away
my little girl . . .' she sobbed.

'Compose yourself, Leonie!' he demanded sternly, a

muscle beating in his clenched jaw. 'I am not intending to take Jade from you, that would indeed be cruel.'

'But you said . . .'

'I said I wished you both to return with me to Dhoman. If you refuse to come, then it is *you* who will be abandoning our child.'

'I can't bear the thought of going back there!' she wailed helplessly as Badyr led her shaking figure over to a sofa. 'You know how awful it was for me—who better? I—I've never been so desperately unhappy in my whole life. Shut away in that dreadful, medieval fortress . . .' Leonie buried her face in her hands, her slim figure shuddering at the bitter memories she had tried so hard to forget.

'That was all in the past. You would find your position in Dhoman quite different now,' he replied evenly, seating himself on the sofa beside her. 'As my wife, you will have your own palace and your own servants. You will be free to come and go as you wish, although for your own safety I would insist on your having a bodyguard with you at all times. There are still one or two rebels at large,' he explained. 'The guards would only be there for your own protection.'

'It still sounds like the same old Dhoman that I loved to hate!' she retorted, fiercely blowing her nose. 'And why now? Why this sudden desire for your child, when you've managed to ignore us all these years?'

Badyr gave an impatient sigh. 'I have spent a good part of the evening so far, explaining exactly why I "ignored" you and my daughter.'

'Hogwash!' she lashed back angrily. 'I can read the papers, you know! That war of yours was finished a good year ago, so why the sudden interest in reclaiming your daughter, huh?'

'I am touched to learn that you have been taking such an interest in the affairs of my country,' he drawled with heavy sarcasm. 'However, your mother's wedding has merely brought forward my plans. I always intended that both you and Jade should return to Dhoman.'

'My—my mother's wedding?' Leonie looked at him in astonishment.

He shrugged. 'Of course. When your mother contacted me . . .'

'She *what* . . .!'

'Your mother was very worried about the future of yourself and the child. It was quite right and proper that she should let me know how matters stood, and she was absolutely correct in assuming that I would take responsibility for you both.'

'Oh God! How could she do this to me?' Leonie wailed, jumping to her feet in trembling agitation. 'No wonder you were laughing your head off back at the Embassy—you knew very well that my mother wasn't ill—you swine!'

Badyr's lips curved into a sardonic smile. 'Yes, I must confess to having been amused by your—er—inventiveness!'

'I bet you were! Well, let me tell you that Jade and I need you like a hole in the head—far less, in fact! Jade will be going to school in about six months' time and . . . I've got a job that I love. You can't . . .'

'I am well aware of your success in the wholesale oriental rug market,' he murmured blandly. 'I have been pleased to hear of how well you have progressed with your firm, and of Dimitri Kashan's trust and confidence in your ability.'

Leonie glared at him, her hackles rising at his condescending tone of voice. 'Don't you patronise me—you . . . you bloody man! Yes, I'm good at my job, and if I'm successful it's due solely to my own effort and hard work. I don't need you, or your millions, and I've absolutely no intention of throwing up my career and going back to Dhoman with you—*none at all!*'

'If you wish to continue to exercise your mind, there

will be plenty that you can do to help me in Dhoman,'
he said quietly.

'Oh, for heaven's sake, Badyr—you haven't been
listening to a damn thing I've been saying!' she
exploded, pacing back and forth about the room.
Trying to calm down, she took a deep breath and
turned to face him. 'Surely . . . surely you could allow
us to remain here, in London?' she said as quietly and
as reasonably as she could. 'You must be so wealthy
now, that for you to fly over here to see Jade as often as
you like, would hardly make a dent in the petty cash!'

'But that is not what I want, Leonie. I have told you
that I wish my wife and daughter to live with me.'

'I'm sick and tired of hearing what *you* want!' Her
blue eyes flashed dangerously, regarding his casually
lounging figure with utter loathing. 'Why don't you get
yourself another wife? The world is full of women
who'd jump at the chance of marrying a real live
Sultan!'

Badyr shook his head. 'I want you,' he remarked
flatly.

'Why, for God's sake?'

'Maybe . . .' he hesitated. 'Maybe, because I wish to
have a son, hmm?'

'Don't be ridiculous! All you have to do is to find
another wife and possess yourself in patience for nine
months.' She gave a shrill laugh. 'As far as I'm
concerned, you can forget it! I'm *definitely* not prepared
to . . .'

'Enough!' Badyr rose slowly from the sofa, his deep
voice cutting abruptly through her breathless protest.
'As I promised, I have listened to what you have had to
say about the termination of our marriage. Nevertheless,
my mind remains unchanged. Both you and our child
will accompany me back to Dhoman immediately after
your mother's wedding. You are my wife, Leonie, and I
shall exercise a husband's rights, as and when I feel
inclined to do so. I am confident that with Allah's

blessing you will bear me many sons. There is nothing more to be said.'

Leonie gasped with outrage. 'I won't . . .'

'Oh, yes, you will.' He moved forward, placing a hand beneath her chin and tilting her face up towards him. 'It is foolish of you not to acknowledge that I hold all the cards in this affair.'

She stared up at the face so close to her own, her eyes filled with the grimly implacable, unrelenting expression on his harsh features. Badyr was right. He did hold all the cards. He knew, with absolute certainty, that she would never abandon her child.

'God—I hate you! I'll never forgive you for what you are doing to me,' she hissed through clenched teeth, unable to control the furious, impotent rage which was shaking her slim body. 'And . . . and both you and Allah will have to wait a bloody long time—because I'll never, *ever*, willingly submit to your so-called "husband's rights"!'

'No?' he whispered softly as he lowered his dark head, his mouth feathering tormentingly across her lips and reawakening the aching memory of just how she had once responded to his light caresses.

Her mouth was suddenly dry, her nerve ends screaming and every muscle tensed against his calculated, deliberate assault upon her senses. *She must get out of here!* Twisting away from Badyr's arms, she tried to control the involuntary trembling in her legs as she walked towards the door.

'Surely you cannot be leaving so soon, Leonie?' he drawled, his voice heavy with mockery. 'Have you forgotten that I wish you to dine with me tonight?'

She turned to face the tall, elegant figure who had caused her so much heartache in the past. He was so sure, so arrogantly confident of her capitulation, that it was all she could do not to scream with frustration.

'I have forgotten nothing—especially those dreadful few months of our marriage. And the thought of eating dinner with you makes me feel sick!' she flung at him bitterly. 'I'm going home now, and unless you intend to use force and cause a scandal in this oh-so respectable hotel, I suggest that there is damn-all you can do about it.'

His figure stiffened, radiating a menacing force, and for the first time that day Leonie sensed the unleashed power of the anger her words had aroused, trembling at the realisation of just how ruthless and dangerous this man could be. And then he relaxed, smiling sardonically as he picked up the phone and ordered his chauffeur-driven Rolls to be brought around to the front door of the hotel.

'Do not make the error of trying to escape, my dear Leonie,' he warned her softly as she left the suite. 'I have infinite resources at my command, and let there be no doubt in your mind that when I return to Dhoman, I shall most surely be accompanied by both you and my daughter.'

Later that night as she lay in bed, staring blindly at the ceiling, Badyr's taunting words ran like an evil refrain through her tired mind. Driven back to her home in solitary splendour, she had been filled with misery, her only crumb of comfort being the contemplation of exactly what she was going to say to her mother on her return. But even there she had been frustrated, unable to relieve her exacerbated feelings. The house had been empty, with merely a note from her mother—the coward!—explaining that she and Jade had gone to have dinner and spend the night with old friends of the family on the other side of London.

Leonie felt totally exhausted by the events of the day, and yet the blessed relief of sleep evaded her. Try as she might, she could find no avenue of escape from the inevitability of her return to Dhoman. Even wild schemes, such as escaping with Jade to some secret destination, failed to stand up to more than a moment's contemplation. Badyr had stated no more than the truth: with unlimited money and resources at his command, he would manage to track her down sooner or later. And then what? His anger at being defied would undoubtedly result in his immediate abduction of Jade. As ruler of his country, Badyr had absolute and total power over his subjects, and she knew that once her child had been taken to Dhoman, she would never see her again.

Dhoman! The very name of the place was enough to make her shudder. Ever since she had escaped from that country, she had done all she could to expunge the painful memories of her brief marriage. But now there seemed nothing she could do to prevent them from rising like ghosts from the past, powerless to stop the haunting nightmares from filling her mind to the exclusion of all else.

CHAPTER THREE

IT was now clear that her first meeting with Badyr, when Leonie had been so young and innocent, had been nothing but a disastrous, malign twist of fate. If only she hadn't been quite so anxious to prove her worth to her new employer, Dimitri Kashan, by exceeding her instructions and delivering a precious carpet to the wrong address and the wrong person—but she had and she did!

'No, I can assure you that I am *not* Mr Wilding!' The tall, outrageously handsome man had regarded her flustered face with amusement. 'However, I am sure this little matter can be easily sorted out. So, why not sit down and have a calming drink, while we consider what to do about the problem, hmm?'

Leonie had looked nervously around the luxurious sitting-room of the penthouse apartment, her mind filled with her mother's dire warnings about what happened to young girls who accepted drinks from strange men. Not realising that the expression on her lovely face, and the alarm reflected in her sapphire blue eyes had so clearly echoed her agitated thoughts, she had been startled when the man standing before her gave a short bark of laughter.

'I can assure you that you are quite safe!' His shoulders had shaken with amusement. 'You have my word of honour that I do not make a habit of seducing pretty young girls—even one as beautiful as you! So, let us be very correct and introduce ourselves, hmm?'

'I'm ... er ... Leonie Elliot,' she had murmured, staring fixedly down at the rolled-up rug she was carrying, and miserably aware of the deep flush staining her cheeks. This man must think that she was very silly and gauche. How she had longed to be a sophisticated woman of the world and able to make cool, clever conversation, instead of standing here tongue-tied and helplessly uncertain of what to do next.

'Very well, Leonie, you may call me Badyr,' the man had said, gently leading her stiff figure towards a soft leather chair. 'Now if you will make yourself comfortable, and give me that piece of paper containing what is clearly the wrong name and address, I'll see if we can't solve the mystery, hmm?'

He had left the room, Leonie hearing a short buzz of conversation before he returned with a tray containing tall glasses and a jug. 'I have asked my assistant to make enquiries and here, in the meantime, is a cool drink of orange juice—which I can promise you contains no wicked alcohol!'

Smiling shyly up at the man who was regarding her with a calm, friendly expression on his face, Leonie had found herself beginning to relax. It was really very kind of him to take so much trouble on her behalf, and she haltingly told him so.

'Think nothing of it, my dear Leonie,' he had grinned, sitting down on a wide sofa near her chair. 'It is clearly my duty to help a damsel in distress. Now,' he had added, filling her glass again, 'tell me all about yourself.'

'There's ... well, there's really nothing much to tell,' she had begun, but under his skilful questioning she had soon found herself becoming more loquacious. It had been somehow very easy to talk to this man about just how much she missed her father and how, not knowing what she wanted to do on leaving school, she had been so grateful when an old friend of her father's, Dimitri Kashan, had offered her a job in his firm training to be an oriental rug broker. Since most of her school holidays had been spent in Iran, where rugmaking was an important part of the national economy, and where she had spent many hours visiting small village

workshops watching the weavers at their looms, Leonie
had jumped at the chance of working with such
beautiful objects.

'Training to be an oriental rug broker is perhaps an
unusual career? Especially for such a beautiful young
girl, hmm?'

Leonie had been able to feel herself blushing, her
heart beginning to beat in a hurried, nervous response
to the increasing warmth in his voice. 'I . . . er . . . I'm
not sure whether I'll still have a job after this mix-up
with the carpet,' she had muttered unhappily. 'What on
earth am I going to do?'

'What you are going to do, is to allow me to drive
you home,' he had said firmly. 'I know Mr Kashan, and
I can assure you that when I have spoken to him, there
will be nothing for you to worry about.'

Leonie had spent a sleepless night wondering about
what her employer would say, and also disturbed—not
to say appalled—by the strange churning in her
stomach, the hopeless longing and trembling excitement
whenever she thought about Badyr. She had been sure
that such a handsome, older man would have been
bored by her youth and inexperience, and quite
convinced that she would never see him again.

She had, therefore, been astounded when Dimitri
Kashan had welcomed her the next morning with a
beaming smile, and even more amazed to find that the
man in the luxury apartment was a valued client of the
firm. Prince Badyr of Dhoman, she learned, was the
only son of a wealthy Arab sultan and had been
brought up and educated in England. Her head had still
been spinning when she returned home from work to
find a huge bouquet of red roses awaiting her, together
with a note from Badyr asking her to join him for
dinner that night.

The next few weeks had been ones of halcyon
enjoyment and happiness. A serving officer in the
British Army, Badyr's regiment was based at Chelsea

Barracks in London, and he had insisted on seeing her every day, either taking her out to dinner or having a meal prepared by his Arab servants in his penthouse suite overlooking Hyde Park. Leonie had never tired of hearing about the past history of his country, Dhoman. She would sit curled up beside him on the sofa in his apartment as he told her how his country, situated at the foot of the Arabian peninsula overlooking the Arabian Sea, had once been a great sea-trading nation.

'People imagine that it is only a desert, but the south of the country is a wide, fertile green plain, once known as the Incense Coast because it provided the world with frankincense and other rare spices. Nowadays, our chief export is oil, although my father adamantly refuses to spend the revenues as he should—completely ignoring his people's dire need and poverty,' he had added bitterly.

That had been Leonie's first intimation of the strained relationship betwen father and son. Having sent Badyr to be educated in England, and encouraging him to take up a military career, Sultan Raschid had clearly not realised that such an education might well lead to his son taking a more democratic, liberal view of the responsibilities of a ruler.

'The days when one can run a country as if it was one's own private estate are dead and gone!' Badyr had exploded angrily as they returned to his apartment one evening. He had gone on to say that he had been given permanent leave of absence from his regiment, and he intended to return to Dhoman almost immediately.

'There has been constant trouble in the western part of my country for the past few years, mainly due to my father's dislike of all development—such as roads, hospitals and schools,' he had explained. 'Now, however, matters are becoming far more serious, and I have been informed by British army intelligence that both Russia and China are pouring arms into the area. I must go back and stand by my father's side, whether he wishes it or not. He needs me at such a time.'

Leonie had suddenly felt cold as ice, immobile as if she had been turned to stone. Ever since they had first met, Badyr's handsome image had seemed to haunt both her dreams and every waking moment, causing her to be so absent-minded that her employer, Dimitri Kashan, had been forced to protest: 'May the Good Lord preserve me from young girls in love!'

Was she in love? She had wondered how anyone knew if they were *really* in love? Leonie had only been aware that life had seemed to take on a new dimension when she was in Badyr's company, and without him she was somehow incomplete. However, since he had never attempted to do more than give her a chaste peck on her cheek as he delivered her back to her home each evening, she had had no idea of his feelings towards her.

Now, however, all doubts regarding her own emotions had been swept away. As a shaft of bitter agony pierced her heart, she had realised that she loved Badyr, and that she could not live without him. Gasping with pain, she had buried her face in her hands to hide the tide of desperate misery which racked her slim figure. A moment later she had felt his arms closing about her.

'Do not weep, my sweet Leonie,' he had murmured as she sobbed against his shoulder. 'Tell me what is wrong, hmm?'

'You are g-going away and . . . and I c-can't bear it. I love you s-so much . . .' she had stuttered, a deep blush spreading over her pale cheeks as she had realised just how she was betraying her feelings for him.

'Ah . . .' Badyr's tall frame had shaken as he gave a deep sigh. Lowering his head, his warm breath had fanned her flushed cheek as his lips had gently touched the corner of her trembling mouth in a soft, gentle caress. 'I too, my darling,' he had whispered. 'It is a very serious thing, is it not, for a man of my age to fall so completely in love—and with such a young girl?'

'*Oh, Badyr!*' she had exclaimed ecstatically, throwing her arms about his neck. 'I love you and . . .' The rest of her words had been lost as he had clasped her tighter, his mouth possessing hers with passionate intensity.

She had had no idea how long they stood locked together, but eventually his hold had slackened. 'I think that we had better sit down before I do something that we would both regret—like immediately taking you to my bed!' he had said hoarsely as he led her towards a sofa. 'I can see the headlines now,' he had grinned. '"Arab man rapes young girl in Hyde Park apartment"—I somehow don't think your mother would approve!'

A hectic flush had swept over Leonie's cheeks. Although she had been strictly brought up, and had always concurred with the moral principle of chastity before marriage, for the first time in her life she had understood the driving force and power of sexual desire. Badyr had mentioned rape, but she had known that once she was clasped within his arms, she would have no other impulse but complete and total surrender to whatever he might demand of her. Emotionally excited and thrilled beyond words to find that he loved her, she had been so immersed in her own ecstatic thoughts that she had almost missed his next words.

'. . . as I intended. I had hoped that we could be married and spend many happy years together here in England, before I would be forced to take up my responsibilities in Dohman. But it is not to be. I cannot ask you to wait for me, neither can I expect you to accompany me to such a medieval, backward country, where life is so very different from that in England.'

'Oh, please! Please take me with you, Badyr,' she had begged. 'I . . . I'll die if you go away and leave me, I know I will!'

'Ah, my darling. When you look at me like that I am sorely tempted,' he had murmured thickly, gathering her slender body into his arms. 'I, too, cannot bear the idea of life without you by my side. But you will find the life so different, so restrictive, that I hesitate . . .'

'I love you so much,' she had told him earnestly. 'I don't care what Dhoman's like, just as long as you and I are together.'

Badyr had sighed heavily. 'How can I possibly resist such a plea, since I too love you with all my heart? Very well, my darling, it shall be as you say. I will ask your mother for permission to marry you, and then we will leave for Dhoman, together.'

'Oh, Badyr . . .! I'm . . . I'm *so* happy!' she had murmured, tears of joy filling her eyes.

'I hope and pray that you may always be so,' he had said quietly. The dark eyes gleaming down at her had become shadowed, a troubled expression flickering across his face for a moment, before he had smiled and bent to kiss her soft lips. '*Insh'allah*, my beloved Leonie. It shall be as God wills, hmm?'

They had been married a week later at the Regent's Park Mosque, followed by a simple register office wedding and a lavish reception afterwards at the Hyde Park Hotel. Leonie had drifted through the day in a hazy state of bliss, only truly aware of Badyr's tall handsome figure, and her almost unbelievable joy at being married to a man whom she loved with all her heart.

It had taken a great deal of persuasion, on Badyr's part, to gain Mrs Elliot's permission for the wedding to go ahead. She had not been at all happy to learn that her daughter was intent on marrying an Arab, and even more disturbed to learn that the happy couple would be going to live in a far-off and isolated part of Arabia.

'Not that I've got anything against Badyr, himself,' her mother had said. 'He's a charming man, and I know that he will always take the greatest care of you—his assurances to me of his love and devotion were genuinely touching and obviously sincere. But, darling, you are so young—only eighteen!' She had frowned anxiously. 'And who has ever heard of Dhoman? Not only that—I'm told that Arab society is very, very different from anything we know in the West. It will be a totally strange way of life, and learning to live with someone else can be difficult enough, without adding cultural stresses and strains to the relationship.'

But Leonie had been adamant that their love for each other would surmount all obstacles, refusing to listen to any words of caution or the plea that she should wait a year before getting married, so as to be absolutely sure of her decision. And because she loved her daughter very dearly, Mrs Elliot had sighed and said no more.

Almost before she knew it, Leonie had said her emotional farewells, and was boarding the privately chartered aeroplane with her new husband, bound for a week's honeymoon in Paris before travelling on to Dhoman.

Leonie had never had any doubts about her physical response to Badyr, but his experienced lovemaking had been a revelation, an exquisite fulfilment that surpassed anything she could possibly have imagined. Knowing that she was a virgin, he had slowly and with infinite gentleness led her from one emotional delight to another. Beneath his skilful expertise, as his mouth and hands savoured every inch of her slender, quivering body, she had begun to comprehend the true meaning of emotional ecstasy. Eagerly welcoming both the pain and then the pulsating pleasure of his hungry possession, her conscious self had become submerged in a raging storm of desire as he raised her, emotionally and physically, to the very peak of passionate sensuality.

Day after day and night after night, Badyr had clearly demonstrated his inexhaustible desire for her body. Under his masterly tuition, she had learned to finally discard all her virginal inhibitions, wantonly responding to the piercing sweetness of his lips, wildly and passionately returning his intimate caresses.

But all too soon, it seemed, their idyll was over. Badyr had arranged that they would break their journey at Abu Dhabi, spending a night with his father's youngest sister, who had married a member of Abu Dhabi's ruling family.

It had been Leonie's first real glimpse of Arabia, and she had found it disconcerting. From the modern, futuristic design of the airport building which looked like a giant, psychedelic mushroom, to the shimmering glass-towered office blocks surrounded by shady parks and gardens overflowing with tropical blooms in riotous colours, it had seemed light-years away from her previous notions of what constituted a desert city.

Later that evening as Leonie had stood on the open balcony of their palatial bedroom, she had felt the first stirrings of apprehension and unease. Badyr's aunt couldn't have been kinder to her. A small, bustling woman, she had kissed Leonie enthusiastically on the cheek and seen to the girl's every comfort. However, it had quickly become apparent to them both that Leonie hadn't the faintest notion about the traditional customs or what was expected of women in Arabia. She hadn't known, for instance, that it wasn't usual for men and women to eat together—even husbands and wives having separate meals with members of their own sex. Nor had she been very successful at disguising her shock at having to wear a black veil covering her face when strange visitors called. She had also been clearly bewildered by the fact that among the guests at the aunt's female-only dinner-party—all of whom seemed to be clothed in dresses from the top Parisian fashion houses, and wearing magnificent jewellery the like of which she had never seen before—most of the women did not use a fork, but scooped up the food with the fingers of their right hand. Trying to teach Leonie to eat the same way, the women had screamed with laughter both at her awkwardness and the resulting mess on her clothes.

'I must have a long talk to Badyr as soon as possible!' his aunt had exclaimed in some agitation at the depth of the English girl's ignorance. 'How much has he told you about my brother, the Sultan, and the life that you will be expected to live in Dhoman?'

'Nothing, really,' Leonie had murmured, feeling tired and exhausted by all the cultural shocks of the day.

'I see,' the older woman had frowned. 'Well, if we have time before you leave tomorrow, I will try to tell you all I can.'

Which was very kind of her, Leonie reflected, unable to repress a shiver even though there was no breeze to disturb the hot night air. She had been so immersed in her thoughts that she had not heard Badyr's approach, giving a start of surprise as she felt his arms go about her slim waist.

'I must talk to you,' she had begun. 'I didn't realise . . . I mean, it's all so very . . .'

'Come to bed, my beloved,' Badyr had whispered, burying his face in the fragrant cloud of her red-gold hair.

'Please, Badyr, I'm worried, and . . .'

'Tomorrow. We will talk about what worries you tomorrow, hmm? Just now, I am far more interested in other matters!' His eyes gleamed in the darkness as he had turned her to face him, his mouth coming down to possess her lips in a warm, lingering kiss. 'Ah, my darling, I fear I am insatiably addicted to your delicious body,' he had breathed huskily, his hands moving slowly and sensually over the full curves of her breasts. As she had gasped and trembled at his touch, he had given a soft, low laugh, sweeping her up in his arms and moving swiftly over to the bed, where his vigorous, erotic lovemaking had quickly banished everything from her mind, save the driving need to ardently respond to the passion that flared between them.

Waking late the next morning, she had dressed and gone downstairs, drawn to the sound of voices coming from an open door. Standing in the doorway, she had been startled to see the small figure of his aunt, angrily yelling at Badyr who stood rigidly silent, growing pale as the tirade continued. Leonie had thought she heard her name mentioned once or twice, but it was impossible to be sure among the stream of incomprehensible language issuing from the mouth of the small, furious woman.

Badyr had gestured towards Leonie, and his aunt had fallen silent for a moment. 'Well,' she had sighed, speaking in English, 'I have done what I can. No one can say that you haven't been warned. But I do beg you to be careful, Badyr, because the situation is now very, very dangerous.'

'What's dangerous?' Leonie had asked, feeling suddenly frightened by the serious note in the older woman's voice.

'Nothing that need concern you,' Badyr had replied curtly. His dismissive words were clearly nonsense, and Leonie could feel her hackles rise at being treated like a child. However, his aunt was loudly clapping her hands for coffee, and it had proved impossible to pursue the matter any further.

There had been little time before they left Abu Dhabi for Badyr's aunt to do more than show Leonie how to wear the *abaya*, the black covering worn by Arab women outside their home. That, and her whispered injunction, when Badyr left the room for a moment, to contact the older woman if there should be trouble of any kind, had left Leonie in a state of apprehensive confusion. Badyr had not chosen to give a sensible answer to any of her questions during the flight to Dhoman, and so she had been totally ignorant of what lay ahead as their small plane prepared to land, circling over a mountain range in front of which lay the sandy plain and deep blue sea of her future homeland.

They had been met at the airport by one of the most ancient-looking cars she had ever seen. Wheezing and gasping as if at its last breath, it had moved slowly along a winding road behind their official escort—an equally old Landrover—which had raised such a cloud of blinding dust that it wasn't until Badyr tapped her on the shoulder that she had realised that they had arrived at the Sultan's palace.

Peering out of the car's dusty window, she had been amazed and struck speechless by the sheer size of the mammoth, grey stone fortress-like building, hardly able to believe tnat this was where she was going to live. Built in the sixteenth century by the Portuguese to guard the entrance to the port of Muria, the capital of Dhoman, it was still heavily dominating the old walled city all these hundreds of years later.

Later that evening, as she and Badyr were changing their clothes prior to the first official meeting with the Sultan, Leonie had shivered as she gazed at her surroundings. Despite the heat, the stark grey stone walls gave off an unpleasant, clammy chill—accurately reflecting the frigidly cold welcome to her son's wife extended by Badyr's mother, the Sultana Zenobia. The only cheerful face had been that of his sister, Maryam, a pretty young girl of fourteen, who had given Leonie a shy smile of welcome.

When she and Badyr had walked through the great Moorish arch into the castle—the heavy wooden door thundering ominously as it was closed firmly behind them—he had mentioned that his father, the Sultan, had his own private apartments, and that they would be living with his mother whose large, private quarters were known as the Harem.

Leonie had felt inclined to giggle at first hearing of such an archaic arrangement, far more reminiscent of the Caliphs of Baghdad than the modern-day world! However, after what little she had seen of the palace, all desire to laugh had abruptly vanished. As for Badyr's

mother—while clearly doting on her son, the older
woman had made it instantly and quite unmistakably
obvious that she did not approve of his marriage.

Later that evening, Leonie had still been trying to
dismiss the lump of depression in her stomach and think
positively about her situation. It hadn't been easy. As
she had wandered disconsolately through the suite of
rooms which had been allocated to them, she had
shivered at the sight of the dank walls, bare of any
ornament or decoration. All this place needed to make
it a real home from home, she had thought almost
hysterically, was a rack and some thumbscrews!
Defiantly humming a tune under her breath in a vain
attempt to try and keep up her spirits, she had slowly
retraced her steps into the bedroom

Pausing on the threshold, her eyes had widened as she
gazed at her husband. Badyr had finished dressing, his tall
figure clothed in a simple, long white robe, edged about
the neck and down the front by bands of gold thread. A
large, curved ceremonial dagger, whose hilt and scabbard
were made from heavily engraved solid gold, had been
plunged through the front of the thick, wide gold belt
clasping his slim waist; the only splash of colour being the
length of shimmering multi-coloured silk wound
intricately about his head to form a turban, the fringed
end of which rested on his left shoulder.

Watching as he slipped on a flowing white silk cloak,
edged like his robe with thick bands of gold, Leonie had
blinked her eyes several times in an effort to clear her
stunned mind. Talk about the Sheikh of Araby! Badyr
had looked . . . well, there was no doubt that he looked
absolutely sensational!

Unfortunately, it had seemed that Badyr took a less
than enthusiastic view of her own apparel. His mouth
had tightened with annoyance as he viewed the low-cut
bodice of a long, sapphire-blue chiffon dress, supported
by thin strips of satin tied in a bow on her bare
shoulders.

'Wallahi—Leonie! You can't possibly wear that!' he had exclaimed in a harsh, rough voice. 'Don't you realise that my father would have a fit if he saw you in that creation? You must wear a dress that has long sleeves and which completely covers all your flesh. Surely you have such a garment?'

'In this climate? Are you crazy? Of course I haven't!' she had snapped. It had been a long, tiring day and she had felt as if she was going to burst into tears at any moment.

Badyr had taken no notice of her outburst, striding over to the heavily carved wardrobe, the only piece of furniture in the room other than the huge bed, to look swiftly through her clothes.

'You are right, there is nothing here that is suitable,' he had muttered. 'However—yes, this will do.'

'That . . .? But . . . but it's only something to wear on the beach!' Leonie had looked with dismay at the plain black, flimsy garment. Made from fine lawn and cut in the shape of a caftan, it might be just the thing to wear over a swimsuit, but there had been no way it was going to be suitable for this evening's reception.

'Beach—what beach?' Badyr had given a harsh, sardonic laugh. 'Where do you think we are, the South of France? Surely you can't have been so foolish as to imagine that you will be allowed to sunbathe or go swimming, here in Dhoman?'

'But I thought . . .'

'You're not expected to think, Leonie!' he had snapped curtly. 'Just do as you're told, and put that dress on as quickly as possible. My father is a great stickler for punctuality and will be furious if we are late.'

She had been much too shocked by the sudden and completely unexpected change in her husband's personality to do more than snatch the material from his hands and run blindly towards the bathroom. How could Badyr, who had always been so kind and gentle,

talk to her in that harsh, caustic tone? And why she had
to wear this caftan, she had had absolutely no idea.
Wiping the tears of self-pity from her eyes, she had
contemplated the black sack-like dress with distaste.

'Well, I hope you're satisfied!' she had grumbled, as
she had walked slowly back into the bedroom. 'As far
as I'm concerned, I think I look simply awful.'

'We have no time to worry about how you feel, it is
far more important not to keep my father waiting,' he
had retorted sternly, taking her hand and leading her
swiftly from the room.

Her first meeting with the Sultan had proved to be
something of an ordeal. A small thin man, he had
slowly entered the large room where she and Badyr,
together with his mother and sister, were waiting.
Moving in majestic silence towards a low throne, he
had completely ignored his wife, his daughter and the
son whom he hadn't seen for some years, as he
beckoned Leonie over to sit on the carpet beside him.
She hadn't known what to do, so she had remained
sitting quietly, peering up cautiously through her
eyelashes at the austere, melancholic expression on his
face.

After an interminable silence, he had turned towards
her, his large dark eyes almost sleepy-looking beneath
their heavy eyelids, and politely asked if she had
enjoyed her journey, and was there anything that she
required?

Leonie had been struck dumb, completely nonplussed
by his question, which had been spoken in perfect
English. What on earth was she supposed to say? A
quick glance at Badyr's stern face had given her no
assistance, although his dark eyes seemed to be trying
to tell her something. But what? She had hesitated and
then, remembering how she hadn't been able to
understand a word of the argument between Badyr and
his aunt, she had asked if she could have a tutor to help
her to learn Arabic.

The sudden, electrifying tension which swept through the room as she voiced her simple request had been very frightening. Nobody had moved, nobody had spoken a word, yet all the members of his family had seemed to be waiting with bated breath for the reaction of Sultan Raschid.

'Hmm,' he had murmured, after a lengthy pause. 'I do not normally believe in education, and especially not for women, of course!' he had added, giving her a wintry smile. 'Perhaps you are not aware of the interesting fact, but it is precisely because the British were so foolish as to educate the masses in India, that they lost their empire.'

The Sultan had seemed to be expecting an answer. 'No, I ... didn't know that,' she had mumbled, wishing that she had never opened her mouth. There was no doubt that Badyr's father was a very peculiar old man, but this was clearly neither the time, or indeed the place, to publicly disagree with his nonsensical statement about education in the Indian sub-continent.

'However, learning to speak our ancient language is something of which I am prepared to approve,' Sultan Raschid had said, after another long silence. 'It shall be arranged.' He had stood up. 'I will now retire and hold a private conversation with my son.'

Surprised and bewildered by the palpable sighs of relief with which the Sultan's pronouncement had been received, Leonie had scrambled to her feet on legs which felt numb; it had been obvious that sitting on a hard floor for any length of time was an art she had yet to acquire. By the time she had risen, the Sultan had whisked himself out of the room, with Badyr moving swiftly in his wake. Looking around, she had been disconcerted to receive an ice-cold glare of dislike from Sultana Zenobia, before she had spoken sharply to her young daughter. Maryam, who seemed the only normal person in the extraordinary palace set-up, had smiled

and given Leonie a friendly wink, before she hurried
away from her mother.

Left totally on her own, Leonie had had no idea what
she was supposed to do. After many false turnings and
getting completely lost once or twice, she had found her
own suite of rooms. Sitting all alone for what seemed
liked eternity, she had eventually taken off her dress
and crawled miserably into bed. There had been no sign
of Badyr, and she had finally drifted off to sleep, her
cheeks damp with unhappy tears.

That first evening at the palace in Dhoman had been
a precursor of all that was to follow: long periods of
silent loneliness, interrupted by occasional meetings
with the Sultan, who had surprised everyone by taking
a considerable interest in his son's new wife. Other than
copies of the Koran—printed in Arabic, of course—
there had been no books in the palace, and since Leonie
had omitted to bring any reading material with her to
Dhoman, she had frequently given thanks to whatever
had prompted her request for tuition in Arabic. She had
been convinced that without the daily lessons she would
have gone stark, staring mad.

Badyr's mother, Zenobia, had made life in the palace
as uncomfortable for her son's wife as she possibly
could, never letting up on what Leonie came to see as
the older woman's relentless, guerrilla warfare. Meal
times would be suddenly and unexpectedly altered for
no reason, and more often than not Leonie would go
downstairs to find that all the food had been eaten.
After a while it had seemed easier to arrange for her
personal servant, Hussa, to bring the food to her
rooms—thus increasing her lonely isolation.

The main pinprick, until Leonie began to master the
intricacies of the extremely difficult language, had been
her mother-in-law's refusal to speak to her in anything
but Arabic, although Leonie knew from Maryam that
the older woman possessed a good command of
English. The servants, of course, only spoke in their

own language, and she had been reduced to spending hours acting out the simplest requests, which often resulted in tears of frustration on her part unless she could find Maryam and gain her assistance.

It had been Maryam, a bright and amusing fourteen-year-old, who had helped Leonie to retain her sanity. It had seemed that there was nothing the young girl didn't know about what was going on in the palace, and also in the country at large. It had been through Maryam that she had first come to know that the Sultan had another wife, the Sultana Fatima, and two other young daughters who lived in a far wing of the palace.

'Mother and Fatima get on very well. Fatima's so fat and lazy that she always agrees with everything Mother says,' Maryam had grinned. 'However, the most important aid to their friendship is that Fatima hasn't produced a son, who might have threatened Badyr's chance of succeeding my father as Sultan. That's been my mother's featest fear. She didn't want Badyr to come back here,' Maryam had added with a worried frown. 'Not when father's so . . . well, so odd—if you know what I mean?'

Leonie had known exactly what she meant. Sultan Raschid, who at first sight had seemed to be such a benign, if somewhat peculiar old man, had turned out to be not only odd and eccentric, but a man of whom his wife, Zenobia, was clearly terrified. When Leonie had seen that hard, tough and ambitious woman quailing with fear in his presence, she had recalled the words of Badyr's aunt in Abu Dhabi. Had it been Sultan Raschid to whom she had referred as 'very dangerous'?

The edicts issued by the Sultan: banning such items as sunglasses, the live playing of music and radios, cigarettes, dancing, all travel between towns without a permit, and even the wearing of trousers by men, had been irritating but relatively harmless. However, it was his fierce, obdurate refusal to spend any of his vast oil

revenues on important and necessary items such as
schooling or medicine that had led to the present
unrest and rebellion in the western part of the
country. There were, apparently, only three small
primary schools in the whole of Dhoman, and no
hospitals or health service other than that offered by
a small clinic in Muria, run by a dedicated group of
American doctors.

Outside the Sultan's palace, his subjects were living a
life of unrelieved hardship, their dire poverty compounded by the dreadful conditions in which they lived.
Malaria was rife, tuberculosis and trachoma—that
dreadful, blinding disease of the eyes—were chronic
conditions which affected most of the inhabitants.

Inside the palace, the old grey walls almost shook
and trembled with the ferocity of the daily rows
between father and son. Badyr, who was growing
increasingly tense and angry at his inability to persuade
the Sultan to distribute some of his wealth among his
people, had told her that the infant mortality was
among the highest in the world.

'No wonder my father doesn't bother to build any
more schools,' he had raged one evening when they
were alone in the privacy of their suite. 'Judging by the
way the poor, tragic little babies are dying, there will be
no need for more school places. Is it any wonder that
many of our people are beginning to listen to Marxist
propaganda? Who can blame them for seeking to
overthrow my father's unjust, uncaring rule?'

Quite apart from her imprisonment within the harem
quarters of the palace, and the deliberate unkindness of
Sultana Zenobia, Leonie's difficulties had been compounded by the fact that Badyr was so often absent. He
rose early, and only returned to their rooms in the
palace late at night. She had no idea where he went or
whom he saw, since he categorically refused to discuss
the matter. It had only been from Maryam that she
learnt of his secret talks with some of the influential

tribal Sheikhs, and even more secret meetings with members of the Sultan's army and air force.

Increasingly, it had seemed as if the only moments she and Badyr shared together were those when he slid silently into bed at night, often waking her from an uneasy sleep as he sought the comfort of her arms. As the weeks had passed by, his lovemaking became more intense and more strained. It had been as though he wasn't making love to *her* any more, but somehow trying to exorcise his increasing frustration and anger with his father, by demonstrating his ruthless dominance of her body.

She had tried very hard to be understanding. She had known how frustrated Badyr was by his father's obstinate refusal to discuss the affairs of the country, and she had realised that his position was becoming even more untenable than her own. But there appeared to be little she could do to prevent herself from becoming increasingly resentful, both of the way he had virtually abandoned her in this vast palace, and his use of her body to gain physical and emotional relief.

Being able to wear a king's ransom in jewellery, and clothed in the rich silk and satin gowns given to her by Badyr, meant nothing—not when compared to the loss of her liberty and the increasing tension between them. Eventually, of course, she had rebelled; rejecting his approaches and refusing to respond to his demands. And it had been then that their relationship quickly disintegrated into what seemed a war of attrition. Badyr had no longer whispered soft, sweet, tender words of love. With savage, bitter determination he had broken through the barriers she tried to erect between them, and using all the sexual mastery at his command he had aroused her weak flesh until she had been helpless, unable to do anything but respond feverishly to his lovemaking; her eyes filling with tears of shame and humiliation as night after night he had cruelly demonstrated her physical weakness.

'We can't go on like this, Badyr—we simply can't!' she had cried hopelessly one evening, impotently beating her fists against the hard body pinning her to the bed.

'Why not?' he had demanded with bitter ferocity. 'Your body is crying out for my touch!'

'No . . .!'

'You lie,' he had grated thickly, grasping her wrists and pinning them above her head. 'I'm an experienced man, Leonie, and I *know* when a woman is crazy with desire for me,' he had added cruelly.

He had been right, Leonie admitted to herself later, writhing with self-contempt. There had seemed to be nothing she could do to prevent herself from submitting to his demands. He had only to look at her and she trembled with desire, her flesh melting at his slightest touch.

Despite her pleas, he had made love to her that night with a desperate intensity that far surpassed anything she had experienced before. It was as if he was demanding not only her submission to his bodily needs, but her total subjection to his will, withholding complete satisfaction until she begged and pleaded for mercy. The passion that exploded between them following her moaning, abject capitulation had been savage and brutal, leaving Leonie to mourn the final nail in the coffin of all her hopes and dreams; weeping for the loss of warm, tender love as she found herself trapped in the dark forces of a living hell.

It couldn't go on, of course. He was destroying every shred of her pride and self-respect, and so lonely and desperate had she become that she knew she must escape from both Badyr and Dhoman. She had had no idea how she was going to manage such a task, but in the event matters were taken out of her hands. After a final, terrible argument with his father, Badyr had suddenly been placed under arrest. He had requested and been granted five minutes with his wife, and Leonie had been taken to a small room where Badyr, looking pale and strained, quickly took her into his arms.

'My beloved, I have no time to say anything, but to beg you to forgive me, and to remember that I love you,' he had whispered urgently as they both tried to ignore the guards at the door. 'Be calm and very, *very* careful of my father. Always present to him a smiling face, whatever you might feel in your heart. And always remember that I will return—you may be very sure of that. When that day comes, we shall begin our marriage again, hmm?'

Her eyes had been blind with tears as he was marched away, and it wasn't until some days later that she had learned that Badyr was under house arrest in one of the Sultan's palaces, far away in the south of Dhoman. Her terror for his safety had been compounded by the news which filtered through into the Harem, that one of his uncles had mysteriously disappeared, immediately after protesting about Badyr's arrest.

The removal of her son seemed to have aged Sultana Zenobia overnight. She had no longer bothered to make life difficult for Leonie, but stayed hidden away in her rooms, seeing no one. The silent, gloomy palace had been filled with whispers about the flood of people leaving the country, especially the young sons of the ruling sheikhs, and the daily rumours of sudden arrests and executions had led to an atmosphere of ever-increasing fright and terror. Apart from her own desperate worries, Leonie had been distressed to see Maryam's bright personality dimmed by the menace and tension which seemed to ooze from the very walls of the fortress. Leonie had encouraged the young girl to spend more of her time in the warm, comfortable quarters of Fatima, the Sultan's second wife. There, with her half-sisters, Nadia and Sara, she could escape from the unpredictable rages to which her father was becoming increasingly prone. In fact, it had been Leonie who was most often called upon to bear the brunt of these tirades. It was as if the old man was using her to continue the arguments with his son, now imprisoned so far away in the south of the country.

It wasn't until a month after Badyr's sudden arrest, when she had found herself feeling sick and dizzy in the mornings, that Leonie had realised that she must be pregnant. Almost collapsing with despair and loneliness, she had rallied her forces enough to swear Hussa to absolute secrecy, and had waited for an opportunity to ask the Sultan if she could join Badyr in his captivity. Although they had been so miserable together in the old palace, maybe the knowledge that she was going to bear his child would help them to overcome their past difficulties? And no prison could be worse than the strain of having to face the Sultan as he harangued and shouted at her, night after night.

When Leonie had finally summoned up the courage to make her request, Badyr's father had replied by laughing in her face.

'Oh, no! Oh, dear me no, my pretty one,' he had cackled with mirth. 'Why do you think I continue to keep you here under my eye, eh? Haven't you realised that you are the surety for my son's good behaviour? He has been told that I will consign you to a dungeon if he even talks to anyone, let alone attempts to escape!'

Leonie had watched in horror as wild laughter shook the old man's thin frame, his head nodding and jerking with maniacal glee at the cleverness of his evil stratagem.

Shaking with tension as she made her way back to her lonely suite of rooms, Leonie had thrown herself down on the bed in despair. She now knew that she had no alternative but to escape from the palace—and Dhoman—if she and her unborn child were to survive. She had grown desperate as three more terrifying weeks had dragged by and then, just as she had almost given up hope, she had been summoned to Sultana Zenobia's presence, where she had been astounded to hear the older woman address her in English for the first time.

'Allah knows I wished to have nothing further to do with you, but it now seems I have no alternative. How could Badyr have been so foolish as to have married you? A foreign woman!' she had snarled venomously. 'Oh, yes. It is entirely your fault that my son has been banished.'

'That . . . that's not true!' Leonie had protested. 'It's the Sultan. He's mad—completely deranged! You, of all people, must know that.'

Zenobia had blanched as Leonie's passionate outburst rang around the room. 'Be quiet, you fool, these walls have ears!' she had hissed, glancing quickly over her shoulder. 'Guard your tongue, or I will never gain my son's release.'

'Can . . . can you really help Badyr to escape?' Leonie had breathed, hope leaping in her heart at the older woman's words.

'Eventually, yes. However, none of my plans can be put into action—until you leave our country. Therefore your departure from Dhoman must be arranged as soon as possible. Unless . . .' Zenobia had paused, her dark eyes narrowing as she stared at the trembling figure of the pale English girl. 'Can it be that you are expecting a child?'

'No—no, of course not!' Leonie had lied quickly, certain that if she told the truth she would be forced to remain in the palace for ever.

'That is good,' the older woman had nodded to herself. 'Very well, you may go,' she had waved dismissively. 'You will be contacted soon.'

Anxiously waiting, Leonie had almost given up hope when Hussa had woken her one night. Cautioning silence, the servant had led her through one winding passage after another, until they had reached a small wooden door set in the outer wall of the fortress. Releasing the rusty bolts, Hussa had begged Leonie to hurry, leading the way through the silent streets to the waterfront. From there Leonie had been taken on board a dhow, and hidden among a pile of oriental rugs and carpets. Violently sea-sick, she had no idea of the length of the voyage, the fishing-boat eventually delivering her and the rugs to Badyr's aunt in Abu Dhabi, where she had been fed and clothed and put on a plane to London. His aunt had insisted that she keep the carpets, which she had subsequently sold to Dimitri Kashan. The money from their sale, and her old job he had offered her back after Jade's birth, had released her from all financial worries, leaving only the torture of her constant heartache for Badyr to burden those first years after her return.

Even after the birth of Jade, she had clung to Badyr's promise of a happy future together—continuing to have faith in his words. However, when she read reports in the newspapers of the coup and his assumption of power in Dhoman—and had still not heard a word from him well over a year later—she had realised that their marriage was over. During the years that followed, she had finally accepted the brutal truth that Badyr had never really loved her. She saw that her patent adoration, coming as it did at a time of great stress in his life, had merely been a salve to soothe and assuage his anguish over the future of his country.

It had been a hard lesson, but she had learnt it well. The experience had left such a scar on her mind and body, that Leonie had determined never to become emotionally involved again, concentrating all her energy on her job and her little daughter. Now, with Badyr's sudden reappearance, the carefully constructed edifice of her new life lay in ruins about her.

God knew how she was going to endure living in that dreadful country, but for Jade's sake, she had no alternative but to return. Gasping with pain at the thought of her future lonely existence, Leonie rolled over to bury her head in the pillows, her slender body racked by deep sobs of bitter, wretched misery and desolation.

CHAPTER FOUR

LEONIE slept fitfully, tossing and turning in the night, her mind and body racked by painful recollections. Waking early, and feeling far too agitated to even think of trying to go back to sleep, she slipped into a warm dressing-gown and padded downstairs in search of a soothing cup of tea. The silence of the empty house felt strange and lonely without Jade's bright morning chatter—providing confirmation that she had taken the right decision last night. The thought of returning to Dhoman with Badyr was almost unbearable, but she had no doubts at all that to have risked losing her little daughter would have been a totally unacceptable alternative.

The realisation that she had chosen the lesser of two evils proved of little comfort to her sorely tried nerves. The aspirins she had taken for the headache that throbbed and pounded in her head didn't seem to be working at all, and she was still feeling like death warmed up when Mrs Elliot returned to the house an hour later.

'Hello, darling. Shouldn't you be at work? I've just dropped Jade off at her playschool, but goodness, the traffic—it gets worse every day . . .'

'Okay—you can relax, Mother!' Leonie snapped, her voice cutting ruthlessly across the older woman's breathless stream of words. 'There's no need to pretend that you didn't know Badyr was intending to meet me last night, because your precious son-in-law has already spilt the beans. I understand that it's all thanks to you, that the dreadful man has come back into my life— *thanks a bunch*!' she ground out through clenched teeth.

Her mother gave her a quick, nervous glance.

'Now, darling, there's no need to be so upset. I knew you'd be cross, but . . .'

'Cross . . .! I'm not cross, for heaven's sake—*I'm bloody livid!*' she shouted, before wincing as the sound echoed in her aching head. 'How could you do it to me? That's what I don't understand. You know what a state I was in when I managed to escape from that ghastly country. So, how can you possibly have conspired and . . . and plotted behind my back with Badyr to make me go back to Dhoman?'

'That's not fair!' Mrs Elliot protested sharply. 'I certainly didn't "conspire", as you put it, but I have been very worried about you and Jade. What's going to happen to you both after I'm married to Clifford, and living far away in Florida?'

'For heaven's sake! I've told you that we'll be fine.'

'You haven't managed to find anyone to look after her, have you? And what sort of life is it, being left all day with a complete stranger?'

'Oh—stuff and nonsense!' Leonie retorted. 'Thousands of women go out to work, and their children are perfectly all right. In any case, she'll soon be five and going to school all day—so that particular argument doesn't hold much water, does it?'

Her mother's mouth tightened into a stubborn line. 'Jade still needs her father. I knew you wouldn't like it, so I didn't tell you that I'd been in touch with Badyr during the last year. I never mentioned anything about you,' she assured her daughter earnestly. 'Only sending him photographs and information about Jade—she is his child, after all. I've made no secret of the fact that I've always thought it very, very wrong of you to keep all news of her from him. Can't you try and think about Jade and not yourself, just for once?'

Leonie gave a deep, unhappy sigh. 'Oh, Mother, you simply don't understand, do you?' she said, burying her face in her hands for a moment. 'How can I convince you that Dhoman isn't anything like a normal Arab state? It ... it's going to be like going right back into the Middle Ages! Jade and I will be trapped in a harem, never going anywhere or seeing anyone.'

'Badyr assures me all that has changed,' her mother interjected quickly. 'He told me that he has never ceased to love you, and that your life will be quite different from what it was under his father's regime. He's built a new palace for you, and there are now schools and hospitals and ...'

'"Never ceased to love me"? *Hah!*' Leonie snorted in derision. 'How can you believe such rubbish? Did the swine also tell you that he had every intention of snatching Jade away from me, if I didn't agree to go back?' Her voice wobbled as she fought back the tears. 'Were you really part of that blackmail plot?'

'*No!*' Mrs Elliot looked at her with shocked eyes. 'I can't believe that he could possibly ...'

'Oh, yes—he threatened to do just that! And you thought he was such a reasonable man, such a charming son-in-law?' she laughed wildly. 'Well, I could have told you that you needed a very long spoon when you dined with that particular devil!'

'Oh, darling, I never thought ...'

Leonie sighed again and wearily shrugged her shoulders. 'There's no point in my going on about it, is there? How could I let him abduct Jade—to have her taken away and never to see her again? So, I have no choice but to agree to give up my job and return to Dhoman, do I? Apparently we're scheduled to leave right after your wedding—*isn't that nice?*'

Mrs Elliot flinched at the bitter, caustic tone in her daughter's voice. 'What are you going to do?' she muttered, hurrying after Leonie as she walked away into the hall. 'I can always phone Clifford and postpone the wedding.'

'Absolutely not!' Leonie said, slipping on her overcoat. 'There's no point in mucking up two lots of lives. You and Clifford really love each other, and I'll be furious if you two don't settle down and live happily ever after. As for me? Well, I shouldn't have married Badyr in the first place, should I? I wouldn't listen to any good advice then, so I've got no one but myself to blame for having got into such a mess.'

'But where are you going?' her mother asked anxiously.

'I'm going to phone the office and tell them that I won't be in today, and then I must see Dimitri Kashan to give him my resignation in person—it's the least I can do after all his kindness. After which ... I'm intending to have a quiet walk in the park until it's time to pick Jade up from playschool. But don't panic! I'm not going to drown myself in the Round Pond—if that's what's worrying you,' she added wryly, and then immediately felt ashamed of herself as Mrs Elliot's face blanched at her words.

'I'm sorry, Mother,' she sighed heavily. 'I suppose you only did what you thought was best for us all, and with the very best intentions.' She bent forward to kiss the older woman's cheek. 'I ... well, I'm just so upset that I can't seem to think straight at the moment, I'm afraid.'

'What are you going to do about telling Jade?'

'I don't know, that's one of the things I'll have to think about,' Leonie muttered as she picked up the phone.

Gwen, her secretary, was calm and reassuring, confirming that there were no clients requiring her immediate attention, and that any letters or paperwork could easily wait until tomorrow.

Leonie had been dreading the interview with her employer, but in the event the old man had been kindness itself.

'There is no need to worry, Leonie. I am much better and can easily come back to work next week—I have been itching to do so, in any case!' he laughed. 'Well, well, so you are going back to Dhoman, eh? It is, of course, quite understandable that your husband should wish you to return, hmm?'

His keen old eyes searched the girl's face. There was clearly more to this affair than was apparent on the surface. The story she had given him—of a sudden reconciliation with her husband—did not exactly ring true. Not when he was well aware that the couple had not seen or communicated with each other for the past five years.

'However, my dear Leonie,' he continued, 'if ever the need should arise, do not hesitate to come and see me. And you may rest assured that your old job will always be waiting here for you.'

Later that morning as she walked slowly through Kensington Gardens, her boots scrunching over the skeletons of dead leaves, her mind seemed to be bursting with all the things she had to do, all the arrangements that must be made in the short time allotted to her by Badyr. It wasn't just a matter of clothes for herself and Jade, it also meant remembering to pack all the hundred and one everyday items which had been completely unobtainable in Dhoman. Locked up inside the Harem, she could well recall the frustrating difficulty in even trying to obtain such a simple thing as a toothbrush.

With a heavy sigh, she sat down on a park bench, stuffing her cold hands deep into the pockets of her coat and trying to impose some sort of order on the chaotic thoughts racing through her brain. Badyr had assured her mother that everything was now changed in Dhoman, but she couldn't believe that he had been able to alter such a system—a way of life which had been in existence for hundreds of years. She could remember, only too well, the stupefying boredom, the hours and hours of what amounted to solitary confinement, and the ever-increasing strain between Badyr and herself.

The past was past, she told herself firmly, thrusting aside the bitter memories. Of far more immediate importance was the necessity to tell Jade that Badyr was now here, in London, and that in under two weeks they would be returning with him to Dhoman.

Leonie had always taken the greatest care to see that her daughter knew she had a father—just like other little girls. She had also tried to stress the point that if he wasn't living with them, it was only because he couldn't leave his country, so far away on the other side of the world. Leonie knew that this simple explanation, first voiced when she still believed that Badyr would eventually get in touch with her, wouldn't satisfy Jade for very long. Although only four years old, the child was bright, very intelligent and already beginning to ask some awkward questions. Such as: why didn't her daddy get on an aeroplane to come over and see her? And: if he couldn't leave his country, wouldn't it be a good idea if she and her mummy went to see him? Leonie had fielded those very reasonable enquiries as best she could, but now the crunch had come, and she had no idea of how Jade would react to Badyr's sudden arrival. Nor, for that matter, how he was likely to view the daughter he had never seen.

Leonie's mouth curved into an ironic smile at the thought of her husband trying to cope with Jade's boisterous spirits, her non-stop chatter and the interminable questions. If he thought that he was due to meet a sweet, demure little girl—well, he was certainly going to be in for a surprise!

Glancing down at her watch, she gave a small yelp of dismay. She must stop day-dreaming here in the park and hurry back to the car, otherwise she would be late in picking up Jade from her playschool.

When they returned home, it was to find Mrs Elliot in a thoroughly flustered state.

'Thank goodness you've arrived! I don't know what's going on—I really don't ... I mean—where am I going to put everything? And what about insurance ...?'

Leonie looked at her mother in astonishment.

'What's the matter?' she asked, hanging up Jade's coat as the small girl ran off into the sitting-room.

'It was all those men, you see.' The older woman sighed and brushed a tired hand through her grey hair. 'You've simply no idea—I mean, the doorbell hasn't stopped ringing all morning! It was: "Sign here" and "Sign there", till I thought I'd go mad.'

'Mother, for heaven's sake, calm down! I haven't a clue what you're talking about and—*Jade . . .!*' Leonie gasped as her daughter came back into the hall. 'What *do* you think you're wearing?'

'There—you see!' Mrs Elliot exclaimed as she and her daughter stared at the small girl pirouetting in front of them. What appeared to be a diamond tiara was set on her dark head, while two long, glittering strands of a diamond necklace dangled down over her short blue dress.

'Mummy—Mummy! Do look at me. Don't I look stu-pen-dous?' Jade laughed happily as the tiara slipped sideways to hang drunkenly down over her ear.

'Take it off, at once,' Leonie commanded, before turning to her mother in bewilderment. 'They can't possibly be . . .? I mean—they aren't *real* diamonds, are they?'

'The man from the jewellers assured me that they were. But that's not all—not by a long chalk!' Mrs Elliot said. Catching hold of Jade, and ignoring the little girl's protests, she firmly removed the sparkling jewellery. 'The sitting-room has become nothing more nor less than an Aladdin's Cave! Come and see for yourself.'

'Oh, my G-God!' Leonie stuttered, as with incredulous eyes she viewed the overflowing boxes piled high on every table and chair. 'Where did all this stuff come from?'

'Well, all the jewellery comes from Aspreys,' Mrs Elliot waved a distracted hand towards a mound of black leather cases. 'They are mostly sapphires and diamonds, I think, although maybe there was an emerald necklace as well.' She shook her head. bemusedly and walked over to the drinks cabinet. 'God knows, I don't usually drink in the middle of the day, but I suddenly find myself in dire need of some alcohol!'

'But . . . but who . . .?'

'Well, dear, I really think it must be Badyr, don't you? I mean—who else do you know with enough money to buy all these things? Her mother sighed heavily and took a large sip from her glass. 'Now, what else? Oh, yes,' she added as Jade excitedly delved into a large box and pulled out a dark brown fur coat. 'When the man from the shop told me how much that sable coat was worth, I nearly had hysterics! And as for all those parcels of pure silk and satin underwear from The White House, they must have cost a fortune. Of course, it's wonderfully generous of Badyr,' she added quickly, 'but where on earth are we going to put everything? You should see the dining-room—it's full to the brim with what must be at least ten years' supply of cosmetics! Do you think you could possibly have a word with him and . . . er . . . explain that we haven't much room?'

'Damn right, I will—*the rat!*' Leonie snapped furiously, before remembering that Jade was in the room. Hastily clamping her lips tightly together, she removed the fur coat from her daughter and took Jade out to the kitchen to give the little girl her midday meal. When she rejoined her mother some time later, she found her sitting slumped in an armchair.

'You really must be careful not to . . .'

'I know, Mother,' Leonie sighed. 'I shouldn't have said what I did in front of Jade, but I was just so mad at Badyr! He knows—only too well—that the temperature in Dhoman has got to be at least a hundred degrees in the shade, and I'll need a fur coat like . . . like a hole in the head! As for chucking his money around like an oriental millionaire—those diamonds alone must have cost enough to feed everyone in his beastly, fly-blown country for at least a month. What a swine the man is!'

'Leonie! How can you say that when Badyr's been so ... so ...'

'Diabolically sure of himself?' Leonie gave a shrill, hysterical laugh. 'You can't possibly imagine that Badyr went out and bought all these things this morning? There's no way he could have completed the purchases *and* had everything delivered by now. In fact—I haven't a shred of doubt that the bloody man had already ordered everything *before* he saw me last night. He knew damn well that his blackmail couldn't fail—and all these things,' she added, glaring about the room as she lifted the telephone receiver. 'They're nothing but sugar icing on the bars of my prison cell!'

Her call to his suite at Claridges was answered by Sheikh Samir. 'Would you kindly tell my husband *not* to send me items for which I have no use!' she snapped. 'It's a quite ridiculous waste of his time and money, and ...'

'Ah, Leonie.' Badyr's rich, dark voice came on the line, interrupting her carefully prepared speech. 'I wish to talk to you about seeing my daughter.'

'There's nothing to stop you seeing her whenever you wish, and it's certainly a better use of your time than buying up the whole of Bond Street!' she grated angrily.

Infuriatingly, he merely gave a low, mocking laugh as he ignored her caustic remark. 'Since you clearly have no objection, I will call and see Jade tomorrow, at three o'clock. We will take her to Regent's Park Zoo, yes?'

'No.' Leonie knew that she was reacting childishly, but why should she have to keep jumping through his hoops? 'It will ... um ... be much too cold at this time of year,' she improvised quickly, desperately trying to think of an alternative venue.

'Jade is unwell?'

'No, of course not—she's in perfectly good health!' she retorted quickly.

'Then you will only need to wrap her up warmly, hmm? As for yourself, you now have a fur coat, my dear Leonie. I therefore suggest that you wear it!' His sardonic laugh was cut short as he put down the phone before she could think of a suitably crushing reply.

Both Leonie and her mother spent some time that evening explaining to Jade that her father was in England, and would be coming to see her tomorrow. The little girl was so excited at the prospect that it proved a difficult task to persuade her to go to bed, and a long time before she at last fell asleep.

Leonie discovered that she also found sleep elusive, and subsequently she overslept the next morning. Thereafter, the day seemed to be one in which she never quite managed to catch up with the work awaiting her at the office and, as always happened when she needed to get away early, the phone never stopped ringing. As a consequence she was late arriving home, noting with dismay the large chauffeur-driven limousine that was parked outside the house.

She felt sick with apprehension, but was determined not to show it as she took a deep breath and entered the sitting-room. She found Jade sitting happily perched on Badyr's knee, busily engaged in placing his black patch over her own small eye.

'How do I look, Mummy?' she demanded, before jumping up and running over to stand on a stool, regarding herself critically in a mirror for several moments. 'I don't think I look as nice as Daddy,' she added thoughtfully, running back to climb up on to her father's lap.

Leonie couldn't say anything for a moment. There seemed to be a large lump in her throat, her body trembling with shock at the sight of the two dark heads so close together. Why had she never realised just what a strong resemblance there was between father and child?

Badyr smiled lazily down at Jade, idly playing with a lock of her black, shoulder-length hair. 'She is very much my daughter, hmm?' he murmured softly, accurately reading Leonie's mind.

Who else's daughter should she be? Leonie wanted to scream, biting her lip with frustration as she realised that to relieve her feelings by snapping at Badyr would only upset Jade. The little girl was bouncing with excitement as she wound her arms about Badyr's neck.

'It's so nice to have a real daddy, at last!' she sighed happily. 'Are we really going to Ar-ab-ia? Mummy's pretty, isn't she? She was very cross about the fur coat and the diamonds. In fact . . .' Jade grinned at her mother, '. . . I heard her say some *very* naughty words to Grandma—I really did! Are you going to give me some diamonds too? I do hope so, 'cos you see, Jill— she's my best friend at school, although I hate her really—well, she has a pink pearl necklace. But, if I had some of those stu-pen-dous diamonds, then she would be terribly cross . . . I'd like that!'

Leonie could barely manage to repress a malicious grin as she watched her husband mentally reeling under the rapid fire of Jade's artless conversation. 'Very much your daughter, I think you said!' she murmured, before telling the little girl to go and get her coat.

'Is she always quite so . . . er . . . talkative?' he enquired with a broad grin.

'Oh, no, not at all!' Leonie deliberately made her voice saccharin-sweet. 'Jade's still feeling a little shy, of course, but when she knows you better, I can promise you that she'll be *far* more forthcoming!'

'Then I can see that life will certainly not be boring!' His broad shoulders shook with laughter as Jade danced back into the room.

'Hurry up, Daddy. I want to see the camels and the snakes and . . .'

'I am quite ready, little one. We are merely waiting for your mother to put on her fur coat, are we not? The one about which I understand she was so ... er ... cross, hmm?'

It would have given Leonie great pleasure to have been able to slap the mocking smile off his handsome face. As it was, there was nothing she could do but go and put the damn thing on! And as much as she hated to admit it, even to herself, she couldn't help but relish the warmth and feel of the luxurious fur as they left the car to enter the zoo.

Preoccupied in keeping an eye on Jade as she scampered off towards one of the cages, Leonie looked up startled to see Badyr's tall figure standing in front of her.

'You must be careful not to catch cold,' he said, his voice heavy with irony as he reached forward, lifting the shawl collar of her coat about her ears. 'Incidentally, if I should decide to give my wife some jewellery, or dress her as befits her station in life, I do not expect her to argue with me. Do I make myself clear?' he murmured with soft menace.

'Please let me go!' she demanded, trying in vain to move her head away from the firm grasp of his hands beneath the fur collar, the words coming from her throat in a tremulous, hoarse whisper and not the imperious command that she intended. As he continued to stare searchingly down into her blue eyes, she desperately tried to steel herself against the dynamic masculinity exuded by the man standing so close to her quivering figure. But there seemed nothing she could do to prevent a deep flush from staining her cheeks, or her breathing from becoming ragged and uneven.

He gave her a slow, sensual smile. 'How very, very remiss of me—I have not yet thanked you for giving me such a lovely daughter, and for bestowing on her such a beautiful name. Can it be that you still have my ring, Leonie . . .?'

'I ... er ...' she faltered, her sapphire blue eyes unable to meet his dark gaze. She was only too well aware of the large jade signet ring, carefully wrapped in tissue paper and buried at the bottom of her small jewel-box. On leaving Dhoman she had gladly left behind all the jewellery she had been given by Badyr, retaining only his signet ring which he had put on her finger a day before their wedding; the purchase of an engagement ring having been forgotten in the hasty preparations for their marriage.

'No matter,' he murmured, his voice breaking into her confusion and rescuing her from having to reply. 'If Jade grows up to be as beautiful as her mother, I shall indeed be happy.'

The husky note in his voice should have warned her, but Leonie was too concerned with striving to control her own wayward emotions to react in time. Almost before she knew what was happening, she found herself clasped tightly in his arms and responding without thought to the seduction of the firm lips possessing her own. An ever-swelling tide of excitement raced through her body, her senses reeling swiftly out of control, and it was only Jade's impatient pull on the fur coat which brought her back to reality.

'Do come and see the elephants, Daddy—they're gi-nor-mous! What are you kissing Mummy for? I'm awfully hungry, so can we go and have an ice-cream, please?' Jade clasped Badyr's hand as he released Leonie's trembling figure, tugging him off towards a kiosk.

Damn, damn, damn! Leonie cursed silently as she turned away to gaze blindly at a pair of long-necked, languid giraffes. What on earth had come over her? It was no good trying to pretend, even to herself, that she hadn't been responding to his kiss—because she most certainly had. And in the middle of the zoo, for heaven's sake! What was more: that stupid, emotional gesture of naming her daughter after Badyr's ring—

something which had once meant so much to her—
seemed to be giving him *quite* the wrong ideas! A deep
tide of crimson flooded over her face as she recognised
the ache in her treacherous body, the reason why her
legs felt like jelly and her hands were shaking so badly.
She had been so sure, so positive after all these years,
that Badyr's strong physical presence would no longer
have the power to disturb her. A heavy lump of shame
and depression gripped her stomach as she realised just
how wrong her assumptions had been.

She somehow managed to stagger through the
remainder of their visit to the zoo, careful to avoid
meeting the mocking, sardonic gleam in Badyr's dark
eyes. The only morsel of comfort, despite any worries
Leonie might have had, was that Jade had enthusiastically taken to her father, who seemed to be equally
enslaved by his daughter.

'Yes, I promise that I will see you tomorrow, little
one,' he assured the child as they arrived back at the
house. 'Maybe you would like to come and have tea
with me in my hotel?'

'Oh, yes, please!' Jade breathed ecstatically, leaping
out of the vehicle and dashing into the house to tell her
grandmother all about her wonderful day.

'I'm afraid that my mother will have to accompany
Jade tomorrow,' Leonie muttered nervously as she
prepared to get out of the car. 'I'm very busy at work at
the moment, clearing my desk and . . .'

'Relax, Leonie!' Badyr murmured, catching hold of
her elbow and halting her hurried exit. 'Once we have
returned to Dhoman, we will have all the time in the
world to be alone together, hmm?'

'No!' she gasped. 'That's not what I meant at all. I
really am busy, and . . .'

'I know what you meant,' he interrupted smoothly.
'But I also meant what I said to you the other night.
For the moment, and until such time as we return to my
country, I will permit you to enjoy your single bed.

However, let there be no doubt in your mind,' he warned her with cool, silky menace. 'When you return to Dhoman, it will be as my wife—in every sense of the word!'

'Who do you think you are—God's gift to women?' she demanded breathlessly, her blue eyes flashing with rage. 'I ... I've told you, quite clearly, that I can't possibly ... that I won't ever ...'

Badyr gave a low bark of dry, sardonic laughter. 'Oh, yes, my dear Leonie, you will find that you can, and indeed you will!'

Leonie was still seething, burning with indignation at her invidious position, when she went to spend the evening with Sally a week later. They had supper in her friend's flat, giggling like young girls as they passed on to each other some of the latest gossip about old school friends.

'It's been such fun,' Leonie sighed. 'Just to be able to forget about everything for a few hours has been marvellous.'

'Does your husband really expect ...?' Sally paused. 'I mean, does he really imagine that you can both just resume your relationship together, after all these years, as if nothing had happened?' she queried, having listened earlier in the evening to Leonie's account of Badyr's sudden reappearance in her life.

'I know—the whole idea is crazy, isn't it? We've both changed so much during the last five years. Badyr is now a much harder, tougher character than the man I married, while I ...' She shrugged. 'Well, the past five years haven't exactly been a piece of cake, but I have managed to hold down a good job and support myself and Jade. Let's face it,' her voice hardened with exasperation, 'there's no way I bear any resemblance to the young, starry-eyed girl he married years ago. And how he expects me to fall on his neck with a grateful sigh at being taken back to that hateful country, is quite beyond me! Are all men so conceited, I wonder?'

'Every single one of them that I've ever met!' Sally grinned. 'Still, being showered by diamonds and a fabulous fur coat can't be all bad?'

'That was just the beginning!' Leonie groaned. 'The damned man must have spent I don't know how much money—practically buying up London, for heaven's sake! It seems as though the doorbell has never stopped ringing with the delivery of one huge parcel after another; honestly, Sally, it's completely unbelievable—both Mother and I are becoming demented! The house is overflowing with boxes and boxes: hundreds of pairs of shoes from Rayne, Gucci and Charles Jourdan ... ditto handbags; sapphire and diamond jewellery like you've never seen before in your life; crates of heavily monogrammed linen sheets, pillowcases and towels; huge flagons of my favourite scent ...' She sighed heavily. 'The list is *endless* ...!'

Sally gaped in astonishment. 'It all sounds amazing!'

'Believe me—I can think of other words to describe the state we're in!' Leonie said with a grim laugh. 'My mother is reduced to taking tranquillisers by the handful—just to get herself through the day! And we both spend most of the night lying wide awake, expecting to be burgled any moment! Don't you dare laugh ...' she added as her friend collapsed with giggles.

'I can't help it!' Sally gasped. 'How on earth are you going to pack and transport all those things to Dhoman?'

'Oh, my dear husband has solved that little problem,' Leonie ground out through clenched teeth. 'This morning's collection of goodies contained, among other items, monogrammed leather cases and trunks from Lowe of Bond Street—Jade even has her own set of luggage, but she's not particularly interested, of course. She's far keener on two brand-new saddles and bridles, which were despatched all the way from a shop in Newmarket. I imagine that they are for a pony, but since she hadn't got one and can't ride yet—your guess is as good as mine!'

'How does Jade feel about her father?' her friend asked, wiping the tears of laughter from her eyes.

'Well, obviously she thinks he's the best thing since sliced bread!' Leonie shrugged. 'Actually, to be fair, she'd adore him even if he hadn't a bean and just swept streets for a living. They ... well, they're both very alike, very much in tune with each other.'

'And ... er ... apart from all his quite extraordinary largesse, how do you feel about Badyr, himself?' Sally asked quietly. 'Are you ... well, do you still find him attractive?'

'Are you kidding?' Leonie retorted quickly. 'Absolutely, one hundred per cent not! I really hate the man—anything I once felt for him has long since disappeared. I mean ... how would you feel about a man who virtually abandoned you for five years?'

'I don't know,' Sally replied slowly, staring at the hectic flush on her friend's cheeks. She didn't believe that Leonie was being entirely honest with herself, but there seemed little point in pressing the point and she turned the conversation into safer channels.

However, as she stood chatting to Leonie at Mrs Elliot's wedding reception some five days later, Sally could hardly tear her eyes away from the tall dark figure of Badyr. She had noticed him in the church earlier that morning, and now he was standing across the room talking to Leonie's cousin, Janet, who was gazing up at him with dazed eyes.

'Is that really your husband? I didn't know he was going to be here,' she whispered.

'Neither did I!' Leonie hissed out of the corner of her mouth, glaring at the back of his broad shoulders. 'The damned man simply turned up without any warning. He's supposed to be taking Jade and me away after this reception, so I imagine that he's just making sure we don't have a chance to disappear—the swine!'

'But, Leonie, he's . . . he's *stunning*! And with that black patch and scar, *well* . . .'

'Got a "thing" for pirates have you?' Leonie sniffed dismissively.

'Oh, come on! You, my girl, are protesting far too much,' Sally murmured. 'He's devastatingly attractive, and well you know it! So, I may add, does every other woman at this reception. Look at them—they're all staring at him with glazed eyes. Honestly, Leonie, I've never seen so many bosoms heaving and panting with sheer lust . . .!'

'You always were a nasty, vulgar girl at school, and I can see you haven't changed one little bit!' Leonie sternly told her friend, who merely grinned as Jade came running up to join them.

'Daddy says that we've got to go soon,' she announced excitedly. 'And we don't have to go home and get changed. Daddy says that I look so pretty in my dress that I can wear it on the aeroplane! Don't I look nice, Aunt Sally?'

'You look lovely,' Sally assured her, admiring the flounces of cream satin and lace. 'It's a simply wonderful dress, Leonie. Wherever did you buy it?'

'Me? You must be joking? Little madam, here, took her father shopping in Harrods—where else?—and came home with that small item, among many others!' She smiled wryly down at her daughter. 'Of course, Jade is just a *little* disappointed that she hasn't got a diamond tiara of her own to go with it—but she tells me she's working on it!'

The sound of Sally's laughter was so infectious that despite her general misery, Leonie found herself reluctantly joining in. Until the smile was wiped off her face as she felt a strong hand firmly grasp her arm.

'I think, my dear Leonie, that it is time you said your farewells,' Badyr murmured quietly, his dark gaze sweeping with appreciation over her slim figure in a finely pleated dress of pearl grey silk shantung and the small, veiled hat decorated with grey and pink roses.

'But I can't possibly go before Mother and Clifford leave for their honeymoon. And . . . and I've got to change, and . . .'

'I have arranged matters with your mother and her new husband. There is also no need to change your clothes, since we shall, of course, be driven straight to my aeroplane,' he said firmly.

'But . . .'

'I will allow you five minutes. However, if you are not back by my side in that time,' he added blandly, 'you may be very sure that I will have you forcibly removed from this room.'

She glared angrily up at the man surveying her flushed cheeks and furious eyes with cynical detachment. Tense and trembling with nervous tension, she tried to muster the courage to defy him. But she couldn't. She knew—only too well—that she had no choice but to obey his commands.

Tightly compressing her lips to stop herself from giving vent to her rage and frustration, Leonie turned and walked across the room. Moving like an automaton, she calmly kissed her mother and new stepfather, and said goodbye to all her friends and relatives. It was as if she had become totally numb, aware of nothing but the sickening knowledge which lay heavy as lead in her stomach.

With Jade as his hostage for her good behaviour, Badyr would be able to enforce any and all of his demands for the foreseeable future . . . and there wasn't going to be a damn thing she could do about it!

CHAPTER FIVE

LEONIE lay soaking in the deep, sunken marble bath, gazing at her opulent surroundings with bemusement. After the last two weeks of wretched misery, forcing herself to face up to and accept the inevitability of her return to the dreaded Harem, it seemed impossible to believe that she would be living in this luxurious new palace, whose large airy rooms seemed another world away from the dark, dank old fortress that she remembered so well. This place was ... well, it was magnificent! She had been amazed by the size of Jade's suite, let alone the beautifully decorated, elegant rooms allocated to her own use.

A tired frown creased her brow as she stared up at the pink marble ceiling. Exhausted by the long flight and anxious to settle Jade down to sleep, she hadn't really had the time, or the opportunity, to question Badyr on the exact sleeping arrangements here in the new palace. Was this wing of the building a modern version of the old Harem, where Sultan Raschid had possessed his own private suite, and visited his two wives in strict nightly rotation as laid down in the Koran—the Moslem bible? She fervently hoped that Badyr had separate quarters, otherwise it was going to be extremely difficult, if not impossible, for her to avoid him.

The imperative need to keep well away from her husband's orbit had been only too clearly demonstrated during the long, seven-hour flight from London. Silent and numb with misery as she boarded Badyr's privately-owned Boeing 727, she was briefly introduced to the crew and a sandy-haired, freckle-faced girl called Elizabeth Jackson, who was apparently to be Jade's new governess. Leonie's resentment at her husband's high-handed behaviour in not consulting her about the appointment was further exacerbated by the fact that Badyr gave her no opportunity to object to his decision. Shortly after take-off, and blandly ignoring her rebellious expression, he ordered a young Arab stewardess to escort his wife to one of the small private bedrooms on the aircraft.

'I wish you to rest, and therefore Miss Jackson will be looking after Jade during the flight,' Badyr said, calmly disregarding her protest at being removed from her child.

'But I'm not at all tired, and . . .'

'I am not prepared to discuss the matter. Kindly do as you are told,' he added coldly, before turning away to have a word with Sheikh Samir.

Embarrassingly, aware of the hovering stewardess, Leonie almost screamed with frustration. It was clear that short of having a full-scale row, the only result of which would be to seriously disturb Jade, she had no alternative but to obey Badyr's command. Smouldering with fury, she allowed herself to be conducted to her cabin, and it was of little comfort to realise that the damned man had been right—that she had indeed been tired and nervously exhausted—when she found herself being shaken awake some hours later. Leonie felt confused for a moment and then recognised the continuous hum of the engines and the face of the stewardess, who was placing a cup of tea on the small table bolted to the floor beside her bed.

'The Sultan has asked me to say that we shall be landing at Dhoman in just over two hours, Majesty. Is there anything you require—anything I can do for you?'

Leonie struggled to sit up, brushing a weary hand through her long, curly hair as the young stewardess plumped up the pillows behind her back.

'I . . . I'm fine, thank you. But, my daughter . . .?'

'The Princess is still fast asleep, although I can wake her if you wish.'

'No, I'd prefer her to rest as long as possible. Thank you for the tea,' Leonie smiled at the girl. 'It's very welcome.'

'A pleasure, Majesty,' the stewardess murmured as she left the room.

Leonie reached over for the cup and saucer, sighing heavily as she stared down at the pale brown liquid. All this 'Majesty' and 'Princess' business—she'd have to have a word with Badyr about it as soon as possible. Otherwise Jade, who was a very ordinary little girl, was likely to become a nasty spoilt brat—especially if Badyr continued to give his daughter everything her heart desired. While as for herself? Never in a million years could she become used to being addressed as a queen—although the thought of being called 'Sultana' was even worse!

Getting out of bed and walking through into the small adjacent bathroom, she gazed glumly at her reflection in the mirror. Well, 'a dried-up grape' wasn't a bad description of how she looked at the moment, she told herself, viewing the thick cloud of uncombed hair and the shadows beneath her blue eyes. In fact, she looked simply dreadful! Although—God knows—the strain and nervous tension of the last two weeks would have aged anyone.

However, her spirits began to lift as she discovered that the small bathroom contained a shower. Standing under the fine needle-spray of warm water, Leonie couldn't help worrying about her imminent arrival at Dhoman. Where on earth did Badyr think she was going to wear all those clothes and jewels he had bought in London? Locked away in the Harem, she wasn't going to see anyone—or be seen, for that matter. At the thought of the long years of isolation ahead of her, she had to grit her teeth to prevent the weak tears from sliding down her cheeks. All this luxury was a hollow comfort and meant nothing without personal liberty. And as for the man who was going to lock her up and then throw away the key . . . How could Badyr possibly expect her to feel anything for him, other than fear and animosity?

However, by the time she had made up her face and slipped into a blue silk dress, she felt slightly calmer. There was absolutely no point in giving way to self-pity, she told herself firmly. Why give Badyr the satisfaction of knowing just how miserable she was? After all, this time she knew what she would be facing, and had prepared for it. She managed to grin shakily at herself in the mirror, remembering the grunts and groans of the men at Heathrow as they had loaded up one of her trunks into the aircraft. Only she knew that it was full to the brim with books of every description: from a complete set of the *Encyclopaedia Britannica*, and volumes of self-tuition in over twelve languages—together with all the necessary dictionaries—down to as many paperback novels as she had been able to lay her hands on.

She had calculated that she would have to stay in Dhoman for at least the next eleven years, by which time Jade would be sixteen, grown up and well able to live her own life. Then, there would be nothing Badyr could do to prevent his wife from escaping back to the West, no blackmail that he could exert to keep her in a country that she so detested. And when that longed-for day arrived: she might well be an old hag of thirty-six—but at least, Leonie grimly promised herself, she was going to be a well-educated old hag!

A knock at the door interrupted her thoughts, the stewardess quietly announcing that there was a cold meal awaiting her in the forward saloon, and that Jade was still fast asleep.

Glancing quickly at her watch, Leonie saw that there was well over an hour to go before they landed.

Deciding to let Jade rest as long as possible, she took a deep breath and left the bedroom.

Going into the main part of the aircraft, she saw that it was divided into two, with Badyr, Sheikh Samir and two other men talking quietly together in an office, which was separated from the lounge area by sliding glass walls. Nervously trying to ignore the quick turn of Badyr's head and his searching glance, she followed the stewardess over to the high-backed, comfortable plush chairs surrounding a round dining-table. It was only as she sat down that she realised she wasn't alone.

'It's a long journey, isn't it?'

'Yes ... yes it is,' Leonie answered, looking at the strange girl's friendly, freckled face and realising that she must be Elizabeth Jackson, Jade's new governess.

'I ... er ... I believe that you are coming to Dhoman to teach my daughter,' she said as cold meat and salads were placed on the table. 'Has my husband told you anything about the country?'

'Not a great deal,' the girl smiled. 'However, Jade seems to be a very intelligent little girl, and I'm looking forward both to teaching her, and my first visit to the Middle East.'

'I don't want to put you off before you've even started your job, Miss Jackson,' Leonie said wryly as she passed the salad bowl. 'But it seems only fair to warn you that if I had to think of a word to describe your future surroundings, possibly "primitive" would best fit the bill.'

The girl laughed. 'Well, Mrs ... er ... Your Majesty ...'

'Oh, please,' she quickly interjected. 'My name is Leonie, and I'll call you Elizabeth, if I may, okay?'

'Fair enough—just as long as the Sultan doesn't object to such *lèse-majesté*?'

Leonie found herself grinning with wry amusement at the girl's apt pun, and began to feel considerably more cheerful at the thought of not being entirely on her own in Dhoman. 'Have you always been a governess?' she asked, staring down at her plate with distaste. She didn't feel able to face any food, however beautifully prepared.

'Well, I spent some years teaching in various primary schools,' Elizabeth said. 'And then, two years ago, I took a job as private tutor to the young children of the Kuwaiti Ambassador—which is how I came to be recommended to your husband. I really am a good teacher, even if it's immodest for me to say so!' She smiled reassuringly at the beautiful woman sitting oppposite, who seemed strangely tense and nervous.

'However, I've now reached the age of thirty, and looking back I couldn't see that I'd done anything very exciting with my life. So, I decided that I'd like a challenge, a bit of adventure before I finally became a crabby old maid. Which is why,' she concluded, 'I jumped at the chance of deepest Arabia! I honestly don't care how rough or primitive it turns out to be— and I promise you that I'll make sure your daughter has the best education I can give her. Okay?'

'Okay.' Leonie's lips curved into a brief smile. She privately thought that the new governess was selling herself short. She wasn't a beauty, of course, but with an infectious smile and twinkling brown eyes, she presented a warm, attractive personality.

A slight popping in her ears indicated that the plane was beginning to lose height, and it wouldn't be too long before they landed. She rose from the table to go and see to Jade. The little girl had just woken up, still very sleepy and lethargic as she allowed herself to be changed into a thin cotton dress, before Leonie handed her over to Elizabeth while she went to gather her own things together.

Busily engaged in packing her case, Leonie nearly jumped out of her skin as the bathroom door opened and Badyr entered the room.

'What are you doing in here?' she gasped, noting that

he had discarded his Savile Row suit, and was now clothed in his national dress. The sight of his tall figure in the long white robes brought back such poignant, disturbing memories, that her trembling figure swayed and would have fallen if Badyr hadn't moved swiftly forward to put an arm about her waist.

'Husbands and wives normally share the same room,' he drawled softly as his grip tightened. 'Or did you expect me to change my clothes in the main cabin, hmm?'

'No ... I ...' Leonie swallowed nervously. The elusive aromatic scent of his cologne and the close proximity of his hard, masculine form seemed to be having a disastrous effect on her nervous system, and making her shockingly aware of the emotional response of her own body. What was happening to her? How could she possibly feel like this about someone from whom she had been parted for so long? A man who had threatened to abduct her child, and who was forcing her to return to a country she hated? It simply didn't make any kind of sense—none at all. Turning her head away, she closed her eyes as she fought to control the deep flush staining her cheeks, gasping as she felt him pluck the combs from her hair.

'What do you think you're doing?' she protested nervously as the thick, reddish-gold curls fell about her shoulders.

'Merely admiring your crowning glory,' he murmured, running his hand through her heavy mass of hair. 'And, since we have a bed at our disposal—it would seem a shame not to use it, hmm?' His soft, mocking laugh echoed ominously around the small room. Trying to twist away, she realised that she was hopelessly trapped, his fingers tightening in her hair and holding her head firmly imprisoned beneath him.

Her instinctive denial was smothered as his warm mouth possessed hers, moving softly and sensuously over her lips and evoking a trembling response almost impossible to resist. Every nerve-end in her body seemed to be tingling with excitement, a deep knot of tremulous desire flaring into pulsating life as her arms slid up about his neck and her lips parted involuntarily under the delicate pressure, allowing him to slowly and erotically savour the soft moistness within.

Badyr's husky murmur of satisfaction at her action did nothing to encourage her resistance. She seemed powerless to prevent her body becoming soft and pliant as he moulded it to his own, his hands moving down over her back to span her slim waist before reaching her hips. It was only when he relaxed his grip to lower her down on to the bed that sanity returned. It seemed to require an almost super-human effort to break away from the intoxication of his kiss and the seductive caress of the hands now savouring the rounded warmth of her breasts, but she eventually managed to pull her shattered mind and body together.

'No!' she gasped, jerking back her head and striving to push him away. Panting breathlessly, her dazed eyes noted his sardonic grin as he let her go and rose to his feet.

'Poor Leonie—you look somewhat disturbed!' he said softly, gazing down at her trembling figure. 'It would seem that your claim of amnesia was merely a temporary affliction!' His low, cynical laugh was hateful, adding fuel to the flames of her self-disgust as she quickly rose from the bed on legs which felt as if they were made of cotton wool.

'I don't know what you're talking about,' she muttered, inwardly cursing the betraying, husky note in her voice. Moving jerkily over to a mirror, she attempted to scoop her hair back up on top of her head, the coiled, nervous tension in her shaking hands making the task far more difficult than usual.

'You lie!' Badyr said curtly. 'Your body is crying out for my possession—just as much as mine demands release. It is pointless to deny it.'

She gave a shrill, incredulous laugh. 'You can't
seriously imagine that you're the only man who ...
who ...'

'Can raise you to the height of ecstasy, and far
beyond?'. he queried, moving slowly towards her
trembling figure. 'We both know it is so, and the sooner
you acknowledge the fact, the better it will be for both
of us.'

'You ... you arrogant swine! I'll never do that—
never!'

'Do not try my patience too far, Leonie.' His soft
drawl held a warning that was impossible to ignore.
Viewing in the mirror his tight lips and the stern cast of
his countenance, she felt a frisson of fear shiver down
her spine.

'We shall be landing in Dhoman shortly. I hope that
you will not make the mistake of ever forgetting that I
am now absolute ruler of my country,' he added, his
voice heavy with menace. 'There is no route open to
you, other than to obey my commands.' He paused for
a moment. 'Unless, of course, you wish to lose your
daughter.'

'You ... you *blackmailer*! You're every bit as evil as
your old father!' she hissed through clenched teeth,
shaking and trembling with the effort to control herself
as she stalked over to the door. 'He was a fool to have
locked you up in prison. If he hadn't been so crazy,
he'd have known that he should have polished you off
while he had the chance, and ... and made me a
thoroughly merry widow!'

She might have felt happier if her Parthian shot as
she slammed the door of the small cabin hadn't been
followed by his low rumble of sardonic laughter, the
sound echoing in her ears as she made her way into the
main lounge area.

Later, as she adjusted the straps about Jade's sleepy
figure, Leonie cursed her own folly. She was bitterly
ashamed at her pitiful lack of resistance, her pathetic,

emotional weakness as far as Badyr was concerned. She had taken great care to avoid all meetings with him—ever since that disastrous episode at the zoo—*and how right she'd been!* She didn't know how she was going to evade any further contact with him, but the Harem quarters in that grim old fort were full of deserted corridors and long-forgotten rooms. Maybe, if she kept her wits about her, she could ensure that she escaped his presence?

Carrying Jade down the steps of the aeroplane, Leonie felt as if she was walking into a hot Turkish bath. A wall of heat came up to meet her, the dark night air carrying an unforgettable smell of the lingering effects of burning sun on sand, tarmac and machines, mingled with the evocative aroma of frankincense and other aromatic spices so peculiar to Dhoman.

It was all so extraordinarily familiar, that she half expected to see one of the late Sultan Raschid's old cars come lurching up to the aircraft. Instead of which, a fleet of black limousines moved smoothly forward and together with Elizabeth and Jade, Leonie was led towards a black Rolls-Royce with dark-tinted windows.

'It's all very luxurious, isn't it?' Elizabeth said, looking about the plush interior of the car as it slowly moved away across the tarmac.

'Purdah,' Leonie muttered, in answer to the other girl's puzzled glance at the windows. 'It is the custom in Arabia to make sure that the male sex aren't tempted to run amok with unbridled lust, and so women are hidden from their gaze at all times—hence the dark windows. I suspect that my husband will have failed to mention an important facet of your future life,' she added. 'Namely, that you will be living in a Harem—the women's quarters of the palace—and from which you will seldom, if ever, be released.' She sighed and shrugged her shoulders. 'However—welcome to Dhoman, Miss Jackson!'

Silence fell in the car, Elizabeth digesting the

information she had just been given, while Leonie
cuddled the sleeping form of her daughter and stared
blindly out of the window. It was still night, and there
was little to be seen, although she was surprised to note
that they seemed to be travelling along a wide highway,
brilliantly lit by modern sodium lamps; very different
from the conditions under the old Sultan's regime.

The journey seemed to take a surprisingly long time,
but at last the car slowed down, the wheels crunching
over gravel before the vehicle came at last to a halt. The
door was jerked open, the lights dazzling their eyes as
the two women descended from the Rolls.

'*Wow!*' Elizabeth breathed.

Wow . . . indeed! Leonie thought, looking about her
in utter confusion. Instead of the grim, grey exterior of
the old fort, her startled eyes swept over a long, white,
two-storied modern building. The tall windows, shaped
like Moorish arches, were ablaze with light which spilled
out on to the forecourt and illuminated the wide
expanse of green lawn. She was staring in awed
fascination at the elegant pools surrounding the
mansion, whose cascading fountains were lit from
below, when she saw Badyr walking slowly down the
wide steps towards her, the long white robes flowing
dramatically about his tall, elegant figure.

'Ah, you have arrived at last,' he murmured, his
lips twitching with amusement at the incomprehension
on her face as he led her up the stairs and into the
building.

'I don't understand,' she muttered. 'What . . . I mean,
what's happened to the old palace?'

'It has been demolished,' Badyr said flatly. 'I decided
to build a new home well outside the old town, and this
is now my principal residence here in Muria. It is a
definite improvement on the old palace, wouldn't you
say, hmm?'

'I certainly would!' Leonie gasped, looking around at
the wide expanse of white marble flooring in the

entrance hall, the tall elegant columns which supported the high-domed ceiling way above her head. 'It's absolutely beautiful—and *definitely* an improvement on that ghastly old fort!'

They smiled broadly at each other, Leonie forgetting for a moment her mistrust of the man beside her in the shared memories of the ancient, grimly forbidding old castle. It wasn't until Jade gave a tired moan of protest that she had been recalled to the need to see to her daughter's comfort.

Now, lying here in the warm scented water, Leonie's head was still spinning as she tried to come to terms with her new environment. It was clear that Badyr hadn't, after all, been lying about providing her with a new home. Did that also mean that he would allow her more freedom of movement as he had promised? The brief feeling of optimism which swept through her tired body was sharply and abruptly terminated a moment later. She must be out of her mind! How could she have possibly forgotten the scene in the aeroplane and the other firm promise—the quite definite statement he had made in London . . .?

A knock at the door interrupted her distracted thoughts, the feverish flush, which had swept through her body at the recollection of Badyr's determination to exercise his 'husbandly rights', dying away as her old servant entered the room. She had been delighted to see Hussa again, a happiness fully reciprocated by the Arab woman, who had greeted her former mistress with tears of joy running down her cheeks.

'Ah, Majesty, all has been arranged. Your clothes have been put away in the cupboards and a small meal awaits you in the other room.' Hussa clicked her teeth as she came over and insisted on scrubbing Leonie's back. 'You must not stay in the bath too long. Your skin will become dry and wrinkled—and that will not please your husband, eh?' she cackled with laughter.

'This is a wonderful new palace,' Leonie said quickly,

D

anxious not to discuss her relationship with Badyr. 'Does my husband's mother live here too?'

'Oh, no. The Sultana Zenobia and Princess Maryam have their own palace a few miles away, and Sultana Fatima and her daughters have also been provided with a home. His Majesty has been good to his two mothers, yes? And so busy! The country has changed overnight, it seems. Yes, we are indeed blessed with our Sultan. Day and night he has laboured to make all well for his people. You cannot imagine the miles of new roads from town to town, the new hospitals and schools for the children—it is indeed a wonder what he has achieved in the last five years.'

'Not before time!' Leonie muttered tersely, and then immediately felt contrite. It wasn't Badyr's fault that the reforms so desperately needed by the Dhomani people had taken so long to be put into effect. And if what Hussa said was true, then it would be churlish of her not to give her husband full credit for all his hard work.

'Now His Majesty will at last be truly happy with the return of his beloved wife, eh? And the little princess— so pretty, so like her father!' Hussa gave a deep sigh as she stood up. 'I prayed that you would not lose the baby you carried, and that the child would be born well and strong. Praise be to Allah for his mercy, and for listening to my prayers. I was so worried when you left us, so frightened. You remember how it was, eh?' The old serving woman gave another heavy sigh, and with a stern reminder to Leonie not to remain in the bath too long, she smiled and left the room.

Leonie climbed out of the bath, drying herself with hands that shook with tension. Oh, yes, she remembered how it was—only too well! Was it any wonder that she had been frantic at having to come back to this country, so deeply unhappy at being forced to become involved with Badyr once again?

Slipping into the nightgown and matching négligé

which Hussa had put out for her, Leonie tried to calm her ragged nerves. It was only because she was tired and exhausted after the long journey, on top of the strain of the last two weeks, that she was allowing herself to lose her sense of proportion. What she needed was a good sleep, she told herself firmly, ignoring the food set out in the large sitting-room as she made her way into the enormous bedroom. Too fatigued to examine her surroundings properly, she slid between the sheets and a moment later was fast asleep.

She awoke to find the sun flooding into the room through the arched windows, the gauze curtains billowing in a soft breeze from the open casements. She gazed sleepily at the soft pink walls and the rose-coloured silk curtains which surrounded the windows, and which also fell in elegant loops and swags from the decorated cornice above the enormous bed. A small sound interrupted her lazy inspection, and raising her head she saw Badyr standing in the doorway which led to the bathroom.

'Ah, I see you are awake at last,' he murmured, walking slowly towards her across the white marble floor. Leonie idly noticed that he must have recently had a shower, since his black hair was still damp and he was wearing nothing but a short towel about his waist.

A shaft of sunlight caught his tall lithe figure, illuminating the smooth, golden-tanned skin rippling over the muscles of his arms and broad shoulders, the light mat of dark hair covering his deep chest. The passage of time had done nothing to diminish his powerful masculine attraction, nor the shivering response that gripped her stomach as she blinked nervously up at her husband. It was only when he sat down on the bed beside her that the alarm bells began to ring in her brain, breaking through the sleep-drugged mists of her mind with loud, strident urgency.

'What time is it?' she muttered, desperately trying to pull herself together.

'It is now ten in the morning, sleepy-head,' he smiled, his hand moving forward to toy with one of the tendrils of her long curly hair.

'Oh, my goodness! What about Jade?' She struggled to sit up. 'I must go and see to her immediately, I . . .'

'Be calm, my beloved, there is no need to worry. She has had her breakfast, and is now having her first riding lesson under the competent supervision of my Uncle Feisal and Miss Jackson.'

Leonie's nerves had begun to tingle at the soft emphasis he had placed on the endearment, a tide of crimson sweeping over her face as the gleaming dark eyes roamed slowly over the semi-nudity of her thin silk nightgown.

'It's very late. Oh, dear, I . . . um . . . I don't know how I could have slept so long. I must . . . yes, I must get up and . . . and get dressed,' she babbled, inching away from his tall, dominant figure.

'No, I don't think so, not just at the moment,' he drawled with soft mockery, his eyes glinting with sardonic amusement. 'I have . . . er . . . other plans for the next hour or two!'

'N-no . . .!' she stammered, giving up all attempts to pretend that she didn't fully understand his intentions. 'Please, no, Badyr. You . . . you don't really want me— you know you don't! There must be thousands of other women who . . .'

'Do not insult me, or yourself, Leonie. I can assure you that I know *exactly* what I want!'

The amusement had died from his face. His penetrating gaze, hard and unwavering, sent shock waves spiralling down her spine as she recognised the ruthless determination in the chilly depths of his dark eyes.

'No! Please—*no* . . .!' she gasped, attempting to scramble away across the bed, her progress abruptly halted as Badyr caught hold of her wrist in an iron grip.

She tried to pull away, but she found herself drawn relentlessly back towards his bare chest, gasping as his fingers tightened to crush her fragile bones. A tortured moan broke from her lips, and completely losing her temper she sank her teeth into his hand. Badyr gave a grunt of pain and released her arm, but as she snatched it away, he reached for her again and caught his fingers in the neck of her gown. There was a thin screeching sound as the silk gave way beneath the force of his action and the garment split from top to bottom.

A long silence followed as Leonie threw back her long, wild flowing locks, staring down in numb horror at the display of her own nakedness. She was unaware of Badyr's eyes devouring her glowing beauty: the sheen of her pale skin gleaming like pure alabaster in the warm morning light and the sight of her breasts, full and ripe, rising erotically between the torn fragments of material.

With a deep, husky growl of impatience he tore the towel from about his waist, moving swiftly to strip and toss aside the remnants of her nightgown. The next moment she found herself sprawled on her back, Badyr's hard body pinning her firmly to the mattress as he stared grimly down into her dazed eyes.

'*Wallahi!* Very well, my red-haired vixen—we shall see how long you can defy me!' he breathed heavily. 'And just how soon it is before you are begging for satisfaction, hmm?'

'Never!' she cried defiantly, beating her hands against his broad shoulders and trying to twist away from beneath his heavy weight. With contemptuous ease, Badyr captured first one hand and then the other, holding them firmly above her head and calmly allowing her to exhaust her strength in the vain attempt to escape him.

'I am a *very* patient man, Leonie,' he drawled softly as she lay panting wearily, and bitterly aware from the hardening muscles in his thighs that her desperate struggles had only served to increase his own arousal.

'After all, I have waited for five years, and so a few more minutes are neither here nor there, hmm?'

'I . . . I hate you! It . . . it's nothing but rape!' she gasped, tears of anger and frustration welling up in her blue eyes.

His lips curved into a savage smile. 'No, you do not hate me, nor will I have need of force. On the contrary, my sweet, you will shortly be pleading for the merciful release that only my possession can assuage!'

Her howl of protest was smothered as his mouth descended to cover hers, the bruising, relentless pressure forcing her lips apart and allowing him to savour the inner sweetness in a devastating invasion of her shattered senses. She was scarcely aware of exactly when the pressure eased and his mouth softened, moving over her trembling lips with a sensual languor that ignited a fire deep in her loins.

Leonie desperately tried to ignore the warmth of his lips as he kissed her damp eyelids and willed herself, with all the remaining strength at her command, not to respond to the mouth that trailed slowly over her cheek to murmur soft words of endearment in her ear. But as he continued, his lips scorching a path down her neck and on across the soft swell of her breasts, there was nothing she could do to prevent a helpless moan of pleasure, her body shuddering with ecstasy as his tongue caressed her nipples; the rosy peaks hardening with passion beneath his erotic touch. His mouth left her breasts to brush delicate kisses across her stomach, her body aching and throbbing at the promise of release from its long starvation, tremors of shock quivering through her flesh beneath the explicit sensuality of his mouth and hands.

Her emotions finally reeling completely out of control, she was only aware of the driving need to surrender to the passionate desire racing through her veins, the dizzy spiralling excitement engendered by the masterly seduction of his touch. Possessed by an urgent desire that went far beyond anything she had ever experienced before, her body writhed and arched against him, powerless against the explosive, ever-increasing ache that overrode all thought and action.

'Badyr—Badyr . . .!' The caressing hands and mouth moving over her body paused for a moment as she moaned his name in a helpless refrain.

'Umm?'

'Badyr . . . *please* . . .!' she gasped, tormented by overwhelming desire as she feverishly pressed her lips against his hot, burning skin.

'Do you want me, Leonie?' His thick, husky whisper seemed to fill her whole existence.

'Oh, God! I . . . I . . . *Oh* . . . *Y-Yes* . . .!'

With a harsh laugh of triumph, he swept his hands down over the sweet mounds of her breasts and the warm, undulating curve of her thighs, before parting her legs and possessing her with a thrusting, pulsating urgency that banished all conscious thought as their wild, physical rapture reached its climax.

Afterwards, as she lay silently within his arms, the realisation of her wanton response to his sensual mastery filled her with bitter shame. Fully intending to be as frigid as ice, she had been betrayed by her weak body into a raging inferno of passion.

'You see?' Badyr murmured softly, his fingers surprisingly gentle as he smoothed back the hair from her damp brow. 'There was no need for the "rape" that you spoke of, hmm?'

His words only served to deepen her humiliation. 'I loathe you for what you've just done—only slightly more than I hate and loathe myself,' she grated bleakly, unable to prevent her lips from trembling as tears began to trickle down her cheeks. 'How . . . how often will I have to be . . . be *used* in this way?'

He rolled his hard body over to cover her soft flesh, capturing her face with his hands and forcing her to meet the darkening gleam in his eyes.

'Ah, my beloved, how I love the way you hate!' he taunted softly, his mouth descending to brush away the escaping teardrops, before moving hungrily down to cover her quivering lips.

Her strangled moan was stifled as his kiss deepened, storming her puny defences and sending waves of heat pulsating through her body.

'I want you,' Badyr murmured thickly against her mouth, his words merely underlying the throbbing urgency of his body. 'And I will take you wherever and whenever I please. As for you, my dear wife . . . you will cry out for *my* possession, yearning for the intimate sweet pleasure that only *I* can give!'

Whimpering with despair, she found herself drowning in a deep pool of passion, before the hard pressure of his thighs ignited a flame of desire that was swiftly fanned into a white heat. Raging uncontrollably, it scorched through her body until she cried out—as he had said she would—eagerly demanding and welcoming his shuddering thrust and the sweeping, shattering sensation that exploded the universe around them into fragments of light and power.

CHAPTER SIX

'SWEET dreams, darling.' Leonie leant over to kiss Jade good night.

'Can I ride my pony tomorrow, Mummy?'

Leonie laughed. 'Since you've been riding nearly every day for the last four weeks, I don't suppose tomorrow will be any different, do you?'

'Great-uncle Feisal says I'm very good. He says that I show a natural ap-ti-tude!' Jade beamed up at her mother. 'Did you know that he can ride a camel? Yes, he can, really! He's going to show Miss Jackson how to do it, but he says I must learn to ride my pony first. Great-uncle Feisal is awfully nice, isn't he? In fact,' she paused, before adding the highest accolade in her vocabulary. 'In fact, I think he's stu-pen-dous!'

Leonie smiled. 'Come on, chatterbox. It's time you went to sleep.'

'It certainly is!'

The deep, mocking voice from behind her shoulder made Leonie jump. Badyr moves as silently as a panther—and he's every bit as unpredictable as one of those dangerous animals, she reminded herself, casting a sideways glance through her eyelashes at his profile as he sat down on the other side of Jade's bed.

'Doesn't Mummy look pretty?' Jade said, sitting up and winding her thin arms tightly about her father's neck. 'Are you going out tonight? I do wish I could come too.'

'You are much too young, little one!' Badyr laughed as he kissed her cheek and settled her back on the pillows. 'But yes, I agree that your mother is looking very pretty, and grows more lovely with each passing day.'

'Your father is apt to apply flattery with a shovel!' Leonie said lightly, rising to her feet and blowing Jade a good night kiss as she left the room. Walking back down the corridor, a glance at her watch revealed that there was no need for her to hurry. She had well over an hour to get ready.

Entering her suite of rooms, Leonie wandered over to the arched windows, sighing with pleasure as she gazed down at the wide expanse of green lawn surrounding the marble pools filled to the brim with cool, clear water from the high cascading fountains. Even though a month had gone by since she'd arrived back in the country, she was still having considerable difficulty in coming to terms with both the changes that had taken place in Dhoman over the past years, and her own emotional confusion about her relationship with her husband.

Hussa hadn't been exaggerating when she had spoken so enthusiastically concerning the sweeping reforms which had been instituted by Badyr. During her first week in the country, Leonie had become sharply aware that there was an air of definite purpose, a new spirit abroad in the country, with new industries, schools and hospitals planned or being built in all the major towns. Indeed, not content with simply razing the old palace fortress to the ground, Badyr had also ordered the bulldozing away of most of the decaying, decrepit houses in Muria, replacing them with modern housing estates and brand-new shopping centres.

One of the most astounding sights of all had been a grand, spacious palace set on the waterfront of the capital city. Badyr had told her that it was used mainly for the formal entertainment and reception of important guests, and was also the place where he held his *Majlis*. This, she learned, was one of his innovations whereby, once a week, any member of the population had the right to see the Sultan.

'It may be that they are experiencing difficulties over

family matters, or wish me to settle a contentious dispute with a neighbour,' Badyr had explained. 'Whatever the problem, I feel that it is of prime importance that my people know that I care about them, and that they can always turn to me for help.'

Despite her resentment of the way she had been forced to return to Dhoman, each passing day had resulted in Leonie becoming more and more impressed both by Badyr's reforms, and by the obvious love and affection with which he was regarded by the populace.

Not that she'd been possessed of any such charitable thoughts that first evening after her arrival in the country. Staring silently down at her plate, she had been hardly able to eat any of the delicious food which had been placed in front of her, her whole being filled with deep anger against the man sitting on the other side of the table.

'Well, now . . .' Badyr had murmured as the servants poured the coffee and swiftly left the room. 'We must find something for you to do here in Dhoman, hmm?'

'I thought you'd already taken care of that!'

His only response to her bitter retort was a low, mocking laugh. 'Ah, my dear wife, although I might wish to spend all my waking hours pleasurably occupied with your delicious body . . . I'm afraid that I also have other matters to occupy my time. Alas, one must work as well as play, hmm?'

The urge to open her mouth and scream like a fishwife, telling him exactly what she thought about his notions of pleasure and play, was almost irresistible. Never had she felt so achingly tired and exhausted as she did at this moment, and no wonder, considering that she'd hardly been allowed out of bed all day! Desperately trying to banish the memory of his passionate lovemaking—and the humiliation of her own eager, feverish response—Leonie gritted her teeth as she struggled to control the flush spreading over her pale cheeks.

'Leaving aside your undoubted ... er ... wifely talents,' Badyr murmured with amusement, well aware of her suppressed fury, 'I also know that you are a competent businesswoman. And if you can run Dimitri Kashan's firm, then I am sure you will have no difficulty in organising some of the new projects I have in mind.'

'Such as . . .?'

'Such as the formation of a carpet and rug-making industry; and the setting up of a modern textile industry, concerned not only with producing the cloth but also with fabric design. Dhoman is one of the few places left in the world where the people still use indigo to dye material, for instance, and I thought you might be able to think of a way to make that a commercial proposition.'

Shocked out of her unhappy self-absorption, Leonie looked at him with bewilderment. 'I—I might be able to offer advice on marketing rugs, but Dhoman has no tradition of carpet-weaving. It's a marvellous idea, but it would take years to train the craftsmen needed, and I don't see how I could do that on my own. Besides, I haven't the slightest idea of how things are run in this country.'

'I have discovered that ruling a country requires exactly the same qualities as the management of a large firm,' Badyr said firmly. 'And I would not ask you to start organising new industries, badly needed in the outlying towns and villages, if I did not feel you were capable of doing so. You would have the support not only of myself and my ministers, but we would also make sure that adequate funds were made available as well as any technical advice you might require.'

Leonie stared blindly down at the table, aware of a rising tide of excitement. She could scarcely believe that Badyr meant what he said; that he wasn't going to insist on her spending her days shut away in the Harem. It seemed as if he really was going to give her the opportunity to do something useful with her life. There would be tremendous difficulties, of course, but what a challenge! Her euphoria was suddenly checked as she remembered that she was now living in Arabia.

'I—well, I think it's a wonderful idea, and I'd love to have the opportunity, but I don't see how it can work, I'm afraid. Being a woman in a Moslem country . . .' she gave a shrug of resignation. 'Well, you know the problems as well as I do.'

'I am not going to pretend that you won't occasionally experience difficulties, Leonie, but times have changed, certainly as far as Dhoman is concerned.' Badyr leaned back in his chair. 'Since becoming ruler, I have actively encouraged the return of all those of my countrymen who went to live abroad to escape my father's persecution, and there are also generous terms of employment for foreigners who have the necessary technical skills that we require.' He paused. 'I'm sure you'll be interested to know that we have also given asylum to a flood of refugees escaping from the war between Iran and Iraq—many of whom are carpet-weavers.'

'That's great! We could use their expertise, and . . .'

'Exactly!' Badyr smiled at her enthusiasm. 'Now, maybe you can see why I believe we can start a new carpet industry. And since many of the newcomers to this country have been used to living in more liberal areas of the world, I have relaxed the traditional rules regarding Moslem dress and habits. I am, in fact, hoping to promote a more *laissez-faire* rule in this country. Those who wish to keep to the old values are perfectly at liberty to do so, while modern dress, albeit reasonably discreet, is also freely permitted.'

'Is it working?'

'Most of the time. However, I am aware that I must make haste slowly if I am to unite my people into a cohesive whole, hmm? So, you will find that you are free to go about this country—always provided you will accept the presence of at least two guards, who will be there merely to protect you and not to pry on your business. Moreover, I am not expecting you to wear a veil, and when in our home I am happy to permit you to wear your own western clothes. Only on official occasions would I deem it a favour if you would dress in the discreet manner expected by our guests.'

Leonie hesitated, still trying to assimilate the fact that she was to be allowed some personal liberty, and the opportunity to do something positive. It all sounded far too good to be true—there must be a catch somewhere. 'Why didn't you tell me about all these reforms when we were in London?' she asked.

'Would you have believed me? Since you so firmly persist in regarding me as a wicked, lascivious villain, it would surely have been a waste of time, hmm?'

'Well, I . . . er . . .' She blushed, glancing up through her eyelashes to find Badyr's face creased into a broad smile. A smile of such intimate warmth and charm that she suddenly felt as if she had been stunned by a blow, leaving her feeling dazed and confused.

'I am still waiting for your answer,' he murmured as the silence lengthened between them. 'Are you willing to help me develop my country? Or is it a task for which you don't feel suitably qualified—something that is far beyond your mental and physical capabilities?'

'No—of course it isn't!' she retorted quickly, stung by his dismissive words, and also annoyed with herself for being so susceptible to his overwhelming masculinity.

'So, it is agreed. Excellent!' Badyr rose from the table.

'But there's so much to discuss . . . and I haven't exactly agreed to anything . . .' she protested breathlessly as he took her hand, leading her reluctant figure purposefully from the room and up the long, wide staircase to their suite.

'Oh, yes, you have, and I am quite confident that you will perform the services I require, to perfection.' He gave a low husky laugh as he closed their bedroom door. 'Just as certain as I am that you will perfectly perform the ... er ... service I require—tonight!'

And that had been that! Leonie thought with a wry smile as a clock chimed in the distance, reminding hter that she must get changed if she was to be ready on time for tonight's official banquet.

Walking through into the bedroom, she noted the shimmering white silk chiffon dress which Hussa had placed out ready for her to wear, its dramatic simplicity a perfect foil for the diamond tiara and matching necklace, glowing brilliantly in the velvet-lined casket set on an adjacent table. Leonie had long ceased to wonder why Badyr had bought up half of Bond Street, after she had set eyes on the fantastic clothes worn by most of the Arab women in Dhoman. Maryam and Badyr's half-sisters, Nadia and Sara, for instance, seemed to think nothing of having couture dresses flown over from Paris for special occasions, such as a wedding or a reception and banquet like that planned for tonight.

Slowly undressing, she frowned as she tried to think what to do about her relationship with Maryam, who had changed out of all recognition from the amusing child who had brightened Leonie's days in the grim old fortress. Now nineteen, Maryam had been oddly constrained on meeting her old friend again, and nothing Leonie could do seemed to be able to bridge the apparent gulf between them. It was obvious that Sheikh Samir was very attracted to Maryam—a feeling that was clearly reciprocated by the tall, slender girl— but that was surely no reason for her to be so awkward and nervous with her brother's wife?

Aside from wishing to resume her old companionship with Maryam, Leonie had been reluctant to have anything to do with Sultana Zenobia. However, she had eventually agreed to Badyr's request that she should pay a courtesy call on his mother. It hadn't, in fact, been quite as bad as she had feared, the older woman greeting her with far more cordiality than she had ever shown in the past, and clearly very taken with Jade.

'I do not blame you for hiding your pregnancy from me,' she had said with a bleak, wintry smile. 'We must all do what we think best for our children, something that you must realise by now, I think?' she added, the only time she had referred to the reason behind Leonie's forced return to Dhoman. 'I do hope, however, that you will permit your little daughter to visit me from time to time?'

Leonie had agreed, and Jade always seemed to have enjoyed herself when she returned from having tea with her formidable grandmother.

Sultana Fatima, on the other hand, was a complete contrast. Fatter than ever, she was clearly every bit as warm and jolly as she had always been. She would need all her good humour to put up with her daughter, Nadia, Leonie thought grimly. Now aged twenty-one, Nadia was a spoilt, selfish and discontented girl who was violently jealous of her younger sister, Sara.

It wasn't surprising that no one wanted to marry the shrewish Nadia, whereas Sara, a sweet girl with a soft, gentle personality, had been married for three years to Sheikh Hassan, the older of Badyr's two uncles. The elderly man, imprisoned by the old Sultan for protesting at Badyr's captivity, had been a widower with a young daughter at the time he had married Sara. They appeared to be very happy together with their young son, Ali, who was aged two and the present heir to Badyr's throne.

Leaving aside Hassan's daughter by his first wife, about whom Leonie knew nothing, the only other member of the family was Badyr's younger uncle, Feisal, whose whole life revolved around his precious Arab horses. He and Jade had taken to each other from the start—so much so that the little girl now practically lived in the stables!

Still thinking about Jade, Leonie went through into the bathroom and turned on the shower. Her daughter's obvious happiness in her new life, with a father she adored and her present love affair with her pony and her uncle Feisal, was ample proof that whatever her own problems, Leonie had chosen the right course of action. Not that Badyr had given her any real choice, of course, but she was glad—if only for Jade's sake—that she hadn't been tempted to run away from what she now saw to be her inevitable return to Dhoman.

The cool sting of the water was invigorating after the heat of the day, which had been spent wrestling with problems at one of the new textile mills. It was obviously going to take her a long time to put all Badyr's ideas into action, but already considerable progress had been made, especially with the Iranian exiles. They had been overjoyed to learn that their trade and ancient skills were valued in Dhoman, and several village workshops were in the course of construction.

Stepping out of the shower and towelling herself dry, she caught occasional glimpses of her pale body in the mirrored walls of the bathroom. Even her self-critical eyes couldn't help but notice the rich, silky sheen of her soft flesh, and the sparkling brilliance in her sapphire-blue eyes. There was no doubt that she had never looked better or more radiant in her life.

If she had initially hoped that Badyr's raging desire for her body would fade as the days went by, she soon found that she was doomed to disappointment. No matter how hard she had tried, no amount of firm resolution or downright refusal had any effect. Night after night there had been no reprieve, no respite from his passionate lovemaking.

At first, of course, she had fought him wildly, pummelling his broad shoulders with her clenched fists and kicking any part of his body that she could manage to reach. None of which had done her any good at all! The only response to her defiance had been his low growls of sardonic amusement and a contemptuous disregard of her violent, struggling figure as his hands and mouth had worked their devilish magic. How swiftly, how easily he had been able to turn the protesting body in his arms into that of a pliant, willing slave, moaning helplessly beneath his erotic, sensual touch and and eagerly crying out for his possession. Again and again he had demonstrated his power over her, and after the first few nights, Leonie had been forced to ask herself who she was fighting . . . Badyr or her own emotions? That question now, of course, seemed merely an academic exercise. There was no point in continually asking herself how she could respond so ardently to Badyr—a man who had not only treated her shamefully, but had also blackmailed her into returning to Dhoman. The shocking truth was . . . she no longer cared!

It had taken her a long time, but she could now acknowledge the fact that, despite all that had happened, she had never stopped loving the man she had first met when she was only eighteen. She still didn't understand how Badyr could have virtually deserted her for so many years. Perhaps she never would. However, everything in the past now seemed somehow irrelevant, when set beside the deep feelings she had for the only man she had ever loved. It wasn't just the physical side of their relationship, the driving need to possess each other which seemed to increase in intensity with each passing day. Working together for the good of the country, she and Badyr had forged new bonds of warmth and friendship. She admired his selfless devotion to his people, his care and concern that they should have a better life. She was also irresistibly drawn to the inner kindness beneath the hard, forceful and ruthless personality with which he faced the world. She loved him with all her heart—for his faults as well as his virtues—and that was the beginning and end of it as far as her own emotions were concerned.

But what about Badyr? He was more than frank about his physical need for her, a fact clearly demonstrated by the nights they spent locked in each other's arms. But he had been ominously silent about his deeper feelings. When Badyr had assured her mother that he had always loved her ... had he ... could he have been speaking the truth? Leonie sighed. She must be realistic. As much as she wanted to, it would be folly to forget the long years of silence after she had left Dhoman, foolish to ignore the fact that she was only here because she had refused to leave her daughter. And yet ...

Her heart heavy with longing for what could never be, Leonie leant weakly against the cool mirrored surface of the wall for a moment, before slipping into a silk dressing-gown and trailing slowly back into the bedroom. She was so preoccupied with her thoughts that it was a few seconds before she realised she wasn't alone. Badyr, who had been standing by the windows, turned at her entry, his dark eyes gleaming with amusement as he removed his black patch and tossed it aside.

'I have just been having a long talk with Jade. I have told her that she must be a good girl while we are away for a few days.'

Leonie looked at him with startled eyes. 'What on earth are you talking about?'

'I have decided to visit my summer palace in the south of the country. We won't be away for very long, and Jade will be perfectly happy with Miss Jackson and my uncle Feisal.'

'But I can't possibly leave at the moment. The new textile mill is having real difficulties, and ...'

'While I am full of admiration for all you have done over the past month, it is useless for you to argue with me. We are going to have a break for a few days—and that is the end of the matter,' he said bluntly.

Leonie sighed heavily. It was futile to try and oppose

him once he had made up his mind, but she could hardly bear to think about the problems she would have to face when they returned. Despite all the help given to her by Badyr and his Minister of Development, the new manager of the mill—like every other Arab man with whom she dealt—did not take kindly to being given orders by a woman.

'Jade didn't take the news of our departure very well, either,' Badyr laughed. 'I now know the meaning of perpetual energy—it is undoubtedly her tongue!'

'I did warn you,' she muttered, going over to her chest of drawers to select some frothy silk underwear.

'So you did,' he agreed, swiftly undoing his wide gold belt and stepping out of the loose robes he habitually wore when in Dhoman. Crossing the marble floor towards Leonie, who was standing with her back to him, he slowly ran a finger down her spine. 'I can also remember you saying that you would never—ever—willingly submit to me, hmm?'

It was as if she was paralysed, unable to move or speak as he gently brushed aside the long length of her curly hair, softly pressing his lips to her neck. An icy shiver feathered down her backbone and she was powerless to resist the hands that moved to untie her belt, slowly edging the silk gown from off her shoulders to let it fall in a pool at her feet as he turned and drew her trembling, naked figure to rest against his hard body.

'Well, Leonie?' he murmured thickly, not waiting for an answer as he lowered his dark head to lightly brush her lips with his mouth, the kiss filling her senses with such an aching sweetness that her lips quivered and parted, a soft moan breaking from her throat as her arms crept slowly up to encircle his neck.

He slowly withdrew his mouth, gazing down into the blue eyes cloudy with desire, before giving a low laugh and sweeping her up into his arms to carry her with effortless ease towards the bed.

'No, Badyr, we can't . . .!' she gasped as he intimately caressed her trembling body.

'Oh, yes we can, my beloved,' he breathed huskily, his mouth causing havoc with her senses as it captured first one rosy peak of her breasts and then another.

'But the reception and banquet, and the guests?'

'Without my presence there can be no reception or banquet. So, our guests will just have to await my pleasure, hmm? And since, darling one, my pleasure is to be found here with you at this moment—in the possession of your delicious, quite irresistible body—there is no more to be said!'

They were indeed late, arriving at the reception a good half-hour after all the guests had assembled. Badyr blandly proffered his apologies without bothering to give an adequate excuse, but Leonie suspected that anyone looking at her flushed face and heightened colouring would be in no doubt as to *exactly* what had delayed them. And after receiving a beaming smile from the charming French Ambassador, she was certain of the fact!

She was still feeling embarrassed about the episode, and unhappy about leaving Jade, when she returned later with Badyr to their palace.

'Save your breath!' he said, with an infuriating, mocking smile as he stood aside to allow her to stalk ahead into their bedroom. 'I have not forgotten that it took me two whole weeks to persuade you to leave London! That was a quite exhausting experience which I certainly have no intention of repeating. Now, let us hear no more of the matter. It is time we were in bed and asleep.'

'The day you get into bed and go straight off to sleep, will be the day I drop dead with shock!' she snapped.

'Ah, my poor darling, I cannot face the responsibility of causing you such a sad end,' he laughed, walking over to take her into his arms. 'I can see that I must

make the ultimate sacrifice, and save you from that
terrible fate, hmm?' he added, removing her tiara and
casually tossing the priceless diamonds into a nearby
chair.

'*Oh, you're impossible!*' She glared at him, her heart
beginning to thud as she glimpsed the naked desire in
the dark eyes gleaming down at her. ' "The ultimate
sacrifice"—indeed! You've got a nerve!' she muttered
huskily as he plucked out the combs from her hair,
trying not to respond to his warm, sensual smile. 'You
know what you are, don't you? You're ... you're
absolutely and utterly ... incorrigible!' she gasped,
weakly surrendering to the demanding arousal of the
mouth that descended to possess her trembling lips.

Leonie sat out on the wide terrace of the Summer
Palace, gazing out over the rolling waves of the greeny-
blue sea to the wide, empty horizon where the Arabian
Sea mingled with the waters of the Indian Ocean. The
sun was just setting, the fiery glow turning the long
sandy beach into a ribbon of deep, rich amber as it
wound its way through the palm trees in the coconut
groves along the shore-line.

She had been astounded to find that instead of the
vast, sandy desert of her imagination, the province of
Mazun was an entrancing surprise. Covering an area
about the size of Wales, high mountain ranges formed a
half-circle to enclose a green crescent-shaped, fertile
plain bordered by long miles of sandy beaches that
would make most Caribbean islanders weep with envy.
Badyr had explained that by some strange quirk of
climate, monsoons just touched this corner of Arabia,
lasting from June to September every year.

'The bad news is that during the monsoon, the coast
is covered in cloud and fog. It never seems to stop
raining, and much of the province becomes a muddy,
cold, insect-ridden land of dark, murky gloom!'
His lips curved into a broad smile. 'However, the

good news, my dear Leonie,' he continued, 'is that for the rest of the year, Mazun is warm, green and overflowing with semi-tropical vegetation. Rivers flow through fields of wheat, sugar cane and cotton; mountain streams gurgle their way past groves of coconut palms; the sea is blue, the beaches are golden and it is for me—and I hope for you, also—a land of milk and honey!'

From what she had seen of the province during the drive from the airport yesterday, Leonie could easily understand why Badyr had spoken so poetically about this particular area of Dhoman. The green fields had seemed to be full of abundant crops and the meadows filled with flowers and herds of fat browsing cattle.

Standing amidst lush gardens and directly on the sea-shore, the Summer Palace was a long turreted building, surrounded by and hidden behind high walls. Inside the building, which had been built by Badyr's great-grandfather, Sultan Karim, in the late eighteen-seventies, a maze of inter-connecting courtyards and alley-ways led to rooms of differing architectural styles.

'This really is a lovely place,' she said, smiling up at Badyr as he joined her on the terrace, followed by servants bringing coffee and flickering lamps that glowed in the gathering dusk. 'Has it been in your family for a long time?'

'Every Sultan since Karim's time has fallen in love with the province and this palace,' Badyr said. 'And every one of them has added a room here, or a complete wing there. I was born here, and one way and another I seem to have spent a considerable amount of time in this building.' His lips twisted into a grim smile.

'Was this where . . .?'

'Yes,' he answered her hesitant enquiry. 'This is where my father had me confined after my arrest. It seems very pleasant, doesn't it? But I can assure you that after experiencing two monsoons during my incarceration here, if I hadn't managed to escape, I

would have undoubtedly shot myself from sheer gloom
and depression!'

Although he had spoken the words lightly, the bleak
underlying tone in his voice was unmistakable. There
was a long pause as he leaned back in his chair staring
blindly out into space.

'I have very ambivalent feelings about this lovely
place,' he said at last. 'Maybe that is natural, since no
one would willingly choose to return to their old jail.
Redecorating and refurbishing the rooms has helped, of
course, but nevertheless . . .' He sighed deeply and fell
silent, only the sounds of the sea lapping against the
sand disturbing the still night air.

Leonie sat quietly, hardly daring to move in case she
disturbed his train of thought. For so long she had
wondered what had happened to Badyr after his arrest,
and now, at last, it seemed that he might be going to fill
in some of the missing pieces of the jigsaw puzzle.

'I was brought down here under heavy guard, right in
the middle of a torrential downpour that seemed to last
for months!' he said wryly. 'The place was devoid of
any human inhabitants—other than myself and my
guards, of course. The only benefit of such solitary
confinement was that I had a great deal of time in
which to think about what I wanted to do for my
country, and how to implement the plans I had made. I
must confess that it would not have been too difficult to
escape. However,' he shrugged his shoulders, 'my father
put paid to that notion—rather cleverly, I thought.'

'He . . . he told me,' Leonie murmured. 'He said he
would put me in a dungeon if you even so much as
talked to anyone, let alone tried to escape. I . . . I'm
sorry, Badyr, there wasn't anything I could do to help
you.'

'My dear girl!' he smiled. 'My father was so firmly in
the grip of senile dementia by that time, that not even
all the luscious, shapely houris in paradise could have
prevailed upon his crazed senses! Nevertheless, it

became increasingly obvious I must escape before the country became engulfed in a civil war—my father versus the entire population!—but I had to see to your safety before I made the attempt.'

'You said, in London, that you had arranged for me to leave the country. But, I thought your mother . . .?'

'Let us just say that she and I came to an arrangement,' he remarked flatly, a muscle tightening along his jaw. 'Not one that I would ever normally have agreed to—but I was not in a position that allowed me any choice in the matter.' With a heavy sigh, Badyr rose from his chair to pace silently up and down the dark terrace.

'How I wish . . .' he muttered under his breath, and then gave a harsh laugh. 'If wishes were horses, beggars would ride! There is nothing to be gained by bitterly regretting what is already history in the sands of time. What is done is done, hmm?'

'Yes, yes, I suppose so,' Leonie murmured, totally confused by the underlying savage tone in his voice, and not having the least idea of what he was talking about. 'But you haven't told me how you escaped, or . . .'

'We will leave that for another time. It is growing late and I'm sure you will agree that there are far more important things we have to talk about.'

Leonie peered up at his tall figure, silhouetted against the light of the rising moon. Badyr seemed in such a strange mood tonight, and she couldn't for the life of her think what . . .

His low voice interrupted her confused thoughts. 'Just why do you think that I wanted us to be alone together? You have been in Dhoman for over a month now, and it is surely time that we discussed our relationship.' He came over to stand before her looking down at her pale face lit by the moonlight. 'Can you tell me that it is not passionate desire that you feel in my arms each night?' he said softly. 'Can you deny the soft, tremulous cries of pleasure that haunt my days like a siren's song, calling me back to your sweet body night after night?'

Leonie shook her head, shivering in the cool night air. She couldn't seem to find her voice, but neither could she deny or repudiate any of the things he said.

'Has it occurred to you that, in time, such feelings might become more than a purely physical response?' he asked gently. 'That you might possibly be able to forget the past, and learn to love me again—as I love and have always loved you? Or have my actions in the past destroyed all chance of that happening?'

Leonie gazed up at him, her mind and senses whirling in chaotic disbelief at what she was hearing. Was Badyr really saying . . .? It didn't seem possible, and yet . . . Her heart began a wild pounding, the blood surging and racing through her veins as her mouth suddenly became dry and she swallowed nervously, almost feeling sick with rising excitement.

'I . . . er . . . could you p-possibly repeat w-what you've just s-said,' she stammered helplessly.

'Ah, my darling,' he murmured, drawing her up into his arms and burying his face in the fragrant cloud of her hair. 'I never stopped loving you, never for one minute of my life. I know . . .' he added as she stirred restlessly in his embrace, 'I have treated you abominably. First in not telling you the entire truth about what you would find when you first came to Dhoman, and then, when you had escaped from the Harem, in not contacting you for so long.'

He put his hands on her arms, holding her away from him and staring intently down at her bemused expression. 'Love is very much a matter of trust, hmm? So, I am asking you to trust me, my dearest one. I would not have deserted you, other than for your own sweet sake. Please believe me when I say that I could not leave Dhoman, and it was only because I wished everything to be absolutely right for you, that I did not bring you back here any sooner. I loved you too much to do that. Can you understand that I made what I felt to be the best decision—in your own interests?'

'I don't really understand anything you've been saying, except . . .' She paused. 'You do really love me?'

'Oh, my darling, how can you doubt it!' he whispered thickly, cupping her lovely face in his hands. 'I would never have stolen Jade from you. But when I realised that you had been so hurt, so disillusioned by my desertion that you would not return to Dhoman, I had no alternative but to blackmail you into returning to this country. I have lived in desperate hope that your love for me was not dead, that given time it would come back to life and flower once again.'

'Oh, Badyr,' she breathed huskily.

The next instant she was locked tightly in his arms as he rained fervent kisses on her upturned face. Her heart leapt for joy as all her doubts and uncertainties dissolved and vanished away. Dizzy with the almost unbelievably wonderful fact that Badyr loved her, she wound her arms about his neck, drawing him closer to her trembling body as his hands slid sensuously over her warm curves; aware of his quickening desire and that his heartbeat was as rapid as her own.

'My darling Badyr. I never stopped loving you!' she whispered softly.

With a strangled cry of triumph, he swept her up in his arms. Carrying her as if she weighed no more than thistledown, he strode across the terrace and into the palace, swiftly mounting the stairs two at a time until he reached their bedroom where he laid her on the downy softness of the large bed.

'My beloved Leonie, I have such a great, over-powering love for you,' he murmured, quickly stripping off his clothes before slowly removing the light caftan she was wearing. His long, tanned fingers moved caressingly over her pale skin, casting aside the thin scraps of silk and lace as he exposed her full naked beauty.

'Exquisite!' he breathed thickly, his hands erotically stroking the full ripe curves and thrusting peaks of her breasts and the tender softness of her stomach. Leonie's flesh trembled beneath his touch, a sense of wild exultation at the intensity of his desire flowing through her veins like quicksilver. As if under a magic spell, she floated in a dreamlike trance as Badyr's lovemaking raised her to peaks of ecstasy she had never attained before, sweeping her up in a wild spiral of ever-escalating rapture until, when she was certain she could not bear the deliriously exciting agony a moment longer, his body merged with hers in a heavenly explosion of joyous, rapturous delight.

The long hot days and nights merged together into a shining stream of delight and happiness. It was as if Leonie and Badyr were discovering a completely new world together, one that was encompassed by the high walls surrounding the Summer Palace. Wandering hand in hand through the many rooms, or lying out under the shady trees in a garden full of the scent of exotic flowers, Leonie revelled in the beauty that surrounded her on every side.

'They are nothing to *your* ravishing beauty, my dearest,' Badyr murmured drowsily one hot afternoon as Leonie called his attention to the brilliant, shimmering colours of a pair of humming-birds hovering over a small pool of crystal clear water, near where they were lying on the grass.

'Oh Badyr—do look! Aren't they lovely?'

'I am looking.' He raised himself up on one elbow, leaning over her prone figure as his fingers moved to slowly untie her long, filmy gown, sliding it off her shoulders and exposing the unconfined, sweet curves of her breasts. 'And they are indeed lovely!' he breathed, his eyes savouring her beauty before he bent to touch his lips first to one rosy peak and then the other.

An echo of the previous night's lovemaking rippled

through her body and she uttered a shivering sigh of deep pleasure. 'I can't believe that I can be so happy!'

'Umm,' he murmured, his erotic kiss deepening as his mouth teased her nipples until she gave a small cry of pain. 'Darling?' he looked at her with concern. 'I did not mean to hurt you.'

'No, you didn't, not really. It's just—well, I'm a bit sensitive at the moment. I wasn't sure until a few days ago, but...' She paused, suddenly feeling oddly nervous. 'I think ... in fact, I'm quite sure—that I'm going to have a baby.'

If she had been worried about his reaction to the news, her fears were instantly put at rest by his overwhelming joy and pleasure at the news. 'You wonderful, wonderful woman!' he exclaimed, clasping her rapturously in his arms. 'And I promise you, my darling,' he murmured later as he tenderly stroked her warm flesh, 'that I will be close beside you at all times during your pregnancy. I cannot ever forgive myself for not being by your side when you were expecting Jade.' He smiled tenderly down at the girl in his arms. 'We shall call him Karim, after my great-grandfather.'

Leonie laughed. '"Him" ...? Well, I don't re-commend buying the baby a train-set just yet—*she* might prefer to play with a doll!'

'Oh no,' he said, his hands moving possessively over her stomach. 'You are going to give me a son to rule this land after me. Of that I am quite certain!'

'And ... and if I don't? If it should happen to be a little girl?' she asked, her blue eyes suddenly shadowed by uncertainty.

'Ah, my dearest, I will then have the perfect excuse—if I am ever likely to need one!—to keep on making love to you until we have a great tribe of children.' He lowered his head to passionately kiss her lips. 'Yes, of course I want a son, but if Allah should bless us with another daughter—like my little Jade—then I will be more than happy and content.'

Reassured by his words, Leonie surrendered to the tide of desire engendered by his lips and hands, the long lean length of his hard body as he swiftly removed their clothes. She gloried in the intimate contact of his warm flesh against her yielding softness, the throbbing urgency of his arousal as unable to contain himself, he possessed her there and then on the soft green grass. Only her small moans of excitement disturbed the peaceful setting, the high afternoon sun slanting down through the tall trees to cast long, golden shadows on the figures which lay so closely and intimately entwined together on the green lawn far below.

CHAPTER SEVEN

'ALAS, all good things must come to an end—if only temporarily,' Badyr said with a wry smile as they sat together at breakfast one morning. 'I'm afraid that I have no choice, my darling, but to begin a round of official duties, which means that my uncle Hassan will be joining us tomorrow.'

Leonie sighed. She was still so emotionally caught up in the wonder and delight of Badyr's love, that she resented anyone or anything that interrupted their blissful reunion.

'Besides, you will want to see Jade again. You said last night that talking to her on the radio-telephone was not very satisfactory.'

'No, it wasn't, but at least I needn't worry about her having missed us too much. It sounds as if your uncle Feisal is absolutely her favourite man of the moment. If you don't watch out, you won't be "stu-pen-dous" any more!'

'Where on earth does she pick up these words?' he asked, his mouth twitching with amusement.

'Think yourself lucky! Three months ago, she heard something on the television and it was weeks before my mother and I could stop her shouting "for-nic-ation", at the top of her voice!' Leonie giggled.

Badyr threw back his head and roared with laughter. 'I am sorry, my darling, but I think I really must pray very hard to ensure that our coming child is indeed a boy. Can you imagine what it would be like to have two little daughters like Jade? *Wallahi!* I do not think I could stand the . . . er . . . strain!'

'I hadn't thought of that,' Leonie agreed with a smile.

'Oh, by the way,' he added as he rose from the table.

'It occurred to me that it might be nice for Jade to get to know her little cousin, Ali. So I have invited not only my uncle Hassan, but his wife and son also. You will be pleased to see Sara again, yes?'

'Yes, of course. Although Ali's only two, and just a little young for Jade, who will probably order him around unmercifully,' she smiled. 'I'm very fond of your half-sister, who's every bit as sweet and placid as her mother.'

'We must hope that Sara does not become *quite* as fat as Fatima—my stepmother seems to grow more enormous with every passing day!'

But there seemed no likelihood of that, Leonie thought, as she sat out on the terrace one afternoon a few days later. Sara was still slim and petite, although she had confessed with a shy smile that she was expecting another baby in seven months' time.

'And, maybe you, too?' Sara had murmured that morning, casting a knowing eye over Leonie's glowing skin and the burgeoning swell of her breasts beneath the long filmy gown.

Leonie had wanted to keep her pregnancy a precious secret between Badyr and herself, until such time as it became too obvious to hide. But Sara's unexpectedly shrewd question had caught her on the hop, and she had not been able to hide her blushing, tell-tale confusion.

Now, as Sara's little boy, Ali, played quietly in the sand by the edge of the terrace, she asked Sara not to tell anyone else about the coming baby.

'I feel it's terribly important that Jade hears about the new baby from Badyr and myself, and doesn't pick it up from a servant's careless remark. Although, you know what the gossip in these palaces is like,' she added drily. 'Everyone knows exactly what is going on, weeks before one knows it oneself!'

'Very true!' Sara agreed ruefully. 'But where is little Jade? I have not seen her all afternoon.'

'When Badyr's uncle Feisal invited your husband and mine to go fishing on his yacht, Jade gave him no peace until she was allowed to go too!' Leonie laughed. 'I think Feisal invited Elizabeth Jackson along simply to make sure he retained his sanity!'

'Well,' Sara mused. 'That may be so, but I think Feisal likes Miss Jackson very much. In fact, I wouldn't be at all surprised . . .' She hesitated.

'Oh, no—surely not?' Leonie looked at her with startled eyes. 'He's far too old for Elizabeth! I mean . . .' she paused, horrified by what she had said as she realised that Sara's husband, Hassan, was considerably older than his brother, Feisal.

'Relax, Leonie!' Sara smiled. 'You have an expression in England, do you not? "There is many a good tune played on an old fiddle"! Hassan may have grey hair, but I can assure you that my dear husband is very . . . er . . . very vigorous in every other respect!' she giggled.

'For the love of Allah—can't you two talk about anything else but marriage and babies?'

Leonie bit back a sharp retort as she looked over at the girl lounging on one of the comfortable chairs spread along the terrace. She hadn't been pleased to find that Nadia had invited herself along to the Summer Palace with Sara and her husband, and the girl's malicious, bitter comments were beginning to get under her skin.

'Marriage and babies are a fact of life—literally!' she murmured with a smiling shrug of her shoulders.

'Babies! We poor women find ourselves trapped as soon as we marry!'

Leonie gave a light laugh, attempting to defuse the situation as Sara's small figure bristled in the chair beside her. 'That may possibly be true, Nadia. But when you fall in love, you will undoubtedly find that you are happy to be caught in such a warm, tender trap!'

'Never!' Nadia cast a spiteful glance at the English

E

girl's fair, glowing beauty. 'You may be fool enough to welcome your husband straight from his other wife's bed, but I would never submit to such an indignity!'

'Oh, for heaven's sake! What on earth are you talking about?' Leonie looked at her in puzzlement, only half aware of Sara's hands fluttering in the air as she tried to prevent her sister from saying any more.

'Oh, it's all so stupid!' Nadia snapped at Sara. 'I ask you—how does Badyr think he can possibly keep Leonie from hearing about Aisha? She's bound to find out sooner or later. Surely it's better that she knows the truth?'

'*Nadia!* How can you do this?' Sara cried, jumping to her feet in consternation. 'Badyr will *kill* you! Why must you take such delight in being malicious and cruel?'

'I don't understand.' Leonie looked on in confusion as the two sisters began screaming at each other in Arabic. 'W-what "other wife"? And who is Aisha? I've never heard of her, I . . .'

'Of course you haven't—you poor fool!' Nadia spat the words venomously. 'Your precious husband is no better than any other man. He wants to have his cake and eat it too, doesn't he? Oh, yes,' she gave a wild laugh, 'Badyr's certainly a good Moslem. You should think yourself fortunate, Leonie, that he's only got *one* other wife—he's allowed up to four at any one time, you know!'

Leonie couldn't move. She sat stunned by Nadia's words, not able to comprehend what the other girl was saying. Badyr—married to another woman? Another wife? It couldn't possibly be true. Nadia was just trying to make even more trouble than usual—of course she was! The very idea was too extraordinarily foolish and far-fetched to be worth taking seriously. She'd have to tell Badyr to send Nadia back to her mother as soon as possible. She really wasn't going to put up with any more of the girl's stupid, malicious remarks.

Leonie turned to Sara, shocked to see the girl sitting slumped in her chair with tears streaming down her cheeks. 'For goodness sake, there's no need to cry! Nadia's just being silly, that's all . . .' Her voice died away as Sara turned to look at her, the expression of sorrow and pity in her eyes sending shivers of fear down her spine.

'Yes, it is true,' Sara whispered, agitatedly hunting for a handkerchief to wipe her eyes. 'Oh, Leonie, I am so . . . so sorry. I know that such customs are difficult for western women to understand. But I also know that my brother does love you very much, and . . .'

'But how, why?' Leonie felt cold, icy fingers tightening around her heart. 'And who is Aisha?'

Sara glared over at Nadia, who was sitting back in her chair with a smirk on her face. 'You had better start saying your prayers, you wicked, wicked girl. Because when Badyr finds out what you have done, he will surely tear you limb from limb!' she ground out through clenched teeth.

'For God's sake, Sara, tell me the truth!' Leonie cried, as Nadia merely responded to her sister's words with a defiant toss of her dark head. She suddenly felt desperately sick, and tight bands seemed to be closing about her ribs making it difficult for her to breathe.

Sara gave an unhappy sigh and fiercely blew her nose. 'Badyr swore us all to secrecy . . . but yes, it is true. You see,' she shrugged her shoulders, 'it is traditional in our family for the eldest son to marry his uncle's daughter. Feisal is not married, and so—as expected—Badyr married his young cousin Aisha, the daughter of his uncle, Hassan. I hope you can understand—it is maybe a little complicated.' Sara looked at the English girl with compassion.

'But *you* are married to Hassan.' Leonie shook her head in stunned confusion.

'Aisha's mother died of tuberculosis soon after she was born; a disease that has killed many of her family in the past,' Sara explained. 'It was only after many years, long after his daughter Aisha was married to Badyr, that I married Hassan.

'But how? I mean ... where? And when?' Leonie whispered.

'I do not know all the details, since I was much younger at the time.' The other girl sighed heavily. 'However, I think it was over five years ago that they were married, and she now lives up in the mountains behind Muria. But, Leonie, it is important that you understand.'

What it was important that she understand, Leonie never heard, the full horror of her situation scorching through her trembling body like a blinding flash of lightning. As her brain struggled to comprehend the terrible fact that not only was she bigamously married to Badyr, but that her precious little daughter was illegitimate, something seemed to snap in her brain. The terrace, the palace and the sea beyond began to spin, revolving faster and faster and drawing her down into a swirling void. The last sound she heard was her own strangled moan as she lost all hold of reality, limply falling out of the chair on to the hard stone terrace.

Leonie surfaced from the swirling mists, gazing blindly about her in dazed confusion as she dimly realised she was lying on her bed. The room itself seeming to be filled with a crowded mass of servants, all shrieking at the tops of their voices. A moment later, Sara's worried face swam before her eyes, bending over Leonie's prone body to place a cold cloth on her brow. The noise and confusion suddenly seemed too much for her to cope with, a low moan breaking from her lips as she slipped thankfully back into the darkness once more.

When she finally returned to full consciousness, all the noise and confusion had disappeared. Looking around she saw that the room was empty, save for Badyr's tall figure pacing distractedly up and down by the tall windows. She couldn't prevent a strangled gasp of horror as she began to recall the scene on the terrace, the sound bringing Badyr instantly to her side.

'What has happened to you, my dearest?' he murmured, sitting down beside her on the bed. 'I can get no sense from anyone in this palace! When I returned from the yachting trip, it was to find Sara in floods of tears and refusing to explain matters, the servants hiding in their quarters and wailing as if there had been a death in the family—and all I have been able to gather is that you fainted out on the terrace. So, please tell me what is wrong, darling,' he added, softly brushing the hair away from her brow.

The warm, gentle touch of his hand was almost more than she could bear, the tears welling up to trickle down her cheeks in a steady stream.

'Ah, my sweet, my dear one. I have called for a doctor, and we will soon have you well again.'

'I'll never—ever—be well again!' She turned her head away, burying her face in the pillows, her slim figure racked with sobs.

'Come, this is foolish, Leonie. You have no need to weep.'

'Haven't I?' she moaned. She felt as cold as death although her body was shaking as if in the grip of a raging fever. 'What do you expect me to do when I find out that my husband is a lying, cheating adulterer, and that my child is . . . is a bastard!'

The hands that had been gently stroking her hair became suddenly still, and the faint hope that Nadia and Sara were mistaken—that it was, after all, only a bad dream, a nightmare—drained away in the long silence that followed her tortured cry of anguish.

'It's true, isn't it? You really do have another wife?' she whispered, her hoarse voice echoing around the room as she struggled to sit up.

Leonie's dazed blue eyes stared fixedly at Badyr, noting the blood draining from his face to leave it pale and strained beneath his tan, the deepening lines about his hard, firm lips. It was as if he had been turned to stone, only a vein beating furiously in his temple giving any indication of his inner tension.

'Well?' Her trembling, shaking hand dashed away the tears which were beginning to fall again. *'Have you—or have you not—another wife?'* she demanded harshly.

Badyr gave a deep, heavy sigh, putting his hand to his forehead for a moment as if in pain. 'Yes, Leonie. I cannot deny, however much I might wish to do so, that I have another wife. But . . .'

'But—*nothing!* Or maybe Nadia's right?' she gave a wild, hysterical laugh. 'Maybe you've got at least four of us "wives" stashed away around the country?'

'Nadia!' he suddenly roared, rising swiftly to his feet and striding about the room. 'I might have known that little bitch . . .'

'She may be a bitch—but she was absolutely right!' Leonie cried, anger coming to the aid of her stunned mind as a torrent of rage flowed through her body. 'For God's sake! Just how long did you think you could keep me in blissful ignorance? Someone was bound to tell me that I'm . . . I'm . . . God knows what I am! Some s-sort of c-c-concubine . . .?' she wailed, throwing herself down on the pillows again in a paroxysm of hysterical tears.

Badyr strode swiftly over to the bed and gathered her weeping figure into his arms. 'Oh, my dearest, my beloved one. You are indeed my true wife, that I assure you. And our child is not a bastard! I promise you that she is legally my daughter, as our son will be also.'

'You *promise* me? Your promises don't mean a damn thing!' she cried, wrenching herself away from his embrace. 'And what's "legal" mean in this bloody country, anyway? It's legal for a man to have four wives at one and the same time, and all his children are legal—whoever their mother might be. But . . . but you just try living your so-called legal way of life in Europe or the United States ... and you'd soon find yourself locked up for bigamy! They'd shove you into jail so fast, that even your handsome head would be spinning like a top!'

Badyr rose to stride agitatedly about the room. 'I assure you, Leonie, that you are my first, my legal wife. I give you my solemn promise that our marriage will stand examination in any European or American court. It therefore follows that Jade is my true daughter, and that the child you carry is definitely not a bastard.'

'*Big deal!* Thanks a million!' she lashed back furiously. 'And what about all your other wives and their children? What do you tell them? A version of the same bedtime story you've just given me. God ...! *I can't believe this is happening to me!*' Her cry of pain and anguish echoed around the room, reverberating in her ears like the knell of doom.

'Leonie! I beg you to be calm.'

'Calm? Did you say *calm*!' she screamed, rising from the bed. 'I'll give you "calm", *my fine Sultan!*' she hissed, swiftly raising her hand to give him a resounding slap on his tanned cheek.

'Enough!' he commanded curtly, catching hold of her wrist as she aimed another retaliatory blow at his face. 'I can understand your wish to hit me, but it will achieve nothing.'

'Don't you believe it!' she panted, trying to break away from his iron grip. 'If I had a knife in my hands, I'd plunge it into your black heart without a moment's hesitation!'

His lips twisted wryly. 'Ah, yes, my vixen—I can readily believe that you would.'

'It's no laughing matter!'

'I agree,' he said in a flat, heavy voice, bending swiftly to seize hold of her struggling body. 'Now, we must talk sensibly and calmly, yes?' he murmured as he carried her over to the bed, before sitting down beside her and gripping her hands tightly together between his own.

'I had married no other woman before you, and our marriage is perfectly legal—both here in Arabia and in the Western world. That is the first point I wish to make. Yes, I do have another wife, whom I married according to Moslem law—*after* our marriage—and that is also a legal marriage as far as she and I are concerned. Do you understand me, Leonie?' He grasped hold of her chin, holding it steady as he forced her to meet his dark, troubled gaze.

'Oh, I understand all right!' Her voice wobbled dangerously as she fought to control her pain and anguish. 'I clearly understand that you seem to think that because I was the first of your . . . your paramours, that makes everything just fine and dandy! God—what a swine you are! How many other wives and children have you got—or isn't it polite of me to ask?'

'I have only one other wife, and no children other than Jade,' he replied evenly. 'I know you may not believe me. However, if you consider the matter, you will see that while I have indeed been guilty of the sin of omission, I have never deliberately lied to you.'

'Your definition of the word "lie" and mine are hardly likely to agree, are they?' she grated bitterly. 'As far as I'm concerned the last five years has been one big lie on your part, not to mention that little item: for-nic-ation!'

'My darling, if you would just listen to me.'

'And give you a chance to sweet-talk me into accepting this revolting, bizarre set-up? Forget it! And while I'm on the subject of "sweet-talk", have you bothered to tell your other wife about me? Or have you kept her ignorant of my existence too?'

'No, of course not. Aisha knows all about you, and . . .'

Leonie gasped, nearly choking on the hard lump of dark jealousy which seemed to fill her throat. 'What a jolly little *ménage à trois!*' She gave a cracked laugh. 'I'm sure you've both had a lot of fun discussing me—been seeing a lot of her lately, have you?'

Badyr stared at her for a moment, his face white and strained. 'Yes, Leonie,' he said quietly. 'I've had to. But I've never . . .'

'*Wow!* You're quite the sexual athlete, aren't you?' She began to laugh, and found she couldn't stop. The crazy, shrill tones echoed around the room until Badyr raised his hand and gave her a quick slap on the face.

'I'm sorry, my darling! I had to do it,' he whispered as she hiccuped into silence, staring bleakly at him with eyes that were deep blue pools of misery. 'Please stop torturing yourself—and me—so unnecessarily.'

'Oh, Badyr . . .' Leonie shook her head helplessly. 'Why on earth did you drag me away from my life in London? How . . . how could you be so cruel to make me go through this agony? Why, why?' She stared at him, the blood draining from her face. 'Oh, no! *What a fool I've been!*' she groaned, stiffening with shock and almost paralysed as she was struck by the horrifying truth.

'It's because you need a son, isn't it? Oh, God—I can see it all now! Your precious Aisha hasn't given you any children—and so what do you do? You look around and suddenly remember the girl who was so foolish as to marry you, and whom you've completely forgotten about for the last five years. After all, you got me pregnant fast enough, didn't you? Since Aisha hasn't come up trumps—why not put stupid old Leonie in the family way? She might be a bit of a nuisance—but at least she's fertile! Right, Badyr?'

'For God's sake, *no!*'

Leonie gave him a savage, mocking grimace of a smile, her voice harsh with loathing and disgust as she ignored his sharp protest.

'Wait a bit—the story's just beginning to get interesting! Using his considerable talents . . . mostly

trickery, blackmail and a lot of oily, sexy charm . . .
our handsome hero manages to haul the silly woman
back to Dhoman. And guess what? Yes, fast as knife,
she conceives a baby! And—now this really is the
clever bit—*it's all as legal as can be*! Ho, ho! Our
hero is laughing like a drain, isn't he? He's got his
second wife, whom he's been happily living with for
the last five years, *and* someone else to have his
children. Clever . . . c-clever B-B-Badyr . . .!' she
sobbed, shudders of anguish and torment shaking her
frame as she gave way to tears of overwhelming grief
and desolation.

'Leonie! You don't understand! You are so terribly
wrong—it is not like that at all.' A deep groan broke
from his throat as he seized her tightly in his arms,
kissing her with rough, mounting passion.

Appalled, Leonie realised that her treacherous body
was responding to his firm embrace and inflaming lips.
With an almighty effort she managed to push him
away, far enough to allow her to slip from beneath his
arms and roll across the bed, taking to her heels and
dashing for the bathroom. Slamming the door and
locking it quickly behind her, she staggered over to sit
down on a stool, panting breathlessly as she ignored his
angry demands that she come out and listen to what he
had to say.

'Do not be foolish,' he added in a softer tone. 'You
cannot stay in there forever, and I will be waiting out
here—even if it takes a week. So, be sensible, hmm?'

'Go to hell!' she shouted, trying to control her limbs
which seemed to be jerking as if she had St Vitus's
dance. It was some time before she could even attempt
to pull herself together. Sitting huddled on the stool
with arms clasped tightly about her shivering body, she
was only able to rock herself backwards and forwards
in mindless agony. The shock of being so swiftly and
abruptly transported from heaven to hell—all in a few
short days—was more than she could cope with.

Eventually, her shuddering figure became still, and she tried to think what she was going to do next.

Could she make Badyr divorce her? Would he let her leave the country? She could hardly bring herself to face the fact, but it seemed certain that he would refuse to do either of those things. So, what could she do? She was alone in the country, with no real friends and no help at hand. Badyr was absolute ruler of Dhoman, and what he said was, *ipso facto*, the law. There was no one who would raise a hand to assist her, not when they knew they would inevitably incur his wrath. And yet, to submit to him, to have him make love to her—straight from another woman's bed, as Nadia had so succinctly put it—was so intolerable that . . . Never! she promised herself, gasping with pain. She must never let him possess her again! But how was she to stop him? She knew very well that fight him as she might, his superior strength would always prevail in the end. And even if her body didn't betray her, as she very much feared that it would, his need for sons to follow him on the throne was such that he wouldn't hesitate to rape her if necessary. The baby! Could she possibly use the baby in any way . . .?

Totally exhausted by her storm of tears, she moved over to the shower on legs which felt as if they would collapse any moment. Standing beneath the cool spray, letting the water flow over her hair and body, she gradually found that she was able to begin thinking more constructively. By the time she had dried herself, and wrapped her wet hair in a small white towel, she had managed to formulate a course of action. Although, whether it would be successful or not, she had no idea.

'Ah, I see that you have decided to be sensible,' Badyr murmured, leaning against the open window that led to the balcony. 'I have locked the door of this room, and we will stay here until you give me an opportunity to tell you exactly why I married Aisha, yes?'

'No.' Leonie said firmly, walking across the room to sit down in an easy chair. 'Why should I have to listen to your puerile excuses? I'm not in the slightest bit interested in your relationship with your other so-called wife, whom I will always regard as nothing more than your mistress. Frankly, I have far more important things on my mind than trying to keep up with your sex-life!'

'You stupid girl!' he shouted, throwing his hands in the air in exasperation.

'You are so right! Stupid is exactly what I was, but I've now decided to get smart. So—you, *my dear Badyr*,' she added caustically, through teeth which chattered loudly in her head, 'had better just shut up—and listen to me for once.'

'I will not divorce you. I will not let you go back to England—and that is my final word,' he retorted in a hard, flat voice.

'I've already realised that,' she informed him bleakly, noting a look of uncertainty flit across his face. Taking a deep breath, and trying to control her nervously shaking body, she began to lay down her terms.

'We have been married—if you can call it a marriage!—for six years. We have a little daughter and now I am expecting another child. My mother had always said that Jade needed a father, and the same must apply to the new baby. I am, therefore, prepared to stay with you, to act as your wife and to submit to your possession as best I can,' she shuddered.

'However, you have admitted that you have used me shamefully—as indeed you have! And it is only right that you should make some effort to repair the damage you have caused myself and my daughter. I must insist that you immediately divorce your second wife, Aisha. I've nothing against the woman—if anything I feel damn sorry for anyone involved with you—but my children need the sole attention of their father. To put it bluntly: I'm not prepared to have Jade's view of life corrupted by the sight of her father's flagrant immorality!' She paused. 'Have I made myself quite clear?' she demanded harshly.

'Yes, Leonie. Very clear,' Badyr retorted bitterly, before turning to look out of the window, his tall figure silhouetted against the dying sun. It was a long time before he gave a deep, heavy sigh and slowly turned back to face her once again.

'You are a fool if you do not realise that I would do anything I possibly could to please you,' he said softly. 'But in this case...' He wearily shook his head. 'I cannot ... I cannot do what you ask, my darling. It would be too unkind, too cruel for my Aisha to bear.'

'*Your Aisha*? To hell with your Aisha! What about *our* daughter, and the new baby?' She took a deep breath. 'I don't care about myself, Badyr, I really don't,' she assured him earnestly. 'But what sort of life is it going to be for my children? Surely they deserve more than half a father's love. Do you really want them to grow up in the sort of life and atmosphere that you did? How can you have so quickly forgotten that terrible old palace?'

'I cannot do it, Leonie! You may be right in what you say, but I cannot do it, my darling. If you'd just let me explain ...'

'Okay—that's it!' she snapped grimly. 'I had to try and rescue something from the shambles of our marriage—if only for Jade and the baby's sake— although God knows, the thought of having to live another day with you makes me feel sick! However, it now seems that I have no choice but to give you my final ultimatum.'

'What on earth are you talking about, Leonie? If you'd just ...'

'I'm just going to tell you how it will be from now on,' she said, her voice low and deadly. 'There is, you will agree, a fifty-fifty chance that the baby I'm expecting is the son you want so much?'

'Yes, of course, but . . .'

'Right, let's see how badly you want that child, Badyr. You are going to leave this palace tonight—together with the rest of your family—leaving me, Jade, Miss Jackson, Hussa and sufficient servants to make sure we are all comfortable.'

'No!' he retorted furiously.

'Oh yes—this is where I am going to live—without you, I'm happy to say! I am quite prepared to send Jade to see you once a month, but you will never—*never*—so much as set foot in this palace, ever again.'

'And what makes you think that I will agree to such a preposterous idea?' he demanded angrily.

'Are you a betting man? How do the odds of two-to-one attract you? If you leave me here, I will give you your son—maybe. However, if you make me live with you, forcing your revolting attentions upon me, I will deliberately abort the baby I'm expecting and any others that I might conceive.'

'I don't believe you!' he snarled, his face as white as chalk. 'It would be a sin to do such a thing.'

Leonie shrugged as carelessly as she could. She had to try and make Badyr too angry to think clearly, and to be as convincing as possible if she hoped to get away with her bluff.

'What is sin? As far as I'm concerned it would be a far worse crime to bring a new baby into our present lives. To have our son grow up realising that his father is a bigamist!'

'Don't you dare use that word!' he bellowed with rage.

'The facts speak for themselves,' she snapped. 'However, let's keep to the point. Unless you are prepared to lock me up in one of your father's dungeons, I can assure you that I will terminate this pregnancy. And there isn't a damn thing you can do about it!' She saw that he was hesitating, and quickly pressed home her advantage before she lost her nerve in saying the terrible words.

'Of course, you might be like your dreadful old father—maybe you'd get a *real* thrill out of having me chained to a dank prison wall for the next eight months? It would make the time dear old Sultan Raschid had you confined here, in this palace, seem like a picnic—wouldn't it?' she murmured, encouraged by his hard, bleak expression to go for the *coup de grâce*. 'Ah well, you had better unlock the door and call the guards in to arrest me.'

'My God, you're a clever woman—just like my mother!' he whispered with cold rage. 'That is a very dramatic performance you have just given—you know damn well that any question of prison is ridiculous! What is more, I don't believe for one moment that you would harm our unborn child, but you know I cannot take the risk that you might do so.'

He swore violently under his breath as he paced up and down before the windows, clearly trying to find a way out of Leonie's ultimatum. 'Very well, Leonie,' Badyr said at last, his voice cold as ice as he turned to face her. 'You win—it shall be as you say.'

Despite her total misery and her loathing of the man who had so destroyed her life, she felt a sudden pang as she looked at his bowed shoulders and the lines of strain on his face as he went over to open the door.

'Oh Badyr,' she sighed wearily. 'Can't you see? Can't you understand—that once you deserted me and married another woman, you set in train this ... this ghastly, unhappy mess in which we find ourselves? You talk about winning,' she gave another deep, heavy sigh, 'there are no winners in this affair—only losers, I'm afraid.'

He turned, pausing to look at her for some moments, his face a blank mask. 'I am not a loser, Leonie. And you would do well to remember that fact in the future!'

His cold, harsh warning seemed to permeate the still air of the room long after he had slammed the door behind him.

CHAPTER EIGHT

HUSSA showed the doctor out of the bedroom, leaving Leonie to dress herself in privacy. Checking her make-up in the mirror, she grimaced at the reflection of her heavy figure before walking slowly and carefully down the stairs to the main room of the palace.

'Would you like a cool drink before you go?' she asked Dr Winslow, the brilliant young American gynaecologist at the new hospital in Muria, who had been assigned by Badyr to monitor her pregnancy.

'I'd love one,' he grinned. 'I never need any excuse to delay leaving this lovely part of the country. It sure is a great place!'

'Yes, I'm very happy here, it's so peaceful and quiet,' she said, ringing for a servant and ordering some fresh lime juice.

'Well, I guess you'd better make the most of it. I reckon this is likely to be my last visit before the monsoon sets in, and I gather that there is no way you are going to be able to stay down here in the south when that happens. Besides,' he added, 'you're seven months pregnant now and I'll need to give you more than the monthly check we've been having so far.'

'Oh, no!' Leonie checked her outburst as the servant returned with the cool drinks. 'I'm really very well, and what is a little rain to someone who is used to English weather?' She gave him a soft, cajoling smile. 'Couldn't you persuade my husband to let me stay down here for another month, at least?'

He looked at the lovely girl and regretfully shook his head. 'I sure am sorry,' he said, 'and I truly understand why you don't want to leave. But I just can't do it. I had enough trouble persuading your husband not to

144

haul you back to Muria last month—he'll never go for it again, I'm afraid.'

'But I'm perfectly fit and well.'

'Hmm. Yes, in general I'd agree. But your blood pressure is up a little, and with under two months to go.' He paused and shook his head. 'If it wasn't for the monsoon, I might possibly have been able to swing it— to allow you to stay here for a while. However, what with the bad weather coming soon and the need for more frequent medical checks, I'd have to agree with the Sultan. I'm sorry, but...' He shrugged his shoulders.

Gazing at the beautiful girl's unhappy expression, he wished that he didn't have to be the bearer of what she clearly regarded as bad news. There was obviously trouble between the Sultan and his wife, and it was a shame to see two people tearing each other apart; although after a shaky start to her pregnancy it now looked as if the wife was in better shape than the husband. Still, the Sultan had his own doctors, and it was up to them to tell him to take it easy. He could only be glad that it wasn't his job to try and talk some sense into that austere, taciturn figure. Sultan Badyr, once such a likable and approachable guy, had lately become so hard, tough and bad-tempered, that it would take a brave man to tell him that if he didn't slow down on his work-load, sooner or later he was going to be seriously ill.

Leonie sighed. 'Well, as you said, I'll just have to make the most of the time I've got left,' she murmured, realising that it was unfair on the doctor to protest any more. By getting the last two months' extension he'd already done as much as he could for her, and to push him any further was unreasonable.

Walking slowly through the garden, Leonie sank down on to a bench beneath a wide, shady palm-tree. It was almost six months since she had been left alone in this palace, desperately unhappy and heart-stricken at the discovery of Badyr's second wife. As the weeks had passed slowly by, the peace and calm of the quiet life had provided some measure of balm for her troubled spirits, but nothing it seemed could banish her love for Badyr, or the wretched misery at the choice he had made.

She hadn't—she didn't—wanted to know anything about his other wife, Aisha. But that didn't stop the evil, insidious jealousy from winding its slimy green tentacles around her heart. Night after night she hadn't been able to stop torturing herself with the thought of Badyr making love to another woman—a woman that he had refused to relinquish, and who therefore meant far more to him than Leonie had ever done.

Those first few months, living day and night with the haunting vision of Badyr's long, tanned body lying closely entwined with another woman, his erotic lovemaking arousing and inflaming another woman's passion, had led to a serious decline in her health. Growing daily more thin and strained, her face gaunt and pale with dark shadows beneath her dull blue eyes, she had only been jerked from the dark depths of her misery and depression by Dr Winslow's hard words.

'Look here,' he had said. 'The Sultan has made me entirely responsible for your health during this pregnancy. The baby is fine at the moment, but I can't say the same goes for you! After my last trip, I had to tell your husband that I wasn't happy about you—it would have been worth more than my life not to—and he hit the roof!' He looked at the haggardly beautiful girl with compassion.

'So, okay, I'm not blind and anyone can see you've got problems, but you've got to try and pull yourself together. I'll do what I can for you, but you're going to have to co-operate and make a big effort. Otherwise, I can promise you that the Sultan will override anything I say, and insist that you go back to Muria. You may be able to stop him doing that, but I sure as hell can't!'

The threat that she might be forced to return to Badyr had been enough to help pull her at least halfway out of her depressed state, and the slow march of time had done the rest. She was still bitterly unhappy, but she had made a determined effort to banish from her mind the sensual images of Badyr's lean, hard figure, and to control the overwhelming sexual jealousy, which had been so tormenting her days and nights. She wasn't always successful, of course, but very gradually she had begun to put on some more weight, the colour coming back to her cheeks and the life to her sapphire-blue eyes.

'Attagirl!' Dr Winslow had said on his next monthly visit, looking at her glowing beauty with appreciative eyes. 'Just keep on the way you're going, and you'll be fine.'

A shout in the distance interrupted her thoughts, and she looked up to see Jade racing over the grass towards her.

'I caught a fish—I did, really!' Jade danced with excitement. 'But Miss Jackson said it was only a baby fish, and so I had to put it back.'

'You'll be able to catch it again next year, and it will be much bigger then, just like you!' Elizabeth laughed as she joined them, carrying the fishing rod which was Jade's latest present from her great-uncle Feisal.

'Can we go fishing tomorrow?' Jade demanded. 'Maybe Mummy can come too—oh, please do say that you will, Mummy?' she added, giving Leonie a hug and laughing as she felt the baby moving in her mother's womb. 'I bet the baby would like to go fishing. I do wish it would hurry up and arrive, 'cos I want to show it my collection of shells.'

'Well, you'll have to wait just a little bit longer,' Leonie said as she stood up, and taking Jade's hand began to walk slowly back to the palace. 'Although I think it might be some time before the new baby will be able to appreciate your collection, I'm afraid!'

'Did the doctor give you a clean bill of health?'
Elizabeth asked as they stopped to allow Jade to pick
some flowers.

'Yes, I'm fine. But it looks as if we'll have to leave
here fairly soon. Apparently the monsoon is due to hit
this area of the country very shortly, and when that
happens, we must return to Muria.'

'Never mind. It's been an idyll—as far as I'm
concerned, anyway. And although you may not want to
return, you're going to be so busy getting all the
necessary bits and pieces ready for the baby, that you
really won't have time to think of much else.'

Leonie smiled gratefully at Elizabeth. Looking back,
it seemed incredible that she had once been annoyed
with Badyr for engaging the governess. Elizabeth had
been such a quiet tower of strength during these last
months, that she didn't know what she would have
done without her.

Not that Leonie had confided in the other girl, of
course. But she imagined that Elizabeth must have a
very good idea of exactly why the Sultan and his wife
were so estranged. The governess had been here with
Jade at the Summer Palace when the whole terrible
business—Nadia's revelation about Badyr's second
wife—had blown up in Leonie's face, and there couldn't
have been many there who didn't know the reason why
Badyr had so suddenly ordered everyone out of the
place. Any remaining doubts would have been removed
by the subsequent, monumental row between Nadia
and Badyr.

Leonie had resolutely refused to leave her bedroom,
but even from there she could hear Badyr's thunderous
roars of anger as he vented his rage over the head of the
hapless girl. When Sara had come in to kiss Leonie
farewell, she had been shivering and shaking from the
scene downstairs.

'I warned her,' Sara had muttered through teeth that
were still chattering with nervous tension. 'But, *wallahi!*,

I did not realise just how bad it would be. My brother is as one demented! Oh, Leonie, I am so desperately sorry and unhappy for you.'

'Don't let's talk about it, please,' Leonie had whispered, very near to breaking down again. 'I—I can't face any more discussion of the subject, I really can't.'

'But, surely Badyr explained . . .'

'Oh, yes, he explained all right!' she had grated, before the events of the day proved too much for her and she ran into the bathroom to be violently sick. Sara hadn't wanted to leave her at that point, but Leonie had insisted. Sweet though the girl was, she simply didn't feel she could take any more of Badyr's family. She hadn't of course set eyes on Sara since, and as to what had happened to Nadia, she had no idea.

'Well, Jade and I had better start packing and getting all our things together,' Elizabeth said calmly. 'Little madam, over there, will be overjoyed to return to Muria—and her pony!' She looked over to where Jade had wandered off after some flowers across the glade. 'I haven't said much to you, since there's been no point in making a meal out of the situation, but there's no doubt that Jade has been missing her father a great deal, and finding the monthly visits very confusing, I'm afraid.'

'I know,' Leonie sighed. 'But there hasn't been anything I could do about it—not really.'

'Never mind. She'll soon perk up and settle down when we get back. Children are very resilient, you know,' Elizabeth murmured sympathetically. 'And with her pony and her stu-pen-dous uncle Feisal, she'll soon forget all her worries!'

'Oh, Elizabeth,' Leonie gave a shaky laugh. 'You're a terrible governess! Surely you could have taught her another favourite word by now?'

'Hmm, I have tried, but none of the ones I suggest seem to have taken root in that active little brain. The main trouble is that the interesting sounding words are, more often than not, thoroughly rude—if not downright pornographic!'

'What's por-no-graph-ic mean, Mummy?' Jade asked, having come up without the two women hearing her approach. 'Why are you and Miss Jackson laughing like that? Shall I take these flowers in to Hussa, I'm sure she will like them.'

'I'm sure she will, darling,' Leonie laughed and took her hand. 'Come on, it is nearly time for lunch, and I'm sure you must be hungry,' she added as they walked back into the house.

The young doctor's warning had proved to be correct, Leonie realised, when Sheikh Samir flew down to see her three days later.

'His Majesty suggests that you might consider being ready to leave in four days' time. The meteorological report is not good, and he is anxious that you should be well away from this area before the rains come.'

'I think that is more of an order than a suggestion, don't you?' Leonie murmured wryly. 'However, you may tell the Sultan that I shall concur with his wishes. Where . . . er . . . where exactly are my daughter and I going to live?'

The young sheikh looked at her in surprise. 'You will be taken to your home, of course. To the palace in Muria.'

'I see.'

'However, his Majesty has asked me to tell you that . . . er . . . most unfortunately he will be unable to . . . er . . . welcome you back to Muria in person. It is a matter that I am sure he . . . er . . . very much regrets.' The Sheikh cleared his throat nervously. 'However, I understand that he is about to undertake a tour of the country, and is likely to be away for the next six weeks. He has asked me to assure you that he will, of course, return in ample time to be with you on the birth of his child.'

Leonie sat back in her chair. 'You know, Sheikh, I

really do feel that you are wasted in your present job. The diplomacy with which you so charmingly translate your master's commands and edicts has my complete and utter admiration. You should surely be an ambassador, at the very least!'

Sheikh Samir flinched at the caustic tone in Leonie's dry voice. 'I merely try to convey his Majesty's ... er ...'

'I know,' she said quickly, instantly contrite for taking out her unhappiness and frustration on the young man, who was having to carry out Badyr's orders. 'I must apologise for my bad manners, and I hope you will forgive me for being so tiresome.'

'Of course, Majesty,' he smiled. 'I realise it is not an easy time for you—with the baby's birth imminent, I mean,' he added hastily. 'And I can assure you, with total sincerity, that it has been a very great pleasure to have been able to visit you over these last few months.'

'Oh, Sheikh Samir!' she laughed softly. 'You really *are* a splendid diplomat! Now, do please relax. Tell me—how is Maryam?'

'The Princess Maryam is very well,' he assured her, going on to describe a picnic organised by her Prince Feisal at which, Leonie gathered, the Sheikh and Maryam had been able to spend some time together.

Leonie no longer wondered why Maryam had been so awkward in her company, when she had returned to Dhoman. She now saw that Badyr's sister had known all about his second wife, and due to the friendship between them in the past, had found the necessity of suppressing that knowledge more difficult than the other members of the royal family.

'Do please give Maryam my love,' she said as the young ADC prepared to leave. 'And tell her that I do understand, and despite all that has passed, I hope she will feel she can come and see me when I return to Muria.'

The Sheikh, to his eternal credit, didn't pretend not

to know what Leonie was talking about, but merely
bowed over her hand as he promised to deliver the
message.

Leonie was deeply unhappy to leave, but even she was
forced to see the sense behind their hasty departure
when the heavens opened a day before they left. The
thick fog and the never-ending, heavy sheet of
pounding rain was as depressing as Badyr had said it
would be, and Leonie regretfully resigned herself to her
fate. She found some measure of cheer in reflecting that
the weather would clear in three months' time, when
she would be able to return to the peace and seclusion
of the summer palace.

Maybe because she was heavily pregnant it seemed a
long, hard journey back to the capital city. By the time
she arrived at the palace, Leonie's ankles were puffy
and swollen and she felt weary and exhausted. Wearing
long filmy robes, the traditional dress of Dhomani
women, wasn't just sensible in the heat but might have
been specifically designed to hide the bulky figures of
pregnant women, she thought wryly as she lay soaking
in the bath.

Of course, part of the reason she felt so exhausted
must be due to the nervous strain of having to return to
this place. She had spoken caustically to Sheikh Samir
about his polite explanation of Badyr's planned
absence, but she really ought to be thankful that her
husband had chosen to go away. Having to live cheek
by jowl with him in an atmosphere of ever-present
enmity would have been more than she could bear. And
what was Badyr planning to do when she had given
birth to the baby? Her threats to harm her unborn
child—something she could *never* have brought herself
to actually carry out—would be useless. However,
maybe if she had a boy—a son to follow him on the
throne—he would feel no need of further procreation?
She fervently hoped so.

A noise in the next room broke through her thoughts. It must be Hussa with the light supper she had ordered, Leonie realised, and removed the bath plug before trying to get out of the large, sunken bath. Unfortunately, it was of a different design from the one she had been used to in the summer palace.

'Please come and give me a hand, Hussa,' she called out. 'I think I've got stuck in the bath!' she added with a laugh.

Hearing footsteps approaching, she turned to smile at Hussa and nearly fainted when she saw not her old servant ... but the tall figure of Badyr! Her eyes widened in fear, her body trembling as she saw him pause inside the door for a moment before putting out a hand to collect a large fluffy towel, and walking slowly over the marble floor to where she lay trapped in the bath.

'W-what are you doing here?' she gasped. 'I ... I thought you had g-gone away.' The blood drummed through her veins as she viewed his tall figure, her dazed eyes noticing that he had discarded his black patch and his usual traditional dress, his broad-shouldered frame clothed only in a short towelling robe.

'Unfortunately, I have had no choice but to delay my journey,' he retorted curtly. 'I can assure you that it is not on *your* account, my dear Leonie, that I am still in Muria,' he added in a cold, hard voice. 'God knows I do not ...'

Badyr drew in a sharp breath, his eyes darkening as he stared down at her body, completely revealed as the last of the bath-water gurgled away. Instinctively, she folded her arms, trying to shield the heavy swell of her stomach and the full ripeness of her breasts.

'No! Let me look at you.' He knelt down to grasp her hands, moving them aside as his eyes travelled down the length of her body. 'My child—my son,' he breathed thickly. She flinched as he reached for her, but his touch was surprisingly gentle as he lifted her out of the bath and enfolded her shaking figure in the soft towel.

'How could I have forgotten your gloriously soft flesh?' he murmured, drying her arms and shoulders before moving gently down to the burgeoning swell of her breasts. 'So pale . . . so soft and smooth, like silken velvet.'

'Please, no!' Her low moan of protest was ignored as his hands took the place of the towel, moving erotically over the rosy peaks that hardened and throbbed at his touch.

'Let me go!' she cried, struggling in vain as he quickly tossed aside the towel, adroitly capturing her wrists and holding them in one of his broad hands behind her back. Arching her body towards him, he allowed his other hand to move tenderly and carefully over the taut mound of her enlarged womb, her body quivering and trembling at his touch and the intensity of his gaze as his eyes devoured the sight of her changed contours.

His action and her nervous response provoked a reaction as she felt the baby give a protesting kick. Badyr looked at her with startled eyes, his face pale and tense as he quickly released her.

'Your son—or daughter—is clearly feeling energetic tonight,' she muttered, her teeth chattering nervously as she grabbed the towel; she was still feeling stunned by his unexpected appearance, her senses bemused by the heavy atmosphere of sexual tension which crackled like electricity between them.

'That is really . . .? You mean . . .?' He stared in fascination at her stomach as her trembling hands fought with the towel, clumsily trying to hide her nakedness from his sight.

'Oh, Badyr! Surely you know how babies kick?'

'No—how should I? I was not present when you were expecting Jade,' he retorted savagely. 'And it would seem, would it not, that once again I have been denied the pleasure of seeing my child grow in your womb?'

Leonie was confused by the harsh, bitter tone in his voice. Looking at him more closely, she was disturbed to see the deep lines of strain on his face, and surely ... surely he used not to have silver threads among the black hair at his temples? To her utter consternation, she was suddenly swept by an overwhelming and extraordinary urge to comfort the man gazing at her with such bleak intensity. Without conscious thought Leonie moved slowly towards him, pulling aside the towel as she took his hand and placed it on her stomach.

'You see?' she whispered as the child within her moved again. 'Sometimes babies aren't very active, but as you can see this one—so like its father!—kicks very hard indeed.'

Although he gave a grunt of laughter at her words, there was a strange look of awe on his tanned face. 'It seems a miracle that my child should be growing in such a way, and that he will soon be born into this world,' he murmured. 'But come, Leonie,' he added a few moments later, gently lifting her up in his arms. 'I was told that you arrived very tired and exhausted, so you must now rest.'

'No, please, please put me down, Badyr. I have to oil my body, and really I'm feeling much ... much ...' She couldn't continue, a hard lump in her throat preventing her from saying any more. She could feel his hard chest muscles and the warmth of his skin through the thin towelling, the harsh planes of his tanned cheek so close to her own and the familiar scent of his cologne filling her nostrils. It was all so evocative of their deliriously happy moments together in the past, those deeply sensual, intimate hours they had spent making love to one another, that she seemed incapable of protest as she felt all her willpower draining away.

Reminding herself of his despicable conduct appeared

to have no effect on the languorous, drowsy lassitude which was seeping through her mind and body as he carried her through into the bedroom. Laying her carefully and tenderly down on the bed, he left her to return a few moments later with a bottle in his hands.

'There is no need to worry, my Leonie,' he murmured, sitting down on the bed beside her. 'I will smooth the oil on for you.'

'Oh, no, you mustn't . . . it's quite wrong, and I'm so ugly like this.'

'On the contrary,' he breathed huskily, ignoring her weakly fluttering hands as he parted the towel to reveal her naked body. 'I have never seen you looking so lovely—or so very, very desirable.'

Pouring some of the liquid into his palm, he began to massage the taut skin of her stomach, moving his hands slowly and gently over her flesh. 'How can you think that I would not wish to see your body, especially when it is ripe and swollen with my child?' he murmured, rhythmically smoothing the oil over her skin.

There seemed to be a humming noise in her ears as a lambent warmth coursed through her body. She sighed deeply, incapable of any effort of will or desire to stop his caressing fingers, mindlessly responding to their sensual touch. Cupping her full, ripe breasts in his hands, he lowered his dark head to brush his lips tantalisingly over her taut nipples, Leonie moaning aloud at the thrilling ache deep in her stomach.

'You see?' he breathed. 'We are the two halves of one whole. Hate and loathe me as you will, my beloved, but you cannot deny the innate need and desire we have for each other.'

He was right. However much she wanted to protest and refute his hoarsely whispered words, Leonie realised that she was helpless beneath the erotic mastery of his hands; a soft yet demanding arousal that provoked a quivering, heated response in her traitorous body.

'Badyr . . . no!' she moaned as he put aside the lotion and swiftly removed his towelling robe.

'Oh, my Leonie . . . *yes!*' he muttered thickly, his face a tight mask of desire, the dark eyes glittering with mockery at the lack of conviction in her voice.

The arms that enfolded her trembling body were hard and warm, his mouth descending to kiss away the hopeless tears which had filled her eyes, before trailing down her cheek to seek the soft hollows at the base of her throat. There was a raw hunger in the hands and lips caressing her soft flesh, a devouring, demanding need that met an answering response. It was as if she was in the grip of a hallucinatory drug, every one of her senses, every nerve-end, screamingly aware of his breath on her skin, the heavy pounding beat of his heart and the black silky hair on his chest brushing against the tips of her breasts. Her body shook with an overwhelming desire that she could not possibly deny, her hands feathering down the long length of his spine and moving over the taut, firm muscles of his hips and thighs.

A deep groan was wrenched from his throat at her intimate, caressing touch, his figure shaking as he possessed her lips with an urgency that finally swept aside all the barriers between them. Leonie clung blindly to his broad shoulders, totally abandoning herself to the ardour that flared through her body and murmuring soft, incoherent cries of delight as his lips and hands moved over her flesh with scorching intensity; burning and demanding her total surrender.

'My sweet Leonie . . . it has been such a long time . . . such torture! For God's sake do not deny me, my darling!' he whispered thickly, the words rasping in his throat, his chest heaving as though it pained him to breathe. 'I will be gentle and careful, but I cannot resist your lovely body. I must . . . *I must have you!*'

Neither the moral values of right and wrong, nor the unhappy past nor the uncertain future seemed to have any meaning for Leonie as she feverishly responded to the overwhelming desire which held them both firmly in its thrall. Here and now, the only reality was the hard warmth and strength of his tanned body, and the almost unbearable ecstasy that raced through her veins. Almost unconscious with delirious excitement, she barely heard the low, deep groans provoked by the wanton abandonment of her response; her soft moans and pleas for fulfilment an irresistible enticement, provoking heated shudders that shook the tanned length of his long body as he strove to maintain his self-control.

As he had promised, Badyr managed to temper the urgency of his desire, leashing and controlling the force of his own passion as he gently and tenderly led her from one exquisite delight to another; the mounting pleasure so prolonged and emotionally intense that she cried out, weeping with joy as he at last brought them both to a soaring high plateau of mutual ecstasy and overwhelming rapture. Thereafter, floating on a hazy cloud of warmth and happiness, Leonie drifted aimlessly down into a deep sleep, aware only of the comfort and security as she lay within Badyr's encircling arms.

The sun was pouring into the bedroom when Leonie woke next morning, and she drowsily stretched her languid, satiated body before slowly turning her head to see that she was alone in the middle of the great bed. Her eyes widened with horror and disbelief as she noted the crumpled sheets, the pillow still bearing the imprint of Badyr's head. Inexorably and relentlessly the events of the previous night flashed through her mind like a reel of film out of control, and with a deep groan of despair she rolled over to bury her head in the pillows.

Oh God! How ... how could she? How could she possibly have allowed herself to submit to him? And it was worse than that! *Far, far worse!* She hadn't just weakly given in to his amorous demands, had she?

Leonie moaned with self-loathing and disgust as she remembered exactly how she had responded, how eagerly and lasciviously she had demanded his possession.

Shivering and shaking she turned over, seeking a handkerchief to staunch the tears of bitter remorse which were flooding down her cheeks. A sound attracted her attention and she glanced sideways to see the swirling white robes of Badyr's tall figure as he entered the room.

'*No!* Go away!' she cried hysterically. 'Oh God! How I wish I'd never b-been b-b-born!'

Not able to control the sobs that shuddered through her trembling body, she hung her head, tears blinding her vision as she stared fixedly down at her fingers clutching the sheet in wild agitation.

There was a long silence as Badyr came to a halt beside the bed, staring down at the girl who was weeping so bitterly. His lips tightened into a hard line as he viewed the disordered cloud of her magnificent red-gold hair, her figure shaking as if in the grip of some tropical fever.

'I realise that it is no excuse to say that I could not prevent myself from behaving as I did last night,' he grated harshly. 'The sweet enticement of your body would tempt even a saint—and God knows I am but a frail, mortal man.' He paused for a moment as she buried her face in her hands, shaken by a fresh paroxysm of convulsive sobs.

'Unfortunately, as much as I would wish to do so, there is a very good, pressing reason why I cannot leave Muria at the moment. However, I am not prepared to allow scandal or gossip to touch my house and family,' he declared in a cold, hard voice. 'I must, therefore, continue to use this palace as I have always done, until such time as I can depart on my tour of the country. Nevertheless, my dear Leonie,' he added with savage bitterness, 'you have no need to worry. I can give you my complete assurance that you will be quite safe from what you clearly regard as my vile attentions. I trust I make myself clear?'

Exhausted by her storm of weeping and stunned by the harsh ferocity of his voice, Leonie could do no more than nod her head, waiting with quivering, nervous tension to hear what else he had to say. However, the heavy silence was only broken by the swishing sound of his long, white robes as Badyr spun abruptly on his heel and swiftly left the room.

CHAPTER NINE

TOWARDS the end of what seemed to have been the longest three weeks of her life, Leonie was quite sure she had never before been quite so miserably unhappy, despite all that had happened in the past. It was as though she inhabited a desperately lonely, wretched state of purgatory, where nothing could lift the heavy weight of her despair.

Tension headaches plagued her during the succeeding long hot days, giving her no rest from the terrible realisation that she was trapped: both by the imminent birth of her baby, and a daughter whom she could not possibly abandon, but also by the knowledge of how desperately she yearned for Badyr's arms; a longing which haunted her every conscious moment. He was her first thought on waking and her last at night. His presence even haunted her disturbed, restless sleep as his tall, charismatic figure strode relentlessly through her dreams. His cruel abandonment, his callous disregard and total insensitivity was an ever-present torture—a terminal illness from which it seemed she would never recover.

If only she had not asked old Sultan Raschid for tuition in Arabic, all those years ago. Maybe, if she hadn't been able to speak the language, she might have been spared the knowledge of exactly where and with whom Badyr was spending his days. Unfortunately, she had inadvertently overheard a conversation between two of the palace servants. From what they said, it had been abundantly clear that the Sultan was in constant attendance on his second wife, Aisha, at her palace up in the hills behind Muria.

Despite the painful knowledge of her husband's

scandalous, almost obscene behaviour, it seemed that nothing could destroy the deep feelings she had for him. If, as she did, she constantly told herself how much she hated Badyr, she was also full of bitter self-loathing for her own emotional weakness. She couldn't even accuse him of not keeping his word, given the last time they had spoken to each other. She was always fast asleep when he joined her in the large bed, and had left it long before she opened her eyes in the morning—only the lingering aroma of his distinctive cologne betraying the fact that he spent his nights lying beside her.

Maryam had called one afternoon, the brief visit proving to be a heavy strain on them both. Leonie, whose head was pounding with a migraine, felt quite unable to talk about her desperate situation, while Maryam had been clearly shocked and horrified by the sight of the English girl's haggard beauty, the bleak misery in her sapphire-blue eyes. Keeping their conversation to such innocuous topics as Jade's enthusiasm for her pony and her scholastic progress under the supervision of Elizabeth Jackson, Maryam did let fall the information that a few days previously Sara had given birth to a little girl.

'Uncle Hassan is delighted with his new daughter,' Maryam enthused, before blushing fiercely at her *faux pas*. Mention of her uncle and his new child could only lead to the dangerous topic of his eldest daughter, Aisha. 'I . . . er . . . I went to visit Sara yesterday. She's in the new Maternity Hospital,' she continued quickly. 'It is really a wonderful place, Leonie, and all the nurses—who are British and American—seem to be so friendly. Are you having your baby there?'

Leonie shrugged her shoulders. 'Yes, I think so,' she muttered, realising with a pang that she should have given more thought to the necessary details and arrangements for the birth of her child. 'I'm so pleased that Sara has the little girl she wanted, please give her my love,' she added, feeling ashamed of the envy she felt for Sara who, unlike herself, had the loving warmth and support of her husband at such a time.

The tense, strained atmosphere between them had caused Maryam to cut her visit short, and when the arrival of Sultana Zenobia was announced a few days later, Leonie asked Hussa to make her apologies. The thought of having to go through the trauma of yet another round of polite conversation was more than she felt she could cope with.

'Stuff and nonsense! I have no intention of going away without seeing her Majesty,' the older woman stated firmly, brushing the servant aside as she strode regally into Leonie's private sitting-room. Taking no notice of her daughter-in-law's obvious reluctance to see her, she proceeded to sit down in a comfortable chair, giving Leonie a searching glance from beneath her heavy eye-lids.

'Hmm. I can see that Maryam was quite right. It is plainly obvious that matters between you and my son have reached a desperate state.'

'I ... er ... I really don't want to discuss ...'

'How long is it before the birth of your child?' Zenobia asked, as Leonie slowly raised her ungainly body from the *chaise-longue* on which she had been lying, and rang the bell for a servant to bring in the coffee which was traditionally served to visitors on their arrival.

'About a month,' she muttered, returning to lie back against the soft cushions.

'One would have thought Badyr could see how he is endangering the birth of the son he desires so much—the stupid man!' Zenobia shook her head, clicking her tongue in exasperation. 'Very well,' she added firmly, 'I can see that despite his orders to the contrary, I clearly have no choice but to resolve this unfortunate business as swiftly as possible.'

Imperiously clapping her hands for Hussa, the Sultana completely ignored Leonie's protests as she instructed the maid to bring a shawl for her mistress, before sweeping the breathless English girl out of the palace and into a waiting limousine. Reeling under the swift turn of events, Leonie demanded to know what was going on.

'Despite being motivated by the very best of intentions, I once did you and my son a great injury. I believed that I was right at the time, but . . .' The older woman gave a weary shrug of her shoulders as the vehicle sped through the streets of Muria. 'Oh, yes, I have had years in which to realise that I was wrong—that I had, in fact, made a tragic mistake.'

Leonie looked at her in silent confusion.

'It is important that you understand how it was when you first came to this country,' the Sultana mused quietly. 'I must tell you that I was completely devastated when Badyr arrived back in Dhoman with you as his new wife. I was horrified by what my son had done—especially in view of the past history of the family. Badyr's grandfather married a French woman as his first wife,' she explained. 'And although their child was the eldest son, the ruling sheikhs of the time refused to accept the boy's mixed blood. Ignoring his just claim, they chose his younger brother, by another Arab wife, to rule Dhoman.'

'I really don't see . . .' Leonie looked at her in puzzlement.

Sultana Zenobia sighed with impatience. 'You are an intelligent girl, so surely you can understand how it was? I had schemed and planned to get Badyr out of the country, insisting that he be educated abroad, and made strenuous efforts to keep him well away from his father's increasing madness. And then—what did my son do? *He returned to Dhoman with a foreign bride!*' She sighed deeply.

'But Badyr has no other brothers.'

'I could not rely on that fact. There was no guarantee that Fatima would not have a son, or the ruling sheikhs might decide to adopt Hassan or Feisal on my husband's death—see how Hassan has married Sara, and already has a young son.' Zenobia waved her hand dismissively. 'Besides, after Badyr's arrest, my spies told me that my husband was seriously planning to disinherit his son in favour of Hassan. I had to move quickly, Leonie. It is important that you understand that I had no alternative but to make sure that you left the country—something which, Allah knows, I had tried to achieve since the day you arrived at the palace! Once you had left the country, I would then be able to marry my son off to a proper Arab wife. It would be easy to rally support behind him, once he was suitably married, and ensure that when he escaped from his prison, nothing would stand in his way. There would be no impediment to prevent him from taking over control of Dhoman from his father.'

Leonie gasped. 'You mean . . .?'

'Yes. For Badyr—for my son's life, his safety and the future good of this country—I did what I had to do.'

'So, it is *you* I have to thank for everything that has happened to me!' Leonie ground out harshly. 'My God—I hope you're pleased with your handiwork!'

'No, I have told you that I now see I was wrong. Please, please calm yourself,' she added hurriedly, putting a restraining hand on the arm of the furiously angry girl sitting beside her.

'Don't you touch me, you . . . you evil woman!' Leonie cried. 'Have you any idea of the heartbreak you've caused me? And don't keep telling me to calm down!' she added with a snarl. 'My God—there's nothing to choose between you and your son—*the spineless bastard*!'

'You do not understand.'

'You're damn right—I don't!' Leonie retorted savagely. 'It's quite clear that I've never understood my husband! How could Badyr have let himself be ordered around like that? It's almost unbelievable!' Her voice rose incredulously. 'I knew he was ambitious—but to meekly do as he was told? Tossing me aside and cheerfully marrying another woman?' She couldn't go on, almost choking with rage and fury.

'*Leonie!* Be silent and listen to me!' Zenobia ordered, catching hold of the younger girl's hands and holding them firmly in her own for a moment. 'It was not as you think. No, not at all!'

'Oh, God!' Leonie sighed heavily, slumping back in her seat and closing her eyes. 'Please take me back to the palace.'

'No—I cannot do that.'

'What?' Leonie turned her head to look at Zenobia, a frown creasing her tired brow.

The older woman hesitated for a moment. 'I am taking you to see Aisha.'

'*Oh, no!*' Leonie sat bolt upright, her eyes flashing with anger.

'Yes, yes I must. I have no choice in the matter,' Zenobia shrugged.

'Well, I certainly have! For God's sake—haven't you caused me enough trouble? Let me out of here, immediately!' she added with a sob, looking wildly about her. For the first time she noticed, through the smoked glass windows, that the car was travelling swiftly across a dusty plain towards the foothills of a far mountain range.

'Please, Leonie! I speak only the truth,' Zenobia assured her earnestly. 'I told you that I had no choice—and it is true, I haven't. Badyr's wife, Aisha . . . she is dying!'

It was some moments before Zenobia's words seeped through the chaos in Leonie's brain. 'Aisha? Dying?' She turned to stare at the older woman in bewilderment.

'Aisha made me promise—despite anything Badyr might say—that I would bring you to her. I cannot break a promise to a woman who will soon leave this life. Such a request is a solemn, binding obligation which I must obey.'

'Aisha is dying? But why? I don't understand.' Leonie shook her head in dazed confusion.

'I have been trying to tell you, but you would not listen to me,' Zenobia sighed wearily. 'To understand all, I must explain what happened when Badyr was arrested by his father and sent into exile down at the Summer Palace. Yes, I was frantic with worry for my son—what mother would not be? I knew it would only be a matter of time before my husband disinherited his son—as you know, he was growing more mad and unpredictable with each passing day. Hmm?'

'Yes, I . . .'

'However, while you remained in the palace as a hostage for Badyr's good behaviour, there was nothing I could do to gain his release. My son sent me many secret messages asking for my help to arrange your escape from Dhoman. However, I realised that he was powerless without my assistance, and so I agreed to do as he asked, but only on condition that he immediately took another wife.'

'My goodness,' Leonie's voice grated bitterly. 'What fun for Badyr!'

Zenobia winced at the girl's caustic words. 'I may well deserve your anger, but not my son, Leonie. He completely refused to agree to my terms, remaining adamantly opposed to any suggestion that he should take a second wife until he heard, from sources other than myself, of the pressure which my husband was directing against you. Only then, and because he feared for your safety—indeed, for your very life—did he most reluctantly agree to do as I wanted.'

'Are you telling me . . .?'

'I swear that what I say is the truth. As soon as I received Badyr's assent, I arranged your departure to Abu Dhabi. Badyr had no access to funds while he was imprisoned, and it was his suggestion that you be sent with some precious rugs and carpets. He said you would know how to dispose of them and have enough money on which to live, until such time as he could plan the coup against his father, divorce the wife I chose for him and bring you back to Dhoman.' Zenobia leaned back on the seat and gave a heavy sigh.

'I had no objections to my son's plans. My only desire was to see him safely on the throne and running the country—that is all.'

'And I was just a silly young girl, an expendable pawn in your game, wasn't I?' Leonie said quietly.

The Sultana shook her head. 'You were very far from being a silly young girl—how much easier my task would have been had you been so! No, Leonie, you were too young to realise it, but I saw immediately that you were too strong and independent. Despite all that I did, it was obvious that you were determined not to give in, resolved to survive all the hardships placed in your way. Not even my husband's terrible rages could manage to completely quench your spirit. Oh yes! You possessed the power to defeat all my plans—all my arrangements. I had to be rid of you before you became fully conscious of the fact.'

'*Dear God!* I really do believe you think you're paying me some sort of compliment!' Leslie lay back wearily against the seat. 'I can see it would be useless to even attempt to explain just how revolting I find your mad pursuit of power. Power, position and wealth—all gained at such a terrible cost!'

'You are right to accuse me, Leonie.' Bright patches of red stained Zenobia's cheeks. 'I accept all you say, but in my defence I must ask what you would do if your little Jade was threatened? Or the new baby, hmm? Would you not fight tooth and nail for their interests? And if you feared for their life—as I feared for my son's—can you swear to me that you would not seek to brush aside anyone or anything that stood in their way?'

There was a silence in the car as Leonie remembered how she had tried to make Badyr divorce his second wife. She hadn't cared about Aisha at that point, had she? All she had been concerned about were her children and their future welfare. Desperately wanting them to have the sole protection of their father, she had even offered to stay with Badyr, despite her full knowledge of his despicable behaviour.

She gave a heavy sigh. 'I . . . I don't know. You may be right. But I like to think that I would have been more humane. Not so terribly cruel.' She couldn't say any more as she fought to control the tears which threatened to fall any minute.

Zenobia looked at the girl sitting beside her. 'I am sorry,' she said softly. 'More sorry than you will ever realise. And it is because words of sorrow achieve nothing, that I am taking you to see Aisha today. My son will be furious. He is such a proud man, is he not? Just as proud and stubborn as you, I think!' She gave a harsh snort of wry laughter. 'I doubt that he will ever forgive me for interfering in his life, but Aisha wishes to see you. She has requested that I bring you to see her, because she has something of importance to say to you. And no, I do not know what it is that she wants to say,' she added, forestalling the question trembling on Leonie's lips. 'I am merely fulfilling the obligation she has placed on me—one that I cannot in all conscience avoid.' Zenobia hesitated. 'Come, Leonie. Will you not listen to what I have to say? Please give me a chance to explain how it was.'

'"How it was", is a phrase that seems to haunt my existence!' Leonie muttered grimly, staring blindly out of the window. 'Very well,' she said at last.

With a sigh of relief Zenobia sat back in her seat, pausing for a moment to collect her thoughts. 'After Badyr had agreed to take another wife, and with your departure from our country, it seemed as though all would go well with my arrangements. The choice of

Badyr's new bride was an obvious one. Aisha was the daughter of my husband's brother, Hassan. I knew that she would be approved of by my husband, especially when I pointed out to him, as I did, that the girl would also be a hostage for Hassan's good behaviour. Such a consideration was necessary, since Sultan Raschid was enraged by your escape!' She shuddered at the memory. 'However, I soon discovered that I had made a terrible mistake—not only in seeking to interfere in my son's life, but because I knew so little about Aisha.' Zenobia gestured wearily. 'Hassan had been ruling the north of the country for my husband, and his daughter was brought up there. I, myself, had only seen her once as a small girl and had no idea that the tuberculosis which had killed her mother was also already present in Aisha's lungs. She was a pale, sickly young girl of sixteen when she was married by proxy and sent down to join Badyr at the Summer Palace. There, at the height of the monsoon, she rapidly succumbed to the disease. My husband would do nothing—although I begged him on my knees to send a doctor down to look after the poor child—and she gradually became more and more ill. I know that Badyr and the guards did what they could, but by the time the good weather arrived, it was too late. The disease had gained a hold which it has never lost, and ever since that time, Aisha has been very, very ill.'

'But surely tuberculosis is curable nowadays?'

Zenobia shook her head. 'Badyr has taken her to Switzerland and seen the world's top consultants—there was nothing anyone could do. Eventually, she begged him to allow her return, to let her die in peace in her own country.'

'Oh, God—the poor girl!' Leonie looked at her in distress. Zenobia's story, the description of Badyr's poor sick wife in the throes of a terminal disease, was so far removed from the glamorous 'other woman' of her jealous fantasy, that she was hardly able to fully comprehend what she was hearing.

'And that is why my son would never divorce her. Badyr has always said that it was tragic that she should have been forced into marrying him, and that our family was totally responsible for the sharp decline in her health. He maintains that if Aisha had been left to live in the North, high in the mountain ranges, none of this would have happened to her.' Zenobia sighed. 'And yes, of course he is right, Aisha needs all his care and support for the little time she has left in this world.'

Leonie gave a low moan, hiding her face in her hands as she recalled all she had said to Badyr, the day she had discovered the existence of his other wife. 'Why did he never tell me? Why didn't he explain everything to me in London?' she whispered.

'My son does not confide in me, and there is little I can say that will be of any help to you, I'm afraid.' The older woman's voice was surprisingly warm and sympathetic. 'But I do know that Badyr was convinced you would never, never accept his second marriage—whatever the reason—and he felt he could not bring you back to Dhoman while Aisha was still alive. I can only imagine that when your mother wrote to him about her marriage, and her worries about you and Jade, that he decided to take a chance; bringing you back and hoping against hope that you would never find out about his second marriage.' She gave a wry smile. 'Men are such fools, are they not? But truly, Leonie, he has a great love for you—of that I am very certain.'

Her mind a seething mass of pain and confusion, Leonie's chaotic thoughts were interrupted as she felt the car slowing down to negotiate a series of dangerous bends through a narrow mountain pass. A few moments later they drew up outside a small white, single-storied building set on a cliff projecting out over the valley far below.

'When Aisha expressed a wish to return to Dhoman,

Badyr had this house built for her. The air up here is purer than that down in the plain,' Zenobia murmured as the chauffeur came around and opened the door of the vehicle.

Trying to control her nervously trembling limbs, Leonie found herself being helped out of the car and following the older woman up a wide flight of steps towards a heavy oak door. It was opened by a nurse in a blue starched uniform, who was swiftly joined by a young Dhomani doctor wearing a white coat.

'I'm afraid that it is only a matter of hours,' he murmured to Zenobia, before turning to Leonie. 'You are the Sultan's wife?'

Still feeling stunned and in a state of shock from all that she had heard during the last hour, Leonie was incapable of speech and only able to nod her head.

'Ah, then if you would please be so good as to come with me,' the doctor said, taking her arm and leading her slowly down a long corridor.

'I do beg you, Majesty, not to be alarmed by what you see,' he murmured softly as he halted outside the door. 'The Sultana Aisha is very weak, but I assure you that she is in no pain. Indeed, I am hopeful that your visit may ease her spirit, since she has been most anxious—most determined—to speak to you. So, please do not be distressed by her frailty and remain calm, yes?' he added as he put out a hand and opened the door.

Leonie's first impression was of a large, white-walled and airy room, two sides of which were composed of arches open to a wide verandah overlooking the far mountain peaks. Trembling nervously in the doorway, her eyes were irresistibly drawn past the two nurses present towards the small, frail figure of the girl lying on a narrow bed in the centre of the room.

Why—she's no more than a child! Leonie thought, swept by a tide of deep pity and compassion as the doctor led her over to a chair beside the bed. It was all she could do not to cry out in distress as she found herself staring down at the pitifully gaunt, stick-thin frame of a young girl. Her face, surrounded by long black hair, was deathly pale, only the brilliant dark eyes burned fiercely, glowing feverishly as they surveyed the woman bending over her.

'You . . . you are Leonie?' Aisha murmured, her thin lips curving into a sweet smile. 'I hope . . . I understand you speak Arabic?'

'Yes,' Leonie whispered nervously, lowering herself down on the chair and trying not to show how shocked she was at the sight of the other girl's wasted limbs.

'That is good—my English is very, very bad!' She lapsed into Arabic, once again giving Leonie a sweet smile, her thin chest heaving as she fought for breath. 'I wanted to see you . . . it is very important that I tell you . . . tell you . . .'

'Please! Please don't try to speak too much,' Leonie murmured, her tender heart going out to the frail girl whose laboured breathing was a heart-wrenching sight. Without thinking she took Aisha's thin fingers into her own warm hand. 'Surely you should rest and conserve your strength?' she added.

'No. No, I have no time!' Aisha rasped. 'And I know . . . I know that it is so important I tell you that Badyr and I . . .' She began to cough, a nurse swiftly materialising by her side to gently sponge the perspiration from the Arab girl's face.

'Poor Badyr, he has been burdened with me for so long. Never has he shown the least impatience . . .' She paused to catch her breath. 'Because of his great kindness, and because he is so unhappy and desolate, I knew I must tell you . . .' She faltered, looking up at the girl beside her. 'Yes,' she sighed. 'Yes, you are as lovely, as beautiful as Badyr always said you were.' She gave another heavy sigh. 'I must confess I was always jealous of you. So silly of me, hmm?' Aisha gave a small, wry smile.

'And I of you,' Leonie whispered, tears filling her

eyes as a hard lump of pity and sorrow obstructed her throat.

'Of—*of me?* How foolish of you!' The girl gave a rasping, incredulous laugh which shook her frail figure. 'That is why I wanted to see you. Why I had to tell you that Badyr and I have never ... never lived together. Not ... not as man and wife, you understand?' she panted. 'I knew that it ... it was important that I tell you this, yes?'

'Oh, Aisha!' Leonie grabbed some tissues from a box beside the bed, fiercely blowing her nose and wiping the tears from her eyes.

'Poor Badyr. He has loved you so long ... and so well. He was always so kind to me ... but he could not bring himself to touch me ... could not act that which was not in his heart ...'

The girl's voice died away as she lay back on the pillows and closed her eyes, clearly exhausted by the effort of speaking so much. 'Yes ...' she murmured, her breathless voice breaking into the long silence at last. 'Yes, it is true that I love him. I, too, love Badyr with all my heart—even a poor creature such as I! Alas, I can give him nothing.' A sob rasped in her throat. 'But I thought that if you knew the truth, Leonie ...?' The thin talons of her hand gripped that of the English girl, agitatedly trying to raise her thin, wasted body. 'He says little, but I know you are estranged because of my marriage to him. He is so unhappy. Can you not forgive him? His marriage to me was not ... not of his making. Surely you can understand—and learn to love him again?'

Tears were streaming down Leonie's cheeks, her figure shaking with sobs as she realised the depth of Aisha's unselfish, hopeless love for Badyr.

'Please, do not cry.' The breath rasped in Aisha's throat. 'All I ask of you is that you do not throw away his love and devotion. It is so very ... very rare, is it not?'

'I promise you that I never stopped loving Badyr,' Leonie whispered. 'I tried, but I found that I couldn't,' she faltered, swept by a devastating sense of shame. 'He tried to tell me the truth, but I wouldn't listen!' she cried. 'It's all my fault!'

'Oh, no! I too am married to Badyr. I also know him well, you understand? I think he was frightened.'

'Badyr—frightened?' Leonie gazed incredulously at the girl through her tears.

'Oh, yes!' Aisha's lips curved into a wry smile. 'Even Badyr is human! He feared to lose you for ever. And when you discovered our marriage . . . how silly of him not to tell you the truth! . . . and you would not listen to him . . . he became too proud to beg . . . to confess to you why he married me. Yes, I love him, Leonie. But loving brings knowledge of weakness, as well as strength. So, I know he is kind and good . . . but he can also be stubborn and arrogant. Oh yes!'

The two girls found themselves grinning warmly at each other through their tears.

'So, you see? We are friends, yes?' Aisha whispered, smiling up at Leonie.

'Yes,' Leonie nodded, sniffing as she wiped away her tears. 'It is so generous of you to tell me everything. Is there anything you need, anything I can do for you?'

'No, I am just happy that we have met and talked,' Aisha murmured, her breathing becoming less laboured as if eased by being able to tell Leonie at last all that had been on her mind for so long. 'I can see that you will soon be having a baby, hmm?' she added. 'And Badyr says you have a little daughter, whom he loves very much. Please tell me all about her.'

Leonie felt almost too choked with emotion to comply with the girl's request. 'Well, her name is Jade and she was five years old last April,' Leonie began, holding Aisha's hand as the girl lay peacefully back on the pillows and closed her eyes. 'She is very like her father, possessing both his temper and the same

determination to get her own way!' Encouraged by
Aisha's grunt of laughter, she went on to describe
Jade's love of hopelessly unsuitable words, and her
current craze for learning to ride. 'Of course, her great-
uncle Feisal—who is her great hero—spoils her
outrageously,' she was saying as she became aware of
the doctor standing beside her.

Looking up, she saw him lean over the prone figure
of the girl on the bed, staring at him in bewilderment as
he gently removed her hand from Aisha's and slowly
drew the sheet up over the Arab girl's pale face.

No! Oh no!' she cried, swept by a feeling of utter
desolation. 'Oh no ... please say it isn't true,' she
begged helplessly, slumping back in the chair and
burying her face in her hands.

'Ah, Majesty,' the doctor murmured, putting an arm
about her shoulders and helping her trembling figure to
rise. 'You must not weep for the Sultana Aisha. It was
only her determination to see you which had kept her
alive so long. She is surely now at peace, safe and well
in Allah's loving arms.'

'But we had only just become friends, and ... and
there was so much I wanted to say—so many things I'll
never be able to tell her!' Leonie sobbed as he led her
slowly towards the door.

'Death is not to be feared. It is merely a door
leading into a new world for the Sultana. One in
which she has already cast aside the frail, sick frame
with which she was forced to inhabit this life. Her
true purity of soul is now shining whole and beautiful
among the blessed,' he said softly. 'You must not
begrudge her the happiness of which she is now most
surely possessed, nor fear that she does not see and
know all that is in your heart.'

Leonie, the tears streaming down her face, allowed
herself to be led from the room and back down the
corridor. Almost paralysed with grief, she was hardly
aware of being helped into the waiting limousine, and

was still sobbing helplessly when the vehicle arrived back at the palace. Trembling with anguish and remorse, she stumbled from the car—and into her husband's arms.

'Oh, Badyr!' she wailed. 'Poor Aisha—she's ... she's ...'

'Yes. Yes, I know, my darling,' he murmured, holding her closely and gently stroking her hair.

'I've been so stupid! So blind and cruel! And ... and I love you with all my heart,' she sobbed. 'How can you ever forgive me?'

'There is nothing to forgive—unless we must beg forgiveness of each other,' Badyr said quietly. 'By her generosity of spirit, Aisha has given us both the chance of a new life together. Can we not accept and treasure such a precious gift, hmm?'

Raising her tear-stained face to his, Leonie became aware that Badyr was standing very still, a muscle beating wildly in his jaw as he waited for her answer.

'Oh, yes—yes, please,' she whispered, feeling the breath being slowly expelled from his powerful body in a long-drawn-out, emotional sigh before he crushed her passionately in his arms, his mouth covering her trembling lips in a kiss of fierce, hungry possession.

Later that evening, Leonie awoke from a sleep of deep exhaustion, which had claimed her tired mind and body almost from the minute that Badyr, having carried her upstairs, had laid her on their soft bed. Turning her head, she saw his tall, lithe figure rise from an easy chair as he moved over to sit down beside her.

'You are feeling better now, my love?' he asked anxiously.

'Yes, I ...' She faltered as he gently helped her to sit up against the pillows. 'We must talk. I hardly know how to begin to apologise ...'

'What need is there for apologies between us, my darling?' he said softly, as his arms closed gently about her. 'I fell hopelessly and quite irresistibly in love with you—an adorable, innocent and shy young girl—when you called at my apartment all those years ago. From that moment, absolutely nothing has changed the deep emotional feelings I have for you, my beloved.'

Leonie stared down at her quivering hands, before forcing herself to meet Badyr's intense gaze. 'I never stopped loving you, either,' she murmured softly. 'I . . . I did try, but . . .' She sighed helplessly as she leant back against the pillows. 'I know that I've been incredibly stupid at times, but we've had such a very complicated married life, Badyr. Please don't blame me too much for . . . well, for doubting your feelings for me.'

'How could I ever blame you for anything!' he said huskily, taking her trembling figure into his arms. 'So much has been my fault. Right from the first. From the moment we married, our love was put under such an intolerable strain.' He sighed deeply. 'I should have waited. I should have had enough self-control to wait until after the coup against my father before marrying you. But I wanted you so much, my darling! You were so very young, like a rose in bud, perfect and unawakened, and I feared that some other man would steal you from me while I was away. I nearly became demented at the thought of an unknown stranger teaching you the delights of physical love, receiving your first shy responses and hearing those sweet cries of rapture,' he groaned, buring his face in the soft cleft of her breasts.

'I . . . er . . . I did beg you to marry me and take me to Dhoman,' she murmured, gently running her fingers through his black hair.

'Yes, but I should have been sensible enough to know what a disaster it would turn out to be. But where you are concerned, my darling, I am as weak as water.' He raised his head to give her a lingering kiss. 'The only excuse I can offer is that I had been away from this country for so long, that I did not realise the full extent of either my father's despotic rule or his unstable temperament.'

'The poor man,' Leonie mused. 'I feel sorry for him. I realise now that he just couldn't cope with life in the twentieth century.'

Badyr turned to lie on his back, staring up at the ceiling. 'You are more generous than I,' he sighed. 'It is a sin to conspire against one's father, and I shall have to answer for my actions at the day of judgment—of that there is no doubt. But when I used your sweetness to assuage my anger and frustration against my father ... it was right that I should have reaped a full punishment for such cruelty. And I was punished, Leonie,' he added in a low, throbbing voice. 'I do not think that there was one hour, of those five, seemingly endless years, when I did not yearn for your sweet presence.'

'Aisha?' she whispered tremulously.

For a moment there was silence, and then Badyr rolled over to gather her gently into his arms. 'The Americans have an expression: "over a barrel", and that is just what I was—well and truly over a barrel—when I heard how my father was threatening you. I was so ... so damned *helpless*! If I wished to make sure you were safe, I had no alternative but to marry a girl I had never seen in my life. I have learnt to forgive my mother, who only did what she felt was in the interests of the country; but when I took that dreadful decision, every one of us suffered as a consequence. The poor, frail little girl,' he added softly. 'Aisha was so frightened when she arrived down at the Summer Palace. Can you imagine how terrified she must have been? She had no mother, and her father had just been arrested. She had never travelled more than a few miles from her home in the north of the country, and when she quickly became so ill ...' He sighed deeply. 'I knew that I was responsible, Leonie. I had chosen to save you, but in doing so I had unwittingly condemned her. Can you understand?'

'Of course I do,' she murmured, tenderly pressing her lips to the strained lines about his mouth. 'I'm only ashamed that ... that when I discovered her existence, I didn't give you a chance to tell me the truth.'

He hesitated. 'From the beginning I had told her how I felt about you, and that it was not possible ... that our marriage must be in name only.'

'I know. Aisha told me. Oh, Badyr! If only I could have met her sooner. And now it's too late,' she whispered, hiding her face in the warm curve of his shoulder.

'Aisha was a sweet, generous girl of whom I became very fond, and for whom I cared deeply—but she was not you, my darling,' he said simply, his lips kissing away the tears from her eyes.

Some minutes later, Badyr slowly and reluctantly let her go. 'I think I am going to break one of my golden rules,' he said huskily as he got up off the bed. 'Attempting to keep myself away from you has been a damned torture—I've never had so many freezing cold showers in my whole life as I've been having these last few weeks! So, I suggest we have some champagne on ice, which may help to cool my ardour.'

Leonie couldn't help smiling through her tears at his rueful expression. 'Don't you laugh at me, you witch!' he muttered in mock fury, picking up the internal phone and issuing an order. 'Which reminds me,' he added, 'I must have an urgent word with the worthy Dr Winslow. I can see that it might be dangerous at the moment, but when you've given birth to the baby, just how many hellish weeks will I have to endure before I can make love to you?'

'It's no good looking at me for the answer!' she retorted, smiling as his tall figure paced about the room. 'I'll have you know that I led a thoroughly pure life after Jade was born!'

'*Wallahi!* I can't begin to tell you how I worried about *that* fact!' he growled. 'I kept as close an eye on your life in London as I could, but I can assure you that I went through the tortures of the damned, worrying incessantly about your relationships with other men! As soon as I took over the rule of this country from my father, I realised that if I'd been over a barrel before, it was nothing to the situation in which I found myself then. I was damned certain that you'd *never* accept the fact of my second marriage. I know,' he said over her muttered protest. 'You might have been understanding, but it was a hell of a risk for me to take, all the same. On the other hand, I simply couldn't bring myself to divorce Aisha—it would have been far too cruel to treat her in such a way.' He sighed. 'I give you my solemn word that I have never, ever, wished for her death. I realised that I must simply bury myself in the necessary work involved in pulling Dhoman into the twentieth century, and let fate decide what was to happen.'

He paused as there was a knock at the door, and Hussa entered with a tray. Putting it down on a small table, she winked at Leonie and scurried out of the room.

'Hussa is clearly an incurable romantic!' Badyr laughed wryly as he placed a cold glass of bubbling champagne in his wife's hand. 'She never ceased to ask after you, urging me to bring you back to Dhoman. Of course, I shouldn't have taken the risk, but when I received your mother's letter telling me about her marriage, and just how worried she was about you—I decided to take the gamble. I now see that it was incredibly foolish of me, but although I am a patient man, I knew that I could no longer endure life without you by my side. And as soon as we kissed, that first time we met again in the Embassy, I *knew* you still cared for me! That unless something went badly wrong—which, of course, it did—I had taken the right decision. However, being certain that you still felt something for me, was one matter. Trying to handle an extremely difficult, temperamental and obstinate wife—was quite another! Getting you back to Dhoman was one of the most difficult tasks I've ever attempted. It was like trying to woo a cage full of rattlesnakes!'

'Charming! And what's this nonsense about trying to "woo" me?' Leonie gave a sardonic laugh. 'There was nothing lover-like about you—you horrible man! The sound of a door-bell still makes me shudder, and as for that fur coat . . .!'

'Ah, beloved. You looked so beautiful, so ravishingly lovely, that I nearly raped you there and then in the zoo!' He laughed at the bright crimson flush spreading across her cheeks.

'Yes, well . . . I suppose I was in a bit of a state,' she admitted. 'And although I like to think I would have been understanding, if you'd told me about Aisha when you came to London, I don't know . . . I can't honestly say what my reaction would have been.'

Badyr stared sadly down at his glass. 'I want to tell you that those long months, when you insisted on being left alone at the Summer Palace, were a far worse torture than the five years' absence between us. No, I never believed for a moment that you would seek to lose the baby you carried,' he assured her. 'But, not a day went by, when I didn't decide to fly down and *make* you listen to the truth. But always I stopped before doing so. I knew that I was responsible for your deep hurt and anger, but I also—

alas—became angry and stiff with pride. I told myself that if you had loved me, you would have made some effort to understand, and I ... I could not bring myself to make the necessary explanations, a gesture which I foolishly saw as a crawling humiliation.'

'Oh, Badyr ...' Her eyes filled with tears. 'I've caused you—both of us—so much pain!'

'Enough!' he commanded firmly. 'We have both been unhappy long enough, hmm? Sweet, kind Aisha has given us the chance to renew our marriage—a legacy that we must treasure. Not only do we have a lovely and amusing daughter, but we will soon be blessed with another child. With so much for which to be thankful, my darling, let us now look forward to the happy future—not backwards to the mistakes we have made in the past,' he added huskily, his mouth possessing hers in a pledge of warmth and tenderness.

Four months later Leonie sat gazing idly out of the window at the fiery sun slipping slowly down over the horizon. They had been at the Summer Palace for almost a week, and already she had slipped under its lazy, carefree spell. In the distance she could hear the fishermen calling to each other as they left their boats, while nearer at hand Jade was laughing as her father told her a good-night story.

Sighing with contentment, Leonie lowered her head to smile at the baby in her arms. With fluffy, jet-black hair, Karim was the very image of Badyr, the only legacy from his mother being the startling, sapphire-blue eyes hidden now by his drowsy eyelids, as he lay sleepily content and replete at her breast.

'I would find it very easy to become jealous of my son and heir!' a voice said softly. Smiling up at Badyr's tall figure as he walked across the floor of the nursery, she instinctively attempted to cover herself. 'Ah, no, my beloved. Do not hide your loveliness from me,' he murmured, sitting down beside her and gently tracing a path with his fingers over the burgeoning fulness of her bare breasts.

'Your son is greedy—just like his father!' she grinned, wiping a small trickle of milk from the baby's chin. Although she spoke lightly, her nerve-ends tingled and throbbed at his intimate touch. Karim's birth had not been an easy one, and she was aware of just how inhibiting Badyr had found that fact, striving to carefully restrain his ardour when they had resumed their lovemaking. But she was already feeling a great deal stronger, her body becoming eager and impatient to welcome the full force of his passion.

'Ah,' Badyr sighed, regretfully moving his hand as Leonie lifted the baby to her shoulder, gently patting his back. 'Before I become too carried away, I must tell you three pieces of interesting news. First, I have had a reply to my cable, and you will be pleased to hear that your mother and stepfather will be joining us here in a week's time.'

'I'm so glad they can make it—it will be lovely to see my mother again,' she smiled happily.

'And for her to see her new grandchild, hmm?' He gently stroked his son's cheek. 'Karim is a very clever child—did I tell you that he smiled at me today?' Badyr added proudly.

'That was probably wind!' she teased. 'What are the other two bits of news?'

'Well, you may ... er ... remember that I was paralytically angry with that wretched sister of mine, Nadia. In my fury, I sent her off to some cousins in Saudi Arabia. They belong to a very strict religious sect and I thought that life with them might give her something to think about,' he added grimly. 'However, to my utter amazement, I received a letter today from the head of the family, telling me that Nadia has fallen madly in love with an elderly prince, and is requesting my permission to marry him.' A slow smile spread across Badyr's face. 'The cream of the jest is that he already has two wives and countless children! I have, of course, despatched my sincere congratulations—and a huge dowry, just in case the poor man should think of changing his mind!'

'That's really rotten of you!' Leonie tried not to laugh. 'Even Nadia doesn't deserve to get herself into that sort of mess. She's bound to be unhappy before very long.'

'No—I think not. Nadia is the child most like my father. I will wager you any sum you care to mention, that she will quickly manage to persuade her husband to cast aside his two other wives, disinheriting his children in favour of any she may have—and then proceed to make his life a misery. Believe me—the poor man will need all the consolation of a large dowry!' he laughed. 'And talking of weddings: I was approached today by my uncle Feisal. I must confess to being somewhat embarrassed that a man, so much older than I, should feel the need to ask my permission to get married.'

Leonie gasped. 'Not . . .?'

'Yes, he wishes to marry our governess! I have already had a word with Elizabeth, and she tells me that—always provided that Feisal faithfully promises not to bring his horses into their house, or to take a second wife—she thinks she might like to marry a *real* Sheikh of Araby!'

'Goodness—how exciting!' she laughed. 'I must go and have a word with her right away.'

'No—not just at the moment,' Badyr murmured, taking the sleeping baby from her arms and placing him in his cot. 'Having attended to the needs of my son, I think it is time you turned your full attention to the requirements of his father, don't you?' he added as he led her through into their bedroom, firmly closing the door before taking her into his arms.

Laughter gleamed in the depths of her blue eyes.

'Darling, Badyr,' she whispered as she became aware of the passion throbbing in his body, and the rising tide of desire beginning to sweep through her veins. 'How could I possibly presume to disagree with my husband? I wouldn't dare to be guilty of such ... such *lèse-majesté!*'

Bachelors' Babies

Fatherhood Fever!

Available 1st June

Available at branches of WH Smith, Tesco, Martins, Borders, Easons, Sainsbury, Woolworth and most good paperback bookshops